ANGELS OF MARADONA

ANGELS OF MARADONA

GLEN CARTER

BREAKWATER BOOKS LIMITED
JESPERSON PUBLISHING • BREAKWATER DISTRIBUTORS

 **BREAKWATER BOOKS LIMITED**
JESPERSON PUBLISHING • BREAKWATER DISTRIBUTORS

100 Water Street • P.O. Box 2188 • St. John's • NL • A1C 6E6
www.breakwaterbooks.com   www.jespersonpublishing.ca

Library and Archives Canada Cataloguing in Publication

Carter, Glen, 1957-

   Angels of Maradona / Glen Carter.

ISBN 978-1-55081-239-8

   I. Title.

PS8605.A7778A66 2008   C813'.6   C2007-907538-X

© 2008 Glen Carter

ALL RIGHTS RESERVED. No part of this publication may be reproduced, stored in a retrieval system or transmitted, in any form or by any means, without the prior written consent of the publisher or a licence from The Canadian Copyright Licensing Agency (Access Copyright). For an Access Copyright licence, visit www.accesscopyright.ca or call toll free to 1-800-893-5777.

 We acknowledge the financial support of The Canada Council for the Arts for our publishing activities.

We acknowledge the support of the Department of Tourism, Culture and Recreation for our publishing activities.

We acknowledge the financial support of the Government of Canada through the Book Publishing Industry Development Program (BPIDP) for our publishing activities.

Printed in Canada.

Dedicated to my parents,
Muriel Baker and the late Walter Carter.
Et mon fils, Philippe Robichaud.

As a journalist, I have been telling true and compelling stories my entire professional life. This is my first pack of lies.

Glen Carter, November 23, 2007

"There is sometimes a belief that these are demon children, that the father is some sort of animal."

Leigh Minter, Psychologist, U'wa observer

PROLOGUE

THE U'WA DECREE 1973.
JAGUAR FOREST, COLOMBIA.

They felt like knots of clay hardened within the fires of hell, an abomination which brought in Luis Mendoza a deep, awful dread.

The old man of Maradona shuffled through the night, stooped in exertion. Farmer's boots echoed a lopsided beat on hard earth, a pathetic uneven gait which electrified muscles withered long ago. After a second, Mendoza dropped his gaze into cradles formed by his sinewy arms. Two tiny faces there. In shadows. Still sleeping. Mendoza wheezed his thanks, bit at moist air as he lunged through brush as dark as the two little souls.

After another hundred yards the shriek of a night creature high in the jungle canopy caused him to jolt. Sweating and breathless, the old man twisted his head towards the sound and thought again about the screaming women. So shrill, it felt like a hot blade eviscerating him.

Momma, Momma, the babies! Momma, Momma, please!

His own blood. His daughter – the whore. His wife – no better. Her arms flailing, beating at him as he scooped up the children and turned for the door. The stain on his house could not be tolerated, not what the girl had brought into their lives. Not these children.

Against his bare arms the old man felt the warmth of them, festering heat from something in the process of decaying. Certainly not the flesh of innocents.

A new noise made him twist backwards. The old man's eyes widened in panic until he realized it was the pounding of his own heart. Tightness spread across his chest but he knew he could not rest.

The women had fought like animals to stop him. They were U'wa, yet they refused to understand, to accept. Understand that he had delayed too long already. It was what Serpez had warned that very night and Serpez understood. *You risk us all, Mendoza. You know what you must do.*

A tree branch scraped the old man's face, leaving a thin trail of blood on his brown cheek. He swore aloud, drawing the children tighter. Soon, he thought, hunkering lower to protect his cargo from splintering brush.

Mendoza had swept aside his guilt. The millennia of his people soothed his conscience, eclipsing his darkest fears. Besides, the curse had already claimed Pinto and his wife. The two of them strong as bulls before being taken by the mysterious sickness. The co-op had lost livestock; a dozen head were down. Then there were the mangos. On many farms the unpicked fruit was black and shriveled. The agriculture man from Bogotá had come, had rambled on about parasites and such, but what did a bureaucrat know about the U'wa ways?

The two babies were wrapped tightly in thin worn blankets, still in slumber even with the raspy coughs splitting their grandfather's laboured breaths.

Five minutes later. Higher in the cloud forest than he imagined he could run, Mendoza halted in a small clearing. Moonlight crowned him. Wolf-like he snarled, wiping a tremulous hand across his bloody face. The elder Serpez had given him specific instructions about what had to be done. Quick instructions, spoken closely, spit like venom into his face.

Mendoza's eyes darted around the clearing, relief on his wet face. This would be the place, he decided, and not a moment too soon since he was certain now the babies were coming awake. He bent painfully. Carefully he placed the bundles on the ground, one next to the other. A tiny hand brushed his fingers, causing Mendoza to jerk backward, nearly losing his balance until he caught himself against a nearby tree. Mendoza pulled himself straight, glanced quickly upward, his face glistening with sweat and blood. His lips fluttered. Soundless. Then the old man of Maradona spun around, and without a backward glance, he stumbled into the jungle.

The babies gurgled contentedly. Their eyes wide with the erratic flight of fireflies in the darkness, they swiveled their heads in tandem to chase the airborne minuet, faces spotted with pinpoints of light from the luminous insects. Small fingers grasped at miniature wings which hummed impossibly fast and tickled their faces like angel wings fluttering.

Each child was an image of the other, one tiny voice an echo of the second in a singularity of nature's choosing as rare as the nova stars that streaked brilliantly across the night sky.

The babies turned to each other with the sweetness of cherubs – between them a connection that would stretch the vastness of oceans, mountains, and lost decades.

They were not alone.

The Lord of the Underworld was close. Silent as death it moved like a black smudge that melted into the shadows beneath the jungle canopy. Eyes hung like yellow orbs in the blackness. The jaguar cocked its broad heavy head and raised its snout to taste babies' breath on eddies of humid air.

The cat was achingly hungry. The babies were near.

ONE

NEW ORLEANS 2004.

The music was pounding too hard for anyone to hear the door splintering at the back of 52 Avalon Road. Neighbours – no one. The shattering didn't wake the man upstairs, who had decided on earplugs to block out the head-splitting noise, and the teenagers downstairs in the rec room were simply having too good a time.

They clapped their hands – firecracker loud. They whooped and hollered while one of them danced on the sofa, gyrating outrageously and nearly losing her balance.

Thump! Thump! Thump! "Sherra!" someone squealed. "Shake it, Sherra! Shake it, girl!"

Sherra Saunier rocked her hips and spun to face her audience. Pumped her pelvis in a ridiculously rude pantomime that caused some of the other girls to cover their mouths, muffling their screeches.

Good thing too, Sherra thought. Her father had already warned them about the noise, to hit the sack because they had a long drive starting bright and early the next morning. *Thump! Thump! Thump!* Sherra shook her rear end and howled – prayed her father wouldn't wake up and ruin her party.

The rec room was a darkened mess. The floor was littered with empty pizza boxes and half full cans of sticky soda, which the girls had gulped to see who could burp the loudest. Marilee won that contest hands down and grabbed her prize which was a large poster of their currently favourite boy band. They laughed so hard at Marilee when, with exaggerated lust, she smacked loud wet kisses on each of the young pop idols and rubbed the glossy poster against her small breasts.

They were all popular in school and best friends who shared everything, including the secrets that if blabbed would certainly ruin them. Stuff like boys and sex. Two of the girls were experts now after consulting some porn site on the internet.

Roxy screamed, "Marilee, you slut!" Roxy Sparrow's father was a bible-thumping preacher, but Roxy was the only one who wasn't a virgin anymore. The other girls had pestered her mercilessly until she told them, in great horrid detail, what it felt like. Samantha, the youngest one, had squealed and rolled on the carpet clutching her groin at the mention of Jacob Cabochon's erect "thing" and how he had stammered and fumbled until Roxy realized it was over. "Gross," several of the girls had exclaimed in exaggerated revulsion. "Marilee's gonna be the next one!"

The girls didn't want to stop, even though it was late and they should have crawled into their sleeping bags an hour ago. They were too excited to sleep — too pumped with anticipation. The divisional cheerleading competition was the next day in Biloxi and none of the other teams had practiced as hard as the squad from Avondale Heights High. That was for *S-U-R-E*.

They were having such a good time. How could they know someone was in the hallway outside? Sherra and Marilee and the six other girls strutted around in their PJs, dancing to the loud music which obliterated the sounds made by the intruder, including the two gunshots that had already killed Sherra's sleepy dad.

The base deepened until the walls shook, causing the girls to scream even louder with delight.

Outside the door an unseen hand turned the knob slowly.

The girls continued to howl, limbs and hair whipping recklessly into one another. Someone picked up the thread of lyrics, began singing badly.

Screw it, Sherra decided. She danced to the boom box and was about to crank it up when she stopped dead in her tracks. *Daddy?*

The door was suddenly open. Light from the hallway spilled into the darkened room. All the girls stopped to see who it was, squinted at him against the outside light. The man standing there was too tall and too thin to be Sherra's dad. He never swayed like he was drunk, and why would he be holding *that?*

Thump! Thump! Thump! Music pounded the walls, but the air was deathly still, frozen like ice around the eight screaming girls and the man pointing the gun.

TWO

They were only four minutes to air when Jack Doyle spotted the fat man and the politician, a pair too oddly coupled to mean anything but a curious shift in the story. Something delicious. The coroner for Orleans Parish normally rode in a grey sedan, not a long black limousine, but that was how the senator traveled, and when Doyle spotted the shiny car sneaking in through a dirt laneway near the back of the house he knew the story would need updating – fast.

After a moment he turned and cocked his head, a gesture caught by his field producer. Kaitlin O'Rourke was normally reluctant to bother the talent so close to air. Normally.

"What's wrong, Jack?" She couldn't resist. "You look like you've seen a ghost."

For a moment Doyle said nothing, bunched his eyebrows while he tried to make sense of what he had just observed – the Hitchcockian form of the good doctor Richelieu stomping through the rose garden with Louisiana's senior senator in tow. Laurel and Hardy, Jack thought, although that might have been cruel given the circumstances. Still, Doyle managed an inward smile as he turned to his producer. "We need to give Senator Robicheaux's office a quick call," he said.

Kaitlin stared at him suspiciously. She'd become accustomed to Jack's little surprises, the timing of which often threatened their ability to make deadline. It was her ass if they didn't. "You know something I don't?"

"Yep. Ask the flak why his boss just walked into the bloodbath on Avalon Road. It's possible we missed one."

Kaitlin searched the scene beyond Jack, beyond the lights, the television staging area. Seeing nothing that satisfied her curiosity, she grabbed her cell phone and flashed it to her ear.

Bloodbath wasn't actually a word Jack planned to use. It was a hackneyed word that he'd already tossed aside, though it still held currency in war zones where whole villages were laid to waste by religious zealots. There were few words to describe what had happened at 52 Avalon Road. *Slaughter* was too ugly a word when children were involved, and not nearly potent enough. *Unfathomable?* Maybe. Jack wrote it down, glanced at his watch, and realized it had been only six hours since Walter Carmichael had sent them out the door – with minimal information. "Get to the airport. Shit happening in New Orleans. Bad one, Jack. Call from the plane, we'll have wire stuff for you."

Jack stowed a suit bag in his office for the times Carmichael wanted his best reporter in the air, quickly. They said clothes made the man and that was especially true when you measured your audience by the millions. He was tall and darkly handsome with a crooked disarming smile but would never have been mistaken as a pretty boy or meat puppet, thanks largely to his hard-earned reputation as a story breaker who was never satisfied. Black hair, laced with grey, as well as warmly inquisitive blue eyes earned him a loyal and gold-plated female demographic.

Unlike the overdressed talent, chase producer Kaitlin O'Rourke traveled light. Her laptop and a couple of changes of clothes because stories never lasted more than a couple of days, even stories of this magnitude. Doyle smoothed the wrinkles on his pale blue shirt and straightened his tie, watching as she worked the phone. Who would have guessed Kaitlin, daughter of that fireplug-of-a-man Argus O'Rourke, would turn into such a knockout? Not Doyle. Anyway, what difference did it make? The Irishman had never been a big fan of the Doyles, something that started a long time ago with Doyle's father. Bottom line: Kaitlin O'Rourke was a damn good producer, and that meant more to Doyle than her bombshell looks and the long history between them. Still, Doyle had had to twist the screws on his imagination on more than one occasion.

The corporate Citation aircraft had shot them from New York to New Orleans in three and a half hours with just enough time for that first police briefing and for George to shoot the B-roll. Kaitlin had done a superb job of pulling the material together and vetting Doyle's script. It was up to Doyle now.

The *massacre*. Now there was a good word. The *unfathomable massacre* would lead all the newscasts that night. Drug involvement made it even juicier, Doyle thought as he checked his notes, trying to recall the exact words of the president not two weeks ago. *No more of their poison on our streets*, Denton had declared that night. A tough sell, Doyle decided as he jotted it down, considering that even the Drug Enforcement Agency had admitted the borders were leaking cocaine like large mesh nets. Colombia and Peru were the usual suspects.

"DRAGON SLAYER," the next day's headline had shouted in *The Washington Post*, with Denton's photograph located large above the fold. When children were killed, slaughtered like lambs, Doyle thought wryly, a presidential declaration such as that gave the story on Avalon Road strong, strong legs. Stronger than anyone knew, he suspected, allowing his mind to wander to Senator Aaron Robicheaux. The silver-haired friend of the Christian right had business at 52 Avalon Road. Doyle wondered about that as he smoothly recapped his pen and looked at his watch in a gesture Kaitlin didn't miss. "Lay on the charm, O'Rourke. Quickly," he said.

News was a calling like the priesthood, but without the rules on sex and compassion. Mercy too. The pack was hungry. To civilians they'd look like selfish irreverent bastards salivating over the biggest story to cross the transom since that wacko murdered his pregnant wife and got the death penalty. Stories like that sucked a reporter up, but when the juice was gone so were the story's legs. That's when television crews packed up for the next assignment – somewhere else where blood and sorrow were worthy of the lead.

Doyle spied Mona Lasing fifty feet away at the neighbouring satellite truck. Her famous pout. She was mic'd and primping for her *hit* — mirror and hairspray artfully choreographed in a kind of synchronized diva ballet. A dozen or so reporters had been dispatched to New Orleans. To the crime scene on Avalon Road. They were melting beneath television lights that sprang up like glow balls for a hundred yards up and down the street. Doyle saw the Fox guy who always wore black, the colour of doom, with pipes that made every story seem like it was the end of time. CNN flew in the Hispanic kid whose on-air uniform was sneakers, jeans and one of those war correspondent vests with a million utility pockets. His shooter was the been-there-done-that Heath, who was firing off film aboard HMS *Conqueror* when it sent two Tigerfish torpedoes into the Belgrano during the Falklands War. That was before the Hispanic kid was even toilet-trained. Heath looked at Doyle and shook his head, sharing something between veterans who had seen it all.

Half a dozen satellite trucks were parked nose-to-tail like a herd of circus elephants along a narrow strip of black pavement that sashayed its way past postage stamp yards and antebellum town houses. It was a good neighbourhood, not extravagant, but well-to-do and mostly white. The red streetcars that rolled charmingly along Canal Street to City Park and Beauregard Circle didn't come this far, and although Avalon Road was not close enough to Jefferson Parish to be considered a bedroom community, its demographics made it feel that way.

The sharpest bend in the Mississippi was so close you could hear the whistles of casino paddle-wheelers, but Avalon Road was far enough from the Quarter that it entertained neither beaded tourists nor restaurants serving authentic sassafras gumbo and poulet fricassee. The minute Jack Doyle got there he knew Avalon Road wasn't that part of town where bourbon-and-milk punch was consumed by the frosty bucket and certainly not a neighbourhood where the big network stars reported on the bullet-ridden corpses of ripening debutantes.

Those stiffening bodies were still inside the house. At last count eight of them. Not that it made any difference to the live shot, which was about to broadcast a tall detached two-storey with shining white columns, a Tuscan portico and large shuttered windows barely visible behind two ancient vine trees. Flowering azalea bushes perfectly matched the yellow police tape behind which some forensics guys were taking their time dusting a luxury SUV in a driveway bordered by boxwood hedges and tall pecan trees.

The call had come in sixteen hours before from one of the parents, and even though a lot of shifts had officially ended since then, none of the cops seemed in a hurry to leave. District Two uniforms were all over the house, swarming the doorways like bees blindly protecting a dead queen.

The local affiliates were relegated to lousy live positions farther away from the crime scene and were rightly pissed about that. But the networks were king, and they'd already claimed the best live spots, had selfishly monopolized the police communications flak with an unpronounceable Cajun name who was spitting out sound bites like there was no tomorrow, icing them with moist eyes and a quivering lip. *"Mon dieu.* Bodies everywhere."

Three minutes to air Doyle uncapped his pen and decided to rework his intro. The others wouldn't have the new angle. He'd seen the coroner and the senator entering the house from the rear, and they hadn't. That meant Jack Doyle had another exclusive. The others would curse him and complain about the horseshoe lodged in the lower regions of Doyle's anatomy. Doyle didn't know about a horseshoe but he did have the intuition of a carnival psychic, an ability to deduce mountains of information from seemingly unimportant events. Not that what he'd observed was unimportant. The coroner was a busy man who didn't make return engagements to a crime scene unless there was a very good reason. The fact the senator was with him could only mean one thing, and it was a red flag Doyle couldn't miss – even if the others had. Horseshoes were struck with luck, something Doyle never counted on. Nothing was as cruel as the scowl of luck when the competition got the money shot and you didn't, or when your feed window was about to slam shut and you were stuck in traffic. Luck had nothing to do with the exclusive interview they'd knocked off with the father of one of the dead teenagers – a preacher. He'd screeched and wept and damned the "bloodthirsty spawn of Satan," before finally collapsing into someone's arms. "Eye for an eye," he had added, with holy authority. Grief liked to talk. Venting had a way of being therapeutic and Doyle knew scenes like that made for compelling television.

Doyle watched Kaitlin work the phone, fidgeting with his earpiece so that he could hear the control room over the din of reporters and cops and slack-jawed bystanders. Overhead, a couple of news choppers were broadcasting the scene live and Doyle wondered whether they'd caught the arrival of the limo at the back of the house. He guessed not because there were too many trees in the way for an unobstructed shot. Besides, the eyes in the sky seemed to be concentrating on a couple of canine units working the brush about a hundred yards from the Saunier house.

"Well?"

"They've got me on hold," Kaitlin said between clenched teeth. "You sure about this, Jack? Eight bodies – all identified as of an hour ago, remember?"

Doyle knew she was pissed at the implication she would have screwed up something as basic as the body count. "Trust me. Doctor Death's back and he's got company." Doyle checked his watch.

In his ear the director told him to stand by. "Opening in a minute fifteen, Jack."

Kaitlin looked at him, a producer's panic in her eyes. "There's been nothing since the police briefing," she said. "And there's nothing on the wires. I checked."

Doyle nodded slowly in agreement. Sometimes the wires had more information even when you were not fifty yards from the story. The wire guys were always working the phones, ferreting out new stuff because they were feeding the news monster every fifteen minutes. If the wires didn't have it, it was definitely an exclusive.

Doyle jotted down a few notes, silently mouthed words to make sure every syllable flowed smoothly, without speed bumps that caught you up, left you rattled and red-faced. He breathed evenly, scanned what he'd written as he listened to Frank Simmons doing a voice check. "One, two. Talk to me, Jack," Simmons said. "Can you hear me, New Orleans?"

"Clear as the proverbial bell," Doyle replied, fixing his tie and praying nothing would screw up, not even Frank Simmons, who was dumb as a sack of hammers but who had Cary Grant looks and a Doberman agent, both of which had conspired to rob Doyle of what should have been his long ago, even though he was also quite handsome and extremely well represented. Doyle pushed it aside, concentrated instead on the story and getting the facts straight. That was more important than trying to decide if your studio makeup needed more yellow tones. "Got a surprise for you, Frank," Doyle said cautiously.

"What's up?"

"No time to explain." No need to rattle the hair-and-teeth anchor so close to air. "I'm going to tag with the speculation on drug involvement," said Doyle. "You know. Drug violence in a once safe neighbourhood. That kinda thing. Plays great with what the president's been saying about drugs being a threat to national security."

"Gotcha."

"Then ask me where the investigation goes from here."

Felix, the sound guy, stepped up to dress Doyle's clip-on microphone, whispered, "Tell him it's New Orleans, Jack, not New Rochelle." Doyle chuckled despite the tension.

"Perfect, Jack," Simmons said a thousand miles away on the anchor desk in New York. "Nothing like a massacre to bring in the numbers."

Doyle cringed, Felix too. "Frank," Doyle admonished. "We're on the satellite, remember?" Doyle knew the anchor's smile had just vanished, but someone pulls a comment like that off the bird and tosses it on the internet and your career's toast. Fundamental mistake, Doyle thought. Always assume your mic is hot. Jesus, after so many years in the biz Simmons should have known better.

Frank faded from Doyle's ear, replaced by the orchestrated chaos which was normal for the control room when so close to air. "Thirty seconds. Stand by." It was Doyle's executive producer, Jamie Malone, this time. "What's going on, Jack? Don't keep me guessing."

"Hold on a second, Jamie." Doyle looked expectantly at Kaitlin.

Kaitlin snapped her cell phone shut with a report that sounded like a high velocity weapon. A shocked look as she reported, "Robicheaux's flak just confirmed. His daughter, Jack. Her name was Marilee. Fourteen years old. Friend of Saunier's kid. They found her body behind a piece of furniture in a storage room. The senator's office will be issuing a statement in half an hour. That makes nine dead now."

"Damn," said Doyle. "Kid ran, tried to hide." He shook his head. "Thanks, Kaitlin."

"Been a long day," Kaitlin replied, wiping a tendril of long brown hair from her smooth dark forehead. Huge chocolate eyes melting into a pool of humility. "Sorry I missed it, Jack."

"I don't think the others have it," Doyle said with an understanding smile. "Don't sweat it. We got it."

Jamie Malone had heard. Whistled in Doyle's ear. "Holy shit! Jack, we wanna second source this?"

"No need, Jamie. Good as the horse's mouth when it's Robicheaux's flak. No time. Follow my lead, OK?"

"Fifteen seconds to air."

Doyle slipped into the zone, separating the useless facts from the salient, preparing the big picture stuff before the director rolled his piece. "Wish me luck," he said to Kaitlin.

"Like you need it." She smiled, nervously.

In his ear Doyle heard the brassy show opening, then Frank Simmons' first smooth words. "Good evening. A bloodbath in the city of New Orleans. Eight people have been brutally slain in a massacre that defies explanation or reason. CNS senior correspondent Jack Doyle is live at the scene, where police have begun a very difficult investigation tonight. Jack?"

"Cue, Jack!"

When CNN went to commercial Diego grabbed the remote, but checked his urge to hurl it through the television. He'd had enough crap from those mother-fucking talking heads who didn't really contribute shit to what he needed to know at that particular fucking moment, which was what the fuck happened in Avondale Heights and where the fuck was that shit-for-brains little brother of his, Sal. He dropped the remote, shovelled another forkful of rice into his mouth, and twisted his dark features into a sneer. Not enough cilantro. Bitch screwed like a porno queen but couldn't cook worth shit.

Diego chewed noisily and stared out the open balcony door, two storeys above Rampart Street and a couple hundred yards from Congo

Square where someone was squealing on a sax. That or beating someone to death with it. A warm wind carried the smell of boiled crawfish from Hurricane Haul's across the street. Diego decided he'd get his belly full once he dumped the bitch he'd snagged last night on Bourbon. Tonight, he'd work his voodoo at the Funky Butt. Lots of hot senoritas would be hungry for a piece of Enrique González Diego.

He waited for the news to come back on. Before CNN went to commercial, the Hispanic guy, who looked just like his stupid rock-smoking brother, was saying that a bunch of kids were dead. Executed in Avondale Heights. It was reason to worry.

Diego swallowed a mouthful of beer and watched the car commercial playing on his fifty-inch screen. Whatever. Shit, nothin' could touch his '64 Vette. It was cherry red and he wound it out in second gear through the Quarter on the nights he and Sal weren't stepping on product or making deliveries like the kilo they'd dropped off at DB's three weeks earlier. Losers like DB didn't seem to get it, that if you took a kilo of coke, cash was expected at the other end.

Diego watched his "guest" swing her fat ass into the bedroom. Gonna "powder her nose." She was blonde and had real tits, and although she couldn't cook, she didn't yap too much and she did what she was told, especially between the sheets where it really counted.

"Lay off that shit," he shouted. *Gonna give the bitch another fuckin' nosebleed.*

He dropped his fork and drummed his fingers nervously on the table. Where was Salvador, anyway? Simple job. Go find DB and deal with him, because there was no way he was going to take shit from that cocksucker anymore. DB was fucking him around as usual. He'd sent Salvador to make things right, because his dim-witted brother was the kind of moron who enjoyed getting high and fucking people up. Problem was, Salvador wasn't the smartest banana in the bunch, and Avondale Heights was where DB was hunkered down, probably not far from where those kids were butchered. DB was small-time but you get a hundred cockroaches like him and all of a sudden you got a well-tuned machine sucking up a hundred kilos a week and spitting back cash that kept that fat fucker Carlos smiling back home in Colombia. Mostly it worked just fine until someone got stupid, like DB had gotten stupid. Word was the fucker had been spotted making conversation with a couple of the narcotics guys from the Quarter. Those 8th District faggots were probably already on to DB, and Diego knew exactly where that was going to lead. To him.

He tore off a piece of bread. The gringo bitch had brought back baguette. What the fuck was baguette? He grunted. "Right, baby. I come in there in a minute, show you what Enrique can do." He watched a hair commercial roll by, bitches with thick shiny hair smiling at him from the big screen like they all knew he drove a '64 Corvette that was cherry red and that he'd killed a man once for stiffing him on two ounces of product, much less a kilo, which was what that fuck DB had taken him for. Nobody fucks with Enrique González Diego. Nobody, he thought, as he stuffed the hunk of bread into his mouth and wondered if he'd given his shit-crazy brother the right address.

THREE

From behind the camera outside 52 Avalon Road, George pointed a finger in Doyle's direction. *Showtime*.

"Frank. This story has taken another grim turn. CNS news has learned that the daughter of Louisiana Senator Aaron Robicheaux is among the dead in this home, which is both a crime scene and a tomb tonight. It brings to nine the number of people brutally murdered here. The victims were nearly all young women, slaughtered at a teenage slumber party on the eve of a big cheerleading competition. There are no suspects and at this hour there is no apparent motive for this slaughter of innocents."

"Roll tape," the director called. "Stand by, Jack. A minute thirty back to you. Good job."

Doyle breathed deeply, tasted exhaust from the sat truck's generator.

Kaitlin gave him a thumbs up. "Nicely done on the Robicheaux kid."

"Thanks, boss," Doyle replied.

"Funny boy."

Doyle listened to the voiceover through his ear piece while a TV monitor on the sidewalk at Doyle's feet flickered video closeups of weeping parents leaving the police station, hugging, eventually crumbling under the weight of their grief. George had done a good job getting the shots without imposing on their sorrow. Doyle had insisted on that. He looked at George and nodded.

The voiceover continued, "Pierre Saunier was shot and killed in his bed…"

Saunier, Doyle thought. The father was the first to be murdered. No chance to stop what was about to happen. The gunman then moved through the shadows of the house to the basement rec room where he'd shot the kids one by one – sick bastard showing no mercy, nothing faintly human. Doyle could imagine the terror, the disbelief that they were about to die. All kids are convinced of their own immortality.

"The bodies remain inside this house, which is now a grim crime scene," the voiceover said. "Police have no suspects yet, no concrete motive."

A police cruiser screamed away from the scene, its piercing siren pulling Doyle back to the moment. "Thirty seconds to you, Jack." In Doyle's ear the director's voice seemed even more distant. Doyle collected his thoughts, remembered what he'd told Frank earlier about tagging the item. He waited for the out cue, pulled himself straight, and checked his notes again.

A moment later Kaitlin gasped.

What the hell now? Doyle wondered.

Kaitlin brought a hand to her mouth, barely whispered, "Oh my god."

Great, Doyle thought, ten seconds to live, and the power supply on the truck was crapping out or a light was blown. Just his luck. Doyle followed Kaitlin's gaze. *Shit*. A man with a gun. Pointed directly at him.

"Fifteen seconds to you, Jack," the director droned in Doyle's ear. "Tag it out and we'll box you and Frank for a quick Q and A. Good luck."

Doyle couldn't say whether the man with the gun was young or old, tall or short, fat or thin. But the gun in his hand was definitely deadly, with a blue-black barrel that seemed to reach out and touch him. Doyle stood frozen on the sidewalk, oxygen-starved and wordless.

Some people measure their time in minutes and hours, Doyle kept tabs of his by the second. There were thirty frames in a second of video, just enough time for your life to flash by before it winked out. Exactly four seconds elapsed before Doyle slowly brought his hands up and spoke as evenly as he could to the guy with the large weapon pointed at his face. "Would it make any difference if I told you I'm gonna be on national television here real quick?"

The guy looked at him quizzically. "You're that Doyle guy?"

The buzzing in his ears might have been a wonky IFB. Doyle didn't know if it was. Other than that it sounded like business as usual in his ear piece. The control room apparently had no idea what was happening.

At that moment, Doyle had other priorities. "Can I ask you to lower the weapon? Please."

The guy looked around. Not listening.

From the corner of his eye, Doyle inventoried several terrified faces.

"Jack." It was Kaitlin.

"Talk to New York," Doyle whispered. "Tell them what's happening!" Suddenly there was retreat all around him — a chorus of gasps and frantic voices. From down the line came a crash of metal, someone tripping over a tripod or a light. Doyle was aware of his own people. Quiet curses from the audio guy and the satellite truck technician who were both edging away. Not Kaitlin. *Damn it.*

"Staying," she whispered hard.

"Kaitlin," Doyle said between clenched teeth, not willing to remove his eyes from the gun. "Get to the truck. Talk to Malone!"

"Shit, Jack," she protested, then in slow backward steps she disappeared from Doyle's peripheral vision. *Thank God.*

In Doyle's ear. "Ten seconds to you." He was sure the director didn't know what was going on. *Christ.* In ten seconds they'd be broadcasting his execution live on national television. The thought made him nauseated. He chanced a look at George, his cameraman. Still hunched over his viewfinder. Getting the money shot. Like the others. Doyle knew every camera on the street had him nicely framed, and at that moment in households right across the land, he was the subject of breaking news.

"Cool," the gunman finally said, "I seen you on television last week."

Doyle's guts churned. Should have made that pit stop while he had a chance. No one wants to piss himself on national television. He'd be shot dead and the only thing people would remember was the spreading wet spot on the front of his Canali suit.

"John Doyle, right?"

"Jack," Doyle corrected, watching him, dreading the gunman's next move.

"The reporter guy, right?" The gunman stepped slowly towards him. Like he wanted to come on over and shake Doyle's hand, maybe get an autograph.

"Yes. That's right," Doyle replied. "And that gun is making me very nervous."

"Shit," the guy with the gun replied, still not listening.

Things were beginning to register now. The gunman was maybe in his thirties with the physique of a marathon runner, sinewy muscles and wasted skin stretched taut over bony protuberances at every angle of his body. Heroin-thin in worn stovepipe blue jeans and a white T-shirt. He had thinning greasy black hair and hooded eyes as flat as anti-fouling paint.

He was apparently taking the measure of the day and couldn't care less about the commotion or the cops and TV crews. "Guess I fucked them up pretty bad, eh, Doyle?"

Doyle's blood ran cold. *Jesus*. This was the shooter. Jack fought to control his emotions. "Yeah. Real bad," he said. The guy was out of his mind, or stoned. Most likely both.

"No way I'm goin' back to prison."

"OK, I understand," Doyle said as evenly as he could. "What's your name?"

"Salvador."

"OK, Salvador," Jack said.

"Salvador – da man," he hooted. "You got any rock? Just woke up." The shooter pointed towards a park at the other end of the street. "Head feels real bad, all fuzzy and shit, man."

Drugged up mass murderer wants to get high again. "I'm sorry, Salvador," Jack told him. "No rock."

"No rock? Maybe one of your friends. All this fancy equipment. Somebody's got money – got rock."

ANGELS OF MARADONA

Suicide by cop, Jack thought. That was the way Salvador was going to start his day – his last. The gun had to weigh some but Salvador held it at arm's length, unwavering. Real drug-induced stamina.

"Big television star like you got no rock. Fuck is that, man?"

Jack saw the high in Salvador's eyes. Black, dead eyes that seemed to flash intermittently with the remnants of whatever Sal had smoked or snorted or squirted into his arm. "Sorry, Salvador. No one here has any drugs."

Salvador smiled thinly. "Then the party's over."

Frank Simmons couldn't believe his luck. This was a ratings grabber, a double-digit numbers booster. The overnights were going to be unbelievable, and now the daughter of a senator was murdered. Good timing. Right in the middle of contract negotiations too. The bastards were playing hardball, had actually threatened to break off the talks, but they were going to stop the bullshit now, thanks to that man with the gun. Outstanding, Simmons thought as the floor director signaled his mic was hot.

"You're looking at live pictures from New Orleans tonight where senior correspondent Jack Doyle is facing down a gunman outside the scene of last night's horrible cheerleader massacre." Frank rested on his elbows, eyes glued to the live video monitor embedded in the anchor desk. "The man appeared only moments ago as Jack was preparing to wrap up his live report from Miami."

"New Orleans, Frank," the executive producer corrected. "Fuck," he spat, covering the goose-neck microphone that kept him in contact with the on-air talent. "Thirty years in the business and he doesn't know New Orleans from Miami."

Frank Simmons, who'd once confused Abbie Hoffman with Andy Kaufman, brought his eyes level with camera one as script flickered onto the teleprompter. "Just read the prompter," the executive producer droned in his ear.

"Ladies and gentlemen, at this time we can't tell you very much. We don't know yet who the gunman is or why he's threatening our crew. But we can tell you this has just become a very tense standoff. We're now being told police have quietly begun to surround the man...and officers are taking up positions."

The control room expelled a collective gasp. Jamie Malone pounded the console. "Frank," he hissed, "please keep the strategic information off the air." Malone grabbed two cell phones. "George," he shouted, "make sure audio's cut to that monitor at Jack's feet." The EP snapped shut that phone, brought his glistening face to the other. "Kaitlin, the guy gets nowhere near your crew in the truck. Got it? Get the hell out of there before he makes any moves."

"Take it easy, Jamie," Kaitlin replied. "Jack's the one you should be worrying about. And we've already cut audio to the set."

"Great," Malone replied curtly. Then to his crew in the control room, "Folks, we need to regroup. Go to commercial. Open Jack's IFB. Stand by audio," Jamie shouted. "When we hit the commercial I want Jack to hear me."

A moment later, as America watched a commercial for the newest digestive remedy, Jamie Malone rubbed his own stomach and gravely informed Jack that Frank Simmons wanted to speak to the man with the gun.

Salvador lowered the gun, but only slightly. "When I'm gonna be on television, Doyle?"

Jack saw the red light on George's Betacam. "You're on television right now, Salvador." Jack spied several cops hunkered down behind their squad cars, lips moving against hand-held radios. It should have made him feel better. It didn't.

Salvador was mugging for the camera, getting a real charge out of things. "Hey, Enrique, I fucked them up real good," he said, raising his fist. "DB fucked us, man. But I took care of business – just like I said I would." Salvador's eyes hardened as he turned to Jack again. "Not goin' back to prison. Fuckers."

ANGELS OF MARADONA

Jack's stomach felt like it had taken refuge somewhere in his chest. The sound of Frank Simmons' voice in his ear brought a grimace to his face which was plain to see on televisions everywhere. Jack corrected it instantly.

"Jack, this is Frank. We're on the air right now. Can you tell us what's going on?"

Impeccable timing, Jack thought. But before he could open his mouth Simmons was in his ear again. "We're broadcasting live from your camera. The man with the gun...can I speak with him?"

Jack had to think fast. There was no telling how Sal would react to Simmons. Besides, there was no way Jack was going to give Sal a soap box. "Frank, as you can imagine the situation here is very tense." While Jack spoke he watched Salvador and figured he'd have about two seconds to react, to get close enough to grab the gun before Sal got the drop on him. Jack wondered when the SWAT boys were going to get there.

Frank was in his ear again. "We have information this may be the man responsible for last night's massacre. Can you confirm that, Jack?"

"It's quite possible," was all Jack would say. "But I don't think this is the time for that."

Salvador was getting pissed being left out of the conversation. "Who're you talking to, Doyle?" He maneuvered the weapon higher, closed both his hands around it.

"The desk, Sal."

"What desk?"

"The anchor desk. Frank Simmons," Jack replied nervously.

"The guy with the hair, right?" Salvador grinned, seemed to relax a little. Finger still on the trigger though, and Jack calculated a couple pounds of pressure would do it. "That guy. I know him. Tell him Salvador's got a story for him. We got stiffed by that fuckin' cockroach, DB."

This guy is seriously ill, Jack thought, watching Sal's eyes.

"Tell the guy with the wig no one disrespects Salvador and Enrique. Go ahead, Doyle. You got my permission to tell him. An exclusive. That's it, right?"

Kaitlin was in Jack's ear now. "Jack. We've pulled George back. The shot is locked. There's a cop here with me. The police officer says he needs you to move closer. They need to hear what your friend is saying. We need you to do this because we can't boost your audio any higher. Nod if you understand."

Jack nodded imperceptibly.

"That's good," Kaitlin continued. "Jesus, Jack. Be careful."

As careful as you can be with a drug-crazed mass murderer pointing a gun at your head. Jack moved slightly towards the gunman.

"What the fuck you doing, Doyle? You wanna a piece of Salvador or somethin'?"

"You're the star, Salvador. You wanna talk about what happened last night?"

"Shut the fuck up, Doyle," Salvador slurred. "I'm the one doin' the talking." Sal turned to the camera. "Enrique, look at me, man. It's Salvador."

In the CNS satellite truck, Special Ops Captain Stan Billings lowered thick shoulders to avoid overhead equipment. His face showed an intensity that seemed to be seared into his flesh. "Kowalski," he spoke hurriedly into a hand-held radio.

"In position," a raspy voice replied. "I do have a shot. Repeat. I do have a shot."

"Stand by." Billings looked at Kaitlin. "We're going to shut this thing down. Your boy had better do something."

"What do you suggest?" Kaitlin said. As the remote producer she was the ranking staff member in the sat truck. The crew took orders from her. She was trying to keep it together but this cop and New York weren't making it any easier. Not to mention this was Jack out there. "Jack's doing the best he can under the circumstances."

Billings lowered his head towards her. "This guy is about to cave and when he does your man Doyle will be the first to take one."

Kaitlin tensed. Billings was right. Panic rooted somewhere in her gut.

"One more thing," Billings said, almost as an afterthought. "We need you to cut the feed. This isn't going to be pretty."

"You're joking," Kaitlin said.

"I never joke," Billings replied.

Kaitlin didn't doubt it. "There're a dozen trucks here. That means

ANGELS OF MARADONA

a dozen feeds that are live to air right now. Kill ours and the country switches the channel, that's all."

Billings hovered closer, nearly a whisper. "The other trucks have already been taken care of."

So much for freedom of the press, Kaitlin wanted to say. Instead she bit her lower lip and leaned into the console mic. "Jack, we're running out of time. The cops are saying this guy's about to blow. They're gonna cut the feed."

Easier said than done, Jack thought. New York would freak if Kaitlin cut the feed. There'd be hell to pay, and she'd take the fall. It wouldn't matter that the special ops boys had pulled the switch.

All of a sudden, Sal was quiet. Too quiet. Jack shifted his weight and looked sideways at the other sat trucks. Unmanned cameras were pointed at him. He was alone. Just him and Sal. Jack made a decision, something that would end his life or save it. Time was running out so what choice did he have?

Jack breathed deeply. "This guy, Enrique?"

"My brother, man."

"You work for him? He gives you a job to do?"

"DB stiffed us good. We stiffed him back."

There it was again. *DB*. Jack turned carefully to look at the address on the Saunier house. Fifty-two in big brass numbers. Jack understood now what had happened, and it sickened him. "The guy inside. Name's Saunier, daughter Sherra, Sal. Her friends were part of her cheerleading squad. No one by the name of DB was inside the house. No one."

In the sat truck Kaitlin cringed. *Shit*. Could this be possible?

"Fuck you," Salvador spat. The gun came level – eye to eye with Jack. The smell of gun oil swirled around Jack's face. Deadly vapours. "You know that fuck DB or what?"

Jack ignored the question. "Sherra and her dad and seven of her friends were headed up to Biloxi today."

"Like shit. Enrique said DB would be there. DB is always there, case his customers want stuff. So I show up and he's home. So I can take care of business." Salvador pressed the barrel against Jack's forehead. "Only he's got all those little bitches with him – and they need to be taken care of

ANGELS OF MARADONA

too. They think I'm stupid or somethin'. Is that what you think, Doyle?"

Frank Simmons was glued to the studio monitor. "What's Jack doing?" he said quietly.

"Mic's hot, Frank."

Simmons took it as a cue. "Ladies and gentlemen, for those of you just joining us. What we're watching is a standoff in New Orleans where our senior reporter Jack Doyle has been taken hostage by a gunman..."

"Jack," Kaitlin said in his ear, "you're pushing this guy too hard. Ease back."

Jack had just begun to push. It was risky but he had no other choice. "You get the wrong house, Salvador?" Eye contact. Watch for the signs.

Salvador puffed wind between his lips. "What the fuck you talking about?"

"The address, Salvador. You got the wrong address."

"You're crazy, man. Loco."

There it was again, Jack saw. A shift nearly too insignificant to detect in the contour of Salvador's face. Maybe Sal figuring this had gone on way too long. Time to end it.

A cop clamoured up metal steps into the satellite truck and handed Billings a piece of paper. "Salvador Diego, Enrique Diego. Drug boys say they're in the majors," he said.

Kaitlin watched Billings' face as he read. "Jesus," he said, folding the paper and handing it back to the cop. "That's an understatement."

"What does that mean?" Kaitlin asked.

"It means it's time to shut this down – now."

It looked to Jack like Salvador was hungry, really hungry. "Need more rock, Salvador?"

Salvador removed one of his hands from the gun to wipe snot from the end of his nose. "You got rock? Any of you fuckers got rock?" The gun wavered, like Salvador was having trouble deciding which part of Jack's forehead needed a hole in it.

"Put the gun down, Salvador."

"Like fuck," he spat. "I'm a dead man anyway, my brother gets me."
Jack didn't doubt it. He counted silently.

Three.

"You know what, Doyle?"

Two.

"Maybe you're fuckin' right. Maybe the guy wasn't bullshittin' when he said he wasn't DB. He's crying, saying don't hurt us and shit. Then I shot him. Bang, bang."

One.

"Then this loud music downstairs. The bitches dancing and shit and I kinda get into the groove. Bang, bang, bang. I kinda lost it then…don't remember much of that. How many you say were in there?"

Jack had one advantage – no drugs gumming up his synapses. He flashed his hand in a clockwise arc and made contact with the gun. Pain shot through his wrist as the weapon jerked to the right, throwing Salvador off balance. They tumbled to the ground fighting for control of the weapon. Salvador was stronger than Jack expected. Insane with rage as he cursed and grunted and desperately attempted to lodge the weapon between them. Jack knew he was trying for a gut shot.

On the locked off cameras, a blur of movement – flesh slapping and punching with Jack on top of Salvador Diego. The life saver came when the gun slipped from Sal's hand. Jack kicked it away, balled his fists and put everything he had into three jackhammer punches to Salvador's face. He pulled back for a fourth and saw it wouldn't be necessary. Salvador was out cold, a stream of blood spilling from his nose. Jack immediately heard the thump of heavy boots, the clack of ammo being chambered, and the sound of smaller feet tumbling down the steps of the sat truck. *Kaitlin.* The third thing Jack Doyle heard as he slumped onto Sal's unconscious body was Frank Simmon's voice.

"Jack, this might be a bad time, but…"

FOUR

The debriefing by cops took more than an hour. Lots of questions while a detective whose name Jack had already forgotten frantically typed. When he was done they printed two copies and Jack signed them both. There were only four of them left in the windowless squad room which was a blur of manila files, used styrofoam cups and mug shots plastered all over the walls. There was Jack, the two-finger typist, and Billings who watched as a paramedic named Randy patched up an ugly gash that ran along the back of Jack's wrist. "Lucky man," Randy said, "won't need stitches."

"How's Sal?" Jack asked, inspecting Randy's workmanship.

"Badly bruised jaw. Keeps asking for rock," Randy said. "He'll live."

Jack looked at Billings. "I presume you got the senator out of there as soon as the trouble started."

"Had to tear him away from his daughter's body," Billings replied. "Wanted to take her with him."

Jack drained cold gritty dregs from the bottom of his cup and tossed it into an overflowing trash can. He flipped his cell phone open and saw he'd missed five calls, four from the network. "We done here?" he asked, testing his hand for flexibility.

Billings nodded, but when Jack stood to leave, the cop held up a calloused hand. "One more thing."

"Sure."

"How were you so sure Diego got the wrong address?"

"You mean besides the fact Saunier's initials aren't DB?"

"Yeah"

"The mailbox," Jack said.

Billings lifted his shoulders. "Saunier's house has no mailbox."

"That's right, but the house down the street does. D. Bastarache – number 25 Avalon Road. I noticed it when I came in – hard to miss in neon green – probably a flag for his buyers. "

"I'm still not getting it, Doyle."

Jack paused a second to wait for the cop to catch up. "Salvador kept referring to DB, the guy he was supposed 'to take care of.' D. Bastarache. That's the name on the mailbox outside 25 Avalon Road. Saunier's house number is 52. Our genius must have reversed the numbers."

"Jesus," Billings said, his face lighting up like he'd just tweaked to a tough algebra question. He turned to the cop who had taken Jack's statement. "Run the guy's name and address. See what pops up."

"Right on it, Cap."

"Nice work, Doyle," Billings said. "This reporter stuff doesn't work out, you come see me."

Jack had already started to walk out the door.

FIVE

It was close to nine o'clock when Jack got back to his hotel. He paid the cab driver and walked into the lobby. Laughter and loud voices came from the bar on his left. Cap'n Patout's was a popular spot in the Garden District, about a block from the Quarter and right on the streetcar line that carried thirsty riders up and down St. Charles. Jack was hoping to avoid the pack and was making a beeline for the elevator when he heard someone shout his name. "Doyle. Where you goin'?" Mona Lasing held a drink in each hand, a cigarette dangled from her lips. "Get that beauteous ass over here," she shouted across the lobby.

Jack looked to the elevator, then the desk clerk, who shrugged. There was no way of escaping Mona Lasing. Any man who tried was quickly defeated, if not by the strength of her will, then certainly by her former Miss Arizona body. Jack realized his competition had never looked better. "I see the gang's all here," he said, walking reluctantly toward her.

"Everyone except the star of the evening," she said, handing him one of her drinks. "You look like you can use this."

"You got that right." Jack plucked the cigarette carefully from her lips and followed her inside. "No hard feelings?"

"You got lucky on the senator's kid, Doyle. That goddamn horseshoe again." Lasing's look softened. "No hard feelings, Jack. I'm just glad you're still here."

Journalism was thirsty work, Jack thought. Bone-dry back-breaking toil that required large amounts of Cap'n Patout's smooth amber ale and vaporous liquors. He might well have been on the bridge of an eighteenth-century barque on the cusp of mutiny. Reporters, who had three hours before been icons of truth, were now drinking Cap'n Patout's dry.

Jack followed Lasing to an empty spot at the bar where he was mobbed. The reporter for National Public Radio was listing thirty degrees to port when he embraced Jack. "Ladies and gentlemen," Dirk Johnston boomed across the room, "I give you the man of the hour – the prince pugilist – Mister Jack Doyle."

The mention of Jack's name sent them into frenzy. He was suddenly surrounded by a blur of boozy faces and cockeyed grins – hands full of sudsy drinks. Apparently no one held a grudge over Jack's scoop on the senator's daughter.

"Thought you were toast, Doyle." Bill Heinrich was the bespectacled Houston bureau chief for *The Washington Post*.

"So did I," Jack said, "thought you were going to have a new lead for your story."

"Was already working it in my head," Bill slurred before draining half his glass. "But didn't count on that right hook of yours."

Everyone laughed at the little man's joke, then pressed closer to touch Jack's shoulder in genuine displays of affection and relief before dispersing to bar stools fashioned from dark oak rum barrels. Someone rang a bell affixed to a mast in the centre of the bar. "Next round's on the *Post*." The place went up again, only this time louder.

Mona folded a pair of shapely legs, revealing the soft underside of a tanned thigh, and looked deeply into Jack's eyes. "You had us scared for a minute," she said, breathlessly.

"Me too," Jack said, looking away. "Where's Kaitlin?"

Mona shrugged and reached for another cigarette which she placed slowly between full pouting lips. "Be a gentleman, Jack."

Jack took her lighter and watched as the flame cast a golden hue on Mona's pampered features. Dark green eyes softened to turquoise under the glare of light while her platinum blonde hair absorbed rich tones of fiery yellow. "Thanks," she said, allowing her hand to linger on Jack's arm. Gingerly she touched the thick bandage around his wrist. "Ouch."

"War wound," Jack said. "The other guy looks a lot worse."

Mona laughed softly, and then held up two fingers to a bartender who seemed to be locked in her orbit. "Seriously, Jack. Congratulations on the Robicheaux catch. You won fair and square." She leaned forward and kissed him on the cheek. "You get that because you put a deranged killer behind bars tonight."

In the excitement over everything that had happened Jack hadn't even considered the fact he had actually collared a multiple murderer. "Somewhere there's a presumption of innocence, but I believe you're right," he replied. "Given that Sal basically confessed on live television." Doyle swallowed a mouthful of liquor, relishing the warmth that embraced his gut. Hand suddenly trembling he reached for a cigarette, lit it, and exhaled smoke and tension in one breath.

Mona looked at him. "Thought you quit."

"Not tonight," Jack said. "Besides, I beat the crap out of death once today. I figure I'm safe for awhile."

The noise level was an indicator that expense accounts were taking a real pounding. Everyone on the same mental health plan. Drink until the visions of body bags faded. Survival, Jack thought. Easier done in groups, because, like cops and soldiers, reporters coped better in clumps. Jack knew things were getting nasty when he saw Popeye was in trouble. Cap'n Patout's mascot was a macaw, and the sign over the bar said he was seventy-five years old in human years, and he didn't like to be touched, or fed, or even looked at the wrong way. Maybe Ricky, the AP guy, couldn't read because he was maneuvering poor old Popeye onto Bill Heinrich's shoulder. The bird flapped its wings and squawked in protest, and in a flash of revenge loosed a great glob of something roughly the same colour as its plumage onto Bill's three-hundred-dollar Hugo Boss shirt. Everyone howled, including the soiled, Pulitzer-Prize winning, *Washington Post* bureau chief.

Someone yelled, "Give 'em a wipe!" to howls of laughter. "Not Heinrich. The bird."

Jack wanted to tell them to put Popeye back on his perch. Figured, what good would it do? Besides, the bird would survive.

Mona stared at the jokers with the bird and shook her head in disgust. "You missed the White House."

Jack had heard radio clips from the president's address on his way over in the cab. "Denton's on a mission."

"Definitely," Mona added, drawing deeply on her cigarette, casually exhaling a plume of smoke towards the ceiling. "The Christian evangelicals are threatening to pull their support if he doesn't do something about the drug violence, they want the death penalty for drug dealers."

"Voices of reason."

Mona smiled, and then struggled for a presidential voice. "My administration is committed on this issue. To stop the poison that's leaching into our neighbourhoods, our schools and workplaces."

Jack chuckled, took another sip, and was thinking about the president's bluster when Mona leaned over and laid a hand on his knee.

"Jack, we had good times, didn't we?"

The warmth from her fingers felt to Jack like it was melting his flesh. "Sure, Mona. But things are different now."

Mona ignored him. "Remember Kosovo? That villa. Shells exploding all around us. Remember what you said that night?"

He remembered. Also remembered he regretted the night deeply because of the complications it created. "Let's not go there, Mona."

Lasing pouted.

"Fraternizing with the enemy again?" Kaitlin O'Rourke's voice could have seared flesh.

Mona withdrew her hand as Jack turned to see Kaitlin standing behind him with a look that matched the tone of her voice.

"Wondering where you were," Jack said.

"You know how it is. Reporters get the glory, producers get the work," Kaitlin replied, looking around. "Up talking to New York. Malone's pissed at you, as usual."

Jack smirked. "That's what he gets paid for."

Kaitlin glared at Mona, refused to blink until Lasing backed off. She spied Popeye recovering on his perch and then flashed her eyes at the woman sitting too close to Jack. "Poor old bird looks tired. Feathers aren't nearly as colourful and soft anymore."

Shit, Jack thought. Here we go.

Mona straightened. "Cockatoos are—"

"A macaw," Kaitlin interrupted. "Central and South America. A macaw."

Lasing stared straight into Kaitlin's eyes. "Macaw then. Macaws are pretty resilient. Can take a lot of roughhousing. Probably enjoy it. Whaddya think, Jack?"

Jack felt the heat emanating from both female bodies. Made him feel like a piece of burning toast. "Parrots aren't my specialty," he said cautiously, shooting Mona a look.

Kaitlin refused to break eye contact. "We all have our specialties, don't we, Mona? Strengths and weaknesses." Kaitlin punched out the words like hooks and jabs.

Jack cringed. They were treading a minefield. Mona's weaknesses involved a married senator, touted as a Republican contender for the White House. The affair was being kept quiet, but word was the senior senator for California was about to leave his wife.

Mona Lasing stubbed out her cigarette and got up to leave. "I've always had a weakness for good men, Kaitlin, and I can assure you the feelings are always mutual." Mona touched Jack on the arm. "Thanks for remembering the old times." She turned and strode away.

Kaitlin didn't take her eyes off Lasing until she had disappeared in the crowd. She then sat. "That woman," she said, exasperated.

Jack caught the waiter's attention and ordered Kaitlin a drink. "Mona's harmless, Kaitlin, though I don't expect you'll ever believe it."

"It's none of my business," she shot back. "I just think you can do better."

"Now you're sounding like my Aunt Muriel."

Kaitlin ignored the remark. Jack was a shit when he wanted to be.

"Sorry," Jack offered, too late.

Kaitlin didn't care about the baggage that Jack carried in his life. She didn't care about his fling with Mona Lasing, which was now over. Or was it? What irked her was the way Lasing had used her considerable female charms to seduce her way to the network. Brazenly manipulated the men who could help her. One of those men had been Jack Doyle. Kaitlin saw Mona deep in conversation with a good-looking male on the other side of the bar. Jack was watching too.

The waiter arrived with Kaitlin's drink.

"Guess I kind of went to pieces today," she said, tipping the tall beverage between her lips. The softness had returned to her face but not her eyes. She had something to get off her chest, as his friend and producer. "That was a stupid stunt today. Diego was wasted." Kaitlin stared away, waiting for Jack to respond. He was taking his time. She pushed on. "He'd already killed nine times, what was one more to him? God, Jack."

Jack drained what was left of his drink, licked his lips. "Diego's brother Enrique's quite a player."

"Not to be stiffed apparently."

"Nope. Danny Bastarache took him for about twenty large so Enrique sends his intellectually challenged sibling over to make things right. DB has flown the coop, but it doesn't matter because Salvador screws up the address. And the rest is history."

"Sad history," Kaitlin added.

Jack continued, "They nabbed Enrique at the airport with a quarter million and a one-way ticket to Bogotá. And, by the way, about Diego's gun—"

"Big gun," Kaitlin replied with a reproachful look. "What about it?"

"Big...and empty," Jack said. "Clean as a whistle. Remember, I was face-to-face with it. Every chamber was empty."

Kaitlin stared at him in disbelief. "How about the chamber beneath the hammer? You couldn't tell if that one was empty, Einstein."

"Ooops."

Kaitlin shook her head. A moment passed. "Sounds like we've got more work to do here."

"We'll see," Jack replied.

Kaitlin had already turned around and was staring at Mona huddled in conversation now with her burly cameraman. George and the rest of Kaitlin's crew were upstairs cutting a fresh piece for the late broadcast. The incident with Salvador Diego would roll as a separate item voiced by Frank Simmons. Kaitlin had told New York Jack was unavailable for a live pop into the show, and after some raised voices the late-night producer relented, told her and Jack to get some sleep.

Jack was about to order another drink.

"We've got an early morning, Jack," Kaitlin reminded him. "So do these guys," she added, surveying the crowd, smiling inwardly at the sight of Bill Heinrich wiping bird shit from his shoulder. Many a Washington politician would have envied Popeye, she thought.

Jack followed her stare and chuckled. "They gave that guy a Pulitzer. Can you believe it?"

"Nothing in this business surprises me anymore."

Jack studied her for a moment. "You're still a *naif*, Cheri. So much more for me to teach you."

"I'm yours to mould," she said. "But I've got work to do upstairs. Time for me to go."

"A producer's work is never done," Jack said. "If Malone calls tell him I'm in bed."

Kaitlin stared past Jack to Mona Lasing. "Sure, Jack. Whatever you say. Reporters get to sleep now and then."

"Sleep and glory."

"Whatever." Kaitlin walked away.

Jack watched her leave. Past the remnants of the evening, past Bill Heinrich and Roger Jackson who were squinting at their BlackBerrys. Past several more soused reporters representing some of the finest journalistic organs on the face of the planet, and past Popeye who had somehow managed to drift off into avian oblivion.

Jack caught the bartender's attention and ordered another drink. A minute later it was placed before him and Jack brought it to his lips, swallowed half, and then closed his eyes. There was no easy way to explain what had happened that day, no way to make Kaitlin understand. He could have said he was absolutely certain Salvador Diego wasn't going to shoot him. He wanted to explain that unreal ability of his to flash forward during moments like that – his non-linear vision – to see an outcome before it had actually occurred. Once, when he was a kid, his cousin Tommy was hit by a truck. Jack saw it before it actually happened. The younger boy chased a ball into the road, and even before the old pickup appeared from around the curve Jack's brain conjured a fleeting image. It was the shocked expression on his cousin's face in the split second before the truck struck him. There might have been time to scream at Tommy, to warn him back. Jack wasn't sure. Then it happened. Tommy was thrown thirty feet onto some rocks and hit his head. He survived, but was never really the same after that. Jack thought himself open-minded, but he didn't believe in weird notions of ESP and clairvoyance. Whatever he was gifted with wasn't either of those. Maybe hyper-sensitive was a better way to describe it. He didn't waste a lot of time trying to figure it out. Just the way he was, like his dry sense of humour and lazy left eye. Jack was sorry about what happened to his cousin, but he also learned something important that day. Next time, he wouldn't ignore his intuition.

SIX

On Friday morning, July 2, *The Washington Post* carried a large front-page headline "Shooter tied to Colombian Cartel." The kicker said, "Senator in Mourning." The story ran on page three with a photograph of CNS reporter Jack Doyle "locked in battle" with shooting suspect Salvador Diego, who is alleged, the *Post* went on, to have murdered nine innocent people, eight of them high school cheerleaders who, by all accounts, were the bright lights of their families, their school, and the charitable organizations to which they selflessly donated many hours of community service when they weren't otherwise engaged in academics, sports or being perfect young citizens and role models. Now they were dead, and a senator's family was among the grieving.

The article, which took up most of the space above the fold, also included photographs of the victims – bright-eyed, attractive all-American kids with their lives ahead of them until thirty-four-year-old Salvador Diego "is alleged" to have broken down their back door, and brutally executed them one by one. Forty-seven-year-old Pierre Saunier, owner of a New Orleans accounting firm, was killed first, in a tragic case of mistaken identity. Salvador Diego and his older brother Enrique were both in custody, the elder Diego apprehended while trying to flee the country. Both men had numerous previous drug convictions and were known to have family ties with a major Colombian drug lord by the name of Carlos Ruiz. Sources inside the Drug Enforcement Agency had confirmed all of the above, and went on to say that Enrique Diego headed a drug apparatus that operated from the Gulf Coast west to California and north to Washington state. *The Washington Post* and several other highly respected news outlets also did something that day that greatly worried the handful of people closest to President Frederic Denton. They declared in stinging editorials that what had happened at 52 Avalon Road in New Orleans was a symptom of a disease that was running unchecked through neighbourhoods and cities large and small throughout America. The disease was illegal drugs, like coke and crank and ecstasy, and the violence they spawned had long ago eroded the constitutional right of Americans to feel safe in their own homes. Something had to be done about it. It had all been said many times before, but not with the same impact, given the bloodbath at 52 Avalon Road.

The "Cheerleader Murders" consumed talk radio and television that Friday morning in a kind of collective venting ritual for the nation's frustrated and angry.

A half hour after kicking the bedclothes off, Jack Doyle had already read the four morning newspapers that had been dropped outside his door. He had a phone pressed to his ear and was suffering his executive producer who was ramping up for another day – another lead – this time without the theatrics of Sal Diego and the exclusive on Senator Aaron Robicheaux. "Denton scrummed on the Cheerleader Murders," Jamie Malone said, too energetically for so early in the morning. "We got great tape."

"You're kidding me," Jack said.

"No shit. Aboard Air Force One. He strolls to the back of the plane and Rankin tosses it. Denton bites hard. Called it 'a heartless attack on innocent children by the spawn of Colombian drug lords.'"

"Pulling no punches as usual."

"Has he ever?"

It was 8 am in New York and Malone was cresting a caffeine high. "Huxley says something's up."

Jack cradled the cell and reached for the carafe of hot coffee, filling two cups. Cream, no sugar for both. "Huxley may be overreacting...the janitors forget to turn out the lights and Huxley's convinced the Pentagon's drawing up plans to invade Canada."

"He's been right about plenty, Jack."

"What about Iraq? You call that fair."

Malone coughed into the phone. Jack heard him drag deeply on a cigarette and guessed his executive producer was already well into his first pack of the morning. "He predicted the day and hour for the first shots. He won the pool."

"He's the Pentagon correspondent, for Christ's sake. He got tipped," Jack said. "That's his job."

"Whatever."

Jack heard the shower. He looked fondly at something made of lace at the foot of the bed and smiled. She'd been great, but now Jack had something important to discuss with Malone.

"The story here is over, except for the funerals," Jack said.

"Funerals make great television, Jack," Malone replied. "Not to mention good profile. That's important for you right now."

Jack sat on the edge of the bed and blew at the wisp of steam rising from his coffee. "That's downright ghoulish," he said.

"That's reality," Malone replied. "Have you seen the numbers lately? They're tanking. Carmichael's getting nervous, and you know what? So is Mr. Hair and Teeth."

Jack chuckled. "Thirteen years is a long time."

"Apparently not long enough for Frank Simmons."

Jamie was right. It was no secret Frank Simmons was on the way out, and profile was going to go a long way toward deciding who his replacement would be. The bigger the story, the bigger the profile. Huxley had the Pentagon. That was big and so was the White House where Rankin was becoming a star. But Jack Doyle had been in the trenches and that was where the real stories happened, not public relations bullshit and managed media events at the Pentagon and aboard Air Force One.

Malone dragged on his smoke. "There's talk a change could be coming soon, Jack. And your name is being mentioned a lot."

Jack flexed the muscles in his damaged hand – his bonafide war wound. The only danger plaguing Huxley and Rankin was the threat of paper cuts. "Rankin and Huxley both have more years than me," Jack said.

"And your point?"

"Seniority."

"Seniority's worth squat if you're not the right person for the job."

Right again, Malone, Jack thought, wanting to move on to his story proposal. Malone would have to be sold on it first. "I'm thinking it's time to take it back to the front lines in the drug war, Jamie," Jack said. "Take the Cheerleader Murders to where the seeds were planted."

"Go on," Malone said.

Jack paused. "Denton's got a lot invested politically. Then there's his son."

"Latest numbers say he's at forty-eight percent approval rating," Malone cut in.

"Forty-nine," Jack corrected. "Everyone feels the man's pain." Jack walked to the bed, pushed newspapers out of the way to find the remote. The television flickered to life and he punched up CNN. He continued, "I'm thinking it's time we went down there and got our hands dirty. You know the story – country disintegrating into lawlessness, violence, forty years of civil war. The cocaine economy. Everything."

"Don't know about that, Jack," Malone said, sucking even harder on his cigarette. "Lots of dead people down there, especially reporters. A guy got stabbed to death last week."

CNN was running visuals of Jack's hand-to-hand with Diego. Nice take-down, he thought. Malone was purposely refusing to talk about the hostage drama because of the blowout on the telephone after it happened. "This is what I'm thinking," he continued as if Malone hadn't said anything. "We'll put four or five minutes in the can, and use it when Denton plays his ace. Who knows? Maybe he'll invade Colombia and we'll all look like prophets." Jack chuckled, though he knew it made perfect sense. Malone would have to agree.

"Sure, Jack, turn Colombia into another Vietnam? You and I know

ANGELS OF MARADONA

there's not much chance of that. Anyway, Carmichael will never go for it." Malone dragged on his cigarette. "You'd be walking into a bloodbath. Besides, you're not finished there yet."

That's what Jack expected him to say. "Bring in McCoy."

"That's not a good idea."

"Jamie."

"Listen. Ya know what I think of that guy. There's no way I'm going to let him screw this story up too."

Jack stood up and walked to the window, then turned as the water was turned off in the shower. The bathroom door remained shut.

"Jack, McCoy'd fuck up a funeral."

"That's not funny," Jack replied.

"I'm serious."

And right about McCoy, Jack didn't say. Jamie stopped a moment. Jack knew he was catching his breath, probably reaching for another cigarette. "Carmichael likes him," Jack continued. "Someone to follow in my footsteps when I replace Simmons, right, Jamie?"

"McCoy's just plain stupid, you know it," Malone said angrily. "Besides we're missing the point here."

Jack knew this was coming. He grabbed his jacket and slapped at the pockets. No smokes. He'd quit a month ago but the habit was hanging on like a phantom limb. "What point?" He said after a moment.

"None of the networks are touching Colombia. You know that...not even the Italian newsrooms and they'll go anywhere. The more bang-bang the better."

"One of those newsrooms lost a photog in Kabul, didn't they? It's no wonder they're gun-shy." Jack heard the scratch of flint through the phone. Malone sucked deeply before responding. "Everyone's gun-shy," he said. "And this network can't afford to lose its best reporter."

"Thanks for caring," Jack said.

"No worries. Anything for a friend."

Jack considered what to say next. The cheerleaders' story was gaining momentum quickly, but nothing could be gained from pictures of coffins being lowered into the ground. The story was much bigger than that, much more complicated. Getting it might mean some danger pay. What the hell? It's what Jack did. He'd already made up his mind. Better to ask for forgiveness than permission, he decided. But Jack wouldn't leave an assignment uncovered because that was a career killer. "Bring in McCoy to do sidebars. The high school's holding a memorial service tonight, the governor's going to be there, the senator too."

"Jack."

"We're gonna be full tilt with the other stuff," Jack lied. "It's a no-brainer. Even McCoy can handle it." Jack knew he was making sense. The silence on the other end of the telephone meant Malone knew it too.

"He's a stupid asshole."

"Put him in front of the camera. He'll say what he's told. That's what producers are for."

Malone ignored the remark and continued, "Speaking of producers, have Kaitlin call me as soon as you touch base with her."

"Sure…now what about McCoy?"

"You win," Malone surrendered.

"Thanks, Jamie. You're too hard on him."

"Whatever. Gotta keep Carmichael happy, I suppose."

"Now you're getting it."

Jamie coughed, punctuating the end of their conversation, and then hung up.

Jack was going to Colombia, because that's where the story was now. It was going to create a huge headache for Jamie Malone for a couple of hours. But it was going to pay off in spades. Jack was sure of it. The story would take a couple of days at most and when Jack returned they'd have a ball-breaker. The other networks would shit when they saw the piece – especially the exclusive interview Jack intended to get with the leader of the FARC rebels. Jack was certain Jamie Malone would eventually thank him for showing the initiative, and would probably take a large measure of the credit for sending Jack in.

Jack sipped his coffee and thought about the story. Kaitlin was going to love it. He was thinking about her when the bathroom door opened and Mona Lasing stepped into the bedroom, her hair and body wrapped snuggly in thick white towels.

Mona allowed one of the towels to drop casually to the floor. Watched

Jack's face for his reaction.

"Let me guess," she said, "Malone mayhem."

"In spades," Jack replied, taking in the full measure of her.

"My guy's a tornado too," Mona said. "And if I don't call him soon, he'll have a stroke."

Jack frowned, then looked at her lustily. "He'll survive."

Mona smiled back at him. "You're insatiable and incorrigible."

"I'm a flawed man," Jack replied. In pursuit of a huge story, he added silently to himself.

SEVEN

It was another perfect morning on the estate outside Medellin, where three of Colombia's most vicious drug lords were assembled, soon to be joined by a man more powerful than the three of them combined, who had chosen to watch them for a full ten minutes from the window of his study while they waited impatiently.

None of the three would have won any beauty contests, especially not Zebe Bonito and she was the only woman among them. She hadn't always been repulsive. In fact men once paid good money for her. She'd been beautiful then but that was before the ridge of angry red flesh that snaked from below her right ear to the end of her narrow chin. Even her disfigurement didn't blacken the memory of her first kill, when she fought savagely to fell the drunken fucker who had slashed her. Dropped him with his own knife in a motel room and emptied his pockets while he pumped out.

Miguel, her "manager" was drunk when he sewed her wound shut with six-pound fishing line, oblivious to the muscle and delicate nerves that ran beneath her face. It was five years before she hunted him down, and returned the favour.

Bonito gingerly traced the mangled flesh with the tip of a finger while studying the faces of the two others.

Carlos Ruiz, the smiling fat man of Medellin, made small talk while Ungaro Alvarez of Cali sat ramrod straight and swiveled his head like a bird of prey searching for its next meal. Furtive eyes bracketed a beak of a nose.

Montello's man Suarez approached, gently placing a tray onto the marble table. He distributed fine porcelain cups and then positioned a silver carafe in front of them.

"Senor Montello begs your forgiveness," he said. "An important overseas call has delayed him." He nodded his head, turned and retreated over freshly cut grass towards the main house.

Ruiz poured for all of them and then sat back. "You're looking well," he said to Bonito with not a trace of sincerity in his voice and unable to take his eyes from her ruined face.

She looked at him with undisguised loathing. "We're fucked because of you," Bonito spat.

"Cordial as usual," Ruiz said, wrapping stubby fingers around the dainty porcelain cup. "What about it, Alvarez?" he added, bringing the cup to his lips, slurping the thick brew. "I'm sure you have an opinion."

Alvarez stared elsewhere. "My opinion is shared with few, Ruiz… not you."

"Debate is healthy," Ruiz replied.

"I didn't come here to debate," Alvarez said. "What you have to say is of no consequence to me."

"Still, there is this problem of ours," Ruiz added. "It can't be ignored."

"The problem is yours, Ruiz," Bonito barked, jabbing a finger in his direction. She swallowed the rest of her words, realized too late that he was trying to draw them out, to measure the strength of their positions.

Ruiz looked only slightly disappointed. "What is it the Americans say?" He looked to one, then the other, grinning. "Shit happens."

"And soon it'll be happening to us." Alvarez sneered. "Don't underestimate the Americans and their self-righteous president. Anger and grief are powerful incentives…Ruiz."

"There are new risks, I agree," Ruiz replied. "But let's not overreact."

Alvarez shifted his tall frame slightly. "Have you not been paying attention? They speak our names in the same breath as Hitler, Stalin... Hussein. And that was before your cousin's little stunt in New Orleans. A fucking senator's daughter was murdered!"

Ruiz shifted to restore blood flow to the lower regions of his four hundred pound body. He continued to smile. In fact, in nearly every one of the DEA surveillance photographs of Carlos Ruiz, the Medellin drug lord has a smile on his face, displaying a mouthful of glistening white teeth like Chicklets embedded behind lips that resembled dew worms. He never shied from the camera, and once gave the finger to a DEA Blackhawk helicopter as it swept low over his mountain villa. Analysts who studied the photographs later laughed at the hairy fat man with the teeth, wearing a Speedo bathing suit like "ten pounds of shit in a five-pound bag."

Montello approached silently from across the lawn, unnoticed until he reached the table. "I see everyone's here. Good," he said as he sat. "Nice of you to come." Montello pushed a button to raise a lead-lined patio umbrella and then reached for his coffee.

His three guests cast perfunctory glances around the table, a trinity of blank faces that gave nothing away except their distrust of one another. None of them would engage in further pleasantries.

"You're already wasting our time, Montello." It was Alvarez who spoke first, checking his watch, the birdman seemingly transfixed by its shiny gold strap.

"That's unlikely," Montello responded, bringing the fine blue cup to his lips.

Montello gazed across the lawn to the house where Suarez stood stone-like beneath a royal palm. He would waste no time. "You would be smart to listen," Montello said, silently counting their bodyguards. "The Americans have been posturing again."

"Fuck them," Bonito barked. "More empty threats."

"Normally, yes," Montello agreed. "But this time there are additional incentives." He pointed at Ruiz. "You, my friend, know that better than all of us."

"No one can hold me responsible for what happened."

"Maybe. Maybe not," Montello said. "But it was your people who got sloppy."

"And they're dead men," Ruiz shot back. "They bring the DEA down on my house, I'll eat their hearts."

Bonito wanted badly to lunge for the knife strapped around her ankle. Pin his jaw shut with the blade. No more shiny teeth.

Montello smiled inwardly. The anger divided them. This was a good thing. Ordinarily what had happened in New Orleans would be inconsequential. Not now. Ruiz refused to understand the implications for all of them.

"Why should we listen to you?" Ruiz displayed his wonderful teeth, looked to the others for agreement. "You would have us all devalue the product." A look of smug contentment on his ruddy features.

"To enlarge our market, Carlos," Montello said with a forced smile. "Simple economics."

Ruiz slapped a thick meaty hand against the table. "You shifted how many loads last year, Montello? Twenty-five percent in excess of our output, I'll wager. You're paying less for your paste because you've got half the farmers in Colombia supplying your coca leaves, not to mention the Bolivian producers. You can afford to talk about lowering prices."

"Make the product more accessible," Montello shot back like he was trying to instill common sense in a child. "Enlarge our markets, increase our profits."

Alvarez and Bonito both fixed their attention on Montello. None of this was the point of the meeting. None of it would matter if they didn't deal with the problem at hand: how to defeat the extradition treaty and avoid ending up in an American prison.

Ruiz waited a moment before speaking. "None of us needs a lesson in simple economics."

Montello wasn't listening. Ruiz would never get it. None of it would matter if they couldn't stop the forces which were aligning against them. Ruiz would be the only hold out. He was a liability.

Montello's demeanor shifted slightly. "You have no ability to appreciate the strengths we have as a unified organization. You forget the lessons taught us twenty years ago."

Alvarez and Bonito grunted agreement.

Montello looked to both of them, saw the tide was shifting in his favour. The diffuse light beneath the umbrella seemed to soften the savaged flesh on Bonito's face, but only slightly. Montello signaled Suarez in a gesture too insignificant for any of them to detect. "Six months from now the countryside will be crawling with US marines. None of us will be safe," he said, shifting his attention from one to the other. "They will bring their Rangers. They will rappel their Delta teams onto our heads. And they will finish us. What will markets, prices, or any of it matter then? That's why we need the Russian."

"We have resources of our own," Alvarez interrupted, sniffing the air with contempt. "We have the revolutionaries on our payrolls, enough money to supply more than they need to turn Colombia into another Vietnam. None of the Americans forgets Vietnam." Alvarez swiveled his head, beady eyes locking on a pair of bright blue wings on currents of hot humid air over the tree line. The others nodded.

"We've been through this before," Bonito pronounced. "No one forgets the last time Bogotá decided we were not welcome in our own country. The *violencia* lasted for years."

"The three J's," Ruiz chirped up. "Judges, journalists and justice ministers. You remember how many died. The government's surrender."

Montello looked slowly around the table. "Things are different now. Our enemies won't be cowed. The American president's using sacred terms like 'national security.' He'll act, he's got no choice."

One right-wing newspaper had even dredged up the name of the brazen Carlos Lehder. "Cocaine is Latin America's Atomic bomb," he had said once. Another editorialist had described crack as a "weapon of mass destruction." Republican hawks were pushing for dramatic measures — maybe even a US-led invasion of Colombia. It was even possible the Pentagon was about to launch surgical strikes against Colombia's drug barons. Those who survived would no doubt be brought before American judges. Montello understood the danger they faced as well as the dramatic measures that would be needed. The Russian had offered an insurance policy, and even though the price was outrageous, Montello had agreed. A lot had to be accomplished first, and time wasn't a luxury they had.

Montello leaned forward and shot his cuffs in a move designed to remind them who was in charge. "You saw what the Americans did in Iraq. Saddam's forces were formidable, and in the end they pulled the little hairy man from a hole in the ground."

Ruiz chuckled. "A megalomaniac who taunted the Bush men." He lazily lifted a sausage-like finger to touch the centre of his forehead. "Made himself a target."

"And we haven't?" Montello paused, looked with mild rebuke at the three of them. "We've become the monsters that this American president must defeat. It's what the voters said to him. Choke off the supply. He will have Colombia's permission to do what has to be done, you know that. It's already begun. They have units here already. 'Advisors.' Last week those 'advisors' engaged FARC soldiers not fifty miles to the south of Bogotá. Thirty-two revolutionaries were dispatched without casualties to the enemy." Montello lifted his head slightly to view the line of trees where clusters of heavily armed bodyguards stood watch. Each of the three drug barons was under escort by large protection details. There had been twenty-nine men in all, twelve fewer now by Montello's calculations. Ruiz had no clue his men were gone. He was both stupid and blind. No different really than the pathetic cowards who begged for Montello's mercy while he kicked them into unconsciousness and stole their money in the dark alleys where he hunted as a teenager.

For a moment none of them spoke. Montello could see the doubt beginning to lay roots in them, even Ruiz, whose perpetual smile was fading behind the fleshy folds of his face. Though in his eyes, a flicker of challenge.

"The Americans have no stomach for body bags. No guts for another useless war," Ruiz insisted.

Montello allowed the statement to settle, to find its place among them. Allowed them to sample its flawed logic, and unsound reason, to mine whatever false hope they could extract from it. When Montello spoke again it was as if arrows had launched towards Ruiz, pinning him to dark oak.

"The Americans have no tolerance for dead children either." Montello watched their reactions closely, saw eyes narrow in stern faces. "They're dead because your cousin did something which was totally unnecessary, and phenomenally stupid. We'll all pay now."

The two others waited for the fat man to defend himself, which would have been a stupid and useless gesture at best.

Ruiz said nothing, just stared at Montello like he'd been slapped. A challenge that had to be met.

Bonito was longing for her knife, the heft of it. She imagined the feel of its blade melting through layers of fat. She brought her fingers to her face, ran a nail along that part of the scar that began just below her earlobe. Blood seemed to be pulsing there. Ruiz was an idiot who threatened them all.

"I am prepared to die to protect my country," Ruiz said, folding fat arms across his massive chest.

What a fool, Montello thought. No one would win that kind of fight.

Even the former Soviet Union, with its mighty nuclear arsenal had eventually surrendered. But the Americans had made the mistake of calling it a "war on drugs." Wars have winners and losers and coca could not be defeated. For a long time it had been used legally around the world, as a cure-all in everything from wine to sinus medicine. Even American drugstores had once dispensed it in its purest form to recreational users. No. Coca could not be defeated.

Montello doubted Ruiz would ever understand the stupidity of his bluster. "Noble gesture, Carlos," he finally said. "But, irrelevant."

Ruiz burned his eyes into him, stubby fingers drained of their blood as he pulled himself forward in his chair. "You ignore my family's brave history."

Montello appeared calm and confident but beneath the façade boiled pure anger. He gripped the arms of his chair to keep from lunging at the fat man who was now testing him. "Long dead soldiers, Carlos. Another time. Noble then, not now."

"You insult their legacy," Ruiz responded, his face reddening. "That means you insult me."

"Noble and perceptive, as well as stupid," Montello challenged, coldness gathering in a steely gaze.

The fat man seemed to be calculating something. He twisted his thick neck to scan the tree line, saw immediately that something was wrong, and seemed to deflate before their eyes. He recognized none of the men holding the guns, his bodyguards were nowhere to be seen. Twelve of them, gone. A sheen of sweat appeared on his ruddy forehead like the dawn's dew on a granite headstone. Shiny white teeth disappeared behind sneering lips as if they had never existed. He turned to look at the others, saw the deception. Understanding fired in his eyes like a magician's flash paper – then turned to hatred as black as soot. "Fuck you," he was able to say in the second before Branko Montello casually dropped his napkin to the ground as a signal. The rifle shot echoed like a cannon across the finely manicured landscape, shock waves shimmered across an acre of glass at the back of the mansion, and from one window on the second floor a puff of smoke emerged from the end of a weapon that never missed its target. Hernan Suarez slowly drew the weapon inward and disappeared into the room's shadows.

The fat man seemed now to be laughing, but the white teeth were gone, so were his lips and half of Carlos Ruiz's lower face. A large red gaping hole, a final, jovial, open-faced guffaw for the fat man.

Montello felt no need to disguise his satisfaction. Neither did Bonito or Alvarez. Bonito would have smiled if she could have. But her mirth was stymied by a deep paralysis that had been slashed into her face a decade ago. Instead she picked up a napkin to wipe droplets of splattered blood and pulverized flesh from her clothing. She then looked directly into Branko Montello's eyes.

"You've made your point," she said.

EIGHT

Her legs pumped like pistons. Footfalls noiseless atop a thousand years of forest decay. Sweat snaked down her face as she ran, clutching tightly what wasn't hers.

It was as sad as anything she had ever known that she would die so soon after becoming wealthy beyond her wildest dreams. It was much more depressing than dying poor, though death without friends was a pathetic end. In her relatively young life, Mercedes Mendoza had never known family, but she had a bounty of friends. In their mourning, her death would not be pathetic.

She gasped for air. Her heart on wings – like a raven burst from her heaving chest. Mercedes punched through foliage that raked her skin, a wet earthy blur that mimicked the passage of her life. In the fragment of a second, a bullet sliced humid air. Deathly close. Mercedes screamed. Ducked lower as she ran.

Faster!

The men chasing her were Montello's. Out-of-shape goons ruined by cocaine. Mercedes shot a desperate look behind, saw one them drop to his knee. The flash of a muzzle was followed by another bullet. It thudded into a tree as she swept by, cleaving slivers of ballistic wood against her face, making her cry out in pain. Two more rounds struck. Drilling into ground near her feet. Dirt pummeled her bare legs, driving her faster through the thick, moist jungle.

Mercedes cursed her luck, wondered how everything had gone so wrong. Gaining access to the estate hadn't been a problem, neither had his study. Quivering, she had punched in the combination, and then with trembling hands she had stuffed her satchel with unbelievable riches. Montello must have discovered the empty safe and then sounded the alarm. Maybe he had known all along and allowed her to bolt for the pleasure of the chase. This was not the time to think about it.

Angry shouts in the forest behind her.

They're closing.

A heartbeat later the killers went quiet. The rush of blood inside her head became a deafening roar. Instead of relief, Mercedes surrendered to dread, then terror as she realized they were forming a net from which escape would be impossible. She thought about dumping the satchel. That's what they wanted. *No!* She clung to the bag more tightly. All or nothing, she decided, as she ducked beneath the limbs of an ancient tree and was swallowed within its shadowy embrace.

A minute passed. Mendoza's pace slowed as she frantically considered her next move. She could go to ground, find cover until nightfall. Pray they'd give up the chase. She shook her head. That was suicide. Mercedes sprang forward, tensed at the report of another rifle shot. The explosive echo created chaos in the canopy above her. A rainbow of wings blurred upon panicked flight. The macaw, the golden parrot and other spectators to her final earthbound moments. Mercedes wished her escape could be so easy.

A short moment later she broke into sunlight, a second wind driving her onward. Her feet pounded the jungle floor for another two hundred yards. She was still moving. Still alive. Her arms and back were drenched in sweat. Frantically, Mercedes spun right and left, tensing at the sight of two hulking forms closing the distance. Their weapons coughed flame and a bullet whizzed past, so deathly close its tiny wake caressed her cheek. The assassins sneered, shouted angrily.

Suddenly there was a new sound. She shuddered when she saw its source. A black silhouette hovered directly overhead, crushing what remained of her hope. A machine gun appeared at the helicopter's open cockpit. Mercedes froze, wasting valuable time as the aircraft maneuvered to a better firing position. Frigate birds erupted from the nearby brush, squawking as they fluttered to higher perches against the maelstrom borne of the beast's downdraft. Terrified, she spotted a figure leaning through the open cockpit door, his face full of menace. Orange fire spat from his weapon – relentless.

Think!

A split second later, Mercedes bolted from cover. Dashing towards thicker brush while bullets snapped at her heels. There was only one way to escape, and Mercedes winced when she saw it. A deep ravine studded with gnarled trees and jagged rock. She stood at the precipice, swayed in the updraft of cool air.

Safety.

The helicopter began its descent – thunderous in her ears. Waves of compressed air beat down upon her. The weapon barked, a rabid animal baring yellow teeth.

Do it!

Mercedes leapt into the ravine and disappeared into a darkness that held life or death. She cried out in pain as branches and rock tore at her body. Slugs slapped into the trees behind her as she curled into a ball, tumbling endlessly downward.

She would not hear the large airborne beast as it increased power and dipped its nose towards the abyss which had swallowed its doomed prey.

NINE

Branko Montello could hardly believe his eyes. He moaned softly, a plaintive dry sound that was absorbed within the open safe. He reached inside to touch the spot where they had been, allowing his hand to linger there as if plumbing the extent of her betrayal. He then slammed shut the thick lead door, massaged the loathing from his face, and cursed her.

Montello moved swiftly into the hallway, nearly colliding with his chief of security. Hernan Suarez was sweating and breathless.

"We had her on motion sensors and video." Suarez fought for oxygen. "She made her run during a shift change. Unfortunately, it was to her advantage."

Montello studied the Uzi strung across his security chief's shoulder. "Show me her body," he demanded. Clenched teeth.

Suarez seemed not to hear. He wiped rivulets of sweat from the side of his face. "Nanez was already in the south quarter when he spotted her. We weren't thirty seconds behind."

Montello folded his arms in warning. Suarez gulped. "We engaged her, but there's no blood trail."

"The body!" Montello spat, unwilling to accept what he was hearing.

"I boarded the chopper personally," Suarez assured him. "And we spotted her at the ravine."

Montello sensed a possible shift in the outcome. Maybe Suarez had gotten lucky. The chopper would already have been in the air patrolling the jungle around the villa when Suarez called it in.

"The fuel light," Suarez continued, seeming to shrink in advance of what he had to say next. "The pilot was already on vapours when he landed to pick me up. Two minutes later we had to break off the pursuit." Suarez stepped back in anticipation.

Montello slapped the wall. The sound reverberated through the empty hallway outside his study.

Suarez wisely paused before reporting that Range Rovers were continuing the hunt, but so far his men had found no trace of her.

"She dies, or you die," Montello said evenly, before cursing her again.

TEN

Miraculously, she was alive. Though Mercedes Mendoza had tumbled hard. Her hair was matted with dirt and blood. Her limbs were scraped and bloodied in a half-dozen places. As she lay there, shock set in, sending shivers through her entire body.

    Mercedes breathed deeply, grateful she hadn't broken anything, though her head hurt and her ears were ringing, leading her to suspect she might have blacked out for a second. Carefully she sat up and began to take stock of her situation. The satchel lay next to her, still intact. The sun hung nearly directly overhead, causing her to squint when she looked skyward. The helicopter was gone and on the ridge above she heard nothing of her pursuers. Why had they broken off the pursuit? Mercedes struggled with understanding. Eventually, she surrendered to the mystery. What mattered was she was alive. Painfully so. Her ankle throbbed. She rubbed it for as long as she could and then, grabbing the satchel, she rose unsteadily.

    It took her ten minutes to reach the main road, a serpentine stretch of black pavement that already shimmered with the oppressive morning heat. She moved as quickly as she could, hugging the tree line, and twice she darted into the cool underbrush to hide from passing cars. Her ankle throbbed and Mercedes wanted to sit. But that would be a deadly mistake. Montello's men would be aboard Range Rovers by now, continuing the hunt.

Five minutes later she found the spot where Nestor had promised to leave the car. Mercedes breathed deeply, relieved to see a headlight protruding from beneath a camouflage of thick heavy palm leaves. The car was well hidden about fifteen feet from the highway, just as the gardener had said. Nestor had taken a great risk, and although he had wanted no payment, Mercedes made a silent promise to take care of the man and his family. His daughter had been one of Montello's housekeepers, until recently released. Nestor had not told her the reason, though Mercedes could tell he was deeply troubled. It was the hard cold look in his eyes when he spoke about it that made her decide to trust him. He'd asked no questions and eagerly agreed to do what she asked. The car *would* be there.

The keys were in a small magnetic box beneath the rear bumper. Mercedes pulled them out and opened the trunk. She breathed a sigh of relief when she saw the small suitcase stuffed next to soiled rags and an old gas can. Mercedes tugged it from the trunk and threw it into the back of the car. She placed the satchel on the floor behind the driver's seat and covered it with a small patchwork blanket she found on the rear seat.

Mercedes prayed the engine would start, and after growling in protest, on the third try, it coughed to life. *Thank you, God.* She stomped on the gas, spraying dirt and rocks as the little car leapt onto the pavement. Mercedes knew Branko's men would be close behind and the thought of them made her lean forward as if that would make the car go faster. If she was going to live Mercedes had to find the old road. Nestor had told her about it. "A wooden gate three kilometers up the highway," he instructed. "That's the way in."

Mercedes balled her fists as the engine revved. She had to find the gate, knew that the gate was life. *Please, please.* Any minute she'd see the Range Rovers in her rear-view mirror, and the barrel flashes that would end her life.

The gate. *Quickly.*

It was another five excruciating minutes before Mercedes spotted it, hidden beneath vines and tall bushes. She wanted to scream with joy when she saw the gate and the entrance to the abandoned road. It was long forgotten, except by the old gardener who had traveled it hundreds of times when his back was still strong enough to harvest the hundred-year-old shading royal palms for which the resort owners paid a king's ransom. Mercedes was well along the hidden road before she felt she could breathe again. Still, she kept one eye on the rear-view mirror and the other on the narrow stretch of gravel that would take her twenty miles to the main highway again. The farther she traveled from Montello's villa the safer she would be, the better her chances of survival.

Mercedes wanted music, any music would do. She fumbled with the knobby radio dials, and a moment later loud music drowned out the monotonous thrum of the four-cylinder engine and the splash of grit and gravel against the bottom of the old rusty car.

Mercedes tried to relax as the hand drums of the cumbia carried her backward in time, to the day in her friend's apartment. The cumbia was Selena's favourite music, and for the first time that day, Mercedes actually smiled.

ELEVEN

"This is my music, *amiga*." Selena Santos had beamed with pride, glowing white teeth against her perfect mulatto skin. "The music of my people. We were slaves." Selena rolled her hips, ample breasts thrusting to the beat. "Came on the last boat a hundred fifty years ago to work the plantations and sugar mills." The cumbia left her trance-like, swaying rhythmically.

Mercedes didn't believe a word of it, and as she drove on Nestor's hidden road she remembered that she had laughed at Selena. "You were no slave. No slaves in your family either." She also remembered what Selena had said next. "Uncle Orlando said his grandfather had scars. Cane strips up and down his back. Slaves, Mercedes. I still have relatives in Choco where most of them took their freedom."

What nonsense. They had been in Selena's apartment. Her hideaway in Cartagena which was a world away from Nelson Mandela City where the ancestors of real slaves lived in squalor. Refugees of the jungle war.

Mercedes had laughed at her friend who always managed to make her feel better. They'd been like magnets since the orphanage, but to Sister Evangeline they were "the instigator and the imp." Mercedes thought about the first time she heard it, covered head to toe in thick mud. They'd been at a swimming hole near the orphanage, a forbidden place where both girls had spent a hot afternoon splashing around in the cool water. Mercedes had an idea. "Real sisters should at least be the same colour," Mercedes had said to her best friend slyly.

Selena looked at her warily. "We've got to get back before Sister Evangeline knows we're gone, remember?"

"She's too fat to find us," Mercedes said, grinning. It took her a dozen trips, filling her straw hat with water, to create the messy mud hole.

"What if someone comes along?"

"I'll be covered in mud, silly. No one's gonna see me. The mud'll make me vinsible."

"You mean invisible."

"In-visible, *si*."

Selena helped her friend remove her tiny bathing suit. "Lie down, I'll slop the mud on you, then you spread it."

Dark gobs of cool muck soon covered Mercedes from head to toe. "Real sisters now," Mercedes said affectionately. "Now we're both vinsible."

Selena surveyed their work, satisfied for a moment before the realization hit her. "Now you're blacker than me."

Mercedes nodded, and before Selena could protest she scooped up a handful of thick gooey mud and shoved it in Selena's face. More followed. Both squealing girls slung as much mud as they could before collapsing exhausted, unrecognizable mounds of muck.

The girls had gone quiet and still, their rising bellies the only sign there was life beneath the mud.

Mercedes turned a sharp bend in the dirt road and tried to picture the scene. Both of them had fallen asleep until they heard Sister Evangeline's screech. The sun had disappeared behind some hills, and the mud that covered them had dried hard as cement. Sister Evangeline, who had warned them more than once never to go to the swimming hole alone, had searched an hour for the missing girls.

"Dear God, let them be alive," she cried, breathless from the exertion and the shock when she found them. To the old nun they must have looked like fleshy insects encased in black crusty cocoons.

Mercedes and Selena flipped their eyes open and stared at the corpulent nun with the look of innocents. Then they howled with laughter.

It didn't help.

Sister Evangeline's rage peaked in a wave of red. "You little imp," she wheezed and in one stumbling motion jerked Selena from the ground. "The spawn of Satan," she cried. "And you – the instigator," she barked at Mercedes. "Your idea, no doubt."

Mercedes was astonished at how tight the dried mud felt. She had to pee now too.

"Demon seed, the both of you," Sister Evangeline shouted, tugging both children in the wake of her flowing black habit. "You've missed supper. You won't be getting any."

Mercedes scooped up her bathing suit quickly and stole a glance at Selena. The dried mud on their faces fell away as they giggled.

Selena stopped laughing. "I thought you said we'd be invisible."

Mercedes tried to keep up, her brow wrinkling in thought. "Your Uncle Orlando told me black people are always invisible," Mercedes finally declared. "I guess not to nuns."

Mercedes thought about the day in Selena's apartment when she'd told her best friend about Montello. Told her she was a dead woman if she didn't run. As Mercedes drove along the old logging road she wondered just how invisible she and Selena could become. Pretty invisible, she prayed.

As the little car bounced along the narrow road Mercedes checked her watch and smiled to herself. Decent time. Twenty minutes later she inched her dusty tires onto the searing pavement of the main highway and braked while a pickup truck loaded with farm workers lumbered by belching blue smoke into the afternoon sunlight. A couple of them looked surprised when they saw the little car emerge from the overgrown road and pull onto the highway behind them. Mercedes thought about Selena once more.

"I'm just a poor little nigger girl," Selena had shouted above the din of the music while she danced that day in her apartment.

"Selena!"

"It's the truth."

"A poor little…" Mercedes stopped then. She could never use the word. "A poor little girl who happens to have a master's degree in business and works for the biggest bank in Colombia. An account executive no less."

When the music ended Selena collapsed on the floor and rolled over on her back.

"Still a slave, Mercedes. Still a slave. Different master, that's all."

Both of them had laughed at that. Then Selena became serious, turned her head towards Mercedes with a suspicious look on her face. "What's with the turtleneck? It's hot as an oven," Selena had said.

Mercedes considered a lie but after a moment pulled the top of her sweater forward to reveal the ugly purple marks which circled her neck.

"My god," Selena said, pulling herself to her knees. Anger mottled her features. She leaned forward to take a closer look. "That bastard!"

Selena jumped up. "Don't you move," she commanded, disappearing into the kitchen.

A moment later, Mercedes was startled by the shriek of the tea kettle. Selena emerged from the kitchen carrying two cups of steaming brew. She placed one gently on the table in front of Mercedes and reached over to touch her friend's hand.

Mercedes looked at her with tears in her eyes.

"Tell me what happened," Selena said softly.

Mercedes told her everything. From the beginning.

TWELVE

Branko Montello wore a dark rich suit the first time she saw him. He didn't flash cash or jewelry, though the two bodyguards in his wake suggested a man who would not require a reservation. DeMarco's was full on the night he walked in, without one.

Luigi, the owner, was alight, and had personally ushered Montello to the best table in the restaurant, an alcove saturated in the golden light of oil lamps and the relaxing scent of freshly cut flowers. Mercedes hovered nearby.

Montello didn't seem to notice or care that other patrons had stopped eating to stare at him. Instead he seemed transfixed by fading frescos a century old on the alcove's domed ceiling, and after a few minutes he turned his head to speak to her. "Come here please," he had said in a deep soft voice that sounded equally to Mercedes like a command and an invitation.

Who does this guy think he is? she thought as she picked up a wine list and smiled.

Sister Evangeline would have disapproved sternly of the way Mercedes moved her hips as she walked over. Her heart was pounding by the time she got to his table and gently placed the wine menu in front of him. Montello took a long time before he spoke. "It is unforgivable that the Madonna is showing her age," he said, without looking at her.

"Senor Montello?"

Mercedes felt a dozen pairs of eyes burning into her back. Luigi fidgeted nervously as he watched her.

"The Madonna," Montello said again. "Look how the cracks dissect her line of sight with the Christ child."

She followed Montello's gaze to the ceiling and noticed for the first time that widening cracks had split the fresco. The Virgin Mary and baby Jesus were separated by a deep chasm in the bone-dry plaster. Her cheeks reddened, though Mercedes wasn't sure why and for a moment she was incapable of speech – a child again, on the day she was confronted by Sister Evangeline with her large book of Vatican art. The rotund nun could hardly contain her excitement as she retrieved the dusty tome and placed it on the desk in front of her young student. "The many faces of Christ," she had said, and with eyes wide she opened the heavy book and looked to Mercedes.

Mercedes hadn't known how to react at first. The paintings depicted in the old book seemed so sad, full of angels and people who looked like they were about to cry. Mercedes struggled to find meaning.

"Ghosts," she had said simply after a moment passed.

"In a way, Mercedes…ghosts, yes." The old nun smiled at her as she smoothed her long hair. "But they continue to speak to us in wonderful ways." Sister Evangeline continued, "There's a room in a museum where the Holy Father lives. Pinocoteca Vaticana."

Mercedes tried to repeat the words but quickly surrendered.

"This painting is called *Madonna di Foligno*, can you say that?"

Mercedes fumbled the words and they both laughed. "Sorry, Sister."

"It's all right, child, I'm certain Raphael was a kind soul as well as a great artist. He would forgive you."

Mercedes had spent the rest of the day with her nose in the dusty old book and Sister Evangeline had been pleased at how quickly she learned. "These paintings are so flat," she had said, gently touching a photograph of one of the "primitives," a series of Benedictine panels depicting the life of Saint Stephen.

"They were still learning about perspective then," Evangeline had replied.

"Perspective," Mercedes repeated. "And colour and light too, Sister." She looked to the old nun for approval. "Raphael knew."

Sister Evangeline had looked at her with surprise and said almost to herself, "Yes, child. Raphael understood."

Mercedes was yanked back from her memories by Luigi's cough. She saw Montello was still engrossed by the ceiling frescoes while the fingers on his left hand beat an expectant rhythm.

She tilted her head back. "My favourite has always been the *Madonna di Foligno*."

Montello looked at her in surprise. "You know Raphael?"

"Only what I've seen from the Pinocoteca Vaticana," she replied. "It's more beautiful than anything."

Montello smiled at her. "The ceiling needs restoration. Send the bill to me."

A week later Luigi phoned her to tell her Senor Montello had called. A few guests were having dinner at his estate. Would she care to attend? If so, a car would be sent to collect her.

Mercedes waited a full day before responding, but eventually said yes. *Why not? What's dinner?*

She wore something black and tight and Branko had been there to help her from the limo when it arrived at his vast estate. It was not her custom to fawn over wealth, but in Montello, she had seen something. Another lost soul perhaps. Mercedes suspected that beneath all his pretensions there was simply a good, honest and caring man. Maybe it was fantasy, which she was prone to. But then again, maybe not.

Dinner was more than she expected. White-gloved waiters delivered plate after plate of sumptuous food. The other dinner guests spoke in hushed tones, largely ignored by their host who had insisted Mercedes take the seat next to him. That night he mesmerized her with his knowledge of fine art, of Raphael and da Vinci and Pinturicchio. Once, he gently touched her hand to ask about the curious ring she wore – gold and jade in the shape of a tiny insect.

"It's a firefly," she replied, smiling. "It's for good luck and I can tell you, in the restaurant business you need it."

He listened intently as she spoke about DeMarco's where she was manager. How she desperately wanted to open a restaurant of her own some day. In the meantime, Luigi was a good man who appreciated her abilities. He had given her a large measure of the credit for the two plaques in his office for Restaurant of the Year. Luigi's wife was ill and he'd been musing lately about selling the place.

"It could be a great opportunity," she told him, frowning. "But, I'm afraid, not within my reach right now."

Branko had smiled at that. "Opportunities like that don't come often, Mercedes. You just have to reach a little further."

"I suppose you're right," she said.

For a moment he appeared to be calculating something. "If you like I can have my accountant contact you," he said. "He's a genius when it comes to business plans and he's constantly seeking out new and exciting investment opportunities for me."

Mercedes could hardly believe her ears. "Are you serious?"

"Very," he replied, pouring her more wine. "You're good at what you do. I've already seen that. There's no reason why you shouldn't be enjoying the bounty of your talent. DeMarco's should be yours to own. If this is what you desire, it will happen."

Without thinking, she kissed him, and for the remainder of the meal, Mercedes was too excited to speak. Owning her own restaurant had been her lifelong dream. All of a sudden that dream had tangible qualities and the more she thought about it, the giddier she became.

Branko permitted her a few moments of solitary excitement, turning to speak to the guest on the other side of him.

Mercedes decided at that moment that it *would* be possible. It was only recently that she'd spied the brochure in Luigi's office promoting some retirement complex on the Costa del Sol in Spain. It would be more than stupid not to approach him before someone else did, snapping up DeMarco's right from under her. It was too infuriating to think about. She decided then and there to have a long talk with Luigi about his plans. A smile swept her face. Ecstatic, she picked up her glass and toasted silently the opportunity which had been laid in her lap.

Montello's car came often. Dinners turned into weekends during which they rarely left the estate, except to shop at the local market for fresh produce and meat. Mercedes preferred to do the cooking so on those occasions she insisted the kitchen staff be given the night off.

Once, Montello brought her to the Plaza de San Pedro Claver where the Museo de Arte Moderno stood empty two hours after closing. The curator had greeted them personally and had bowed as Montello stepped through the door so he and Mercedes would have the museum to themselves.

Mercedes had been standing in front of the softly lit painting by Fernando Botero, a life-size portrait of a fleshy small-breasted woman toweling herself dry next to her bathtub.

"Have you ever been to Buenos Aires, Mercedes Mendoza," Branko had asked her.

"Of course not," she had replied. "Why would I go to Buenos Aires?"

Montello laughed softly as he came up behind her. "I suppose you're right." He touched her long hair and leaned inwards to smell the scent of her perfume.

For a moment neither of them said anything.

"This one is by Alejandro Obregon," Montello said after a while, pointing at another work. "He was born here."

Mercedes enjoyed the art and was impressed by what seemed to be Branko's limitless knowledge of remarkable painters. But it also made her feel small in his company, as if she were still twelve years old and asking Sister Evangeline to explain the pictures in her dusty old book.

They spent another hour in the art museum with Montello playing tour guide, but then Mercedes was famished.

"I've hired a new chef from Florence," she told him. "His name is Juliano and he's a genius."

"Then we'll have to test him," Branko said, leading her through the huge wooden archway that brought them outside again.

When they returned to the car, Branko seemed suddenly sullen, a mysterious sadness that Mercedes had seen in him a couple of times before.

They drove past an old convent located in the same plaza as the museum. Its monumental size had struck Mercedes and the beauty of its tree-filled courtyard. As a child she and Father Govia had once passed it on their way to a doctor's appointment in the old city.

Montello was watching her now.

"An old monk they called the Apostle of the Blacks lived there," Montello said flatly. "Spent his miserable life helping the slaves."

"A good man," Mercedes had reasoned, oblivious to Branko's derogatory tone.

Montello looked at her with a coolness that matched perfectly the temperature inside the air-conditioned limo. "An idiot," he said, "who ministered to niggers."

He may as well have struck her, so offended was she by the remark and the hatred that coated it.

How could a man who loved the beauty created by the great masters believe such a thing? She was about to challenge him, but thought better of it. Branko had dark moments, and a lonely quality for which Mercedes found compassion without judgment. But never, ever would she find empathy.

He kept his business to himself, spending long periods of time in a magnificent study that was off limits to everyone but Hernan, his manservant, and occasionally a maid who brought his meals.

Mercedes had asked him once what he did for so long in his study. "Don't bother yourself with things that are not your concern," he had replied tersely.

Still, Mercedes' curiosity would not allow her that luxury.

"You don't even know for sure what he does for a living," Selena had once challenged.

"An art dealer," Mercedes responded, not believing it completely.

In the beginning coca was a possibility that Mercedes had quickly discounted. Branko made more trips to Florence and Rome than to Medellin and Cali where cocaine was brokered like sugar cane and mangos. He was a director at the Louvre in Paris and the Uffizi in Florence,

ANGELS OF MARADONA

honours normally reserved for men much older. The newspaper described him as South America's premier broker for renaissance and religious art. The daily in Bogotá referred to him simply as "The Dealer."

Selena had looked at her incredulously. "What art dealer has bodyguards and his own helicopter?"

Although Branko spoke very little about his business, he seemed engrossed by it. Mercedes was an attractive woman, a knockout, many would say. Yet, Montello seemed to find more sensuality in his paintings. He had not once tried to bed her. Mercedes didn't mind. Intimacy would have been a sticky intrusion. It was her ambition to own DeMarco's which dampened her better instincts.

Luigi hadn't given her a firm answer yet, but she had seen it in his eyes. "Two matadors I have seen gored in Malaga. The most robust and deadly bulls in all of Spain," he had said. "Maybe it is time to become so pampered and fat."

The next day, Mercedes spoke for an hour with Branko's accountant, a man named Kovak. He told her papers were to be drawn up. Lawyers would soon become involved. She'd have no need of a banker.

She would have been even more thrilled were it not for the uneasiness she felt during her frequent visits to Branko's estate. She found herself under constant surveillance, and even when she sunbathed beside the Olympic-size swimming pool she felt violated by human and electronic eyes. There were armed men patrolling the grounds, making her wonder whether she was in any danger just by being there.

Mercedes wondered again about coca. Drug barons were rich beyond words, though many Colombians starved or died of neglect. Father Govia had once told her that the cocaine criminals had more money than the government, and more power, but that hard-working people of God were the real soul of Colombia.

Mercedes was also troubled by the way Branko treated the house staff. When she challenged him on it, he looked at her with eyes that seemed to eviscerate.

"You're smart and beautiful, Mercedes," Selena had once told her. "But you have disastrous taste in men."

"This is business," she replied. "Stop it."

Selena was correct. The lawyer Thomas had been incredibly insensitive and hurtful. Marco was no better, a farm equipment wholesaler who had lost his business and her respect to gambling. There were others. Each seemed right at the time. Mercedes didn't want to think about them or her dismal record. There was a lot she didn't know about Montello. A lot, she guessed, she didn't care to know. She wouldn't think about that either. It was just business, after all. And there was Buenos Aires. *Beautiful Buenos Aires.*

THIRTEEN

It was the first time Mercedes had flown on a private jet and Branko had made certain it would be unforgettable. They toasted with fine wine, and at thirty thousand feet Mercedes marveled at the pristine snow-capped mountains that moved slowly beneath them.

Buenos Aires was big and noisy and Mercedes was still giddy from the wine when they reached their hotel near the spectacular Colon Theater on Avenida de Julio. They were shown to a huge suite trimmed in Brazilian teak and decorated with matching splashes of sensuous red and tangerine. Windows that were curtained in pale gold brocade ran twelve feet high and sparkled with the lights of a dozen ships moored in the Rio de la Plata.

Mercedes was intoxicated by the excitement. "It's stunning," she exclaimed, running to glass doors that led to an expansive marble balcony. She sucked in the night air and held her breath when she spotted her first glistening star. Her eyes were clamped shut when Branko came and stood beside her.

"The wish has to be kept secret," he said.

She kept her eyes shut tight. "Normally yes…but not this wish."

Mercedes suddenly thrust herself at him. "It's my wish that you dance with me, Branko, the tango if you please." Mercedes arched her back, expecting Branko to wrap his arms around her.

He laughed softly instead. "A man doesn't have time to learn the tango." Gently, Branko pushed her away, oblivious to her disappointment. Silence.

It might have been the wine, laced with anger, that caused her to say what she said next. Mercedes wasn't sure, but she instantly regretted it. "A real man would dance with me," she slurred.

The slap stung her face, caused her eyes to fill with tears. Backwards she stumbled, bringing a hand to her burning cheek. Stunned.

"That was a mistake," Montello hissed.

Dizzy and confused, Mercedes swayed, a loud ringing in her ears. She tried to swallow but it stuck in her throat. Oxygen suddenly seemed too thick to breathe. Montello showed no sign of remorse. "How dare you?" she stammered. "Don't you ever—"

In a flash, Branko grabbed her throat, choking off her scream. His face was a mask of rage. "No. Don't…you…ever…" He shook her, fingers tightening vice-like around her neck.

Her universe imploded, jagged shards of light stabbed at her, thunder replaced the ringing in her ears. Mercedes fought for breath, her brain and heart struggled for blood as tiny white specks flashed before her eyes. Night and the black shroud of unconsciousness melded into one. She clutched at his hands, desperate to tear them free. Tears soaked her face as she collapsed to her knees, unable to scream. Montello had lost his mind. Tighter he squeezed, moaning like a wounded animal.

She tasted blood and then blackness overtook her.

He didn't kill her.

Mercedes awoke in a bed, still dressed, her throat swollen and painful. She coughed with the sound of coarse sandpaper. Her pillow was soaked. She was alone.

Had it actually happened? She brought a hand to her throat, felt a shooting pain lodge beneath her jaw. Carefully she sat up, eyeing herself in the mirror at the foot of the bed. Tears came to her eyes when she saw the bruising. Her mind stumbled backward and, reliving the moment, a loud gasp escaped her parched lips. Mercedes took five long breaths and then lowered her feet to the floor. After another moment she walked from the bedroom and moved robot-like into the suite. Sunlight coated everything and caused her to squint.

There was something on the coffee table, appearing at first as a red clump until she was able to focus. Roses. Too many to count. Mercedes walked to them and slowly removed the card. She read it twice, bile rising in her throat, causing a painful cough that echoed dryly through the suite. She dropped the card on the floor and for a full five minutes Mercedes wept. All her dreams had been destroyed. There'd be no restaurant in her future. She'd been stupid to think there would be. She had no intention of allowing this man to become her business partner. Not now. Mercedes permitted herself a few moments more to compose herself before returning to the bedroom and throwing her suitcase on the bed. She considered what to do after that. She didn't know how long he would be gone but recalled him saying something about a business meeting in the morning. The afternoon was set aside for sightseeing and a little shopping. Mercedes dreaded his return.

Her purse was on the bed. She snatched it up and checked its contents. Her passport had been removed. She swore. There was no telling what Branko would do if she simply left. It frightened her to think about it.

Mercedes froze at the sound of the door being unlocked. She prayed it was housekeeping. Footsteps moved towards the bedroom, causing her to back up, to want to hide. A man's form suddenly darkened the doorway.

"I regret what happened," Montello said flatly. "I've ruined your visit."

Mercedes might have laughed under different circumstances. He stood there. Steely eyed in his summer-weight tan suit, hands at his sides, waiting for her to speak. Mercedes sensed his intention. To dominate her, make her feel vulnerable, under his control. It riled her. "It would be better if I returned home," she replied curtly, moving to the bed to collect her things. "I'll find my own way to the airport."

Montello then reached into his pocket. "I had no wish to harm you," he replied as though he hadn't been listening. "But you are still my guest here." He withdrew a passport, flipped through its pages, and then returned it to his pocket.

Guest or prisoner? Mercedes wondered. "I'll go to the embassy," she said, anger lacing her voice. "Acquire temporary travel documents."

"Very well," Montello responded smugly. "Give the ambassador my best. We're old friends."

Mercedes realized she was beaten. To hide her disappointment she spun on her heel and disappeared into the bathroom. When she heard him leave, she turned on the water, removed her clothing, and stepped into the steaming shower. For a full ten minutes she stood there, barely moving, except to rub the sting of salty tears from her tired eyes. She toweled herself dry, feeling a thankful measure of rejuvenation. In the mirror, she stared at the bruise on her throat. He hadn't killed her, Mercedes reasoned. *He could have.* Maybe she could put what happened behind her. Why should her dream of owning DeMarco's be crushed by a singular act of madness? Montello regretted what he had done. Mercedes felt her own regret, for pushing a button in him which she had no intention of ever pushing again. She spent luxurious moments combing her long wet hair and then wrapped it tightly in a thick white towel. The bedroom was bathed in sunlight as she stepped to the window, hugging herself through the softness of her robe. It was still possible, she thought. If anything, she was stronger now. Not weak or vulnerable. When she was a youngster at the orphanage one of the nuns had given her an exam to test her intelligence. "One in ten thousand," the dear old nun had told her afterward.

"Am I smart?" Mercedes had asked at the time.

"Too smart for your own good," she had replied.

Standing at the window, Mercedes wondered whether that was a curse or a blessing.

That night, at a magnificent restaurant he had picked, her soup was cold as she watched him eat. The roast beef was superb, he declared, jabbering on then about a new collection of fine books he was acquiring, oblivious to her disgust.

Branko stopped eating. "Your food is getting cold."

In a reflex she couldn't control, Mercedes' hand went to the spot on her throat where a bluish-purple bruise was thankfully hidden behind a silk scarf. "I'm not hungry," she replied. "I think I might be coming down with something."

Branko reached across the table to place the back of his hand against her forehead, causing her to flinch.

"You do feel warm," he said, unaffected by her start. "I'll call for the car. Take you back to the hotel for a good night's rest. I have some business to attend to."

With that, Branko motioned for the waiter and requested the check.

Twenty minutes later, back at the hotel, Montello poured her a brandy, placed it on the coffee table next to the roses and left her alone in the suite. Mercedes watched him leave. With all her strength and despite herself, she hurled the snifter, smashing it into a thousand pieces against the closed door.

One in ten thousand, she thought again as she stared at the broken glass.

Two days later.

At Montello's estate, Mercedes parked in the shade of a long narrow two-storey garage which housed his exotic cars. She noted immediately that his favourite, a shiny black Italian sports model, was missing. She exhaled in relief and stepped onto pavement, breathing in the potent scent of tropical flowers which sprang up from giant ceramic pots lining the driveway. Mercedes stood a moment, pushing aside the feeling that she should get back in the car and drive away. She'd awakened that morning troubled. The residue of a disturbing dream, she thought, though she remembered none. Anxiety picked at her, a fearful nervousness which she fought to deflect by taking deep measured breaths as she sat on the edge of her bed. Control returned and then a restorative calm which she was grateful for.

Someone called her name.

Nestor, Montello's round-faced groundskeeper, waved at her from his gardening shed, his omnipresent smile warming as always. They had shared something unspoken from her first visit to the huge manicured estate. Nestor had proudly toured her through its countless gardens, pointing out the more unusual species of flowers and plants. His daughter had just been hired for the household staff. He had beamed when he told her. Nestor was a kind man who on several occasions had left freshly cut flowers on the front seat of her car. Mercedes' face brightened whenever she saw him. She waved back.

After entering the grand house, Mercedes made her way up the winding staircase that led to the second floor. Montello had made it easy for her to accept invitations to spend the night. The guest suite was located within the east wing of the mansion, with its marble foyer and a tall arched door which opened upon a large sitting area and separate sleeping quarters. Mercedes walked quickly into the suite and with barely a look around made her way to the bedroom. She eyed her lucky ring which she'd carelessly forgotten on the night table next to the bed. Thankful, she scooped it up, turned, and left. She walked back downstairs, her jeweled firefly safely returned to her finger.

The house was quiet except for muted sounds coming from the kitchen. Mercedes strode along the hallway towards the front door, and as her sandals swept along gleaming hardwood she wondered how long Montello's housekeepers had toiled on their knees, with as much grimace as polish in the mirror finish.

The thought vanished as Mercedes suddenly stopped dead in her tracks. She looked twice. Strangely, the door to Montello's study was ajar. Sunlight from the room bled into the hallway, Montello's sacred heart hemorrhaging the lifeblood of his sanctuary.

Mercedes looked both ways along the hallway. Recklessness had always been her companion but never her friend. She moved to the wall, held her breath, and for a full minute she listened.

Was it a hunger for retribution which pushed her towards the door? Perhaps, she thought. Mercedes decided it didn't matter. As her mind screamed for retreat, she leaned into the room.

Montello's study was empty.

She stepped cautiously through the door, her heart pounding, as if the intrusion would sound an alarm to be rapidly dealt with by an army of sneering armed men. Mercedes stepped farther in and stopped. Amazed, she breathed deeply and took in her surroundings. The oak-paneled room was filled with beautiful works of art. There were sculptures, the largest of which filled an entire corner of the room, a piece that looked vaguely familiar. With shock, it finally struck her. It was a Bernini normally kept in a church near the Vatican. Awestruck, Mercedes allowed her eyes to roam the walls. Fine paintings were hung with gilded frames. Towering bookcases were filled with beautiful tomes. Exotic furniture fashioned in rich leather and rare wood seemed choreographed before a glass wall which revealed the estate's magnificent grounds. She understood why Montello spent so much time in this place. It was dizzying to her, though at the same time, he seemed a plundering invader surrounded by such beauty.

She moved farther in, shuddering at the thought of what Montello would do if he found her here. Still, this invasion of his privacy brought a thin smile to her lips as she gathered her courage and approached his ornate desk. She quickly scanned its surface, and seeing nothing of interest she turned to face his collection of books. There had to be a thousand fine volumes, snuggly aligned row upon row until they reached well above her head. Between two of the tall bookcases was an empty space about three feet in width. In that space hung a painting. Strange, Mercedes thought, as she stepped closer. Such an unusual place to hang a beautiful piece of art. It also looked vaguely familiar to her, something she had seen before. Then it occurred to her. It was that day a month or so ago – over dinner – when Montello had retrieved an old art catalogue to check some date or fact relevant to what he was talking about, which was iconic art, she now recalled.

He satisfied his curiosity and then excused himself to take a phone call. While she waited for him to return she had lingered over the old book, sipping her wine, flipping through it until she stopped at one page in particular. She remembered now. Daddi. Bernardo Daddi was the artist's name. There was something on the page that had grabbed her attention at the time. A moment later she remembered. Then a thought occurred to her.

Mercedes searched quickly. Her watch said two. If Montello was taking lunch off the estate he'd be back soon. Rapidly she moved from one end of the bookshelves to the other, sweeping her hand across their spines, eyes darting high and low, excitedly.

Then she saw it. High up on the top shelf, tucked into a corner and nearly invisible. Mercedes reached for it. *Damn!* It was much too high for her. Frantically now she searched for something to stand on. The chair behind his desk would work, so Mercedes maneuvered it into position as fast as she could and climbed on it. Then she pulled the old catalogue from its place on the highest shelf, and with her throat tightening with anticipation, she opened it.

Bernardo Daddi. 1280 to 1348. She searched through photographs of his work and the biographical notes until she found what she was looking for. A picture of the actual painting hung before her. Saint Ursula, martyred by the strike of an arrow during her pilgrimage to Rome. Three vessels arriving at Cologne. Beneath the photograph three tiny numbers had been neatly handwritten. Strange, Mercedes thought, until she remembered Montello's frequent complaints about his poor memory for numbers. She knew now what they meant. She committed the numbers to memory, replaced the catalogue and climbed down from the chair, which she quickly restored to its original position behind the desk. Then Mercedes stepped to the painting and placed her fingers behind its frame. Gently she pulled, until it swung back, revealing a wall safe. She would have smiled except at that instant, Mercedes froze at a sound in the hallway. Voices came next – tense loud voices. She couldn't make out what was being said, but the tone and timbre she recognized immediately as Hernan Suarez, Montello's pock-faced assistant. She quickly shoved the chair aside and ducked beneath Montello's desk.

A moment later the voices quieted, followed by a footstep at the doorway, the wheeze of breathing followed by a low curse. It was Suarez, probably still fuming at whomever he had scolded for leaving the door ajar.

Mercedes had stupidly neglected to close the door after entering the study. She winced at her mistake and realized now that Suarez would want to satisfy himself that his master's study was undisturbed.

Footsteps, closer now.

Mercedes held her breath and at that second realized her second shocking error, the one that would likely end her life. In her rush, she'd forgotten to push the painting back into position against the wall. Suarez would see the safe and realize he had stumbled upon a serious breach of security. Then he'd summon the guards and search the house – beginning with the study.

She felt like bolting, but what chance would that offer? Panic wasn't an option. Instead she waited helplessly for him to grab the telephone. Seconds passed in terror. Then a full minute. Nothing. He was going to engage in the search himself, Mercedes thought, though that wasn't how Suarez normally operated. Suarez usually retreated to the background whenever she was in Montello's presence, but she had seen enough of him to know he was fond of barking orders to his cadre of armed men.

Still no sign of alarm. Then she heard his muffled voice. A dose of adrenalin shot through her – she'd been discovered and was being ordered to show herself. Sweating and defeated, she was about to crawl out from beneath the desk – to surrender and hope for the best. Then, more muffled words, and a second later came a raspy mechanical reply. It quickly occurred to her that Suarez was never without his radio and was now checking in with his men. From the sound of his conversation he suspected nothing was amiss in Montello's study, and a few seconds later Mercedes heard him walk out of the room and gently close the door behind him.

Slowly, she exhaled. Tension seemed to weep from every muscle in her body. She closed her eyes, and after waiting for a full five minutes, Mercedes emerged from beneath Montello's desk. Rubbing a cramp from her leg she looked towards the bookcases and saw that the Daddi painting was returned to its position over the wall safe. Puzzled, she walked over. She pulled the painting out from the wall and then released it. Slowly it swung inward till it covered the safe. The spring mechanism had saved her life.

Mercedes repeated the numbers she had in her head, and reaching up she punched an electronic keypad until a light flickered green. She turned a knob and pulled the safe open.

It took a moment for her eyes to adjust to the darkened interior of the safe. Then she breathed sharply. Inside were thick bundles of cash. By the looks of it, a fortune in banded US hundred-dollar bills. Several watches, some encrusted with diamonds, were carefully laid out on a velvet tray along with an assortment of gold rings studded with large sparkling jewels. Farther. At the back. There was something else. Mercedes stood on her toes and drew closer. Careful not to disturb anything, she reached in, sweeping her hand along its dimensions. It took her a moment to understand what she was looking at. When she did, she nearly lost her balance.

Mercedes spent too long there. Shaking herself from her reverie she closed the safe, turned, and after listening at the door, she quickly exited the room.

That day in Selena's apartment, Mercedes told her friend about the safe and its contents and then she went silent.

Selena studied her incredulously. "Now you're scaring me," she had said.

"I haven't said anything yet."

"Yes, but..." Selena shook her head, exasperated. "The last time you had that look—"

"We did a good thing," Mercedes cut her off.

"Yes we did. But we could have gone to prison."

"We didn't," Mercedes said too sharply. She apologized with her eyes.

Selena stared a long moment out the window. Storm clouds gathered like veins of rough granite pressing upon the old walled city. A premonition too bold to ignore. Selena turned, showing the futility of resistance. "It's not prison that worries me," she said with sadness in her voice.

Mercedes knew what Selena was thinking. This was considerably more dangerous than the brazen thing they'd done before. Prison wasn't the downside. Death was. Mercedes sat quietly in her friend's apartment and brought a hand to her throat. Her pulse jumped at the thought of his fingers — squeezing the life out of her. She shivered with disgust. Mercedes forced the thoughts aside, allowed the temptation to tickle her as it had that day in Montello's study. Slowly, she told her friend about the contents of Branko Montello's wall safe.

"You are crazy," Selena whispered five minutes later, as if to have spoken louder would have alerted his thugs. "Crazy to be even thinking about it."

Selena might have been correct.

Finally. "Dominique," Mercedes said to Selena. Only one word uttered. It stirred a flicker of excitement in her friend's eyes. Selena's face lightened.

"So sweet," Mercedes whispered. "Father Govia says she's been asking for us again. Thank God, she's getting stronger every day. And it's thanks to us, Selena."

A mist appeared in Selena's large round eyes. An unspoken fondness seemed to swell in her chest.

"The money in that dead account," Mercedes continued. "The heart surgeon and the hospital in Miami. It was Dominique's only chance." Mercedes allowed the moment to dissolve into silence.

Finally, Selena nodded. "We were angels once. Wasn't that enough?"

Mercedes smiled impishly, but said nothing.

FOURTEEN

Mercedes checked her watch. It would take her several more hours to reach the place where Selena was waiting. The satchel's contents excited her. But first they'd need a safe place to hunker down. Mercedes accelerated past the pickup truck she'd been following since Nestor's abandoned logging road. It was early afternoon and she wanted to reach Tayrona before supper. Tayrona meant safety.

Mercedes understood why Selena had agreed to go along with it. It was her need to take something back. Why wouldn't she? Her mother and father had been stolen from her by people like Branko Montello.

Ramon Santos had fallen hard and fast and there was nothing his brother Orlando could do about it.

They worked hard to cobble together the money they needed for their first airplane – a big step for a pair of ex-air force pilots.

The brothers were business partners and shared the flying. In their first year Santos Charters made enough money to pay half the outstanding loan on that first Cessna. But then there was too much money, too fast. Ramon made those deals.

The second aircraft was a twin engine and carried a lot more cargo. That's when Ramon started to change.

It wasn't the easy money that killed Selena's father. It was the coke. His shiny new Beechcraft punched through rain and clouds and ended up in the side of a mountain. Searchers waited two days for the weather to clear.

"Uncle Orlando said he should never have taken off," Selena told her once. "He was too stoned to make the right decision."

Her mother was gone too. A day after the crash she emptied the company bank account and disappeared. A couple of times she came back to scream at the nuns about her daughter while Selena hid under her bed. "*Mi hija*. Do with her what I want." When she showed up it was usually Father Govia who chased the wretch away. Selena's Uncle Orlando was a good man. Brought her jars of sweet *melao* and *chirimoya* and told Selena her mother was crazy sick with the coca and that Selena was better off where she was.

Further back, Mercedes kept another memory. Faint. Undefined in shape and substance. A time before Selena and the orphanage. Softly pulsing lights suspended above her. A forest. Someone is with her. *Who are you?* The answer was always beyond her reach, though it tickled her with an extraordinary feeling that she was not alone and never had been. Sometimes when she was a child, strange animal sounds woke her in the middle of the night. She'd throw the covers off and run to the window, her awestruck face a canvas of celestial radiance. She listened raptly to the coyote pups in the forest, howling like babies. She had had a family once. She couldn't remember, but Father Govia had told her. They went to Heaven when she was only a baby, he said. To Mercedes the orphanage was home, Father Govia and the sisters were the only family she had ever known. Sometimes when the coyote pups howled, Mercedes sat frozen by her window, enthralled by fireflies in their erratic flight through Father Govia's flower garden. *Who are you?* The answer teased her, until she eventually dozed off, usually to be awakened at her window by Selena or one of the sisters.

Mercedes thought about the day she told Selena about Montello and what she'd discovered in his safe. The cumbia faded and disappeared from the car's tinny speakers, leaving the sound of wind and an uneven knocking from the engine to fill the void. Mercedes checked her rear-view mirror and saw the old farm truck far behind her. Taganga was where Selena was waiting. Where the work of angels would begin. But first they had to survive, and Mercedes knew the only way to do that was to become invisible.

FIFTEEN

The Bahia de Taganga sparkled like a sheet of crusted green emeralds in the hot Colombian sun. Around the horseshoe-shaped bay fishing boats pulled in evening catches, and here and there large orange buoys carved out parcels of water for scuba-diving schools that advertised coral diving at the cheapest rates in the country. Mercedes downshifted, wiped her hand across tired eyes, and reached for the half-empty bottle of water on the passenger seat.

As she descended into the tiny village along the mountain road she heard loud music from Taganga's busy beach bars. Sun-drenched tourists enjoying ice cold beer and fried fish. Mercedes was famished and tired, but stopping was out of the question. She had another twenty miles before El Zaino, the gateway to the Parque Nacional Tayrona. Mercedes checked her fuel gauge – half a tank – and was thankful she could skirt the busy village without having to stop for a fill-up.

Parque Nacional Tayrona had been a good idea. Mercedes remembered it. The bumpy bus ride that seemed to last forever from the orphanage to a campground just inside the park's entrance. For two days Mercedes, Selena and the other children begged Father Govia to take them home. They were bored.

"But children," Augustus would say, his laughter booming, "We are surrounded by God's splendor. He would be unhappy that you are not enjoying it."

The isolation and privacy that bored them as children was the reason Mercedes pointed it out on a map and assured Selena it was the best place in Colombia to hide from Montello.

Selena thought she was brilliant.

It would take Mercedes another hour to drive from the Bahia de Taganga to the mouth of the Rio Piedras where she would enter the park at the foot of the Sierra Nevada de Santa Marta. As she left Taganga the landscape hardened into an arid terrain dotted by light-brown hills and xerophytic plant species – the most common of which were the cacti which were denied rainfall for all but two months of the year.

It took Mercedes less time than she expected to reach Calabazo, the mid point along the highway where the river turned sharply right to run parallel with Tayrona's southern rainforests.

Soon, she thought.

Mercedes needed food and a good night's sleep, but she knew Selena would be too excited to do anything but discuss their daring plan. Mercedes couldn't blame her, really. Selena was fearless, and Mercedes was thankful some of that was rubbing off on her.

FARC rebels controlled most of the national parks and Mercedes prayed she'd avoid their roadblocks. That's where they were fond of "miracle fishing." Everyone was netted, and the big fish were kept for ransom – gringos fetched the highest prices. If she was caught by the paramilitaries they'd likely just shoot her. If you were fortunate enough to avoid both of those warring armies, there were bandits to worry about, and they were normally more bloodthirsty than any of the murderers who wore uniforms.

So far she'd been extremely lucky. Until that moment.

When Mercedes mounted a rise in the highway, she saw them, and cursed.

Three armed bandits were blocking the road fifty yards ahead. Mercedes gasped when one of them leveled a rifle at her car. She slammed on the brakes. Two rusted heaps were parked nose to nose across the highway. Quickly she looked behind her just as a third vehicle darted onto the road to block her escape. Heading to the ditch wasn't an option. Mercedes' lips parted in a moan. She was trapped. Alone. Her stomach collapsed into a knot when she saw the looks on their faces, mean hungry stares that had already begun to devour her. *No. God, no.*

The bandit with the rifle swaggered to the car, slammed his palm against the hood and shouted, "Get out!" Mercedes sat. The pounding of her heart created a thunder inside her head that excluded everything except the excruciating screech of the door being ripped open. Greasy hands reached in and tore her frozen fingers from the steering wheel. Mercedes lost her voice, her ability to breathe. Paralyzed. A rabbit cornered by wolves. She stood shaking, her arms wrapped tightly around herself.

They took a moment to study their prize. "Pretty, pretty," the leader said, dropping a hand to his groin. Groaning. "*Toco el gordo.*"

The others laughed through blackened teeth. Inched closer.

Mercedes tried to scream, but the air caught in her throat, causing a choked cough.

Another member of the gang got out of the car that had blocked her retreat. He was huge, with a Mohawk cut and black eyes to match his jeans and T-shirt.

Mercedes shivered at the sight of the lead pipe in his large hand.

She was going to die.

The leader thrust a stubbly chin in the direction of her car and a second later his three cohorts eagerly descended on it.

Everything was slipping away, including her life. The satchel was stuffed beneath the driver's seat and Mercedes knew they'd find it. Stupidly, they'd have no clue about the value of what they were looking at. "I have money," she stammered, touching a pocket in her shorts.

The bandit leader flicked his tongue, looked at her salaciously and turned his attention to her car.

The fat one with the Mohawk pulled out the Louis Vuitton bag and grunted. He dropped it on the trunk of the car and with stubby fingers ripped the zipper open. A moment later he was hooting like a man arms deep in treasure.

Mercedes could see the cream lace of her panties wrapped around filthy fingers as fatso brought her silk underwear to his face and inhaled deeply. Everyone was laughing now, snorting loudly.

The leader poked the end of his rifle into Mercedes' throat. "Sexy lady, eh."

Mercedes felt the strength draining from her legs, willed herself to remain standing. The pounding in her chest beat a cadence for the onslaught of dread.

The leader moved closer, the smell off him as sickening as the garbage bin behind DeMarco's. "Show me how sexy," he hissed. His serpent-like tongue tasted air at her ear.

Mercedes was overwhelmed by hopelessness. They were going to rape her. Her body would be discovered days from now, or what predators had left of her.

For a fleeting moment, Mercedes thought about Selena. She'd be found and killed by Montello's men. Branko would win in the end. Mercedes sadly decided that fighting her attackers would only hasten her grisly fate of rape and murder.

Behind her came a sound that caused her to turn. They'd discovered the satchel. *Damn!* Everything was lost now. Desperation turned to mourning. Sadness numbed her instinct to survive. For an instant she considered her only option, to run, though in her imagination she pictured herself being cut down within twenty feet.

One of the thugs was opening the satchel, muttering something. Curious.

That's when Mercedes mustered something in her gut which felt like courage. She whispered, "Go to hell."

The leader cocked his head as if he couldn't believe what he'd just heard, pushed the rifle barrel deeper into Mercedes' throat, and chuckled. "What you say *amiga*?"

"Go to hell."

The others stopped what they were doing.

Mercedes could no longer control her shaking.

The leader smiled, revealing a toothless black hole.

The others ignored the satchel and came around the car. Something was going to happen. *Cojones* were on the line.

The leader hefted his rifle to the fat Mohawk. Paused. A storm gathering strength. "No. You go to hell," he said calmly and in a flash shot an oily hand to Mercedes' belt.

Mercedes struggled to get free but he pulled her tighter into his body, pinning her arms to her sides. He was immensely strong and Mercedes had no doubt that in seconds she'd be on the ground, beneath him. There had to be something she could do.

Bastard.

There was. She knew it was her only chance. Her knee had a clear path to his groin. She grunted from the exertion, and in a jackhammer reflex Mercedes made hard contact.

The leader doubled over in pain, his face a mask of surprise and rage.

His boys found it funny. They were laughing, cupping their own testicles.

Mercedes knew she had to run, and she would have done so, except at that moment the fat one grabbed her quickly from behind. As Mercedes fought to break his grip he slid a hot greasy tongue across the back of her neck. Even from behind, a fetid stench reached her nostrils. Stale cherry candy and sweat.

"Bitch," he grunted, thrusting the rifle towards his boss.

Mercedes felt dread when she saw the look of deadly rage on the face of the bandit leader. Despite his injury he bolted upright, grabbed the rifle and leveled it at her head. "I'll fuck you when you're dead," he wheezed, a finger tightening on the trigger.

For a second Mercedes thought the rifle had gone off, and somehow, miraculously, she was still alive. The report of gunfire reached them as an echo. The bullet that slapped into flesh came from much farther away.

The bandit leader jerked sideways and screamed in pain. A red blotch appeared against his thigh as he fell to the ground.

Mercedes spotted the open jeep at the same time as the others, racing towards them from the dry barren tract that ran parallel to the main highway.

Chaos erupted.

Mercedes broke free of Mohawk and ran to the front of her car. She dropped to the ground while the bandits fired at the jeep. They hoisted their wounded leader and pulled him towards their rusted vehicles. He was losing a lot of blood and Mercedes doubted – by the look on his face – that he was going to survive.

No. You go to hell.

The jeep sped towards them, leaving a rooster tail of dirt and dust.

The bandits stuffed the wounded man into the back of one of their cars and spun their tires to escape. Mercedes ran to the back of the car and crawled in. The satchel was half open, but thankfully none of its contents had been disturbed. She closed the zipper and pushed the package under the seat, then pulled herself from the car as the jeep skidded to a stop at the side of the road, shrouded in a cloud of dust. The two men who jumped from the jeep wore uniforms.

"Are you all right?" The one who spoke first had a swagger that matched perfectly the deep resonance of his voice.

Mercedes was still shaking as he reached her.

"Thanks," she said, doubling over to catch her breath.

The man studied the fleeing vehicles while his partner sprinted to the spot where the bandits had been blocking the road. He dropped to one knee and touched the pavement.

"Good shot, Juan," he shouted.

Juan spied the blood trail. "Radio the hospital," he shouted back. "Tell them to expect a gunshot. Notify de Santo."

He looked more closely at Mercedes as if to convince himself she was really OK. "Lucky girl," he finally said.

Mercedes wiped perspiration from her eyes, stole a look at the patch on her rescuer's sleeve. "*Policia?*"

"Park ranger," the man replied. "I'm Juan Rodero," he added. Then, pointing in the direction of the escaping bandits, "And that was Hercule Prado."

Mercedes cocked her head questioningly – the name meant nothing. The face she would never forget.

"Raped and murdered a British hiker near Guachaca," Rodero

reported grimly. "He would have done the same to you."

Mercedes quivered at the memory of his filthy hands tugging at her, the rifle stuck in her face. She had been lucky all right. "That's horrible. Why isn't he in prison?" she stammered, trying to slow her breathing.

Rodero's jaw tensed. "We've been hunting him and his crew for months now but he continues to find ways to evade us." Rodero looked back to confirm his partner was working the radio. He then walked over to Mercedes' car. "We were on our way back from Taganga when we spotted you," he said, seeming more interested now in the vehicle. Rodero stopped at the trunk where the Louis Vuitton case was ripped open. Lace panties caught his eye. Respectfully, he pretended not to notice, walked past. "What the hell you doing out here alone, senora?"

"Mercedes Mendoza," she said. Embarrassed, she walked briskly to her bag, stuffed its contents out of sight. "I'm...meeting a friend in the park...near Canaveral."

Rodero lowered muscled shoulders and leaned into the back seat. He spoke as if he hadn't heard her. "The fat one's name is Aldo. Likes little girls mostly. First he gives them sweets. Afterwards he threatens to kill their parents if they talk. Usually they don't."

Mercedes wiped the back of her neck. Her stomach heaved as she thought of his slimy tongue and the sickening incongruous amalgam of odours on Mohawk's breath. *Cherry candy. Decay.* She badly wanted to shower.

From the back window, Mercedes followed Rodero's eyes as they locked on the satchel protruding from beneath the driver's seat. She had foolishly neglected to replace the blanket. *Shit.*

She zipped the Louis Vuitton and dragged it noisily from the trunk. "Excuse me," she said, impatiently swinging the bag against the back of Rodero's legs.

The Ranger pulled back from the car, allowing Mercedes to toss her bag in. "The other two are new recruits," he continued, making a show of closing the car door for her. "Real gentlemen."

Rodero's partner revved the jeep's engine. Shouted above the roar, "Let's go, hero."

Rodero ignored him. "We'll follow you to the park gates," he told her, and for the first time Mercedes noticed the boyish shock of black hair that fell across his forehead, his sculpted cheek bones and soft green eyes. Sensuous lips. His last name was sewn above the breast pocket of his uniform. *Rodero.*

The cowboy, Mercedes thought, and for the first time she offered an appreciative smile. "You saved my life. Thank you. But an escort won't be necessary." What was she saying? A normal woman would have collapsed sobbing into this man's arms, begged him for protection.

Juan Rodero looked at her quizzically. "But—"

"I doubt the man you shot will be back. You'll probably find his body somewhere along the highway – if we're lucky."

Rodero stared at her, doubtful. "Prado's a survivor."

So am I.

Rodero placed his hands on his hips, seemed to swell in size with the gesture. "If you're not at the park entrance in forty-five minutes I will send someone."

Hopefully you, Mercedes didn't say as she watched him walk away. He jumped into the jeep, fixed concerned eyes on her. Then they sped away.

SIXTEEN

Thirty minutes later Mercedes breathed a sigh of relief as she reached the main gateway to Parque Nacional Tayrona. The ranger who took her admission money looked her over and smiled. Mercedes didn't doubt he'd be reporting her arrival to Rodero the minute she drove off.

Canaveral was only two miles away. Safety. A hot shower and a soft bed.

Mercedes drove past the park's administrative centre and campground and five minutes later she saw it. It was a small wooden bridge she immediately recognized from the picture Selena showed her. The narrow paved road on the other side of the bridge was the way in.

The car rumbled across the loose planking of the old bridge and disappeared behind a wall of gargantuan trees and undergrowth. Mercedes was plunged into darkness until a moment later when the canopy thinned. Sunlight splashed on black macadam which rolled beneath the car. The narrow road turned and twisted for another mile until the first cabin came into view. An old couple relaxed on a small porch, taking in the dregs of the day while sipping tall drinks. Husband and wife, tourists, Mercedes guessed. Strangely out of place. They waved and smiled as she passed.

Mercedes winced at the stiffness in her lower back and legs. Her stomach growled and she prayed Selena had made dinner. She'd shower first. Hot steamy water and luxurious creamy soap to soak away the day's grime. The scum who had touched her. It was going to feel wonderful.

She was still savouring the thought when she spotted Selena's car in front of the bungalow and exhaled in relief.

"They could have killed you," Selena gasped, refusing to release her friend's hand.

They were in the kitchen beneath a rack of hanging copper pots. Mercedes was sipping rum, straight over ice. Selena had dinner on, but she demanded Mercedes hold off on the shower until she told her everything.

Selena couldn't believe what she was hearing. "Jesus, Mercedes."

"Guess I got lucky."

"Lucky, *si*. Thanks to your Romeo."

"Rodero," Mercedes corrected, raising the amber liquid to her lips.

Mercedes hadn't had a chance to look around yet, but she knew the bungalow came with three bedrooms, a sizable living room and a den that served as an office. It was owned by one of Selena's well-to-do clients who had kindly offered his getaway for as long as she needed. He'd e-mailed a map and a photograph of the way in.

For the moment, neither of them was interested in the satchel that Mercedes had unceremoniously dumped on the kitchen table. Mercedes talked, Selena listened. The day from hell was recalled from its beginning. The deadly run from Montello, the bandits. Rodero.

Selena shook her head. "So much for well-laid plans."

Mercedes nodded. The plan had gone immediately to hell.

The plan was to raid the safe while Branko took his morning coffee on the patio. Then she'd grab one of the Range Rovers and tell the armed guard at the foot of the driveway that she had an early appointment. She'd dump the Range Rover in the same spot where Nestor had hidden the little car. That way they'd be looking for the wrong vehicle. The plan. Nothing happened the way it should have. Almost nothing. Montello must have returned to the study and discovered the safe looted because everything went to hell really fast. Mercedes had the satchel and only one way to escape: out the back of the estate and across the lawn where she disappeared into the trees.

She'd been lucky all right. That was one way of looking at it.

For a full five minutes neither of them spoke. Then Selena pulled the satchel to her. "My god, it's heavy."

Mercedes shrugged. "Back-breaker."

Selena slowly unzipped the bag and pulled it open. She let out a gasp. She took a moment before she reached in with both hands and removed the bearer bonds. Gently she placed them on the table.

They saw two things immediately. Bank of Zurich and the denomination of the first bond. Ten thousand dollars US currency.

Selena couldn't believe her eyes. A stack of bonds nearly three inches high, hundreds of them. Her math failed her.

"How much?" This time it was Mercedes asking the question.

"A lot more than we thought."

"How much?" Mercedes asked again.

Selena went to work. She divided the pile in half and began silently to count. All the denominations were the same. The arithmetic was astounding — too much to comprehend. Twice she looked into Mercedes' expectant face, her eyes wide with disbelief.

Five minutes later she re-stacked the pile of bearer bonds and looked at Mercedes coolly. "Would you believe fifty million dollars?"

Mercedes inhaled sharply and extended a shaking hand to touch the stack. "Some art dealer," was all she said.

SEVENTEEN

Hernan Suarez enjoyed the sound. A powerful destructive thump that splintered wood. It took only one kick to bust her door in. No one screamed. No one home. It was a disappointment to Suarez that neither of the bitches was there, since cap-toed Corduras made an even sexier sound when they struck female flesh and bone. Too bad. The pleasure would be denied to Montello's man that night.

There were the three of them. Suarez and two louts he had rousted from bed in that part of the villa where the crew bunked. "Get up. Got a job to do."

"Night off."

"No nights off when you work for Montello. Get your asses out of bed, fuckers. Work to do."

It took them an hour to find the place.

The noise from the broken door got some attention. A neighbour poked her head out to see what the racket was all about. Eyes wide with fear she ducked back after seeing them standing there in a cloud of wood dust. "Nosy bitch," Suarez said, stepping across the threshold into the dark apartment.

There was no need for a flashlight. Suarez slapped at the light switch and waited for his eyes to adjust.

The apartment was small, five rooms at the most. The living room was cramped and trendy. Plain white furniture with blue cushions. A woman's place, with discount store wall hangings of ocean vistas at sunset. The window above the small sofa revealed an unremarkable view of the old city, a few twinkling lights from the love hotels and brothels of Getsemani.

Light work, Suarez thought. "Either of you want to piss out the beer you drank tonight, bed's in here." Suarez was standing at the door to her bedroom, sniffing to catch the scent of her. He spotted something on the dresser and walked over to it. A framed photograph. Everything else he swept onto the floor in a crash of broken glass and debris. There were two people in the picture standing next to a small airplane. Smiling. An older man with his arm around a younger woman. Both of them black. It had to be her. The older nigger didn't matter. Suarez sniffed again, tried to fix a scent to the woman in the picture. Something else reached his nostrils. He turned around and saw lout number two pissing on her bed.

Suarez looked again at the picture, paying close attention to the airplane before he smashed the frame and gingerly removed the photo which he placed in his breast pocket. Her closet was next.

It took no time at all for Suarez and his louts to destroy her little home. The furniture broke apart like kindling; the kitchen came apart in an explosion of shattered glass and china. Lout number one was having a good time using his new blade to lay open anything with foam or feathers. They didn't find what they were looking for, which was her, but then again Suarez didn't expect to.

There was a room at the back of the apartment, a small den where lout number two was about to deliver a killing kick to the only electronic device that was still working. Suarez shouted at him to back off.

The computer blinked at them.

Suarez circled it for a moment and then sat.

When he touched the keyboard the screen came to life and Suarez smiled like a new father. A few minutes later he was still getting nowhere. The more he pounded the keys the more frustrated he became.

Hernan Suarez was computer illiterate.

When lout number two realized this he said, "Ricky's good at it."

Suarez looked at him like he was stupid. "Ricky?"

Lout number two jerked his chin in the direction of the kitchen where they could here the tinkle of breaking glass. "Computer school. Lots of bitches on the internet."

"Get him."

Ten minutes later Ricky was working the keyboard. There was an e-mail from someone named Orlando.

Suarez smiled. "Print it," he commanded, already heading for the door.

EIGHTEEN

Bogotá.

Neil Braxton was pretty sure he knew what happened to his guy from the Darien Peninsula. He had a bad feeling about him. Like a jammed M-16, or an RPG in your tailpipe when you're bingo on fuel and two of your men are bleeding out on the deck. Bad feeling all right.

Rudy hadn't been heard from since he crossed over from Panama nearly a week ago, which meant he was either on a protracted drunk, which was unlikely, or dead, which was probably the case. Braxton knew it wasn't because union organizers had a lifespan shorter than a fruit fly in Uraba. Not this time.

Braxton stabbed at his keyboard and waited for his password to kick in.

It was Sanchez, the mule, who called him with the heads up. Sanchez, who ran paste to coke labs protected by the insurgents, told him Rudy Orilio had likely been whacked by the paras. *Murieron*. That's how the food chain worked in the Darien. Especially if you were a union man.

Sanchez said he'd spoken to Orilio's wife. "Said two big ugly fuckers came to the house looking for him. Broke both her arms when she didn't tell them what they wanted to hear."

Not even Orilio's wife knew he was in the Santa Marta Mountains asking around. Anything he could find out about the Russians. Only Braxton knew that. Today was Friday and Orilio was two days late making contact. Braxton admitted to himself that he'd underestimated Orilio's vulnerability, and it pissed him off. He checked his e-mail again. Nothing.

Braxton swiveled his chair for a better view through the bullet-proof window of his embassy office and thought again about the phone call. "He had four kids," Sanchez had told him. "His oldest is an assassin in Medellin. He sends home pesos in return for his mother's blessings. She'll survive."

Braxton knew who was to blame for Orilio's disappearance, and it wasn't the paras. It was the "ugly fuckers" who broke his wife's arms. They were Raspov's freak show. The two brothers were on Montello's dime. Montello, who'd lost seven drug labs because of Orilio, and that nice shiny DC-3 full of product. Braxton was sure that Orilio's body was in a river somewhere with his fingers or hands missing. The Russians. Freaks, all right. Braxton wanted more than anything to neutralize the sick bastards. Raspov too. Fidel's intelligence guru was dipping his beak into Montello's business, big time. Braxton knew something was up. Moscow station too. They were having a hissy-fit because of what they were hearing through the pipeline. Raspov was up to no good and everyone was working overtime trying to figure it out. Langley had ordered Braxton to find the bastard, and the brothers grim. That's when he'd sent Orilio because Orilio was the best he had.

For a moment Braxton fixed his eyes on one of the marine guards at the embassy gate – a kid from Chicago who'd just been red-flagged because his father had a fresh narcotics conviction on his rap sheet. He'd be going home. Couldn't have the son of a convicted drug dealer guarding the US embassy compound in Bogotá, Colombia, cocaine capital of the world. No, my friend, you could not.

Braxton thought about his men and the stuff that happened in the Gulf, Panama, and Afghanistan. Iraq. Some tight spots where good soldiers earned their pay. He smiled and remembered that when you were bare-ass in places like that, you didn't panic. Panic got you killed. That's what happened in Mogadishu, when Operation Gothic Serpent became the pig fuck of the century. It was the politicians who panicked and called the Rangers home before the job got done. Fucking cowards calling the retreat of brave soldiers.

The agency had treated him well. After ten years he ran the show here, but he never lost touch with his past. Braxton shifted his gaze to the framed photograph on his desk. There were ten of them, faces blackened, eager for fresh kills as they knelt in front of the Black Hawk helicopter. He would never forget the mission that followed the snapshot. Two of his men were killed — Murphy and Richards, family men. He had to write the letters to their wives. Brave men who died defending their country, he had told them. In truth, their lives had been wasted.

The insertion into Baghdad had gone according to plan and surprisingly the Iraqi informant had been dead on. Hussein was exactly where he had said he would be. The bunker was located beneath one of Hussein's palaces in the centre of the city. It could have gotten him killed but Braxton demanded that he laser the target that guided the bombs onto the building. There wasn't much left for Braxton's men to clean up, a few stragglers who stumbled into the Delta's line of fire and were cut down like weeds. Twenty minutes later they found the maze of tunnels that led them to Hussein's private quarters. Reese, the explosives man, made short work of the reinforced steel door, and when they broke through they ran into Hussein's last line of defense. There were two Republican Guards and one of them got lucky, fired the shots that killed both of Braxton's men.

Braxton returned fire and wounded both of them, then personally delivered the killing rounds at point-blank range. He would have emptied his weapon into them except there wasn't time.

The Deltas bundled up their prize and got the hell out of there.

Three minutes and thirty-six seconds later Braxton was calling in the helo for extraction when his headset buzzed with an order he couldn't believe. It still angered him to think about it. "Mission abort. I repeat, mission abort."

"Fuck! You kidding me?" It was Reese saying exactly what Braxton saw in the eyes of the others.

"Eagle One repeat." Braxton held up a hand for quiet.

"Washington says leave the merchandise. Come on home."

Braxton had looked skyward with cold hard eyes at the AWACS orbiting in the blackness eight miles up. That aircraft was shooting infrared video to the Pentagon, where the generals and politicos were keeping tabs on his mission. Braxton wondered if they could see the heat signature from Murphy's and Jackson's cooling bodies. *Washington Idiots.* For a moment Braxton considered disobeying the command. He wanted to stuff the cocksucker into the chopper and say, "To hell with it. Let's go home."

The others would have cheered. They would have shot Hussein where he stood. Two of their friends were dead. In the end it was a tough call. Braxton refused to sacrifice himself and his men by disobeying a direct order. They would leave Hussein – alive. He would stay.

"You live for now, motherfucker," he'd screamed, shoving the bastard into the dirt. "But we'll be back."

"Fuck you, Yankee," Hussein had screeched, smiling back at him as the Black Hawk lifted off into the damp Iraqi night – carrying eight bitter Delta soldiers – and the bodies of two more.

In the end there were no prizes in that first Gulf war – not Hussein, not Baghdad – and certainly not the honour of Braxton's men, living or dead.

Braxton tore his eyes from the blackened smiling faces in the photograph and thought again about Orilio. A dead man whose wife would receive no sympathetic letter from a commanding officer. The last time Orilio had earned his pay, a Blackhawk helicopter intercepted one of Montello's DC-3s on a run to Panama. Somewhere near the border there was a plane wreck with corpses and a lot of ruined cocaine inside.

Braxton smiled because he knew he'd ruined Montello's day. Likely Raspov's too. He reached over and keyed in another computer password, this one to burrow deeper inside the embassy mainframe. A list appeared on the screen. He ran a finger down the smooth glass, stopping here and there to consider the code names and profiles of his confidential informants. That day several would be contacted and given a task – a simple order. Watch for a man – three men really – and keep your ears close to the ground. There was talk the Russian would be "in country" any day now. Something was up. Montello was running scared and desperate and that meant things would begin to happen – bad things. Braxton felt both excitement and dread as he fixed glacial blue eyes on his computer screen and wondered what Cuba's intelligence chief and Colombia's most vicious drug lord were up to.

NINETEEN

Jack Doyle hadn't cried since the day Whopsie O'Brien pushed him down, cracking Jack's head open. Whopsie laughed hard, so Jack got right back up and punched him in the stomach, glanced his hand off his big silver belt buckle which hurt almost as much as his head. Later, his dad and Whopsie's old man got into it. Jack and Whopsie both got grounded.

He was just a kid then. Not anymore. And there was no way he was going to let her see him cry.

They were in the big room at McTavish's Funeral Home, standing in front of his mother's coffin. Jack was trying to hide red puffy eyes.

Their fathers were on the other side of the crowded room. To Jack it looked like they were mad at each other. Jack's father kept rubbing his face, while Argus, Kaitlin's dad, leaned against a wall with his arms folded. Jack wondered whether it had anything to do with Kaitlin's uncle, the one who'd died on his father's boat.

"Do you think she looks like herself?" Kaitlin stood next to him in front of the shiny wood coffin, covering her nose because, "It smells funny."

Jack looked at her like she was the stupidest person in the room. "Who else would she look like, dummy?" Stoic, brave Jack holding back a dam that threatened to burst under the weight of more tears. Alone and frightened, he rubbed at his stomach where an ache settled in like hot lead.

"Just asking, Mr. Clowny Pants." Kaitlin's lyrical taunt wedged itself between grief and anxiety. Jack's face was a mask of both. He was being watched. Familiar faces full of pity. Poor lad. Mother gone. Just his father now, and what good can you say about him, even at his wife's funeral?

Kaitlin was dark as a summer berry, wearing a dress that made her look like a doll. She had her father. Like Jack had his.

"My dad says in Ireland dead people like to drink," she proclaimed, smoothing the front of her dress. She looked down at a smudge on her left shoe, and rubbed it against the back of her leg.

"That's called a wake," Jack corrected.

"Awake?" Kaitlin's brow furrowed in confusion, and she tugged at her hair.

"A wake...a wake. Two words. And it's the family that likes to drink, not the dead person. Besides," he said, "my mother never drank, cause Dad did all the drinking there was." Jack looked off, seemed to be calculating something. "Cancer killed my mother four days and thirteen hours ago," he said, "and I miss her a lot. What's that on your shoe, dummy?"

Kaitlin pretended not to hear, pushed her chin up over the edge of the coffin, and was surprised by her courage. The late afternoon sunlight shone through a cracked picture window over the casket and cast a golden hue across her face.

Jack thought she was pretty, but would never, ever have told her so.

"My mother was a princess. My dad says so. Do you know where Colombia is?" Kaitlin thought he was very handsome in his new suit and marveled at the sharp crease in his pants, though she wished he would stop tugging at himself.

"South America...it's in my atlas." Jack tugged. "It's where they grow coffee."

"I'm going to go there some day to find my mom," Kaitlin trumpeted. Daring Jack to challenge her.

"You'll have to get your dad to take you...cause it's really far." Jack paused, looked down again. "It's dog poop."

"Excuse me." Kaitlin's eyes widened.

"On your shoe," he said. "It's dog shit." Jack wrinkled his nose and looked away.

"That's not a nice thing to say at your mother's funeral," Kaitlin intoned. "She didn't teach you that."

Jack swiveled his head towards her. "My mom showed me where South America is, and down there I'll bet people don't step in dog shit."

Kaitlin glared at him. "Sorry about your mother," she said, as she lifted her chin and stomped away.

Kaitlin saw Jack again years later when neither of them would have remembered exactly the conversation beside his mother's coffin or the dog shit on Kaitlin's shoe.

It was during dinner, and Kaitlin had a date. Henry Slumberger was a veteran of the crime beat who smelled of musk oil and looked uncomfortable in a rented tux, but to Kaitlin, who was a junior reporter, he seemed like a god. Kaitlin also knew Slumberger's reputation for liquor and ladies. He'd spotted her at a news conference where she was badly over her head and told her simply: "Don't be crushed by the facts. Melt them down. Crystallize them until you have the essence of the story."

It was good advice. Kaitlin made page three – with a byline. She was ecstatic.

"Congrats," Henry had said to her when he phoned her the day after. "Let's have dinner."

Dinner was the New York Journalists' Gala, an annual hoedown full of egos and resentment between print reporters and the glamorous TV types with their perfect smiles that seemed to light up the room. The politicians who were invited had a field day watching the fireworks.

Slumberger ignored the filet but went big time for the scotch. He was red-eyed and slurring his words and generally being an asshole when they ran into Jack.

Kaitlin could tell Henry was itching for a dust-up.

"Lookie here, Kaitlin. The meat puppet." Slumberger could barely stand and was leaning heavily on her as Jack approached.

Kaitlin immediately recognized the woman on Jack's arm.

Jack acknowledged Kaitlin with a warm smile and a friendly hug.

"Hey, Henry, the police chief and the mayor are getting into it over the budget. That's your beat, isn't it?" Jack glanced at Kaitlin with a look that said "better duck."

"You know the rules," Slumberger responded thickly. "Everything here's off the record."

"Never bothered you before," Jack responded, and without waiting for a reply made introductions. "Mona Lasing... Kaitlin O'Rourke. Henry, you know."

The women exchanged curt nods with barely concealed curiosity. Kaitlin knew Mona Lasing was Jack's competitor at the other network and Kaitlin guessed the competition ended at the bedroom door.

Slumberger ignored the pleasantries, pulled himself straight, but was still a good six inches shorter than Jack. "Saw your piece from Somalia last month. Not bad."

"That's high praise coming from you, Henry," Jack replied, turning to Kaitlin. "Saw your dad last week," he said quietly. "Said you're going home for Easter."

"I'll bet that's not all he said," Kaitlin replied, smiling.

Jack chuckled.

Kaitlin loved Bark Island. Loved her father. But Argus O'Rourke wanted his daughter home – for good. That wasn't going to happen. She'd worked hard to earn her way. Honours in journalism at the country's best J-school had led to a coveted position with *The Telegraph* – a junior position for now.

"The islanders are a stubborn bunch," Jack replied with a look of empathy. "Argus will come around...eventually."

Kaitlin had never told Jack that he was the reason she'd gone into journalism in the first place. The hard-nosed reporter who dropped in from time to time to check on the house, and his boat. A big shot telling big stories and winning Emmys no less. Her father had a business to run. Wanted her to take over when the time came. Kaitlin would never forget the look on his face when she told him about the scholarship, about her decision to become a newspaper reporter. "Look at Doyle," he had said, his voice thick with resentment and worry. "Always off somewhere knee-deep in blood and guts."

"It'll be different for me," Kaitlin pleaded, gently. "Covering city hall is a long way from Jack's wars."

Argus eventually relented. What choice did he have?

Kaitlin showed talent early. It was only a matter of time before her editors noticed. Others saw it too, including Jack Doyle. "The network is looking for hot young producers," he had told her on the telephone a week after the gala. "I'm putting *Scoundrel* in the water at Easter. Let's talk about it then. Shanks and Francis can't wait to see us."

A week later at Finnegan's on the island they had beers and fish 'n chips – strictly business. Tommy and Mulligan were due to arrive any minute so Jack laid it out for her. "The pay starts at fifty grand and there'll be travel. You'd run interference, set up the interviews, keep your ear to the ground." Jack finished off the last of his chips and caught the attention of Mert Finnegan, who was cleaning tables nearby. "A couple more beers, Mert," he said, smiling at Kaitlin. "Big ears that one."

Kaitlin smiled at the older woman and nodded in agreement. "Make a good reporter."

Jack chuckled. "It's hard work but you'll love it. And there's nothing to say you won't end up in front of the camera someday. No disrespect intended but you definitely got the look."

"That's the nicest thing you've ever said to me, Jack." Kaitlin laughed.

"Hey, I tell it like it is."

It took Jack weeks more to break down her reluctance. Then Kaitlin said yes.

They kept her close to home at first – Washington and New York, where she shuttled between the state department and the United Nations, quickly earning a reputation as a producer who didn't quit. The reporters she worked with had affectionately called her the pit bull.

Kaitlin had once dogged a UN whistle-blower for three days straight before he agreed to be interviewed. Heads rolled when that yarn went to air, and although it was the reporter who was credited with the scoop, anyone who counted knew Kaitlin O'Rourke had broken the story. Even Frank Simmons was impressed. Left Kaitlin a voicemail message telling her "Great job. Go get 'em."

Seven months after Finnegan's fish 'n chips with Jack Doyle, Kaitlin heard from him again. She was searching for a long-lost notepad on a desk piled two feet high with old newspapers and files when her extension rang. It was a Monday. "Having fun yet?" was all Jack said when she picked up the phone.

"Where are you?" Kaitlin had asked him. "It's been months." She'd regretted it as soon as she'd said it. Cringed at the plaintive tone in her voice. "I mean…"

Jack laughed. "Jordan."

"Jordan who?" Kaitlin asked.

"Jordan…the country."

Flushed with embarrassment, Kaitlin wanted to gently replace the phone at exactly that moment and to pound her head on the desk. To pretend she had never picked it up in the first place. Instead she forced a laugh. "That's nice."

Jack must have sensed her discomfort. "Doing a piece on the royal family," he said from half-way around the world. "Was falcon hunting with the King today."

Kaitlin placed a hand over her mouth. "Jack, that's terrible. Falcons are beautiful birds."

Jack chuckled softly. "Weren't hunting falcons, Kaitlin. Falcons were doing the hunting. It's a custom here."

They both had laughed at that, making Kaitlin feel better. Her embarrassment disappeared. Replaced by something she couldn't or wouldn't identify. It tugged at her with the familiarity of an old friend. She'd known Jack all her life, but what did that matter? She'd worked hard to get where she was. Any feelings she had for Jack Doyle would remain irrelevant in the timeline she'd drawn up for her career – her life.

Kaitlin twisted a length of silky dark hair around her finger as she considered this. Then after a moment she said, "So, to what do I owe the pleasure of this phone call, Doyle?"

Jack sensed the change in her, sounded his disappointment with a sigh that faded into the distance between them. "Has Walter talked to you yet?"

"About what?"

Jack whispered a curse. "Then he hasn't."

"Jack. What's going on?" Walter Carmichael hadn't talked to her about anything. In fact she hadn't seen the Vice President for News Operations in over a week.

"Let's just say there's going to be an offer made, and I hope an offer accepted."

"You're teasing me, Doyle," Kaitlin said. Her mind raced with possibilities. "What kind of offer?"

Jack paused a moment as if considering what to say next. "Kaitlin, I've got to follow protocol here," he said, waiting for it to sink in. "Sorry I brought it up. You'll know soon enough…anyway take care. Gotta run. The Queen is sending a car over. We're shooting the interview over lunch. Catch ya later."

"Jack!"

"Gotta go."

The phone went dead.

Damn Doyle, she thought. Damn him. What made him think he could play with her like that, especially when she hadn't heard from him in so long? He was the reason she'd taken this job. His persuasion. The least he could have done was stay in touch, offer her advice now and then. Carmichael was a ball-breaker. What had he meant about an offer? Kaitlin sorted the possibilities. The Los Angeles bureau needed a producer. Rosie was on maternity leave and Carrerra wasn't the kind of reporter who was capable of going it alone. He'd be whining about now for a fill in. Kaitlin considered it for a moment further, and then shook her head. That guy in Houston. He was next in line for the L.A gig. Kaitlin knew Carmichael was a big believer in the pecking order and it was unlikely he'd deviate for her.

It was exciting. Kaitlin spent half the morning thinking about what Jack had said when her telephone rang again. This time it was the vice president for news and Walter Carmichael had an offer.

Two weeks later, Kaitlin was riding the right seat in a Cessna skimming tree tops on final approach for a jungle landing strip. No one knew she was afraid to fly.

The pilot was stone-faced as he kicked in forty-five degrees of flap, pitching Kaitlin forward in her seat and driving the air from her lungs.

We're going to crash!

He adjusted the throttle to bring the tiny aircraft's nose back up and looked across at her. "You not like my flying, senorita?"

Kaitlin replied with a yelp when tree tops brushed against the aircraft's underbelly.

The guy laughed, then reached behind the seat and retrieved a half empty bottle of something. He thrust it at Kaitlin. She stared at the bottle for a second then swiveled her head in disbelief.

The pilot flung the bottle backwards and then shouted in Spanish to tighten her seat belt.

They bounced twice on touch down and Kaitlin could swear she heard something snap in the landing gear. The pilot shrugged, stomped on the brakes and the little plane slid to a stop with its nose wheel buried in five inches of Mexican dirt. Kaitlin exhaled her relief, brought a shaking hand to wipe the perspiration from her eyes, and inwardly prayed her thanks. A second later a dusty face appeared at her window, grinning. The door jerked open and the face smiled. "How was your flight?" Jack shouted.

An hour after that, Kaitlin O'Rourke had forgotten the flight from hell. She had entered it.

The earthquake had leveled an entire town and six hundred people were dead. The assignment was a blur of corpses. Grey, dusty bodies and weeping relatives. In a home for unwed mothers dead women cradling breathless infants were pulled from mountains of rubble.

Jack was stoic and businesslike. Seth Pollard, the cameraman, was efficient. Inside, Kaitlin was a mess. But the job got done. Shoot, edit – feed. New York was happy.

They took off from the same airstrip where Kaitlin had landed three days before – same Cessna – same pilot. No one spoke, but this time it was Kaitlin who reached for the bottle. They circled the devastated town twice while Seth shot aerials, and by then Jack and Kaitlin had finished it off.

TWENTY

The day after the New Orleans Cheerleader Massacre, Jack and Kaitlin boarded the CNS corporate jet. They had been scheduled to return to LaGuardia when the story was done in New Orleans. But Jack knew the elements needed to advance the cheerleaders' story were found in Colombia, not the Big Easy. The Diego brothers had Colombian connections and the White House had been making a lot of noise lately about stepping up CIA and DEA resources in Central and South America. Jack wanted to see what the face of the enemy looked like, and to show that face to the American people.

Jack stared out the window at an approaching coastline. He'd already made a couple of phone calls to his contact at the American embassy in Bogotá. *Could he have ten minutes face time with the Ambassador? What were the chances of an interview with the DEA honcho?* Not surprisingly, the press attaché had been noncommittal, though Jack was confident that things would line up nicely once they were into the story.

As the Citation jet banked hard Kaitlin looked at Jack with a worried expression. "I still don't think this is a good idea," she said. "Malone's not gonna like the fact we left the funerals to McCoy, and Carmichael is going to kick our asses."

Jack, on the other hand, was betting Carmichael was still enough of a journalist to appreciate the initiative, the enterprise. "When Walter was in Nam he basically refused to even acknowledge the fact he had an assignment editor – did his own thing for months on end without even taking messages from him. He still loves to talk about how he ran his own show," said Jack. "Pissed off the 'tall foreheads' back in New York."

"You're sure about this?"

"I think so."

"Doyle you–"

Something thumped beneath their feet.

Kaitlin squeezed the armrest.

"Landing gear," Jack chuckled. "We're about to land."

The executive jet was buffeted hard as it descended. Kaitlin closed her eyes and whispered a prayer. "It's OK for you, Jack," she said after a moment. "You're the star. You can afford to be petulant. They'll just slap you on the wrist. Me, on the other hand…" Kaitlin allowed the sentence to trail off. Doubt joined the apprehension that laced her face. "I'm screwed."

Jack looked into her eyes and remembered the promise he'd made to her father. A promise he intended to keep. "Simmons is gonna love it," he said after a second. "And Malone won't stand up to Simmons. Malone will say 'yes sir, it's a great idea. Send our man Jack into Colombia before the other guys know what hit them. One step ahead. Exclusive story.'" Jack gave her a reassuring look. "Simmons will love it – so Malone will love it. Don't worry anymore about it. Case closed."

"If you say so," Kaitlin said uncertainly. Anyway she was done with the subject. What was the point? Jack would have his story. She'd probably be fired and that would be the end of it. In the meantime, there was a shoot to set up. That was her job, and she intended to do it. Kaitlin slung open her laptop.

Jack smiled inwardly, certain she would come around. He looked down. The Citation's shadow streaked across the Caribbean Sea. Frothy waves lapped at white sand, and even at their current altitude he could see the customers at a number of palm-thatched beach restaurants. A fleet of snorkeling boats bobbed lazily on glistening cerulean water thick with coral in stunning hues of pink and green.

The pilot increased power to level the aircraft, then banked hard left. "Five minutes more we'll be on the ground," Jack said, tightening his seatbelt.

Kaitlin did the same, though it did nothing to diminish a growing sense of unease that had seeded in her gut the moment they boarded the aircraft in New Orleans. At first she thought the feeling had everything to do with their renegade detour to Colombia. Another of Jack's adventures that would have a happy ending. It's what Kaitlin told herself again and again though she was still unable to shed her anxiety.

The Citation bumped gently onto the runway, and for a fleeting second Kaitlin O'Rourke wanted to race to the cockpit and tell the pilots to add power, to gain speed again and lift off for home. To escape whatever was waiting for them. Whatever was waiting for her.

It was while they were being processed through customs a short time after landing in Cartegena that Jack noticed the strange looks. Lingering stares at Kaitlin that made Jack uncomfortable. The customs officer who took her passport demonstrated a special interest. His head bobbed from her passport to her several times before he muttered something and stamped Kaitlin's documents.

Kaitlin didn't seem to notice. Within minutes of clearing customs she was working her cell phone, trying to confirm that the freelance shooter from Bogotá was on his way. Her plan was to try and get an interview with General Rosso Jose Serrano, a reportedly incorruptible police commander who had led a team of commandos against Pablo Escobar's mighty drug empire. The guy had juice and Kaitlin knew he'd be more than happy to cooperate with the gringo news network if it meant some positive PR.

They rode in air-conditioned comfort through Las Murallas, the parapet walls that had protected the old city for more than three centuries. Sunshine broke through low clouds, bathing brightly coloured outdoor cafes and cobbled plazas that stretched to the Convento de San Pedro Claver, a 17th century convent that was home to the monk Pedro Claver. She told Jack he was the first person to be canonized in the New World. Kaitlin smiled at the sight of Cartagena's stately old mansions with overhanging balconies and shady patios, the legacy of Spanish colonialists. Jack remained silent while she absorbed it all, every brick, every hue, every square inch of stucco in a bewildering maze of shades and shapes. "Jack," she said, "it's beautiful."

Jack nodded.

A moment later Kaitlin's cell phone chirped. She took the call and when she hung up announced the general was available to be interviewed the next afternoon. He asked if the gringo reporter cared to see how Colombia dealt with the blight of cocaine labs. They'd tour one the next day – watch his soldiers burn it to the ground. Two gunships would accompany the general's private chopper. He assured her that danger was nonexistent. Jack smiled his agreement, and of course Kaitlin was ecstatic, getting into the groove now as things were beginning to shape up. "I'll make some other calls. And maybe this afternoon we can knock off some of your standups."

"Standups?"

Kaitlin had the upper hand now. "There's a clinic in the centre of town that treats *campesinos* addicted to coke. It'll be great stuff." Kaitlin flipped open her laptop and began typing furiously. "Though we'll wait till we get to the drug lab to do the opener and closer."

Jack reached up to close her laptop. "There's lots of time."

"And lots to do," she replied testily.

"Eventually, yes," Jack said, tapping the cabbie on the shoulder. He had a detour in mind before they reached their hotel. "There's only one thing we need to do right now," he said, smiling like a devil.

TWENTY-ONE

Café Umbria was highly recommended by the hotel concierge while Jack checked them both in. He was friendly enough, but stared too long at Kaitlin. Jack watched him watching her as she rolled her suitcase towards the elevators. "Say again," Jack said tersely.

The concierge turned to him. "It's a favourite of this hotel. I'm sure you'll enjoy it." He offered to make reservations for seven o'clock.

Jack told him seven-thirty, then added, "A guy's gonna be here in about an hour asking for me. Send him to my room when he gets here, please."

"As soon as he arrives, senor," the concierge responded, catching another glimpse of Kaitlin before she disappeared inside the elevator.

"What's up with him?" she said when Jack pushed his way through the doors.

"Who knows?" he replied. "It's like he zoned out for a moment. Either that or he was mesmerized by your beauty."

Kaitlin caught a glimpse of herself in the mirrored elevator. She needed a shower and fresh clothes. She felt sluggish. It was three days since she'd clocked a five-mile run. Tomorrow, she decided. In the meantime she couldn't wait to pour herself into the new dress she'd bought. Kaitlin had protested when the taxi pulled up in front of the exclusive dress shop in the El Laguito district – Jack's detour. She was reluctant to buy the dress at first, but when Jack insisted, she decided to treat herself.

"Two weeks' pay," she intoned. "Let's get out of here."

Two hours later Jack arrived at her room and knocked, then stood there like a prom date feeling slightly foolish.

"I still think it was too expensive," Kaitlin said after opening the door and studying his reaction, "but, oh well."

Jack was speechless. The dress was cut low and slim and revealed every curve of Kaitlin O'Rourke's beautiful body – a cream-coloured satin that seemed to morph into flesh where it was taut against her hips and flat tummy. Kaitlin's hair was swept back and up in a fashion that made Jack wonder why he'd never noticed the gentle lines of her face, her shoulders and the transition between her delicate throat and the heave of her breasts. She was gorgeous, and Jack was thankful she'd relented and bought the dress.

It took ten minutes for the taxi to travel from the Santa Clara Hotel in the old city to the Boca Grande district where Cape Umbria was located near Avenida San Martin . It was a busy tourist area full of outdoor patios and tropical gardens. The hot humid air was thick with the smell of meat searing on charcoal fires. Jack breathed it in.

They walked a cobblestone street and Kaitlin was quiet. Occasionally she stopped to speak Spanish with old women who sold jewelry made of seashells and coral. Jack saw the curiosity in Kaitlin's deep brown eyes as she casually scrutinized those old faces, listening for nonexistent clues in the sound of their voices. Jack knew what Kaitlin was wondering – understood her inquisitiveness.

They were standing on the sidewalk outside Café Umbria when she spoke next. They'd been watching a lovers' sunset that left them both feeling a little awkward.

"I know what you're thinking," Kaitlin finally said.

"I was wondering when you'd bring it up."

"I've been thinking a lot about her," she continued.

"I'm not surprised," Jack said.

"Not now. OK, Jack?"

"Sure, Kaitlin." Jack thrust his hands inside his pockets. "I understand."

They stepped beneath a stone archway and walked to the front door, past the milky light of soft patio lanterns. Jack sensed edginess in her, could feel it in her back as he led her towards the door. Something suddenly unnerved him about her mood. She had been on the phone when he went to her room to collect her. Before he knocked he heard her, speaking to someone about something that didn't sound like business. Now he was wondering about the call. When he asked her about it she told him it was the front desk. "Wondering if I'd be staying in for dinner. Would I need reservations somewhere?"

Strange, Jack thought, since he had already asked the concierge to make reservations at Café Umbria for the both of them.

As usual Jack was able to talk his way to a great table. It was in a stone nook with hanging vines situated in an open-air courtyard at the back of the restaurant. Half a dozen tables closest to them were buzzing with conversation, while a legion of waiters darted around like schools of fish. The maîtred' left them with menus. "Smells great," Jack said.

Kaitlin nodded as she surveyed the restaurant, taking in the atmosphere, the odours of freshly baked bread and garden herbs, steaming plates of pasta and flaming desserts that smelled of caramel and vanilla. A huge basket of big red roses and yellow lilies hung nearby.

Jack remembered they were the flowers that Kaitlin loved. He watched her checking out the other women, but it was Kaitlin who had turned heads on the way to their table. "Wine first?" he said.

"Wine sounds great."

Jack straightened his tie, checked the knot and gave her a stupid grin. Was it hot in here?

Kaitlin saw his discomfort and smiled to herself. "What about Pietro?"

He informed her of Pietro's arrival. The cameraman had shown up demanding two thousand American dollars a day, especially if they were going to be flying with the Colombian army. "FARC has now an arsenal of shoulder-mounted stingers, thanks to the Russians," Pietro announced grimly over a beer in Jack's hotel room. *Suicidio*.

"Is he with us?" Kaitlin asked.

"Yeah, he's with us," Jack responded, continuing to read something strange in Kaitlin's tone. He ignored it. "At two grand a day he better be."

Kaitlin had already turned her attention to a troubadour playing a mandolin in the corner, serenading a beautiful young couple who listened in rapt silence.

"Merlot OK with you?"

"Sure, Jack," Kaitlin replied. "Whatever."

Jack looked at her quizzically and then caught the waiter's attention.

The newlyweds at the other table were holding hands, eyes locked over a crystal goblet that sparkled from the light of a stout candle.

Another awkward moment intruded. Kaitlin smiled and then allowed her gaze to fall away, somewhere between the olive oil and a basket of bread. Pinpoints of light reflected from her eyes.

"Something on your mind?" said Jack.

"Tomorrow, I guess. Probably all this talk of rebels with missiles."

Jack understood her concern but they were being escorted on the flight to the drug lab by some pretty impressive firepower. "Have you ever seen what a gunship can do?"

"Yes. And that works as long as we see them before they see us." Kaitlin reached for the menu.

Jack watched as she read. It was startling the things he'd not noticed before. Her long lashes and sensuous almond-shaped eyes. Too late he realized he was being obvious.

"What's wrong?" she said.

"Did you confirm our interview at that drug clinic?"

"Yes, as I already told you, remember?"

"Good," Jack replied. *Shit*.

Why the hell did he feel like a high school kid on a first date? His mind pulled him back to that day on the island and one of those rare times they had actually run into each other. It seemed funny to Jack how he could still remember the flush that swept through his body when he spied the astonishing Kaitlin O'Rourke – the woman. He was sitting on his sailboat at the marina Kaitlin's father owned. Another war assignment was done and Jack's world was righting itself again. His thirty-two foot ketch, *Scoundrel*, and that saltbox of a house where he grew up were the reasons he was home again. Bark Island. Always home, no matter what.

"I heard you were back," Kaitlin had said to him that day, stopping at the transom of his boat to say hi. She was wearing faded blue jeans and a T-shirt, and when Jack looked up at her the book he was reading just tumbled out of his hands like his fingers were fashioned from slippery wood. The long-legged wide-mouthed kid had blossomed into something special.

Jack took a moment to align his words in a doomed plan to play it cool. "Argus says you're home for a good time...I mean for good this time."

An embarrassing millisecond passed between them.

"Don't know yet," Kaitlin replied a little too quickly. "I guess you could say I'm considering my options."

They both smiled at that and Jack allowed the moment to spend itself as he tried to recall the small-town newspaper she wrote for. Somewhere near Seattle, he thought. Eventually he gave up and invited her aboard. "Got some great steaks from the butcher and the beer's cooling down below," he said. "I promise, no shop talk. How about it?"

Kaitlin shifted her long legs in a gesture that caused fireworks to explode inside Jack's head. After that, the rejection was nearly too much to bear. "I promised Dad I'd straighten out his books tonight. Thanks anyway."

Jack ate alone that night.

Kaitlin did too. Her father couldn't account for twenty-six hundred dollars. But Kaitlin's mind wasn't on the money. Jack was, the slightly arrogant, Emmy-winning network reporter who had liked what he'd seen and had casually invited her to dinner. Sorry Jack. Kaitlin O'Rourke could have postponed the bookkeeping, but she chose not to. The last thing she needed was the complication presented by Jack Doyle, who would probably be gone before the week was out. A man whose world existed somewhere else, save for the rare trips he made back for his boat.

A week later Jack was on a plane for peace talks in Ireland.

TWENTY-TWO

Adriano Sarantis drove like a demon towards his own death. Cursed for the legions of Spaniards slaughtered by his people centuries ago. His ancestors were eventually sliced into ribbons of flesh and trampled beneath the thundering hooves of the enslavers' obsidian mounts.

Now Adriano Sarantis was about to join them.

The man sitting next to him jabbed a gleaming silver revolver hard into his ribs. "*Vamos*," he grunted. "*Vamos*, my little friend."

Adriano gasped in pain.

In the distance, the city seemed dreamlike to him, a blanket of coloured lights, vile and full of whores and *cocaina*. He was a good man whose only sins, until this moment, were the little white lies he told his wife to make her feel young even though she was not yet twenty-three. The foreigner had promised to spare his family, a promise Adriano clung to as mightily as he gripped the steering wheel.

It was the two large ones who had scared the children the most after the first one kicked in the door to Adriano's house, splintering wood across the kitchen as they ate supper. That's when they strong-armed Adriano to his knees, causing Miranda and the children to scream. Raul made a hopeless run at them. Brave boy – a fighter already. They simply swept him aside and then pointed their weapons at his head. Big ugly cowards against a nine-year-old.

The foreigner had grabbed the back of Adriano's neck, squeezed hard and yanked his face up. "You die. They live," the foreigner said, pressing a gun to the side of Adriano's head. "Easy choice, *amigo*."

It was agony for him to leave his wife and children with the two large ones, but what choice did he have? He rubbed the pewter crucifix that hung on a thin strip of rawhide around his neck and then downshifted into a sliding right-hand turn.

"Take it easy," the foreigner said, twisting the gun into Adriano's side. Concentrating as best he could, Adriano snapped the wheel hard to the left, red-lining the engine as he downshifted. Cotton and sugarcane fields shot past, his life flashing beyond his reach, and for an excruciatingly indecisive moment Adriano considered turning the car around and killing them all, especially this one. He had slapped his woman and laughed in his face.

Adriano stomped on the brakes to regain control of the car. He would die and they would live. The foreigner had promised. And the honour of an evil man's promise was all he could now offer his family.

Heads turned when the four large bodyguards walked into Café Umbria. Dark crew cuts and black linen suits, stepping gingerly around tables while they spoke quietly into their sleeves and eyed everyone with equal suspicion – even the teenaged girls cleaning tables.

Jack watched them, unable to see the VIP who was in their wake. He shoved his curiosity aside and noticed that Kaitlin was clearly preoccupied by something entirely different. She'd turned both sullen and anticipatory, to the point of distraction.

Kaitlin looked at him, offered a weak smile, and then drifted off again.

Jack understood perfectly what was on Kaitlin's mind, and he didn't blame her. Colombia was more than an assignment to her. It was the place where she was born. Her flesh and blood might still be alive here. Jack adjusted his watch so that it was perfectly positioned on his thick wrist and decided to make her an offer. "Why don't you just stay for a few days?" he said. "You deserve the time off. And besides I can handle what needs to be done with the material once it's in the can and back in New York."

Kaitlin frowned. "Why would we want to do that?"

That surprised him. Professional pride, but more likely stubbornness, he guessed. Getting in the way of a great opportunity. "You know why." He waited. She didn't answer. "We can hire a private investigator. This is what they do," said Jack. "All they need is a name and they run with it. We can find someone in the morning – before the drug lab thing – and get him working on it. Whaddya say?"

Kaitlin broke eye contact, picked up a fork and turned it over as if to inspect it for cleanliness. "I'd better stick with the job at hand. Thanks anyway."

Jack was disappointed. Despite his desire to help, he knew better than to push the issue. "It was just an idea," he surrendered.

Kaitlin offered a smile. "And I appreciate it a lot. Thanks again."

There was no way she could tell him where she had gone that afternoon, her cab ride to the municipal building where they'd found no trace of a woman named Eva Mendoza. She'd been told that the records were kept in district offices, but civil record keeping was sometimes not the best depending on the town or village where the birth, death or marriage had occurred.

"Maradona," Kaitlin had told the clerk at the counter, behind him, aisle upon aisle of dusty files stuffed on shelves that ran to a fourteen-foot ceiling, some shamefully spilling their documents.

"That's near Santa Marta," the clerk informed her. A bald chubby man in his fifties with a round face that seemed to inflate when Kaitlin smiled at him. "I know the notary public there. Perhaps if you left the relevant information I would be willing to make a call."

Kaitlin gave him the information as well as the phone number for her hotel and he'd promised to call if he found anything useful. Perhaps, instead, they could meet for coffee, he had suggested.

Kaitlin reinforced her appreciation with a warm handshake, but told him a phone call would be fine. She thanked him, and then returned to the hotel.

It was about two hours later when the phone rang in her hotel room, but the voice on the other end wasn't the records clerk Kaitlin had spoken to. For a full minute she listened, sitting carefully, her hand on her mouth. After some time the man asked her a question. Then provided instructions. And a warning. The call lasted no more than three minutes. Kaitlin couldn't tell Jack about the phone call, and definitely not what she had to do now.

A waiter arrived with their wine. Jack tasted, nodded his approval, and waited while he filled their wine glasses and then disappeared. Kaitlin sipped, then circled the rim with a fingertip. "I'd feel better if we had something to show for today – except this dress," she said.

Jack held her gaze. "Pietro's shooting up in Bellavista. You remember? Two years ago that rebel rocket attack? That Italian guy fed us a couple of minutes and a double-ender the day it happened."

"I remember. It was horrible."

More than a hundred innocent civilians had died, including forty children. Now the village was trying to rebuild. It was good material for their story.

"We should be with him," Kaitlin said. "Instead of..." Holding up her glass. "Fine wine, food. You know. I guess I feel guilty about being here."

Jack removed his jacket. "Pietro's used to working alone. Besides, he's probably shot three tapes by now, so relax." He tore apart a roll, careful to keep chunks of crust from scattering across the checkered tablecloth. "You're gonna appreciate the down time and the good food when we're knee deep in that cocaine lab with General what's-his-name. No rest then. And we'll be eating ether fumes."

Kaitlin knew he was right, and appreciated the fact he was worried about her. "You're a good man, Senor Doyle," she said, passing him a small saucer of whipped butter.

"It's what I've been telling you all along," Jack said to her. "Keep the butter."

Kaitlin pulled a strand of her long dark hair away from her full lips and laughed softly.

"Hungry?"

"Let's order," Kaitlin said.

He had always puzzled her, Kaitlin thought, watching him section his roll into tidy thirds, which he placed carefully on his plate. In some ways he was so organized, especially when under pressure. You needed to be in order to survive deadlines. But this was the same man who also wore odd socks and could misplace his car. Was he really as hard-shelled as he seemed? Not likely, Kaitlin suspected. There was that charity he spent time with. Teenaged drug abusers getting straight at a horse farm upstate. Kaitlin thought it would make a good feature story, but Jack wouldn't hear of it. "The last thing they need is a camera shoved in their faces," he had told her. "Besides, there're lots of rich neighbours who barely tolerate the idea that drug addicts are living down the road. Suppose they're afraid they'll be murdered in their beds. Find a rehab that wants the publicity."

She respected Jack's enormous talent and hoped he also felt the same way about her. So far, though, it had been all business between them and Kaitlin wanted to keep it that way.

Jack's cousin Frannie – whom she refused to call Mulligan like Jack – had condemned any notion of a romance.

"Don't even go there," Frannie would say to her, though she loved Jack deeply. "This is Jack, remember? Gotta-plane-to-catch Jack."

Both of them would laugh at that, but once, after they'd uncorked their second bottle of wine, Kaitlin admitted she'd toyed with the idea.

"Then just fuck him, girl, and get it over with," Frannie had slurred.

"Frannie!"

Kaitlin stared at Jack's handsome face at Café Umbria and reconsidered her decision not to tell him about the phone call earlier. She rejected the notion a moment later. Besides, she didn't know yet whether *she* believed it. She'd know before the night was over. Could it be true?

"What's on your mind now, O'Rourke?" Jack said, picking up his menu.

"Nothing but good pasta," Kaitlin said.

Jack smacked his lips. "I'm starved."

"So am I," she lied. In truth she was forbidden to tell him about the strange conversation she'd had that afternoon. The man on the phone had made things very clear to her and she planned to do as she was instructed.

"*Solo, amiga,*" the man had demanded. Come alone.

The foreigner spoke bad Spanish. "Not far now," he said in his strange accent.

Adriano pulled hard to the left, causing the tires to slide sideways on loose gravel, then stomped hard on the gas to push the little car past sixty. He no longer felt the passage of distance or time.

When they reached the outskirts of the city the foreigner checked his watch. He then removed a cell phone from his pocket. A moment later he was speaking in a language Adriano didn't recognize, and for a few seconds he was distracted.

The foreigner stabbed the gun at an approaching exit and barked at him.

To make the turn, Adriano bullied his way across three lanes of traffic. Tires screeched and horns blared as they shot beneath an overhead sign which led towards the old walled city. His legs shook. Sweat streaked his face and stung his eyes. Adriano prayed quietly and for a second was able to picture the tiny church in their valley, a home he knew he would never see again.

His tribal ancestors left legacies of gold and stone long forgotten on the *minifundia* where the others of Adriano's kind gave in to leftist persuaders and their brash promises of a better life for the landless and the illiterate. Adriano was neither and could not believe in another man's dream. Only his own. But he was about to commit a horrible sin for another man's evil.

Jack raised his eyebrows as he watched Kaitlin gulp her Merlot.

"Thirsty, I guess," she said, licking her lips. She glanced casually over her shoulder towards the door, then down at her watch. She took another sip.

"Expecting someone?" Jack wondered what the hell was going on.

"Is it that late? I think we'd better call Malone," she replied. "I don't think he was finished with us when he hung up today."

"He'll cool down. He has to. Simmons is behind us, and that means Malone has nothing to say in the matter." Jack drained his glass and thought again about the call they'd made to New York. At first Jamie had been furious. It took Jack five minutes to calm him down, another five minutes before their executive producer began to warm to the Colombia story. Jack knew Frank Simmons was hovering nearby and when he was told of their insubordination, he laughed and shouted for Jack to hear, "Go get 'em, Jack."

Jack looked at Kaitlin suspiciously. It wasn't Malone she was worried about. She knew full well the newsroom pecking order.

Kaitlin leaned over and whispered, "Back in a minute."

At that moment he was aware of the heat from her body, a hint of scent when she got up from the table and walked away. She looked back and smiled strangely before disappearing around a corner towards the washroom.

Jack sat there. What was that all about? He inventoried the possibilities but came up empty. He rolled the empty wine glass between his hands and decided, what the hell — relax — follow some of your own advice and enjoy the evening. Tomorrow was going to be a back-breaker of a day. Jack planned to cover the bullshit drug lab photo-op and then head into the mountains where Marxist insurgents were operating what was basically a protection racket for the cartels. They were all in it together — a multi-billion dollar consortium of the greedy, and the brutal. That was the real story. He planned to pitch Kaitlin on the new elements of the yarn when she got back. In the meantime, the ambient clatter in the restaurant was peaking, muted voices and silverware striking fine china, the plucking of mandolin strings. Jack picked up another roll, unconsciously rubbed the taut muscles of his belly, and then dropped it again. He scanned the room. Lots of narco cash in tight silk and Italian suits. Big white smiles everywhere. Everyone was rich or well on their way. He'd seen the pride of exotic cars parked in the grid of alleyways that surrounded the restaurant — the Ferraris, Jags, and a couple of Lamborghinis, polished so brightly they seemed to throb with power.

"To Jaeger and Sasha." An older gentleman at the table next to Jack's raised a glass. He was wearing large sunglasses in candlelight. Jack turned at a commotion near the front door. Six men walked in, including the four who reconnoitered the premises earlier. They were apparently satisfied with what they saw because one of them said something into his cuff and a moment later a tall slender man with grey hair and glasses was ushered into the restaurant. He was followed by a woman and a young girl. Wife and daughter, Jack guessed. The three of them were swept along with the phalanx of bodyguards to a private dining room, trailing a wake of stares and murmurs. Jack recognized the man as Miguel Amillo, Colombia's maverick justice minister. Jack wondered if Amillo would be part of the drug lab photo-op. Perfect! He'd score an exclusive interview aboard the VIP chopper. If he survived till then. This guy was one hell of a target and apparently had big balls given that he was threatening the drug lords with extradition to the United States. While other politicians would have gone into hiding, Colombia's justice minister told a reporter he wouldn't be intimidated by "thugs and criminals."

Jack shouldered aside his uneasiness, moved the butter dish farther away from the candle's flame, and wondered how long Kaitlin would be gone.

Adriano stopped the car exactly where he was told, between two parked cars at the end of a long narrow cobblestone street. On his left the owner of a jewelry store turned a handcrank in rapid circles, noisily lowering a metal cage in front of his shop. Farther down the sidewalk an enormous doorman ushered a pair of long-legged women into an English pub. Lilting laughter punctuated the click-clack of stiletto heels on wet pavement until the two beauties folded into the man's thick arms and vanished in a blur of blonde hair and black leather inside the bar. Adriano looked with dread at the murderous cargo they'd placed carefully in the back seat. He thought again about his wife and two children. They would live. It was the only reason he'd been able to say goodbye, even when Miranda clung to him and begged him not to leave. That's when the man had slapped her, and pressed the gun against her head when Adriano struggled towards him. Adriano would have surrendered his soul for a chance to kill him. Slowly.

The foreigner just sat there, staring at a restaurant at the end of the street. Waiting for what? Adriano saw men outside the restaurant. Five of them leaning against large black trucks parked at the sidewalk. Adriano guessed they had weapons. Men like them always did. Adriano could see the sign in front of the restaurant and wondered what kind of people ate there. Were they rich? Then he froze. Were there children inside? Suddenly overcome by shame and sadness, he buried the thought quickly and followed a string of soft lights that led to the front door of the restaurant.

After five minutes a man left the restaurant carrying what looked to Adriano like a case for an instrument of some kind. The man stopped briefly on the sidewalk to talk to the security men, then lit a cigarette and ambled up the sidewalk as the men watched him walk away.

The foreigner smiled. He spun his head to check the large greasy cache of explosives on the seat behind them. "Start the car," he commanded.

Adriano hesitated.

"Fucking little monkey." The foreigner reached into his shirt pocket and removed a shiny photograph, one of those instant pictures. Shoved it in Adriano's face. "*Mirar! Mirar!*" he growled between clenched teeth, grabbing Adriano's hair, painfully jerking his head back. "Your beautiful wife. Look." The foreigner snapped his teeth together, sucked at air. "Your wife will live."

The Colombian's faced twisted. Sobbing, he pleaded. "Please, mister," Adriano stared at the photograph — snot and spittle spraying on the front of his shirt. "*Ilo hare...idejelos ir!*"

"They live. You die." The foreigner shook the photograph at Adriano. "For her! For the little monkeys!" The foreigner jerked the door open and climbed out into cooler air — inhaled long and deeply. He leered at the photo of the Colombian's wife. Her naked body, a helpless mass of flesh and duct tape, eyes wide with fear with the gun barrel pressed to her temple. The foreigner quietly shut the door and bent to the open window. He nodded slowly and smiled. "When they start shooting — duck," he said and was gone.

Adriano was not a murderer. Until this moment. As he pushed down on the gas pedal he prayed again for forgiveness. Heart pounding, he struggled for air as the tiny car raced down the narrow cobblestone street. Adriano whispered their names on hot sour breath. Feeding his courage on the images of his wife and children. He knew he would die quickly, and so he didn't fear any pain. All that mattered was they would live. Adriano wiped a ragged sleeve across his mouth, a shaking hand downshifted. *They will live.*

The armed men hoisted their weapons and fired. Too late. The car struck two of them, knocking them to the street where they rolled into the gutter – lifeless. The three others continued to fire. Bullets shattered glass and thumped through metal. Adriano crumpled sideways as the car flew onto the sidewalk. Plate glass crashed onto the hood in a thunderous concussion that drowned out the sound of screaming.

The tables closest to the window were crushed beneath spinning tires and hot exhaust pipes, scorching flesh and bone. The smell came to him. The horrible noise, so numbing he shrank from the terrifying scene and was strangely at the beach with his family, turquoise waves chasing the children from their doomed sand castles. Adriano moaned, as if coming awake. Bodies crested the car's hood, headlights flashed on stunned expressions. The car stopped inches from a table full of people. A young dark-haired woman pulled herself from the wreckage, furiously wiping the front of her fine dress. She reached for a dinner napkin, incredulous at the red stain pumping from her jugular. Feet away her dinner companion was already dead.

The sounds of dying faded. Then came silence. It was Miranda's voice Adriano heard. Little Antonia and Raul, too. They would live. He was able to picture them for only a second before a hand he couldn't see stabbed a button on a small transmitter and sent Adriano Sarantis, a righteous soul, straight to hell.

The crash at the front of the restaurant was followed by a flash of blinding light. Then a deafening concussion which was like nothing Jack had ever experienced. The shock wave moved with incredible speed, crushing everything in its path. Bodies jerked like marionettes on invisible strings, spilling blood and entrails upon fresh crisp linen and shattered crystal.

The floor erupted beneath Doyle's feet. He was suddenly weightless, in a world without gravity as he collided with the ceiling. His head struck with a crack that shuddered through his body. Falling now. A lifeless sack striking the floor. A sulphur breath was punched from his lungs and consciousness dissolved to the prologue of a dreamless night where light and sound did not exist.

Doyle had no idea how long he was out. His eyes opened to complete darkness. The air tasted thickly of dust as well as gaseous vapours that seemed on the verge of combustion. Instinctively he shuddered at the new terror. Jack coughed through a blockage in his throat, reached weakly to his head where he felt something warm and wet. No pain. Yet. His face was pressed against something cold, something that might have been cement or stone. Human sounds began to reach him. Moaning. A cacophony of life's final seconds. Doyle commanded movement but felt none. He surrendered to a paralysis that he prayed was the imperative of his mind, and not his body.

Eyes closed as if upon sleep. Thunder rolled across an imaginary darkening landscape. Shutters slammed on the rogue winds of a perfect storm. *Not yet. Jesus, not yet. Kait...*

It was his last conscious thought.

TWENTY-THREE

Doyle came awake as blank as a starless sky, a canvas that depicted nothing but his thickening confusion. Time was indefinable, with no discernable difference between days and decades. He was prone and tightly wrapped, bringing him warmth and comfort. There were the sterile odours of a hospital room, the feel of soft bandages, a mélange of heedless voices, a two-fingered jab into the vein that throbbed in his neck. Cold hard fingers.

Desperate now to open his eyes, he could not. Someone had glued them shut. Something was being strapped around his arm, squeezing, pumping. The airy swish of a bellows. The pressure faded in a long mechanical sigh. More muffled voices. He tried to talk, but the words were stillborn inside his chest. When he was finally able to open his eyes, pry them free of swollen skin, an apparition spoke to him.

"*Buenos dias*," it said. Fuzzy and bobbing. The smiley face on a party balloon. Coming closer. "I'm Doctor Estrada. How are you feeling?"

Without his patient's response, Estrada swept a tiny light across Doyle's eyes. "*Momento*," he said, stretching an eyelid until it hurt. Jack grunted his discomfort and a couple of silent seconds later the light winked away.

"Good news," Estrada reported. "Your reflexes are healthy. But we'll need another CAT scan to confirm that there is no brain damage." He patted Jack's arm. "You'll live." Estrada then handed his clipboard to the nurse next to him. "*Analgesico?*"

"*Si*, doctor," she replied.

Everything was hazy, like the world was layered with petroleum jelly. Everything in soft focus, undefined. The doctor was thin. The nurse had long dark hair. The room contained one bed. Sunshine through light-coloured curtains. That was it. Jack's head hurt. He brought his tongue forward between slippery lips, tasted an ointment of some kind and swallowed. His hand moved weakly at his side. He wanted to say something.

It took a full minute before Estrada understood. He lowered his face. "More painkiller?"

"Kaitlin." It was all Jack could say, the name trailing off on the ghost of a breath. Nothing. Silence. Like he'd just shouted an obscenity in church. Jack knew then. He had survived. Kaitlin hadn't.

He didn't open his eyes again for a full day, swirled in and out of consciousness. Demerol brought him silky comfort, and when reality shouldered forward he simply summoned a nurse and rolled over to signal his need for more dope. Two days later, when Jack awakened, a man was standing in his room. He said he was from the American embassy in Bogotá. His name was Braxton. Neil or Norman, Jack wasn't sure which. He was a tall man with an angular face and closely cropped military hair. He seemed out of sorts in a dull grey suit even though it fit like a uniform. He looked at Jack — a general without his armies.

Braxton asked Jack how he was feeling and stood at the foot of his bed as emotionless as a lobotomy patient. He dropped a large envelope near Jack's feet. "E-mails," he said, and then walked stiffly to the window. Jack looked past him, to the heat waves rising from terra cotta rooftops, the silver and glass highrises spiking into blue sky. "Thanks," he whispered hoarsely.

"No worries," Braxton replied. He poured a glass of water and held it out. Jack took it and maneuvered it carefully to his lips. "Your boss,

Walter Carmichael, will be arriving tonight," Braxton said matter-of-factly. "He'll be taking you home and making whatever arrangements need to be made."

Jack already knew that, and he wasn't looking forward to Carmichael's arrival. One of his producers was missing and they feared the worst. He'd make sure Jack was fine and then – in punishment for his insubordination – he's strip the flesh from his bones. A velvet cushion covered in thorns.

Jack couldn't figure out what Braxton wanted – exactly. Any low level embassy staffer could have dropped off the e-mails, so Jack guessed Braxton was CIA – Station Bogotá, or maybe DEA. One thing for sure, he didn't appear the type for small talk. Jack watched him for a moment, and then asked the question he was hoping Braxton could answer. "What about the woman I was with?"

Braxton turned his back. "You remember a couple of years ago… that night club bombing? Three hundred and thirty pounds of explosives. Ka-boom. Thirty-three people dead." Braxton's bedside manner was as bleak as his suit.

Jack remembered the attack and wondered where Braxton was headed.

After a moment Braxton continued, turning to stare at Jack's face. "Never found half the victims."

"I remember," Jack said. "So?"

"We figure Café Umbria was a much bigger load. Four hundred pounds, maybe more." Braxton stopped a second to let that sink in. "They haven't found all the bodies yet. The ones we did find are so badly–" Braxton stopped. "We don't know yet whether we can separate the DNA from the woodwork."

"Jesus," Jack muttered to himself.

"Yeah. Jesus is right." Braxton folded his arms, continued. "The Colombians should be really good at this stuff by now, but they're still rank amateurs. We offer our help and they take it. But what's the point really?"

Jack shut his eyes while Braxton returned to his place at the window. For a full minute neither of them spoke. Jack looked to see whether Braxton had disappeared out the window.

A nurse poked her head in the door to check on her patient. Braxton smiled and said something in Spanish. The nurse walked in and poured two pills into Jack's hand which he promptly swallowed.

"The justice minister walked in shortly before it happened," Jack croaked. "I remember that."

"He's dead, along with his wife and kid," Braxton replied, waiting for the nurse to leave. "Amillo should never have been there in the first place, but he's...*was* a stubborn sonofabitch. He brought his family. Can you believe that? The man was out to prove he wouldn't be intimidated and in the process they all get wiped out." Braxton looked over his shoulder. "You're a sonofabitch too, Doyle, a lucky one. Lucky you sat where you did, right next to a thick load-bearing cement wall. It's the only thing still standing by the way."

"Yeah. Lucky me," Jack said quietly. "Who's taking credit for the bombing?"

Braxton turned to face him. Arms straight against his sides. "No one yet, and that's the problem. There are so many players here it's impossible to tell. We know why. Amillo was the biggest target in Colombia. We warned him – he blew us off." Braxton shook his head. "The who? We don't know yet. But it's an easy guess." The CIA man walked closer to Jack's bed and looked down at him. Hard eyes, a shade of green like the fungus Jack once found in the bilge of his sailboat. "The most likely culprit is FARC," Braxton said. "Revolutionary Armed Forces of–"

"I know who they are," Jack interrupted.

"Right," Braxton said. "Anyway, Amillo was on our side. He was spearheading support for the extradition treaty and right now, as you now, the White House is chomping at the bit for that little bit of paperwork."

"And spearheading his credentials for a run at the presidency," Jack added.

"It was looking that way," Braxton said. "Too bad for him and too bad for us." Braxton wandered over to a vase of flowers on a table at the foot of Jack's bed, studied one of the blooms like it was some kind of alien creature. "Coming here was a bad idea, Doyle. Embassy staff are being sent home. Christ, even the DEA is evacuating non-essential personnel. It's not a real safe place to be right now."

Jack shook his head. "I took precautions."

Braxton chuckled. "What they're saying back home is you're a renegade who takes chances."

"Who're *they?*"

"Some of your friends," Braxton replied. "You're big news. They were talking about you on CNN last night. One of those panel discussions where the reporters get to say what they really think. They really think you're a junkie for the bang-bang. Afghanistan, Sri Lanka, Iraq. I know the feeling. Been there. Done that too. Usually in the company of soldiers with guns and stuff to make sure everyone comes home."

Doyle cringed. "You're saying I fucked up."

"I didn't say that," Braxton replied. "They did."

Doyle looked away.

"Anyway, sorry about your producer. Too bad she won't be going home."

The condolence washed over him, a wave tugging at his lifeless body. He wanted this guy to leave now.

"She was Colombian?" Braxton moved closer and sat down. Rigid in his chair like an interrogator. Creases in his pants sharp enough to cut bread.

"Born here," Jack replied without looking at him.

"Some homecoming," Braxton continued, like he hadn't heard him. The CIA spook reached inside his jacket to adjust the Glock nine mil Jack was certain was holstered there. "But the good news is you'll survive," he said.

"Great news." Jack felt woozy. His tongue a sponge. The painkiller was kicking in and he wanted Braxton to leave.

It didn't take long for Braxton to get the message. He told Jack the FBI would want to interview him and that he was to get out of Colombia as quickly as he could. Braxton looked down at him. "Listen to me on that, Doyle," he said. "Leave and don't come back."

For a moment Jack was sure there were two Braxtons. Strong stuff, he thought, as the CIA man walked out of the room.

TWENTY-FOUR

He had called her Angelica. A name that might have implied sweetness and light beneath gossamer wings, a spiritual being or Renaissance messenger. She couldn't say whether she was any of these things, but Angelica was what the old man had called her, so that must have been her name. She quietly repeated it, allowed it to roll across her tongue to taste it for familiarity. Though she found none in Angelica.

It was the only word he had spoken when she shuffled into the room, barefoot on floorboards that were split and cracked, worn with what appeared to be decades of dirt.

Angelica was not a name for the dispassionate, or uncaring. She knew little else, but she was sure of that. She had no idea who he was, but for the moment he didn't appear to mean her any harm. There wasn't much she did know, except for what she saw.

He was small, a life-sized knobby wooden sculpture in an old checkered shirt and colourless pants, clutching a straw hat with his large brown fingers. His feet were covered with ratty leather sandals, his toes a collection of bony spurs, their nails black from injury or neglect. The old man had shoulder-length silver hair that was tied back tightly, revealing a bald crown the colour of mocha. He looked at her with eyes that were black as tar, sunken beneath thick bony brows. Ravens perched in the shadow of a rocky ledge. Those eyes followed her as she stepped into the room.

"Angelica," he repeated with the hint of a smile.

She shuffled farther into the room until dizziness forced her to a chair beside a large stone fireplace.

Angelica.

A rhythmic throbbing at the back of her skull clawed its way forward and blurred her vision. She rubbed her head, waited for the pain to settle. She had awakened wearing a simple cotton dress with swirls of red and yellow. Odd and ill-fitting. She had no recollection of it, no memory of dressing in it. She looked at the old man, her face a question.

He dropped his stare to the dusty floor, redness blooming in his sunken cheeks, muttering quietly. Angelica wondered how she'd gotten dressed. And about the man.

She locked arms across her breasts and shivered even though the room was stifling. It wasn't much of a house – just a shack really. There was a plain door, with a small open hole where the door knob should have been. A piece of rope kept the door shut. Two small windows revealed little beyond the hewn wooden walls. She heard dogs barking outside in the distance.

He continued to stare at her, casually loosing a dark glob that landed with a thud in a bucket next to his feet.

Angelica averted her eyes.

There were other rooms, a couple of closed doors that might have been a bathroom and another bedroom. The kitchen was a mess with heaps of soiled dishes and the detritus of half-eaten meals. A cracked enamel stove had one burner. A huge porcelain bowl served as a sink, and assorted bottles containing unidentifiable substances were lined up like ragged soldiers in a lost war. Angelica covered her nose as if just becoming aware of the stench. Too many smells to identify, the heaviest being an indescribable rot.

Her arms and hands were covered in dirt and soot and lined with fine rivulets of dried blood. She became aware of a dull ache in her legs and carefully she drew the thin fabric of her dress above her knees, revealing tiny scabbed scratches.

The old man thrust balled fists into the air. His eyes flared as he barked.

Angelica struggled to understand. She struggled to find her voice. "Who are you?" she finally whispered, sampling the sound that came out of her. "Where am I?"

The old man cocked his head, eyes narrowing in a face that gave nothing away in his intentions.

Angelica showed him her hands, motioned towards her badly bruised legs. "Did you do this?"

The old man's expression flashed with mortification. "*¡Dios mio! ¡Dios mio.* No, senora. No!" Gnarled fingers cleaved the air in front of his heavily lined face. "No, senora." His breathing quickened and the old man tightened his grip on the straw hat, like it might sprout wings and abandon him. "No, senora. *¡Dios mio.*"

"*¡Dios mio,*" Angelica repeated to herself. She understood. How was that possible? She rubbed at the pain in her head, moaned in exasperation. How was it she knew simple Spanish, but had no idea who she was, or where? She wiped at tears that seemed to be bleeding from her throbbing head and realized for the first time since walking into the room that her mind was utterly blank. Nothing. Simply vacant. Her hands shook as she rubbed the point on her skull where the pain seemed to be digging in. Thinking made it hurt more. Blackness filled her mind, a void as deep as space. Angelica looked to the old man, saw pity forming in his face. The tears rolled down her cheeks, falling to the floor where they created tiny impact craters in the dust.

It might have been the horrible headache playing tricks with her ears. She wasn't sure. But she thought she heard a voice in the other room. A muffled cry, weak and plaintive behind the closed door. The voice called out again. A name...Kaitlin. But it had no meaning to Angelica.

Angelica was going to faint. Whatever it was the old man had brewed for her was making her feel a lot better, but lightheaded. When Angelica stood she'd had to steady herself against the chair.

"Take it slow, little one," the old man said to her in Spanish. "Finish your tea. It'll make you well again." He'd said nothing when the voice called out from behind the closed door. Just got up to prepare his concoction.

"I'd better sit," she whispered, feeling slightly foolish as she collapsed into the chair. It took a moment before the lightheadedness went away. Angelica looked at the steaming cup suspiciously as she brought it to her lips and swallowed again.

Even though he was busy with something in the kitchen, Angelica saw the old man was keeping a watch on the closed door. Worry etched across his face. Angelica wanted him to sit, to explain things. At least to tell her his name. The better she felt, the more urgent it became, the more she needed to know. Who am I? Where do I belong? How did I get here? She was vacant, unable to recognize the house or the old man who was wiping brown gnarled hands with a dirty dishcloth. He walked to his chair and sat down again, gave her an understanding smile. "We're not used to having company," he said. "You were a surprise to us. A very nice surprise, I might add. How are you feeling?"

Angelica stared into her cup and replied in Spanish, "Whatever you gave me seems to be working."

"It's an old recipe," he offered.

Angelica nodded. It was crazy to be talking about the tea. "Who am I?"

The old man leaned forward as concentration furrowed his brow. He waited a moment before speaking. "The explosion," he said, pausing. "So many were killed. You were spared."

Angelica had no idea what he was talking about. Explosion? So many killed? What did he mean?

The old man sat back in his chair without taking his eyes off her. "Truly an angel," he said softly, "like your name."

Angelica's headache had disappeared, though the lightheaded feeling was coming back. She decided she'd had enough of his cure. "Where am I?" she asked, trying to keep panic from her voice.

"You don't know," the old man said. A statement. "Of course – no."

Angelica's eyes flicked to the door. She might be able to run, but what was outside? Maybe others, more dangerous than the little man who apparently meant her no harm – for now. Angelica couldn't identify what she was feeling. Surreal. Was it the tea? Panic crept closer. "Who are you?" she repeated, wiping perspiration from her forehead. It was all so strange. The dress, the old man, the dirty little house and the fact she didn't know even her own name. Questions twisted and swirled like sand in a windstorm, stinging her face and eyes.

"My name is Alejandro. I'm your friend, Angelica. Please. Nothing will harm you here."

It brought her a small measure of relief. She breathed deeply. Angelica. The name again. "Angelica?" she repeated as much for herself as for him.

"It's your real name, not the name you were given for the American. The name of your birth, like your beautiful grandmother. She was U'wa. Like me. Like your grandfather." Alejandro frowned, like he had just swallowed something vile. He reached inside his pocket and pulled out a small brown sack and a packet of papers. He opened the sack and extracted a pinch of tobacco which he rolled quickly and efficiently. The match appeared out of nowhere, flaming against the end of the cigarette. Alejandro drew deep, and then exhaled. For a second he vanished behind a cloud of smoke. It hung like fog in the space between them. Alejandro's disembodied voice emerged through it, deep and smooth. "Her name was Angelica…your grandmother," he said, taking another draw. "She was my sister."

Angelica listened blankly.

Alejandro stopped for a moment, placed both hands on his knees and looked directly at Angelica with warmth he hadn't yet revealed to her. "I see her in your eyes."

Her grandmother? What did he mean? Angelica watched him smoke. The sweet smell of tobacco filled her nostrils.

After another moment Alejandro crushed the cigarette beneath his sandal, got up and opened the front door.

Angelica was drawn to the sunlight and when Alejandro stretched his hand towards her she stood slowly and moved towards him.

Alejandro allowed her to find her strength. Carefully he took her arm as Angelica stepped gingerly from the old porch onto ground that was dry and cracked. She stopped a moment to survey her surroundings. They were in a large clearing bordered by tall trees and brush. What lay beyond she couldn't tell. They walked slowly past a large crumbling shed which was filled with junk hung on rusted hooks and rope. There was a beaten-down pickup truck, its chrome grill dulled and broken.

They made their way along a well-worn path that led into woods next to the main house. Angelica breathed deeply, happy to be shaded from the brutal morning sun. Cooler moist air filled her lungs, made her feel normal for the first time since waking. In the daylight, she guessed Alejandro at seventy or more. He stooped to pick up a stick. "Not far now," he said, jabbing at the wide sunlit opening at the end of the shady path.

"Where are you taking me?"

"You'll see."

They didn't speak again until they emerged from the path into the harsh sunlight once more. They were on a grassy plateau which sloped gently downward towards vast tracts of unbroken forest. From a dozen rooftops, Angelica spied thin trails of smoke which rose from chimneys like silver string. There were people too. Like insects as they went about their business.

"Maradona. Santa Rita. Bellavista," Alejandro intoned. "They are U'wa, but so many have been killed, who can say how long before we are all gone?" He shook his head. "The Spaniards murdered us by the thousands. Now the rebels soak their hands in our blood, like the oil companies suck the blood from our ancestral lands."

Angelica listened intently, not wishing to interrupt while Alejandro spoke.

"Coca," he continued, the timbre of his voice thickening. "Bogito owns the farm there." Angelica followed Alejandro's gaze to a squat dwelling situated in the middle of a modest patch of cultivated land far away to their left. "It pays for two of his sons at university in Caracas."

She didn't dwell on Bogito's little farm, fixing her eyes instead well beyond Maradona to a breathtaking range of snow-capped mountains.

He watched her for a moment before changing the subject. "Your grandmother's people have been here two hundred years. The old house was over there." Alejandro pointed in the direction of a clearing to their left, bare now except for a broken column of stone that might have been a hearth and chimney, overgrown by tall grass and woody brown weeds.

It seemed like a dream to her. She needed to sit, but at that moment Alejandro took her hand again and gently pulled her forward. Angelica was content to follow. Every step, every word, seemed to lessen the anxiety she felt. After a hundred yards or so, Alejandro stopped once more.

Angelica tried to make sense of what she was looking at. She turned to Alejandro, waiting for an explanation. He said nothing, though Angelica sensed a darkness in his mood that had not been there previously.

They stood on the edge of a field containing a hundred or more blackened and cracked tree stumps. Grey dirt at her feet, the whole scene made Angelica think of giant stubble on the face of a corpse.

Alejandro continued his silence. He'd become so quiet and somber that Angelica wanted to ask him the reason for the change in his mood. For some reason she felt sorry for the old man. If any of what he had said were true he was her grandmother's brother — her great uncle. How unreal it was as Alejandro marched away, leaving her alone.

Angelica didn't see the grave markers until they stepped through knee-high grass into a small clearing not far from the destroyed tree stumps. She felt dread at the sight of them, wanted at that moment to tell Alejandro it was time to return to the house.

Alejandro let go of her hand and gently knelt at one of the alabaster slabs. He ripped a handful of tiny invading weeds and touched the marker like it was living flesh. Alejandro spoke to it, breathless words in an urgent whispered cadence that made Angelica feel like she was intruding on his privacy. Occasionally he stroked the grave marker with what Angelica saw was deep love and respect. When Alejandro looked up at her, his eyes were red. "Come meet your grandmother," he said as he reached out to her. "She died when you were just a baby."

Confused, Angelica bent slowly, grimacing at the pain which stung her knees. She leaned forward to look more closely at the names which were barely readable. Luis Mendoza. Angelica Gabriella Mendoza. The date of death was the same for both of them: June 23, 1973. Accident, or fire, or something else. Angelica was curious. She looked at Alejandro for explanation.

Overhead, a low flying crow squawked at them, ebony wings flapped against a darkening sky, and Alejandro looked sourly at the second grave. "The remains of your grandfather," was all he said.

"They both died…the same day?" asked Angelica.

Alejandro remained silent, watched as the crow disappeared behind distant trees. "The weather is moving in. Time for us to go now." With that, Alejandro got up and walked back in the direction they had come.

Angelica had to quicken her step to keep up with him, across the plateau and to the shady path which was much darker now beneath a canopy of blackening cloud. When they entered the tunnel the temperature plummeted. Angelica rubbed her bare arms, shivered slightly as the first raindrops began to *tap, tap, tap* on the thick foliage above their heads.

"We could stay here and wait it out, but she must not be left alone. She pains at this weather." Alejandro slowed for a second so Angelica could catch up.

What the hell was he talking about? Angelica was tiring of this. "Who?" she demanded. "Who do you mean?" Angelica took hold of his arm. "Tell me. Please."

Alejandro stopped dead in his tracks. Looked at her with the gentle impatience of a loving father. "She doesn't like to be left alone…not in this."

"Who?" Angelica demanded again. "Who doesn't like to be left alone?" *Tell me, damn you!*

Alejandro waited a moment. His raven eyes fixed on hers. "Eva," he finally replied. "Your mother."

Angelica froze. Like cement hardening around her ankles. But before she could speak, Alejandro abruptly turned, dashing quickly along the gloomy path until he disappeared into the downpour.

TWENTY-FIVE

Alejandro led her into the room, to the foot of a small bed where a slight form was covered by blankets, unmoving. "She eats so little she vanishes," he said sorrowfully.

The darkness settled over her like a harbinger of death. Angelica immediately sensed the neglect. She was horrified.

Thick curtains, like funeral shrouds, covered the room's only windows. A smell of sickness invaded her nostrils, so dour she wanted to retch.

"My God, open the window." Angelica coughed, bringing a hand to cover her mouth. "She has to have fresh air. At least you can do that."

Alejandro's eyes hardened. "You don't understand. Everything possible I have done. But she is very sick."

Angelica shuffled to the window and shook the curtains apart, releasing a blizzard of dust so thick she held her breath. Light washed over them. Angelica grunted from the strength it took to pull the window open, allowing fresh wet air to blow into the room. She swayed and would have fallen except that Alejandro took her arm and helped her gently into a chair next to the bed.

Angelica took a moment to decide what needed to be done. "Clean up that mess in the kitchen and bring food," she demanded.

"She doesn't eat...she sleeps—"

"Now!" she ordered, sending Alejandro from the room.

A single blanket covering the frail body rose and fell nearly imperceptibly, making Angelica wonder where the woman found the strength to breathe. She reached across the bed to pull back the blanket, allowing fresh air to reach her face. The woman was pale and drawn with dark circles around her eyes, sunken cheeks. Long dark hair, streaked with grey, spilled onto the pillow, framing the soft features of her face. Her lips were drained of blood but even in their greyness Angelica could imagine them generous and flush as cherries. The woman might have been beautiful once.

After a moment, Angelica reached beneath the covers and took up one of her hands, gently rubbing her long, finely sculpted fingers. Was there familiarity in them? Angelica let go of the woman's hand and spied the small mirror and hair brush that sat like abandoned artifacts on her night table. Tentatively she reached for the mirror and brought it to her face. There might have been a resemblance, but Angelica couldn't say for certain. She was full of doubt, unwilling to accept anything Alejandro had told her. He was a crazy old man, she decided, taking advantage of her vulnerability. What was he trying to accomplish with his fanciful lies? Were they for cruelty or profit? A way to control her while ransom was being demanded? Who would pay it? Who would be looking for her?

Exhausted, Angelica wept. Tears streaked her face as she sobbed quietly into her hands.

TWENTY-SIX

Jack couldn't shake it, no matter how tightly he squeezed his eyes shut. A kind of looping videotape, a vignette of dust, smoke and bodies, moving towards him, heaps of grey bloody flesh, crawling forward, moaning through shapeless mouths and begging for mercy. The images burned like acid on silk.

There were noises outside his hospital room: a doctor being paged, trays clanging on a lunch trolley. Jack opened his eyes and stared vacantly at the feeding tube which snaked from a bag of colourless liquid into his arm. The drip punctuated time, like a funeral march. A thick soft bandage was wrapped tightly around the top of his skull, and for a moment Jack thought about the Mexico earthquake, the old guy with the head wound who went into cardiac arrest while they were shooting video inside the makeshift hospital. While a doctor pumped the man's chest, Jack checked his watch to see if they were going to make deadline. Kaitlin punished him with her incredulity.

At the time, he guessed, he would not have even registered on the humanity meter, but then again, if you weren't careful, those stories stuck to you. Like the Sudan, where in one village the hacked corpses were piled higher than him, the ground red, and still wet. When he got back to camp that day, his boots were covered with dried blood. He didn't judge the butchers responsible because that would have meant laying bare his humanity. How could you do that, when the rivers were filled with bloated corpses? You did what you had to and then got the hell out.

A couple of times during the night they had to change his hospital sheets because of the sweats that soaked his bed. The second time, a nurse brought a cloth and a basin filled with water. She hummed soothingly, the trickle of water reminding Jack of home and those hot summer days when he dipped his feet in pools left by the low tide. He was thankful for the human touch, the warm, damp cloth on his neck and chest.

"You were lucky," the nurse whispered. "In my country no one is so lucky."

Jack was woozy from sleep and the narcotic, and for a moment he wanted to touch her cheek, to tell her everything was going to be fine. When he woke that morning he wondered whether he'd dreamt it.

Alone, Jack stared through the window of his hospital room. Carmichael told him he'd been cleared for travel and they'd be heading stateside before the day was over. "I'll be collecting O'Rourke's things," he'd said before walking out the door.

For the hundredth time Jack thought about her. In his mind he watched her walk away from the table. How many minutes later did the explosion happen? Two, three? Then there was the flash of light and the deafening concussion. The sirens were muffled at first and then so loud his ears hurt. Wetness. A warm bloody webbing on his dusty face. Jack had no idea how long it took to find him. He remembered the lights, the stifled voices. Uniforms stumbling through black smoke and stepping carefully around small gas-fed fires. *Muerto*. That's what he heard them say again and again as they picked through the rubble. Then they found him, placed him on something hard. A gloved hand forced itself into his mouth, feeling for something – maybe his tongue. Someone jabbed something into his arm and stupidly he tried to pull away. That's when they strapped him down.

Jack had a hard time sorting it out, especially the disturbing belief that Kaitlin was keeping something from him in the moments before the bomber struck.

TWENTY-SEVEN

Branko Montello cocked his head to catch the sliver of sunlight slashing the Michelangelo and brought a lingering hand to his chin as if he were realizing its brilliance for the first time. He felt something he didn't recognize, a quality that wasn't part of the repertoire of feelings he'd mastered so he could live among other humans. The thing he felt now was unfamiliar. It might have been humility in the presence of such genius, though Montello cast the notion aside like a prince presented with pauper's clothing.

He was oblivious to everything except the paintings aligned on the walls of his inner sanctum, a place were no one was permitted, except a few hand-picked household servants. Montello understood their fear of him, nurtured it. Sometimes you needed fear to survive, though arrogance and cruelty he found much more comfortable, and thankfully those things were the dominant parts of his being.

Montello picked up his cup, grimaced at the light ring it left on the polished wood and made a mental note to tell Suarez to fire the new maid. He strolled to the large window, squinting through the sunlight that glistened off the morning dew, an ocean of moisture that formed one droplet at a time on manicured gardens and grass that stretched farther than he could see. He dropped his eyes to stare at Nestor. The old gardener looked up and then quickly averted his eyes to the task of emptying a wheelbarrow. Branko Montello smiled to himself, a smile that had all the warmth of a man encased in ice.

Montello wore a fine black suit – tailored perfectly to fit his tall slender physique – and a white silk shirt which was open at the neck. There was aristocracy in his long narrow face, his high forehead, and aquiline nose. Dark flat eyes seemed orphans of the blood and flesh that made up the rest of his face. He turned from the window and without moving swept those dark pits across the gallery of art. The Picasso had been his only indulgence to the century in which he was born. He preferred the early masters: Leonardo, Donatello, Lorenzo and even Botticelli who foolishly surrendered his talent to the zealot monk who condemned his vanity to fire. Those Renaissance masters had had a rich patron. The Medici brought them perspective through Brunelleschi. Brunelleschi, the heretic, had brought Florentines their great puzzling dome. Montello was proudly a patron too, a protector of the genius that hung on the walls of his study, most of which had been stolen and was now hunted by Interpol and half a dozen other investigative agencies. Paying for fine works such as these would have made him a pimp and the great masters nothing but whores. Montello hoarded for good and honour, he thought, as he drained his cup and moved to a thick leather sofa the colour of oxblood.

He was only thirteen years old when he killed for the first time. Quemarropa. He could still feel the gunbarrel against the man's head, still hear the mewling sound that came from the body after the bullet punched into his skull and splattered Montello with blood. The other *sicarios* watched from their hiding place across the street and howled with approval when the man collapsed onto the sidewalk. Montello felt nothing, except regret that he had done it for food. He was no better than the other urchin assassins who roamed La Terazza killing for Escobar. Montello promised himself then that others would do his bidding.

In time his power came. Slowly at first. When he put a bullet into the head of a police chief, Pablo noticed – and invited him into his world.

Montello shifted easily into Pablo's existence, a world of hatred and beauty where Montello was awed not by the exotic cars or the horses or Escobar's many whores, but by the works of art that hung like medallions of gold around the necks of gods.

Escobar had explained it to him this way, "Art moves across borders easier than cash. Customs agents don't know fuck about the value of a good piece of art. So sometimes I take what's owed me in paint and canvas. Simple." To Escobar art meant currency. His homes were lavishly styled in works by the great masters, but Pablo was a rough man who got his start stealing tombstones and reselling them. What did he know about art? Montello had absorbed more about light and brushstrokes and perspective in one afternoon wandering the hallways in just one of Escobar's villas than his mentor would have learned in a pathetic lifetime.

Montello was eighteen years old when he soiled his hands with murder for the last time. He returned to find his payment: a gift. He gently removed the wrapping paper, but flung the card on the floor unread. It was a Picasso – a small one – signed but undated. Montello spent two hours alone in his room that day studying the confused human features, twisted in a fashion that reminded him comfortably of the chaos inside his own mind.

Montello never knew his birthday. He chose December 2. That was the day Pablo Escobar was killed, and it was not long after that Montello commanded others to murder. The victims were unimportant – a drunkard and a whore who hadn't cared for the whereabouts of their son since he vanished to the streets when he was still a boy. Montello remembered neither of his parents' faces. His father's fists, his mother's hands, he never forgot.

There was a soft knock at the door.

"Come."

Hernan Suarez was late. When he walked into the room Montello's security chief shrugged a set of powerful shoulders in apology and with one hand gently placed half a dozen newspapers on a coffee table.

Montello reached for a copy of *The New York Times* and nodded in the direction of his empty cup. He snapped open the paper and read. "Our friend does good work," he said, while Suarez poured.

Suarez handed him fresh coffee and sat. Grim satisfaction on a face that reminded Montello of dried mud. "It was the Russian's contact within the government who confirmed Amillo's dinner plans. Their assets are second to none. Ears everywhere," said Suarez.

Montello read for a moment. "Amillo's death buys us some time but others will have to be taken care of in a similar fashion. Quickly. The message we send to Washington will be clear and unequivocal."

Suarez nodded. "Misunderstandings won't be an issue if the Russian can deliver what he's offering."

"The Russian," Montello replied, lowering his newspaper, "will need to be paid for what he's offering. Amillo was a taste, his way of proving he can deliver."

Suarez appeared to be pondering this.

"So, Suarez. Where's my money. Where are the bonds?"

Suarez wiped sweaty palms against the front of his khaki shirt. "A hundred men are looking, but the girl has simply vanished. It's likely she had a team waiting for her."

Montello pounded his fists. "What kind of fool do you think I am?"

Suarez flinched.

"She had no team!" Montello shouted, glaring. "I, on the other hand, had a small fucking army which she has so easily evaded." Montello's face darkened. "Bonito and Alvarez will try for my head when they find out some peasant girl has fucked them, eh, Suarez? Fucked me." The jackals would sniff his weakness and join forces to move against him.

Suarez gritted his teeth, bones that formed the joints in his jaw popped in and out with the cadence of battle drums, but he remained silent.

"She makes me a fool," Montello sneered, standing. He stiffly paced. He had invited her into his world, and she had betrayed him. In his mind, her beauty had blackened into wickedness and rot. She'd soiled both his reputation and honour, and Montello wanted the pleasure of killing her, himself. But first, she'd have to be found and the bonds retrieved.

Montello exhaled. Mendoza was a distraction from his brazen plans. The work was already begun with Amillo. Much more blood would be spilled, as much as it took to protect what was his. Raspov held the key and soon it would be his. Montello's lip curled into what might have been a smile.

Suarez picked up his coffee and began his report. There was no sign of Mendoza at her apartment. No bonds. No surprise.

Montello remained silent, now and then simply nodding so that Suarez would keep talking.

They had taken the owner of DeMarco's for a ride.

"Luigi...a good man," Montello said.

"Clueless about her...now dead."

"Go on," Montello demanded, thinking Mendoza had been stupid to leave her acquaintances so vulnerable. Her mistake was his gain.

Hernan continued, "No parents. No family that we know of, but we're still looking."

Montello thought for a moment. There was that orphanage she sometimes talked about. Somewhere near Santa Marta. Trinity, it was called. Montello regretted he hadn't asked her more about her past. Family and friends would have been easy conduits to her – her fleshy weak spots. Though he'd never had to think about such things before. The others were easily dealt with when he tired of them. They were simply made to disappear. This one had gotten lucky, like a wild sow bolting into the underbrush when she caught the scent of a predator.

Suarez stood to leave. "She has a friend," he said. "We paid her apartment a visit and found something that might be useful."

"Find her, Suarez," Montello said. "If you do not..." He allowed the words to trail off, his warning unmistakable.

Suarez nodded and quickly left.

Montello needed to calm himself. Fists clenched, he paced. The truce had been necessary to end years of war – on all sides hundreds of their men had died – a needless waste of resources. But now fresh bloodshed was leading to a growing protest and the government was under increasing pressure to do something about it. Ruiz had been careless – once too often. Besides, he was their soft spot. The fat man had been secretly negotiating surrender with the Americans. In return, there was to be a lesser prison sentence and an agreement that would have allowed him to keep a large measure of his cocaine fortune. Alvarez and Bonito hadn't believed it at first, until Montello provided the surveillance photographs. He'd laid them on the table in dramatic fashion. The first shot was of the assistant deputy director of the Drug Enforcement Agency walking into the US embassy in Caracas. The second photograph – Ruiz, being escorted through the same gate by marine guards. One could only imagine the damage he would have caused.

Consensus came quickly. A truce. Agreement that Ruiz would be eliminated.

The truce had been shaky at best. Montello had no intention of being one of three. Alvarez and Bonito would also die, but only after the Russian made good on his delivery – and was paid for it. The muscles in Montello's face twitched as he thought about her. His money. Her betrayal.

There was another knock at the door. Suarez, the fool, was testing his patience. Montello moved forward and was about to open the door when the teenaged maid stepped into the room, oblivious to her crime.

Montello looked at her in absolute disbelief. Speechless.

"Pardon, senor." The maid lowered her eyes. "Your tray, *por favor.*"

Montello inspected her, his rage building. She had violated him. Like the other one had. It sickened him to think about it. They were whores. No different than the whores he beat and robbed when he was old enough to wield his fists.

Montello nodded in the direction of the silver tray with its croissants and fruit untouched. His appetite had vanished, replaced by a knot of rage that felt more natural to him than hunger.

When the maid moved towards the desk Montello was on her, a flurry of punches before her face could register shock, before she was able to protect herself, or even cry out. When she fell to the floor he dropped too, swinging his fists in wide arcs that connected with flesh and bone. Gobs of blood, mixed with snot and saliva flung onto the front of her uniform. It wasn't her face, but another woman's he saw. She would be punished too. Montello grunted softly, the earnest look of a man swinging heavy tools, a hard day's work hefting a sledgehammer, or a pick axe.

After two minutes he was spent and she was still. Montello got up, walked slowly to his desk and dropped heavily into the chair. She was still breathing, and he was glad he hadn't killed her, not in this room. She was suddenly conscious, weeping, and for a second he wanted to finish what he'd started. Instead he languidly poked at his uneaten breakfast. The sticky coffee ring. That had been her first unforgivable mistake. Entering his study without invitation was her second.

Montello lifted the phone and punched in a number. Suarez answered on the first ring. "I want you to fire the new maid," he said, and hung up.

TWENTY-EIGHT

BARK ISLAND.

"Into God's arms we commit her," Father Faustus Doherty exclaimed with the holy imperative of a Vatican prince. "In our hearts Kaitlin lives on," he cried. "A rainbow forever brilliant."

Doherty's face glistened as he locked eyes with the half-blind Jimmy O'Connor and with Irvine Jones who was plagued since childhood with a dark disposition and never missed a chance for the company of grief. "Amen, Father. Amen," they replied in unison.

There came a simple nod from the bug-eyed mute Aggie Dunn, who was impossibly good at ciphering the words that fell from other people's lips and who synchronized her blinking with Father Doherty's breathing and his syntax, so she wouldn't miss even one syllable of the priest's moving oratory.

Father Doherty continued, "Our Kaitlin was sunlight."

A murmuring of agreement swept through the crowd, a consensus punctuated by the nod of heads and the flash of white linen to red soggy eyes.

Father Doherty paused to savour his own words, sweet and thick as sap from the Cedars of Lebanon. "Sunlight forever warm," he said smoothly.

Jack stared vacantly at the polished granite that bore Kaitlin's name and the dates of her birth and death. A plaque.

Shanks offered Jack an umbrella which he waved away. Mulligan lingered uncomfortably nearby, watching them both.

A snapping Atlantic wind whipped freezing drizzle across a landscape of marble and alabaster crosses, making Jack and the others shiver. His family was sunk into this earth. His mother and father and now the memory of his friend, Kaitlin.

All around him looks shot at Jack, stinging like lead pellets. Even the old priest. "A person's life can touch us in many ways," Father Doherty continued, his ruddy face and quivering jowls punctuating his every word. Tiny glasslike beads of water shimmered on the fine strands of grey hair that disappeared against his colourless scalp. He held an umbrella in one hand, a bible in the other, as he towered over the stone that held the name of Kaitlin O'Rourke.

Jack wiped a hand across his face, sweeping the rain onto the lapel of his drenched jacket, and bent his head towards sodden feet. The priest's solemn words were well meant, but flat, a faint echo. Jack stole a glance at Argus O'Rourke, who had yet to make eye contact. Watery eyes sunken into a face that had taken on the pallor of sour dough bread. Argus. Who had sobbed angrily into the telephone. "Bring her back. You bastard, bring my daughter home."

Jack told him then there was no body to bring home. That's when her father had made that pitiful noise. Like the bleat of a lamb about to be sacrificed.

The service was finally over.

Father Doherty stood before Jack, smelling of sweet wine. He squeezed Jack's hand too hard and shook it roughly. Jack looked into his eyes and saw the pity. "We all loved Kaitlin," Doherty said quietly, then leaning in, "Don't blame yourself, Jack." It should have felt like ointment instead of a scab being torn from his skin. "He's going to need some time," the priest added, turning toward Argus O'Rourke who was being led from the cemetery by a group of men, their wives in lockstep at the rear. "With God's help, he'll come around."

Jack nodded. "Thanks, Father."

Father Doherty walked away.

Jack watched as the mourners dispersed toward warm dry homes nestled in unbroken forest and on wide rocky ledges below. After a moment, he trudged to a narrow stone pathway, leaving behind the polished marble that bore Kaitlin O'Rourke's name. So little evidence of an existence, Jack thought, as he left the cemetery.

TWENTY-NINE

Jack didn't know how long he'd been standing there, dripping water from his ruined suit onto the concrete, where it pooled around his fine Italian shoes. He rested his forehead against the front door and could faintly smell the coat of blue paint he'd applied on a sunny warm morning only four weeks before.

Turn the knob and open the door. Just one more minute, he told himself. That minute became two and when it edged closer to three, he shouldered his way into the small front foyer of his childhood home.

He stood there listening to himself breathe while water accumulated on gleaming hardwood. The slow laboured respiration of a man in a coma. Jack deflected the stillness that shouted for recognition and stomped into the house, shedding his soaked jacket and shoes. There was a box at the front door: the contents of Kaitlin's desk at the network which Jack had volunteered to return to her father. Beneath the notepads and books and assorted knick-knacks Jack had found a photo. They were wrapping up an assignment in Rome. He remembered how she didn't trust him with the settings as she thrust the Nikon at him and found her place among a herd of tourists at the Spanish Steps. "Don't adjust anything. Everything's set."

He took the shot.

"Let me get one of you, Jack," she had said.

"Gotta go. Cab's waiting."

Jack needed a drink. He pulled himself down the hall and lumbered into the kitchen. He grabbed a beer from the refrigerator and cracked it open. The cap skittered across hardwood into a corner. Jack took a swallow, then a second, and then moved to the window above the sink. A wall of fog was closing in from the bay. It was as thick as the day they brought his father back. Only his father. Jack gulped his beer and remembered that day. The others were lost and Jack's mother had cried just as hard as the three widows. Jack didn't understand why until the start of school when Whopsie Jones beat the crap out of him and called his old man a "stupid drunk" and a murderer for cracking his boat up like he did.

That was the day Jack knew he'd be leaving Bark Island for good when he was old enough to find his way through the soup. There weren't many Doyles left to leave, although they'd clung like barnacles to slate, and built stout little ships from the dark wood rooted in three hundred acres of the family's land. They were boats fashioned from sweat and curses, and the pride of Jack's father and grandfather until the inshore fishery began to disappoint and many came ashore to find other ways to make a living. Jack's grandfather retired his tools and his spirit, but his father had one more boat to build – his own. Jack still remembered the crowd that gathered the day she was launched. He was mesmerized when the little ship rolled down her slip, snapping logs and splashing into the still waters of Ragged Hole Bay. "You're in charge, Jack, while I'm gone." Jack didn't like it one bit, his father leaving, but he knew his old man had to go – things had gotten hard. He'd never eaten so much homemade jam and hard tack. Besides, other fathers went up to Nova Scotia to fish. Shanks and Mulligan didn't seem to care. Their fathers were gone for weeks at a time. Jack remembered the both of them the day of the launch, crouched behind a dogberry tree trying to light a cigarette, Mulligan slapping Shanks on the back so hard he coughed up his breakfast.

Caleb Doyle's last schooner was a fine sight. Her carvel hull glistened rich amber, her wheelhouse was stained mahogany red. "She'll be yours someday, Jack," his father had said proudly.

Jack stood at his kitchen window and remembered how he'd lit up that day, lit up so wide he thought his face would split. He rubbed at the scar on his hand, an ache that drifted in and out like the tide of his memories.

"Reminiscing, Jack?"

When he heard the voice, Jack spun around. Argus O'Rourke. Slouched in the doorway, dripping wet in the threadbare suit he'd worn to his daughter's funeral. He swigged from a half-empty bottle and clenched his teeth like a man bracing for battlefield surgery. "Thinking about your old man?"

Jack gritted his teeth, tried to decipher the intent in his ruddy face, though instinctively he knew what Argus had come for and he wasn't surprised at the sight of him in his kitchen. Still, Jack was dreading this visit, not because Argus was a violent man, which he was not unless pushed to the brink. Years at sea had given him a sailor's wits, and fists, both of which had saved his ass on more than one occasion in deadly waterfront hangouts from Hong Kong to Athens, places where merchant seamen became legends and corpses.

Argus was a squat man, made mostly of shoulders and neck. A broad face swung up, then down. "You don't look too bad for the wear and tear."

Jack ignored the remark, but the man's disdain jabbed at him. "How'd you get in?" he said.

"The door. The door was left wide open." Argus took another swallow, reminding Jack of his impressive capacity for liquor when he opted to drink, which was not frequently. When he did, and when he was thirsty for it, the rum exposed an ancient deep brogue like wood grain glistening beneath a coat of Murphy's oil. In a good mood, Jack couldn't say whether Argus liked or hated him. Indifference the best he could hope for. He was not a man prone to pleasantries, and certainly not affection, except when it came to Kaitlin, who was his admission to humanity, the rose-coloured glasses through which even a diseased hairless mongrel

ANGELS OF MARADONA 172

appears healthy and huggable. Glassy eyes glared at Jack from beneath thick fiery brows. He hiccupped, puffing air beneath a wide and well-manicured mustache, his strongest feature and some would have said his only vanity – except for his daughter.

It was from her Colombian mother that Kaitlin had gotten her delicate cheeks, ripe lips and earthy colouring. Certainly not from the fire hydrant of a man swaying in front of him, dripping on the lino from a twenty-year-old suit that looked like he'd had to kill it before forcing his thick limbs through all of its available openings.

Jack lowered his arms, his beer bottle swinging from the tips of his fingers like a metronome keeping both time and score. "You're drunk," he said. "Go home."

Argus widened his feet, pulled his arms tight to his massive chest. "Go home. Not likely. Besides, why would I want to go home? What's there for me at home now? Memories of my dead Kaitlin and my lost brother?" Argus looked falsely like he was having a sober moment. "Aiden was a good man. He'd be fifty-two today had he been the one to come back – instead of Caleb."

"I'm not in the mood for this, Argus."

"No mood for remembering?" Argus tugged the bottle to his mouth, licked his lips as the amber liquid slammed into his gut. "I remember. Me and those widows remember."

"You're drunk. Go home," Jack repeated, tightening the straps on his temper.

Argus paused, as if to regroup. "Like father like son, eh? Caleb and Jack. Though, Jack, you've got more adventure in you. Traveling to all those places. Getting your face on television. Some kind of star that Jack Doyle. The only place Caleb saw his face was his reflection in a bottle."

Jack stiffened at that. His father was a drunk. It was difficult for him to admit it, less so for others who found it convenient to paint him that way in order to fortify *their* image of *his* villainy. It had happened a lifetime ago, but Argus still came off righteous as communion from last Sunday's mass. Jack didn't care that Kaitlin's old man was desperate to deaden his pain with the booze and the blame. He had no right to dredge up the past as an indictment in the present. And on the day of his daughter's funeral, no less.

Argus sagged. "You know what the goddamn priest said to me? 'Your girl's gone, Argus.' Just like that – gone. And you. What you promised that day down on your boat."

Jack turned his back on him, stared out at a sheet of gunmetal grey. Yes, he remembered. It seemed a foolish thing for Argus to say at the time, but Jack had humoured him. "Of course I'll watch out for her," Jack had told him. "She's in more danger riding in that pickup of yours."

Huge raindrops struck the kitchen window and flattened into tiny silver cascading rivers. He turned around and saw that Argus was having trouble standing. Kaitlin's father shuffled a couple of steps and fell against the wall, a prize fighter trying to regain strength before his opponent moved in with the next flurry of hooks and jabs.

Jack stepped towards him, wanting to take the bottle from his hands, sit him down somewhere and put on a pot of coffee. He felt a deep sadness for the man, and wanted a chance to close the chasm that had torn open between them. Kaitlin would have wanted that, he was sure. No words, just a tentative step signaling an armistice. "Argus," Jack said, reaching out, "give me the bottle. You've had enough."

O'Rourke swung the bottle, sliced the air inches from Jack's face.

"Take it easy!" Jack shouted, raising his hands to protect himself.

Argus pulled himself straight; veins suddenly appeared at his temples. "And you were warned about going to that hellhole," he slurred. "I'm hearing that and more."

Argus was right. Jack looked down, unable to find words. The networks had pulled back. No insurance company wanted to issue the coverage that the newsrooms needed to send their crews into Colombia. "We knew there were risks," he said, inwardly cringing.

"Damn you," Argus boomed. "No story's worth my daughter's life! Her boss in New York said you weren't even supposed to be there."

Jack looked him straight in the eye. "I'm sorry, Argus. She was my friend. There's nothing more I can say."

"Sorry?" Argus laughed at that. "Like that means anything at all coming from a Doyle."

"Argus," Jack replied. "That's old news. If you want to talk about ancient history, let's talk about Kaitlin's mother."

ANGELS OF MARADONA

"That's none of your goddamn concern."

"It was Kaitlin's concern," Jack shot back, turning to face him. "She had a right, Argus, and you know it. Her whole life, wondering about her."

Argus took another swig, swallowed, his eyes distant, making Jack believe a truce was somehow still possible.

"Her mother," Argus said quietly, wiping wet hair from his forehead. "I couldn't tell Kaitlin about her mother. Better for her not to know." Argus seemed to be considering how much more to say and after a moment, as if finding temporary purchase on a rocky ledge, he continued, "I had more than Aiden. There was our sister too. Was the prettiest girl… even prettier than Jimmy O'Connor's girl, Meghan. Dolly was her name. She grew up fast and the last we saw of her she was on a street corner in Dublin. She didn't recognize either of us."

Jack had had no idea.

Trance-like, Argus then shifted to a time after Ireland and Dolly, past the years he'd spent at sea and after Aiden was drawn to Bark Island by Duey Whelan's daughter, who taught school, and committed herself to lifelong grief when Aiden died at age twenty-four. These things were well known to Jack – and the fact that Argus abandoned the sea lanes and joined his brother and his new wife and baby at Bark Island. Six months later Aiden was lost aboard Caleb's schooner.

Argus was reaching back to that time. "When Aiden was gone I left again. Signed on aboard *Caledonia*. We brought salt fish to Jamaica and Colombia. Came the other way with coffee and rum." Argus hoisted his bottle. "Not this stuff."

Jack snatched a quick breath, suspecting the storm's eye had just settled over his kitchen.

For the moment, Argus seemed content to tell his story – his own audience. "The captain and me went for a hundred pounds of mangos. The old bastard – Bergsten – a Dane, got the scurvy once when he was a boy and couldn't get enough of 'em. We found a market. Kaitlin's mother was on the truck with the fruit. Beautiful. Much more than a lad from Dublin could hope to have." The hint of a smile appeared on O'Rourke's lips. "We saw each other three more times when my ship was in and then nothing. She just wasn't there anymore. I didn't even know she was pregnant until she wrote me the letter telling me I was a father. Argus gazed down at the floor, remembering. He looked up and then said, "I took Kaitlin from her mother's arms at a bus station after we docked in Cartagena four weeks after that letter. Brought her back to Boston aboard the *Caledonia*."

Kaitlin was the reason a ship named *Caledonia* was the last entry in the old seamen's book that Argus kept in the office of his marina. It was a soiled and worn relic that reminded him of his years, his ships, his travels around the world.

Jack was confused. He'd heard a much different story. It was none of his business, but as far as he knew, Kaitlin's mother was the daughter of a successful Colombian businessman. Jack surmised that an illegitimate child didn't fit into his world and, as a consequence, the infant Kaitlin was given to the care of her Irish-American father.

Argus looked past Jack to a point outside the window. "The youngster made her mother into some kind of Aztec princess. She drew pictures of castles and crowns. When she turned eight she searched my desk for her address so she could send an invite to her birthday party." It obviously pained Argus to say what he said next. "Truth was, she was a housemaid. Just a peasant who couldn't feed her anymore. That's why she gave her to me." Argus raised his head, revealing moist eyes. "I couldn't tell her. How could I tell her that? Besides, I was all she needed. Not some woman I bedded when I was at sea." Argus fumbled with his pocket, tried to retrieve a cigarette, then gave up. He swung the bottle again, more to remind himself that he was there for a fight, eyes like dark poisonous berries. The storm was back. "My daughter. My brother. Goddamn it. You and that drunk of a father."

Jack had taken enough. He moved quickly forward and was about to show him the door.

Argus flung the bottle against the wall, where it exploded, splattering amber liquid onto Jack's face. "Goddamn you!" the Irishman screeched, twisting around and stomping unsteadily from the kitchen.

Jack wiped his stinging eyes and went after him, heart pounding as he grabbed the door jam and swung himself into the hallway.

He shouted something after him, too late for Argus to hear.

THIRTY

The fog that rolled over Jack's house on the day of Kaitlin O'Rourke's funeral swallowed everything in its path, leaving nothing for the eye to see except silvery wraiths that faded in and out like the illusory bug-a-boos in a child's fertile and restless mind.

Jack slept off O'Rourke's rage, like a bad drunk. Tossing like the fifty-year storms that tore up the island. When his eyes snapped open, Jack realized the fog had lifted. Moonlight bathed his bedroom, giving smooth outline to chunky pine furniture and his wet clothes, which he'd tossed onto a chair before putting on sweats and collapsing into his unmade bed.

Someone was in the house.

He smelled food cooking. Pots clanged and someone was rustling through the silverware drawer. There were muffled voices. Jack swung his legs to the floor, and padded from the bedroom. When he got into the hallway the voices grew louder. They were arguing. No surprise, he thought. Shanks and Mulligan never agreed on anything. It didn't matter what the subject, there was absolutely no chance of consensus, no likelihood of harmony, no possibility of concurrence or accord. The two were opposite ends of a magnet forever repelling. Black was white, white was black, and up was down, and vice versa. When Jack walked into the kitchen, the two of them were toe-to-toe in a pool of blood.

"Nothin' wrong with fat. " It was Shanks who had a slab of dripping meat poised over a cast-iron frying pan.

"I said trim it first." Mulligan had a hold of his wrist, a murderous butcher knife in her other hand.

"What for? Missy no-fat latte got something against a good piece of marbled meat?"

"Your heart's gonna explode before you're fifty. You'll see."

The knife came up and Shanks surrendered. "Have it your way," he said. "Go on. Ruin it."

Jack leaned against the door jam and rubbed his eyes while trying to beat back a yawn. "The onions are burning."

"What?" they said in unison, looking at him now, not a trace of humiliation in their faces.

"The onions." The yawn won. Jack stretched, looked at the mess on his granite island. Vegetable peelings everywhere, copper pots boiling over on the gas stove, and a huge electric frying pan full of smoking onions.

Shanks was in charge of the steaks. Mulligan must have had control of the veggies. The burning onions were her fault. Shanks sneered at her. "You derelicted your duty. If I'd done that in the Gulf War we'd have never won."

Mulligan lowered the knife and grabbed the dial on the electric pan. "You were a shaggin' cook."

"Got a Purple Heart, didn't I?"

"The deep fryer exploded in the mess tent."

"Whatever. Besides an army fights on its belly."

"Moves on its belly, Tommy," Jack corrected.

"Gotcha, Jack."

Mulligan walked up to Jack and embraced him. "You looked like you needed the sleep," she said, "so we thought we'd surprise you with dinner."

"Glad you did," Jack said. "Smells great." He caught movement over the cast-iron skillet. "That's enough salt, Tommy."

"Sorry. Slipped," Tommy said and tossed in the fatty steaks.

Frannie Mulligan stepped back, surveyed Jack's disheveled appearance with a look of concern. "You look like shit."

"Thanks," Jack responded. Truth was Mulligan didn't look much better. Jack could see the beginnings of another good cry in her tired face. He drew her to him. "I know, I know," was all he said, rubbing her back as she shuddered in his arms. Her tears soaked Jack's shoulder for the second time that day.

Shanks pretended to be busy, but Jack could see a trembling hand as it stirred a pot of boiling potatoes – Tommy never taking his eyes off the bubbling mass. Somewhere there was his own grief to be dealt with in private.

Minutes passed. Frannie whispered her grief against his shoulder in short urgent gasps. When she stopped the silence became too heavy for the three of them.

"Gravy or no gravy?" Shanks finally said.

Jack was surprised at how good it tasted and how hungry he was. So were Shanks and Mulligan. They watched as he demolished his own rib-eye, laid thick with onions, and took what Mulligan had left on her plate. He shovelled down potatoes and carrots, and Shanks brought seconds of both. He washed it all down with Chardonnay, and the bottle sat nearly empty on the cluttered table. B.B. King belted out tunes on the CD player.

When the conversation began to slow, Shanks excused himself, gathered their plates and walked from the dining nook into the kitchen where he began the clean-up. He lost the coin toss, fair and square. No argument about that.

Jack and Mulligan watched quietly as he filled the sink with hot soapy water, loaded it up with pots first.

"I can't believe she's gone," Mulligan said, turning her red eyes to Jack.

"Neither can I," Jack replied.

"I talked to her after that little wrestling match of yours in New Orleans." Mulligan frowned. "She was furious about that."

"She didn't say so at the time."

"She wouldn't have," Mulligan said. "She was getting used to your shenanigans."

Jack's six-foot frame seemed to shrink. His shenanigans had gotten her killed.

"You wanna tell me what happened?"

Jack fixed his eyes on the checkered tablecloth. "Bad things happen when you make bad decisions. I made a really bad decision."

"We all make bad decisions, Jack."

"Yeah, we do," Jack replied, lifting his head. "But usually we can walk away."

A moment passed before he spoke again. Quietly he told her about the explosion, the days he spent in hospital hoping that somehow it had all been a big mistake, and that Kaitlin had turned up alive in another hospital. They checked patient lists when he demanded it, more to satisfy him than anything else. Of course, they came back with only bad news. No sign of any Kaitlin O'Rourke among the injured. The embassy did its own work, with the same result. Kaitlin O'Rourke was listed among the dead, but her body and at least a dozen others were obliterated by the explosive.

"Disaster seems to follow us Doyles," Jack said, dejectedly.

"Don't even go there, Jack."

"You grew up without a father, Frannie. Don't tell me it wasn't tough."

"Sure it was tough," Frannie said. "Jesus, it was hard. But what's that got to do with you?"

Jack shook his head. "You saw the looks I was getting at the cemetery."

"Whadda they know?"

"What they think they know is that my father got drunk and drove that boat onto the rocks. That's what they think they know. Colombia was my call. They know that too. They blame me for Kaitlin."

Mulligan bit her top lip and waited, her black Irish features and round caring face a comfort to Jack. "It wasn't your fault," was all she said.

"It wouldn't matter anyhow." Jack looked at her and rubbed the scar on his hand. "It was my story, my career."

Mulligan looked at him. "It was her job, Jack, and she loved it."

He didn't tell Mulligan about the advice he'd received from his friend at State before he and Kaitlin left New Orleans. "Bad time. Even the DEA is closing up shop there. Stay out of Colombia, Jack. No story's that good."

"Got our marching orders," Jack had replied at the time. "Besides, we're media."

"Media," his friend had laughed. "This is a country where judges and cops don't go out at night. You think you're immune because you're bloody media?"

In a national television address the Colombian president had promised war on the cartels. Their reign was over. The cartels responded in bloody fashion. Assassinations and car bombings had turned the country into a killing zone, especially for Americans who were either being kidnapped or murdered, depending on whether a ransom could be paid or a political point scored. There was even talk the United States might be asked to intervene. In the meantime the State Department had placed Colombia "off limits" to anyone who had even the slightest inclination to set foot there.

Jack looked straight ahead, past Frannie who was staring at him with deep sympathy in her black Irish face. "I saw their justice minister in the restaurant," he said quietly. "He was the biggest target in Colombia, especially because of his initiative on the extradition treaty." Jack gripped his glass so tightly Frannie feared it was going to shatter in his hand.

Shanks looked over at them and stopped what he was doing. Mulligan shot him a look that said, "Get back to the dishes." Shanks shrugged his well-muscled shoulders, thrust thick arms covered in fine red hair into steaming water and returned pale eyes to the pile of dirty dishes.

"Stop beating yourself up. Kaitlin understood the risks." Mulligan fixed her eyes on him. "She was quietly planning a trip down there. To find her mother." Frannie shook her head, reached for her glass. "Soon as Argus stopped being such an asshole. The man irks me to no end."

Jack hadn't known. He shook his head, sat back, took a gulp of wine and thought again about that day. The mysterious phone call Kaitlin had lied about. "I think it was possible she was already talking to someone about that." Jack went on, dropped his voice, "I'm sure she lied about a phone call."

"Go on," Frannie said.

"There's not much else to tell. She seemed really preoccupied afterwards at dinner." Jack watched Tommy wiping down the countertops.

After Jack's mother died, when it was just two of them, his father often sat at this table, half-drunk and staring out the window. Singing. Something about a pirate, Jack remembered, hunting for American ships full of gold and ruined by his foolhardy adventure at just twenty-three. It was on one of those nights that Caleb Doyle told his son what had really happened in that storm when they'd smashed up on Sable Island and three men were lost, including Aiden O'Rourke and Arthur Mulligan, Frannie's father. The third man was nineteen. Dunphy, a deck hand from Nova Scotia. Jack never fully understood why his father refused to tell the truth about what actually happened. Even when they called him a drunk like Charlie Bidgood who froze to death not twenty feet from his back door.

"I was the skipper," his father explained carefully to his son that night. "They were my crew. My responsibility. Not a soul, Jack. The bastards would never believe it anyway."

Jack kept the secret and his father never spoke of it again, even though Jack suspected Caleb Doyle was desperate to erase the stain on his family's name.

"Goddamn them all. Right, Jack?" His father would laugh until the laughter became a cough. Then Jack's old man would spark up another filterless cigarette and fill the kitchen with thick grey smoke, like a death shroud smothering his hopeless face.

The house was full of memories for Jack, cold but sweet like the menthol cigarettes his father reached for when the navy cuts started bothering his throat. It wasn't long after, Jack saw the specks of blood on his father's shirts. On a rational level, Jack understood that a lifetime of liquor and cigarettes killed Caleb Doyle, but it was the loss of those men, for which he was blameless, that drove him to the grave.

A day after his old man was buried his Aunt Muriel from Boston came to collect him. "There's nothing here for you now, Jack," she had said. Jack didn't believe that. There was a lot for him here, especially his memories. His mother's old dishes and brick-a-brac furniture – the lingering smells. His mother's framed picture on the mantle. His father's old clothes were stuffed into boxes piled neatly into a corner of the front room, ready for pick-up. They closed up that saltbox house and walked out through the gate, and Jack left Bark Island. Years would pass before he returned to try and reclaim the good memories – and to deal with the bad.

"Goddamn them all," Jack said quietly.

"Sorry?"

"Nothing," Jack replied. "Just thinking about something my father used to say." He then told Mulligan about Argus O'Rourke.

Mulligan shook her head. "Saw that coming."

"Wondered why the place stunk like booze," Tommy said, as he placed three mugs of hot coffee on the table. "Didn't think you were a rum drinker." Shanks blew across the top of his mug. "Saw O'Rourke on the way over, just sitting there looking out the window in his front room. Don't think he'll ever forgive you."

Mulligan was instantly mortified. "Quiet, Tommy."

"Sorry, Jack," Tommy said, as he stared down at the steam rising from his coffee. "Didn't think about what I was saying."

"No worries, Tommy," Jack said. But Tommy was right, and at that moment he decided to keep the promise he'd made to himself in that hospital bed in Cartagena. Jack looked into his cup, nodding to himself as he thought about Argus O'Rourke at that window, a broken man, whose life and gold had slipped away forever.

THIRTY-ONE

MARADONA, COLOMBIA.

The dusk came to Maradona in spectacular shades of gold and orange and darker hues of purple and red that tumbled across hillsides and valleys stretching luxuriantly for miles beneath the rocky peaks of the Santa Marta Mountains.

    A gentle wind dispersed the scent of *mute* and *cabrito*, and from many houses the *guacharaca* and *caja* – and of course the sounds of singing accordionists of the *vallenato* whose *puya* and meringue sweetened evening meals of the traditional soup and grilled goat. Nicolas Mendoza had been one of the best, a master of the German instrument who had won the respect and love of a nation. And Nicolas Mendoza's blood still lived in Maradona.

    The fertile soil here once produced crops that fed the belly: mangos and sugar cane, yucca and maize. But nothing paid like the coca, which was largely an unremarkable looking plant with astounding qualities. It brought many pesos to Maradona and within a generation it was the cash crop that spread prosperity across a peasant's landscape like sweet thick jam. A hundred grams of cocaine paste brought more cash than a ton of maize. Easy math, even for the illiterate dullards who toiled over explosive extraction barrels like geniuses of chemistry.

A patchwork of Maradona coca fields was already descending into the shadows of night, and farmers prayed the fumigation aircraft would not return until the plants were stripped of their valuable leaves. Only then could the lengthy process begin to turn the numbing paste into profit.

When the sun dropped from the sky, Maradona's night creatures began their incessant squawking. In the Mendoza house on the highest hilltop, Angelica – whose name was really Kaitlin – was waking up from a deep sleep and having difficulty clearing away the cobwebs. She must have drifted off, slept away the afternoon, but when she opened her eyes she managed a child-like smile that pleased the one other person with her.

Eva Mendoza was awake and silently inspecting her. "You were exhausted," she said weakly.

They stared at one another for what seemed an eternity. Kaitlin took inventory of her. The woman was beautiful, even though she'd obviously been through a hell of some kind. Eva had managed to sit up and was feebly trying to brush long strands of hair from her face. She looked like she'd been crying.

"I must look a disaster," she said, wiping her face with trembling hands. Sniffling into the blanket, muffled words. "I had more in my mind for our first meeting."

Kaitlin blinked a couple of times while she tried to shake off the sleep. She pressed her teeth hard against her bottom lip and decided that nothing else would matter if this woman didn't get some nourishment into her. "You have to eat," she finally said.

Alejandro had brought food. Bowls of rice and dark beans sat on a wooden tray at Eva's bedside. He'd obviously decided to let them sleep and had disappeared somewhere since the house was now quiet. The meal had gone cold long ago, but Kaitlin was famished, and she hoped her patient was feeling the same way.

"Alejandro's a good cook," Eva said weakly. "But he doesn't clean as well."

Kaitlin handed Eva a bowl of rice and nodded. "The kitchen's a pig sty."

They ate for a moment in awkward silence. Kaitlin watched as Eva brought tiny spoonfuls of brown rice to her mouth, in a process that looked strangely unfamiliar to her.

Kaitlin on the other hand ate hungrily and was already finishing off her rice when she cast a covetous glance at the two bowls of beans.

"You were always the hungry one," Eva said, eyeing her with a warm smile. "Never far from my breast."

Kaitlin nearly dropped her fork. Embarrassment flushed across her face, and she sat back, placing her empty bowl on the night table. "I don't understand."

"It's all right, Kaitlin. There is much you should know." Eva lowered her bowl and looked at her warmly. "But first, let's both of us have some of Alejandro's famous beans."

Kaitlin's hunger disappeared in a flurry of rice and beans and ice cold fruit juice she had retrieved from the refrigerator when Eva said she was thirsty. While they sat there, both of them pleasantly full, Kaitlin felt somewhat normal again. As normal as anyone could feel given what she was going through. She wondered how much to say about that, how much Eva could help her remember. If there was reason to trust, there was reason to hope.

The colour had returned to Eva's face. She reached out to touch Kaitlin's hand. "You hurt your head," she said. "Everything is lost right now."

"Like my life," Kaitlin replied. "Will they wonder where I am?" Kaitlin stopped. Who is there to wonder? As hard as she thought, everything was still a blank for her, everything a mystery, especially this place and the only two people in her life. Maybe her assessment had been wrong. What if Eva and Alejandro meant her harm? What if, what if? Nausea seeded itself in her gut, her headache returned, stronger than before. Kaitlin slumped in her chair, sighed loudly, and searched Eva's face with droopy eyes.

"I think we both need sleep," Eva said, pulling the blanket up around her shoulders. "The mayor's brother is a doctor in Cartagena. He'll be here again in the morning."

Kaitlin nodded and unsteadily got up. When she reached the door, she stopped. Kaitlin wanted to ask her about everything. Doctor? Kaitlin remembered nothing of a doctor. How badly had she been hurt? What was the connection she had with this woman? Alejandro had told her, yes. But that didn't explain how she got here, and certainly revealed nothing about her lost life.

Kaitlin fumbled for the light switch and turned – was about to say something – when she saw that Eva was already sleeping.

THIRTY-TWO

"When are we going to say enough is enough?"

Jack watched blankly.

"When are we going to be safe in our homes again?"

The host of the television call-in show looked directly into the camera and with coiffed evangelical enthusiasm held up pictures of the eight dead girls. "It's too late for Tracy, Alyssa, and Marilee. Too late for Sherra and Krista, Roxy, Samantha and Susie. What did the Denton White House do for them? The mainstream liberal media parrot his empty commitments."

Asshole, Jack thought. Puts Limbaugh to shame. Liddy too. If you believed television and talk radio the nation was under attack. Stoking the story worked. From New York to New Orleans and everywhere from Seattle to Portland to San Ysidro and east to Tennessee, analysts and the so-called experts were feeding the perception that neighbourhoods were under siege, being destroyed by drug violence. Republican Senator Aaron Robicheaux appeared on Russert, tears in his eyes as he demanded President Denton launch surgical strikes against Colombian drug lords.

Jack watched as the talk show host leaned into the camera. "Find me a farm boy who hasn't done crank. Or an athlete who isn't strung out on marijuana or steroids. Last week a third grader in Omaha was caught with an ounce of cocaine in homeroom. Said he got it from his dad. Where does it end, folks? Where does it end? Americans have had enough. America has to protect itself. National security is our sacred right."

Jack grabbed the remote, switched off the television, and for the fourth time that evening he got off the sofa and went to the refrigerator. The beer tasted good and so did the Camels, which he'd picked up for the first time in college even though his Aunt Muriel condemned him mightily for it. Jack chuckled dryly as he thought about his mother's sister with the unfortunate British accent, which was the reason she had left Bark Island. She was thirty-five when she had her stroke and the cockney started before she'd left the hospital. Jack couldn't remember the way she *used* to speak, only the strange accent that came out of her mouth, even though she had never been to England, never watched British television, and in fact had never known anyone whose accent was legitimately English. All of which was duly noted with discomfort, if not disdain, by her former friends who thought she'd turned uppity. It took years for doctors to understand and to give it a name – foreign-accent syndrome caused by traumatic brain lesions. It was a diagnosis that came too late for Muriel, who packed her bags, got on the ferry and eventually found a husband in Boston. Jack thought it could have been worse. The accent could have been German, like the crews of the U-boats which prowled the waters off New England, sinking merchant ships and the occasional unarmed trawler for the terror dividend it paid up and down the coast. Old Paddy White's uncle never made it out of the engine room of SS *Salisbury* when it took a kraut fish amidships. He still pulled a face and hissed lavatorial accusations whenever he hobbled by Klatzel's, a fine Bavarian bed and breakfast overlooking the harbour. To Paddy it might as well have been Hitler's alpine redoubt.

Jack grabbed another cold one, shuffled past a stack of unread newspapers and mail, and headed for the bedroom. He grimaced at his own reflection in the full-length mirror on the back of the door. He looked bad, felt worse. Lately his appetite was off, replaced by headaches, ones that threaded their way through the fabric of his dreams until the pain became too unbearable to sleep. He was told they'd continue until he recovered fully from the concussion. In the meantime he needed another refill of painkillers.

Lately he'd been waking up in the middle of the night, his heart beating so hard it felt like a snare drum was strapped to his chest. He'd bolt upright in bed, toss aside his sweat-soaked sheets and search the darkness for the cause of his panic. When that happened he wasn't able to get to sleep again until he downed a cold beer on the porch at the back of the house. In the distance, moonlight on silver sea, reminding him that Caleb Doyle never left shore again after what happened to his boat – his crew. Jack guessed the manager at Martin's Marine took pity on his old man when he gave him that job fixing small engines. When Jack's mother died it seemed his father's only joy came from the sight of the empty plot next to his wife.

It had been three weeks since the bombing. Or was it four? The MRI on Jack's head showed no lingering trauma to explain his headaches. Jack's doctor shrugged and told him to take a vacation – a long one – because guys like Jack were basically their own worst enemies. "Learn to relax. Take up yoga. Re-evaluate."

Walter Carmichael told Jack to take all the time he needed, which was unusual for Carmichael who sent his wife on vacations without him and had once delayed bypass surgery to ride herd on a network election special. "Get outta my sight, Doyle. Tell Lou Perlman to expect my call."

The next day Jack popped two aspirin, drove eighty-five miles to Boston and boarded the shuttle to New York. He needed to tie up some loose ends with the apartment. His accountant paid all the bills but Jack still spent an hour going through junk mail. He then made half a dozen phone calls to touch base with people he hadn't spoken to in a while. Kaitlin's friend Jesse cried again. She missed her so badly. Jack listened to her sob until she regained her composure, and then he said goodbye – he'd stay in touch. There was a message of condolence from Mona Lasing but not once did she actually utter Kaitlin's name.

He called Jamie Malone and was put through to the newsroom instead. "Malone's done," Dan Finney growled.

Jack was stunned. "What happened?"

The domestic assignment editor lowered his voice. "You know how it is, Jack. His show — he takes the fall. McCoy fucked up bad while you were off chasing drug lords. Got in an argument with one of the fathers. Guy grabbed for the camera at his kid's funeral. That night he intro's his piece from ground zero, and him and George are talking about what happened while the story is rolling. So get this. McCoy says the dead kid's father was being an asshole. Bad move. McCoy's mic was hot. So coast to coast it goes to fucking air. Shit hit the fan. Now McCoy's saying you were AWOL and left him a real mess to deal with. He was frazzled. Jamie slugged him on the way out, screamed at him that he'd literally *fucked up a funeral!*"

As predicted, Jack thought humourlessly. "Shit. Jamie's a good man."

"Great left hook too. Anyway I hear he's still looking," said Finney. "Meantime watch your back, bud. McCoy's in serious ass-covering mode and you're not getting much love these days from the rank and file. Fuck 'em, Jack. You're no prima donna to me."

"Thanks, Finney," Jack said. He called Malone's apartment and got his machine. He left a short message which included an offer of references and then hung up. Doyle was sure Malone would have no problem finding another gig. He was good at what he did. Slugging McCoy would add to his allure.

Jack called half a dozen dailies to suspend his subscriptions, and then placed his last call to Lou Perlman, his agent. "Time for lunch?"

"Always."

Lou was glad to see him, even happier to see the monstrous pastrami sandwich that was being lowered onto the table an hour later at the Four Leaf Clover, which was located near the steps that led to the Brooklyn Bridge pedestrian track. They'd come by way of Lou's old neighbourhood, a rabbit's warren of tall, narrow wood-faced row houses on streets named after fruit. Lou still took warm summer strolls along the Brooklyn Heights Promenade, where he spent long periods as a kid sitting and staring at the Lower Manhattan skyline. He still got that faraway look when he talked about it. "My father always said, 'Nothing there for a Krakow Jew.'"

Jack had heard it many times before.

The Clover was a hamburger-and-gravy death warrant facing, with delicious irony, Lipsky's Funeral Home. Conversation, mostly guttural in nature, rumbled through the smoky grill like artillery. Waitresses in cardboard hats poured coffee by the gallon and did the best they could to sidestep customers who simply belched when they wanted to settle up. A mirror that ran the width of the lunch counter hadn't reflected an honest image in decades except for the undertaker's cracked neon sign across the street.

"Tell Ronny we're here," Perlman grunted to the waiter. "You look like shit," he said, one eye on the sandwich, the other on Jack.

"Thanks for your support, Lou," Jack replied, suspiciously eyeing his own pound of mustard-slathered meat.

"Eat...eat," Lou said, expertly hefting one half of his sandwich towards his face. "You're wasting away."

A glob of mustard splattered on Lou's silk necktie as he stuffed the heart buster into his mouth, a considerable stroke of bad luck considering the expansive target presented by Lou's gut. Jack didn't know if Lou saw, or would even care.

Perlman reached for a napkin, but used it to dab at a film of perspiration that had formed on top of his bald head. He ignored the mustard accumulating at the corners of his mouth, efficiently swept his fat tongue across thin lips.

The lunch crowd at the Clover wore coloured hardhats, like hierarchical crowns that determined which union ass sat in which stained, cracked lino chair. The blue tops got the better tables near the window.

"We're worried about you," Lou said, using the back of his hand to stifle some kind of intestinal event that made his eyes widen. "You haven't returned my calls."

Jack ignored him, pulled at the corner of his sandwich like he was picking the wings off a dead fly. "How are Maris and the kids?"

"Don't change the subject," Lou said, watching Jack fuss with his meal. "I'll eat what you don't. So stop picking at it. Maris and the kids are OK."

"I've decided to take some time," Jack said as he reluctantly lifted his sandwich and tested it for weight and balance. He took a small bite and was surprised at the taste. In smaller portions the fatty spicy meat would probably have been all right.

"Time's good," Lou said, pausing. A worried look. "How much time?"

"I haven't decided yet," Jack replied, dropping his sandwich with an audible thud.

"That might complicate things," Lou said.

"Why?"

Lou stopped talking, pointed his chin past Jack to the reason the floor was shaking. Jack turned and saw Ronny Donnigan stomping towards them, working a bum leg like it was a badge of honour and wiping club-like hands on a stained apron. Jack stood. Donnigan opened his arms and stooped to swallow him in his embrace. "Jesus, Doyle. Good to see you."

"Good to see you too, Ronny," Jack said sincerely.

"Dirty rotten bastards, those Colombians," Ronny said, releasing him. Sympathy etched a face that looked like raw meat, a marbling of various disfigurements. "Never seen the like." Vapours of fried onions and garlic hit Jack like a wake. "You give me the word, Jack. Your say so."

"Thanks," Jack said, "but–"

"I mean it. We've already been talking. A dozen of the lads. We go down there, teach them cokeheads about fuckin' with the Irish." Ronny looked at Jack hard, a mist over eyes like wet stones. He clasped his hands around Jack's head, a reminder that before a bullet shattered his knee, Ronny Donnigan performed this exact maneuver with entirely different results as a union enforcer. "You remember Clancy and his cousin?" Ronny looked around, hair like the shavings from a stump of red cedar. He lowered his voice. "Did special stuff for the IRA. Still good at it. You get my meaning?"

"Thanks, Ronny. I appreciate it." Jack eased back, breathed. "You've lost weight."

"Fuck that. Gained ten pounds. Sheilagh's threatening to leave me and go back to Dublin." Ronny tilted his head at Lou, who smiled weakly. "You still alive? I told that wop in the kitchen to lay on the fat and you're still suckin' in good oxygen."

"The stink in this place will kill me before the pastrami," Lou shot back, popping half a limp pickle into his mouth, smacking his lips smugly. "Good oxygen, my fat ass."

Jack knew the affection between the two men stretched back decades. The Irishman and the Jew were sons of knuckle-bruised Teamsters who wound up on opposite banks of the East River, one because of his temper, which was valued as an asset when you were busting limbs, the second because of his magical talent for negotiating his way into and out of almost anything. If souls were strapped of flesh, Jack thought, Ronny Donnigan and Lou Perlman would have been conjoined.

Ronny looked out through the door where Lou had parked his Mercedes. "Lou Perlman, the fancy agent. Fucking car takes up two parking spots. Goddamn Jew in a Kraut car. Go figure."

"It's called irony," Lou said, smiling more broadly now. "I-R-O-N–"

"Don't get me going, Perlman," Ronny said shaking a fist. Then to Jack. "Don't let him go without leaving a big tip, OK?"

"I won't, Ronny."

"I sent flowers. Get 'em?" Ronny asked.

"Her favourite, Ronny. Thanks."

"That's what they said. Roses and lilies, right?"

"Roses and lilies."

"I remember her, Jack, like it was yesterday. Table number four." Ronny looked to his right, towards the window, half raised a thick hand to point. "Yuppie salads for both of you, right? The guys in the kitchen wouldn't know a hot-house tomato if they shit one."

"Great salads." Jack winced, remembering when he'd made good on a promise to bring his new producer to lunch. Kaitlin thought the place charming – retro, she called it. "It's all original," Jack had told her.

"Nice dame, Jack," Ronny had whispered to him as he and Kaitlin were leaving that day. "You sly bastard."

Jack had simply smiled.

Ronny was now looking at Jack with a worried expression. "I gotta get back to work. You stay in touch, OK?"

"Sure, Ronny."

"And stick with the hot-house tomatos. You'll live longer." Ronny tilted his large head at Lou. "Not like this tub."

"Look who's talking," Lou piped up. "Maybe I'll order the spinach. Get healthy like you."

"A pox on your house, Perlman," Ronny barked, "and don't be late for poker next week. I got mortgage payments."

Lou rolled his eyes.

Ronny dropped a heavy hand on Jack's shoulder. "Jack, anything you need you let me know. The boys still remember the coverage you gave them during the walkout."

"Thanks, Ronny."

"Anything," he repeated conspiratorially. "I mean that." Ronny shot a look at Lou. "Thursday night at eight. Don't forget to bring your wallet. The Giants are playing."

"Gotcha," Lou said with a wink as he watched Ronny turn on his heel and lumber back to the kitchen.

Jack sat down. "A real lamb."

"Play poker with him sometime."

The lunch crowd had thinned, the din silenced like a battlefield armistice. A waitress wandered over to inspect their plates, then left again without saying a word, stopping at a nearby table to light a cigarette and to scoop up a handful of change lodged between some dirty glasses.

They both watched her.

Lou spoke first. "I've gotten a couple calls from Carmichael. He's still steamed." Lou's face became earnest. "I'm getting worried."

"Worried about what?"

"He's hinting they may not be interested in us anymore."

"Us or me?"

"You."

"Just noise," Jack said. "Carmichael rearing up on his hind legs. Normal bullshit at contract time."

"Ordinarily I'd agree. Not this time, Jack. They're pissed off big time. The O'Rourke fellow's got lawyers involved now. They're in a spot and they think you put them there. If it comes to a lawsuit, you become a liability to the network on judgment. Cause you're still on the payroll."

Jack suspected Argus wanted his blood. Not money.

Perlman attacked his sandwich again, left Jack to taste the warning.

"Maybe it's time anyway, Lou," Jack finally said.

"Time for what?"

"Time for a change."

"Maybe you still like the bang-bang, Jack. It's made you famous and fairly well-off, I might add."

"You're a nutcase," Jack said.

Lou wiped his mouth again and looked at Jack's hand. "How's it doing?"

"Hand's fine," Jack said, flexing his fingers.

"You got lucky."

"Got lucky after getting stupid."

"What's important is you got lucky," Perlman said, reaching for the second half of his behemoth sandwich.

"Looks like maybe my luck ran out," Jack said.

"Let's focus on Carmichael." Lou looked around and then stuffed half of what remained of his sandwich into his mouth, chewing noisily while he talked. "He basically thinks you're damaged goods now. Maybe even lost your nerve." Perlman crunched on a pickle, shooting a stream of vinegar and brine across the table. "What should I tell him?"

"Tell Carmichael I did my job, brought in the stories and the numbers like they wanted, and that I should have been handed the anchor desk when it became abundantly clear Frank Simmons was going to run his network into the ground. Tell Carmichael that, Lou. Tell them they missed their chance." Jack stopped what he was saying, a look of surrender crossed his face. "Tell Carmichael their senior correspondent who's been breaking his balls for them for what — ten years now in every shithole on the planet — considers himself a free agent."

Perlman stopped chewing. "Hold on a second. No one said they're not interested. All I said is they're pissed at you right now. And frankly I can't blame them. Colombia was your call, Jack. Your decision. No one's blaming you for Kaitlin—"

"You know that's not true."

"It's my truth, Jack." Perlman leaned forward. "You're my friend. Have been since I got your tape, remember? Market number sixty-two."

Lou had seen Jack's talent immediately in that first brag tape. He didn't have to shop it around for long. Market thirty-two bit first. Then after a couple of years number nineteen came calling. A couple of years after that, Lou called Jack with New York. "Jackpot. CNS wants someone who likes the road and they really like your style."

That was ten years ago. Jack Doyle was now the senior correspondent, able to pick and choose his assignments. Problem was he had a habit of picking the ones that meant at least fifteen hours in an airplane, usually to war zones.

"You were still hungry then. Still are. But when you made the decision to skip out on New Orleans it was your ass you put on the line. Your ass and Kaitlin's and everyone else's – including mine."

"Jesus, Lou, I pay you eight percent for this?"

"Ten percent," Lou said. "Kids and college to think about. Mandy's thinking about med school."

"Lou, all I'm saying is I'm taking a break," Jack said. "I need some time."

For a moment both men remained silent.

The waitress kept her distance, like someone not wanting to intrude on a lovers' quarrel.

Jack looked forlornly at his food and surrendered the last of his appetite, watched as Lou locked his eyes onto a steaming plate of fries smothered in gravy two tables over. "Carmichael will probably cut me loose."

"Let me worry about Carmichael," Lou said.

"Tell him I apologize for screwing up his network."

"He'll get over it." Lou wrapped a meaty hand around a large glass of iced tea, swallowed half its contents. Belched. "So, Ahab, where ya headed?"

Jack smiled at Lou. "There's this whale."

"Now there's a story. Maybe a documentary in it."

"Big white whale."

"Sounds like Jack Doyle's first Oscar."

"No whale stories where I'm headed, Lou," Jack said. "Just me and *Scoundrel* and clear sailing from here on in, I hope."

"I'm your agent and your friend. I'll live with whatever you decide about future earnings. Though my kids will never see college. Mandy faints when she sees blood anyway," Perlman said. "Not to worry. They'll always have me."

"You can hock my Emmys."

"Keep 'em."

"You're a good man, Lou Perlman."

"I'm a shmuck...a fat shmuck." Lou finally wiped his mouth, and then looked over at Jack's plate. "And you need to get your shit together."

"Thanks for the understanding."

"Whatever...heal thyself. You done with that?

THIRTY-THREE

Jack locked up the New York apartment and flew back to Boston the next day. Two hours later he was parked in the crushed stone driveway outside his house on Bark Island. He sat in the SUV for ten minutes listening to the clicking and pinging of the cooling engine, thinking about what Lou had said — Kaitlin's death, his life. Colombia might have been a career killer, the kind of retirement he didn't want. But what the hell? The game was changing anyway, wasn't it? More room for people like McCoy who had no brains and less heart. The smooth-faced "B" team, Jack thought, who cost the bean counters plenty less, and who failed to understand that what they did was a calling, not just a career. Jack rubbed at the fatigue on his face and exited his vehicle.

Three days later he saw Argus O'Rourke at McGonagall's Rope and Tackle. Kaitlin's father looked no better. Their eyes locked for a second and it was long enough for Jack to see that Argus was still full of pain and anger. Kaitlin's father buried his head in a copy of *Fisherman's Monthly* while Jack paid at the counter and walked out.

The next day — four weeks after the bombing in Colombia — Jack compressed his world into gunny sacks and cardboard boxes. "The plants, Tommy...once every couple of days. And if you get a moment, there's that leak–"

"I know, bud...I know. The one over the sofa." Both of Tommy's thick arms were full and he was using his chin to steady the load. "Got it."

"Be careful with that stuff, Tommy," Jack said. "Charts are expensive."

Tommy had heard it a dozen times already and didn't need to be told again. He had already turned and headed out the door. "Jesus, you're worse than my mother."

"Your mother's a saint, Tommy," Jack called out, chuckling to himself. "Don't you forget it."

They'd spent the morning making trips from the house to the dock where *Scoundrel* bobbed like an impatient child. Jack checked his list, scratched off another half-dozen items and wondered whether he was forgetting something.

Anything he wasn't taking was packed or covered. The house was full of ghostly shapes and for a moment he stood very still and tried to conjure the echoes of the past, the sounds of old conversations and laughter that seemed to be trapped beneath white cotton sheets.

Jack had spent two nights charting the legs of his trip. He planned to ride the Gulf Stream to the Caribbean Sea, loiter through the Dutch Antilles and the Virgin Islands. No schedule. No agenda.

"Don't even go there," he'd said to Lou when his friend suggested a satellite phone would probably be a good idea. "You might want to order in. Check the Red Sox. Cry on my shoulder, who knows?"

"Funny boy," Jack told his agent. "I'm incommunicado, Lou."

"Take the phone," Lou demanded. "For safety," he added like it was an afterthought. "It'll be there in the morning. The service provider already has you hooked up. Have a good trip."

It was nearly all loaded now. Provisions for a month, a hundred pounds of books and CDs that Tommy hoisted on his shoulders like a sack of potatoes, a huge pile of foul-weather gear, about half of which Jack knew he'd never use. Better safe than sorry. Jack carefully loaded the weather vane from his father's trawler which he hung next to his navigation table.

That morning Jack visited the cemetery, knelt at her stone and rubbed away a thin coat of dust with the sleeve of his shirt. Told her he was sorry – Jesus, he was so sorry – his guts like a knot of rubber bands.

Jack looked around that dear saltbox house one more time before he stepped into the sunlight and trudged to the wharf where Tommy had his head down checking a locker that held his safety gear.

"Looks good," he said. "Flares are here too."

"Thanks, Tommy."

"Vincent over at the supply store says everything looks clear down to Brig's Point. After that you're on your own."

"That's real good, Tommy."

"But of course you'll probably be swept overboard before that… sailing single-handed. You sure you wanna do this, Jack?" Tommy was looking at him now, an amalgam of worry and sadness had crept over his face. "Look what happened to my Uncle Dorm."

"You know me better than that," Jack replied. "Uncle Dorm was unlucky."

"Yeah, he was that, and plenty more." Shanks came up on the wharf and stuffed his hands in the pockets of his jeans, thankful for somewhere to put them. "Mulligan said she didn't want to be here."

"Mulligan's a cry baby." Jack smiled. "A walking faucet. I saw her last night."

"Yeah…well she said to give you this." Tommy produced a photograph. The four of them, Kaitlin included, at Frenchman's Quay the night last year when they all got drunk and like fools went in the water in sight of a sign that said "No swimming, Riptide." Hamming it up, full of crab meat and beer in front of the driftwood fire, embers floating through the air like fireflies.

"Thanks," Jack said, placing the picture in his pocket.

"Be careful, Jack," Tommy said after an awkward moment.

"I know, Tommy. Thanks." Jack smiled at him and then reached up to touch his shoulder. "Mess tent or not, you earned that medal fair and square. Remember that."

"Yeah. Shit happens, Jack, and everyone knows that it always happens to us good people. Doesn't matter how careful you are. Uncle Dorm was careful."

"And drunk."

"Yeah. Drunk and unlucky."

They both chuckled.

On *Scoundrel*'s transom a flag fluttered on wind born a hundred miles out to sea, spawned by the warm saltwater currents and cooler air that had swirled up and down the coast since the beginning of time. The same wind carried his father and grandfather to the Grand Banks off Newfoundland. His grandfather used to say that when he was a boy the cod were so plentiful you could walk on their backs to shore. A lot had changed since then.

Jack looked up at his saltbox house at the top of the stairs, wondering whether his father ever forgave himself for losing his boat and his crew. He guessed not.

Doyle said goodbye to Tommy with a back-slapping hug that had lasted a fraction too long for the both of them, and as Jack pulled away from the wharf with Tommy still waving, he felt a sudden wave of melancholy. The boat's exhaust stood ghost-like on the water's surface, a blue veil behind which the scene seemed meaningful but suddenly cheerless. Doyle swung *Scoundrel*'s compass in the other direction.

The sound of her engine echoed across undulating ridges of spruce and fir which dipped like fingers into the cool black water. Doyle fixed his eyes on a point far out to sea and spun her wheel to widen the distance from shoreline bedrock which buffered Bark Island against a millennia of destructive Atlantic moods. The truth was he couldn't get away fast enough as he carved his way through the buoys that guided him safely through Ragged Hole Bay and out to sea.

THIRTY-FOUR

It took Jack three days to reach the warm waters of the Gulf Stream where it skirted the Outer Banks. The third day he spent lazily under sail about a mile from shore. For long moments he pressed binoculars to his face, picking out the landmarks that ran along a ribbon of macadam that Jack knew to be highway number twelve. He'd driven it in his third year at university, him and a couple of buddies escaping from the drudgery of campus in a beaten down convertible. Highway 12 is board-straight until it crooks west at Cape Hatteras. That was where Jack and his two friends ran into a trio of flight attendants from Varig Airways and spent two days drunk trying to communicate with their hands. The old lighthouse at Corolla stood like a solitary candle, and past that ran an assortment of multi-million dollar estates that popped up like porcelain crowns on the way to a strange place called Duck. Jack could still remember the thrilling sight of wild stallions on Shackleford Banks and the stilts of Wright Memorial Bridge which crossed Albemarie Sound for the perfect sweet-smelling top-down drive into Nags Head and farther south towards Bodie Island and Buxton. Jack anchored in a sandy bay between Cape Hatteras and Ocracoke, where his favourite local hotel featured a garish lobby statue of Edward Teach, a.k.a. Blackbeard the pirate, who was slain by the British navy in these waters. For a while he watched a squadron of pelicans settling in for the night among thick shoreline reeds near a nameless stretch of sandy beach that might have been perfect for lovers or egg-laying tortoises. Rolling dunes and tall lilting grasses disappeared in the gathering darkness, drooping from his senses like a Carolina drawl.

Jack had eaten light and was contemplating the smoke from his cigar as it drifted over the gunnels and was carried away on a light wind. He reached for another beer and thought about Kaitlin, couldn't stop the fantasy that was forming in his mind. In it Kaitlin is swimming in the moonlight, splashing and teasing him to join her. "Silly Jack can't swim," she says, before disappearing beneath the surface of the water. Truth was he'd sink like a stone for a chance to change what had happened, plunge through layers of darkness till he hit rock bottom. That was the deal Jack would have made for a chance to relive that night at Café Umbria. Amillo. *Dead man walking. We're out of here, O'Rourke.* So much for his hyper intuition, Jack thought. Had he been blinded by Kaitlin's striking get-up? Silly Jack, blinded by his stunning producer.

He thought about her olive skin, wondered how her hair would have smelled as he toweled it dry. Jack shook the foolish sentiment from his skull. He was a pro and so was O'Rourke, and rule number one was that you didn't bed your producer. Still, Jack couldn't deny what he'd felt that night in Cartagena and he wondered whether Kaitlin had had any feelings for him. She'd never shown any. Though once, after four straight days of junk food, chasing the campaign of some senator, Kaitlin looked at him. "I've gained a ton, haven't I?" She had pouted, narrowing her large dark eyes. "Well?"

Jack showed wide-eyed honesty. "It's OK. You needed it."

"Wrong answer." Kaitlin had slapped him playfully on the arm. "Henry Slumberger didn't think so."

"Slumberger's a schmuck. You can do much better. What about that shooter in the Washington bureau?" They'd locked eyes for a tantalizing moment until Jack retreated to rule number one. He had a job to think about. Besides there was never any shortage of women when you were running around the world flashing network credentials.

Jack looked around his boat and thought maybe it had needed a woman's touch all along. Maybe he needed to settle down. He thought about that as he swallowed what was left of his beer. In another hour he'd head below, recheck the weather forecast and jump into the v-berth. With legs tangled in damp bedding he'd try to sleep.

But first he needed another beer.

THIRTY-FIVE

"Traffic at your ten o'clock, Tango Foxtrot Charlie. You are number two. Report on final."

The Aztec pilot acknowledged the control tower's transmission before scanning the sky in search of the other aircraft. It took him a moment to find it. A glint of sunlight reflected back at him from a commuter plane which was now about three hundred feet from the threshold of runway one-eighty at Santa Marta's Simon Bolivar airport. The Apache lowered its nose to trim fifty feet from its altitude, and one minute later banked sharply left to level out at fifteen hundred feet on base.

The sun was directly overhead, and even with the air conditioning at full power the pilot was sweating. He licked his lips as he thought about El Rodadero and the swarm of people splashing beneath him as he swept over the upscale beach district in the city's southern suburbs. Too bad he couldn't stay a while.

There was no one else aboard so the pilot sang to himself. Singing badly as usual, he knew. What the hell. Selena always liked his singing. He glanced at the overnight bag, patted the *chirimoya* and *melao* which always made her smile, then pulled back the throttles until the twin engines were producing eighteen hundred RPMs. He banked sharply left again, checked the tower frequency at one eighteen point seven, and then keyed his microphone. "Tango Foxtrot Charlie on final."

"Cleared to land," the tower replied curtly with information on wind and altimeter settings.

The pilot flared the aircraft on a cushion of air and touched down softly in a perfect short-field landing, even though there was still forty-five hundred feet of runway stretched out before him. Good practice, he thought as he checked his time. Noon. Right on schedule.

She was waiting for him at the Zapata Flight Services hangar, and when he shut down and stepped onto the ground she ran to the aircraft and flung her arms around him.

"Orlando-o-o," Selena screamed in delight.

"Your favourite uncle," he said, squeezing her warmly.

"My only uncle," she laughed.

"It's good to see you, Selena, always good to see my favourite niece."

"Your only niece, silly."

A mechanic jerked his head from beneath an engine cowling a short distance away and looked at the older man and the young beautiful woman locked in embrace. "Lucky man," said his twisted grin.

Orlando ignored him, smiled at his niece and then reached into the aircraft to retrieve a huge jar of custard apple from a bag on the passenger seat.

"Always on time, Selena, and always your favourite," he laughed, handing her the jar. "Now tell me where we're going in such a hurry."

Selena told him and then tossed a briefcase into the back of the airplane.

THIRTY-SIX

George Town, Cayman Islands.

The bank had a purple door and was very private, and had she not made an appointment first she would have been handed a brochure and politely shown the door.

Instead, Swiss National's manager was very glad to see her, despite the fact it was only half an hour till closing, and servicing a new client who desired a fresh account in which to deposit fifty million dollars would require one full hour at least. Even in the Cayman Islands, which currently had about eight hundred billion US dollars on deposit, fifty million was a good reason to keep his wife waiting.

Relief swept through Selena as she handed the bonds to an armed guard who spirited them away to be counted and processed. She sipped lemon tea from a dainty white porcelain cup and made small talk with the manager while his secretary efficiently prepared the necessary deposit documents.

The bank manager introduced himself as Mr. Grito. He was a large man, immaculately dressed, with thinning hair and thick grey eyebrows. In any other job he might have had a sense of humour and an ear-splitting laugh. He hadn't offered his first name but Selena saw Charles Grito engraved on a small stone obelisk that rose from the top of his polished desk.

In another room, visible to them through a wall of glass, two tellers counted the bearer bonds – twice. Small talk exhausted, Selena was given paperwork to complete while her host disappeared to oversee the counting. Twenty minutes later Grito returned to the office and maneuvered his ample form to its position of authority behind the desk. He smiled thinly, more a postmortem twitch. "Your deposit is confirmed at fifty million US dollars," he said. A slight British accent. "We can proceed."

Selena nodded and folded her long legs before speaking. "I hope it won't take long. I appreciate the fact the bank will be closed in a few minutes."

"I assure you that's not a problem."

Not with fifty million American dollars on the table, she thought.

Selena and Grito exchanged perfunctory smiles.

She looked the part of a rich heiress, wearing a finely tailored business suit the colour of latte which had cost her a week's salary. Her long black hair was tied back to reveal a face that needed little makeup. Her large green eyes engaged Grito intently when she spoke. "Then we can begin."

Selena had already produced the letter of reference. The one from Colombia's largest bank was easy. She was an account executive so she had simply written that one herself on letterhead she removed from the president's office while his secretary was at lunch. The second letter was the clincher, but it had taken considerably more time and effort. It started with the internet and a website for the Organization for Economic Co-operation and Development. That's where she had discovered the letter from the Cayman Islands' governor pledging his nation's commitment to eliminate money laundering. It had his signature and his letterhead. Selena downloaded the letter, and with the help of Adobe Photoshop software she created a page which was blank except for the letterhead and signature. With it she crafted a new letter, this one saying she had been granted Citizenship and Permanent Residency and the governor looked forward to seeing her at the formal Citizenship Court a week hence. In the meantime, it also said, feel free to submit an application for a Cayman Islands passport. Signed: Sir Nigel Smith, Governor. "P.S. Give my best to your grandfather." Nice touch, Selena thought.

It was all a well-crafted lie, but Selena knew Grito was unlikely to verify either document. To do so would run the risk of offending a wealthy client. Besides, it was more convenient not to.

In the meantime, Grito was clearly impressed, and despite the fact he was now working overtime, his demeanor lightened. He leaned forward, placed his elbows on the massive desk between them, and positioned multiple chins on his steepled hands. "Then you'll be making Grand Cayman your home?" he said.

"I plan to, yes," Selena lied, and as a fresh cup of tea was placed in front of her, she thought again about what she had to do.

There were countless banks on the Cayman Islands. New laws too. Selena knew that the colony was working to eradicate its reputation as a tax haven for the wealthy and a paradise for drug smugglers. In fact it had now become easier to launder money in the United States than in the Cayman Islands. Selena also knew privacy was still paramount here and was fiercely protected by law.

They'd spent hours working out the details. The bank had been chosen from a long list of financial institutions for one reason, and one reason only. Swiss National maintained no headquarters in Colombia, which provided arm's-length protection from Montello's corrupt influences. Selena was well aware of the degree to which criminals like him held sway within the boardrooms of Colombia's banking system. Even the time of her arrival at Swiss National – just before closing – had been chosen for its strategic advantage.

There were the forms to sign and the standard questions about the purpose of the account and the source of the funds.

It was natural for Grito to suspect drug money. Someone with fifty million dollars, carrying a Colombian passport, would raise a red flag immediately. The suspicion was written all over Grito's face. Selena mustered as much sincerity as she could and said, "I've recently gained full access to the proceeds of a family trust." She then opened her briefcase and produced a manila folder. Carefully she withdrew a series of pages and laid them out on Grito's marvelous desk.

Grito read carefully, occasionally nodding his head as he thumbed through documents.

"Your grandfather was a smart man," he said. "Maximum return on his principal investment with minimum tax liabilities. Of course that won't be an issue here."

Selena allowed a look of nostalgia to paint her face. "Grandfather thought anything was possible. He was a good man and he provided well for his family."

Grito managed a weak smile but quickly cast it aside like a snotty tissue, drawing the papers into a neat pile which he placed into the folder. "He's made you a very rich woman."

Selena ignored the remark. "Two people will have signing authority on the account," she said. "Wire transfers will begin almost immediately."

"Of course. But there is a requirement of seven days' notice before the account is emptied."

She had forgotten about that, but decided it shouldn't pose a problem. "I trust your internet banking is acceptable."

Grito looked insulted. "We're an A-class bank and as such we offer the full range of investment and financial management services for our internet clients as well. You won't have any complaints." Grito nodded towards a large flat-panel computer screen on his desk. "I'll have one of the girls demonstrate the system and the security protocols involved if you like."

Selena told him that wouldn't be necessary. In truth she was already quite familiar with the bank's online set-up.

It took another half hour for the formalities. Then Selena established the computer protocols and passwords she'd need to access the account via the internet.

When they were done Grito rubbed meaty hands together and rose from his desk. "Welcome to Swiss National. Thank you for your trust."

Selena left the bank smiling, and while Orlando held her seat for lunch she walked quickly to a nearby postal outlet and purchased a large strong envelope. She placed the bank documents inside, wrote an address, and purchased enough postage to see it to its destination. She left the postal outlet and headed for the outdoor café where Orlando was waiting. She spotted him talking to a pretty waitress. He turned just in time to see her smile, to return her wave. Selena, the progeny of slaves, was a very rich woman. So was Mercedes. But not for very long, they both knew.

Selena's Uncle Orlando had said hardly a word since they'd taken off from George Town. They were descending from ten thousand feet through darkness towards Santa Marta airport when he surprised her with the question. He turned to her, half angry, half worried. "How long have you been involved with drug money?"

Selena looked at him like he'd slapped her. "What's that supposed to mean?"

Orlando searched her face for signs of deception and then let her have it. "Your father was moving about a ton a week, Selena. Making lots of money too, running the stuff up to Norman's Quay. Partied like a devil until..." Orlando allowed the words to trail off. "You know the story and you know what I mean. How long have you been laundering drug cash?"

Selena should have expected this. She stared out her window as the lights of Santa Marta began to come into focus. Orlando had misjudged her. It hurt — more than a little. But who could blame him? Orlando would be mightily pissed at her for repeating the same mistakes as her father, whose impatience and disposition towards fast easy money killed him. "He risked everything that mattered, Orlando. You lost a brother and I lost a father...we lost so much. Things could have been different, if only..." Selena allowed the sentiment to find its own conclusion.

Orlando nodded. "He loved you dearly, Selena. He always wanted the best for you. Maybe he wanted it too badly." The aircraft banked slightly. "We both worked hard. He just got sidetracked, lost his focus on you and what was most important." A second later Orlando adjusted the throttles, lowering the RPMs until the drone of the engines seemed to soften a touch. The aircraft continued its descent through the darkness. "And now you're making the same mistake," said Orlando. "We both know where the drug money goes. Banks like the one you visited today."

Selena hadn't told him the truth. She'd told him she was doing a favour for a client who owned a cattle ranch in Santa Marta, someone who needed some banking done in George Town. She should have known her father's brother wouldn't believe that. Selena had to tell him the truth – no matter what the consequences. So while Orlando flew the plane Selena told him everything. When she finished speaking Orlando shook his head in disbelief.

Selena told her uncle quickly about what Montello had done to Mercedes. "He would have killed her," Selena said. "She had to run, Orlando. She had to."

Orlando was stunned. "And what do you think Montello's going to do now?"

Selena remained silent.

Orlando rubbed his face. "Don't you realize what you've done. You're both marked for death now. These animals won't stop until they've found you." Her uncle clamped shut his eyes, cursing quietly. A minute later he'd made a decision. "When we get on the ground I'm going to refuel and then I'm going to file another flight plan. You're not safe anywhere here."

His warning shook her, snapped her into a reality she'd conveniently waved away. For the moment she was without words, muted by shame and embarrassment. She understood why Orlando was mad. Anyone would have reacted the same way. But she would never abandon Mercedes – she couldn't – even if it meant dangerous delays while they got Mercedes to safety. She'd work on Orlando after they landed. When he cooled down.

Orlando turned to her, a look of deep sorrow in his eyes. "We could all be dead."

The radio suddenly burst into life. "Tango Foxtrot Charlie…join circuit downwind…runway 36 at fifteen hundred feet." The controller told him he was number one, but to watch for a helicopter crossing the runway at the taxiway adjacent to the flight services hangar. Orlando acknowledged the transmission, banked the aircraft on final, and instructed Selena to tighten her seat belt.

The helicopter was a Bell Jet Ranger with three passengers aboard, and one of them had a torn photograph in his pocket. It was a picture of a man and a woman and an Aztec aircraft with five letters clearly visible behind them on the plane's fuselage. The last three letters were TFC. Tango Foxtrot Charlie.

They touched down with barely a nudge between an old DC-3 and a yellow crop duster — one aircraft carried cocaine — the other carried sprayed chemicals to destroy it.

The irony of that wasn't lost on Hernan Suarez as he worked his large frame from the chopper, crouched low to avoid the rotor blades, and darted towards the flight services hangar. He stopped briefly, waving the pilot off. The helicopter increased power, rose into the air, and dropped from sight at the rear of the building.

Suarez spotted a lone figure standing beneath fluorescent lights in a small office at the back of the hangar, a cavernous corrugated metal structure that held an assortment of aircraft and, strangely, a trailer on which sat one brightly painted cigarette boat with a strip of bullet holes along its port side gunnels. The man was working the night shift, Suarez thought, no doubt the low employee on the totem pole at Zapata Flight Services. The two louts moved quickly behind him when Suarez reached the doorway to the office.

The man was surprised when he looked up to see Suarez and the two others standing there. "Yes, senor. How can I help you?"

Suarez shot him once in the chest. "Just looking," he said as the man collapsed onto his desk. Suarez snapped the light off and pulled the door shut. He turned to the two louts. "You know what to do."

Louts number one and two separated to take up positions on either side of the hangar, hunkering down behind empty fuel drums. Suarez found his hiding place deeper inside the building — a storeroom to the right of the dead man's office. They were here because the photograph produced call letters, which along with cash produced a flight plan, and although they hadn't reacted quickly enough to intercept the aircraft before today's departure, they had managed to get here just in time for the return. Two souls outbound – two souls back. Perfect, Suarez thought, as he waited for Tango Foxtrot Charlie.

The powerful landing lights from the Apache shone white on the broken line that led to the hangar where Orlando planned to fill his tanks as quickly as he could so he could take off again in order to save his foolish but well-intentioned niece from a brutal and certain death.

Selena's uncle hadn't spoken since they landed. He'd opened her door to circulate cooler air and massaged the throttles and brakes to keep his aircraft tracking dead centre along the cracked taxiway. He informed the tower of his intention to depart as soon as he fuelled his plane and said he'd file a new flight plan when he was airborne.

The aircraft came to a full stop behind windmilling propellers and Orlando slapped shut his flight log. "Let's go," he said. "Ramiro will have hot coffee. Maybe some sandwiches if we're lucky."

There was no way Selena was going to abandon her friend. She wanted Orlando to slow down. She wasn't going to Miami or anywhere without Mercedes. What she really wanted was a hot bath and some rest. She'd planned on getting a good night's sleep before heading to Tayrona in the morning. Once there, she and Mercedes would hunker down. That was the plan, whether Orlando liked it or not.

Her uncle was already on the tarmac, waiting impatiently, when she pulled herself through the open door on her side of the airplane.

"The restroom is over there," he said, pointing in the direction of a door at the corner of the hangar. "I'll get Ramiro to pull the fuel truck around."

"Orlando?"

"No argument," he replied sternly.

Selena searched his eyes for concession.

"Go," he commanded.

Stubbornly. "I won't leave without her," Selena declared.

"Her friends," Orlando replied forcefully. "They'll be searching for you because you can lead them to her."

"They don't know about me." They were certain about that. Selena had set out that morning feeling cloaked in her anonymity.

"By now, they'll know about anyone she's ever spoken to," Orlando replied.

Selena was suddenly worried. What if that were true? What if they'd underestimated Montello's ability to reach out to the people in their lives? Selena quivered at the thought.

Orlando continued, "If they know about you, then they'll know about me. I filed a flight plan, Selena. It's an open book with the right connections." Orlando slapped the side of the airplane, a crack that made Selena flinch. "Damn," he said, peering worriedly into the hangar. "We have no time!"

Selena felt cold doubt in the pit of her stomach. Maybe Orlando was right. Tears made their way down her cheeks. Could she really abandon her friend? Mercedes would be left a sitting duck. Her only hope was to flee as quickly as she could. Still, Selena could not leave without her, even if it meant her own peril. Selena was about to say so.

"How long?" Orlando said.

"How long for what?"

"How long will it take for your friend to get here?"

Selena hugged him. "Quicker than anything," she replied. She'd call Mercedes, tell her to pack for both of them and meet them at the airport. It would mean an hour's delay at most. That would be fine. Orlando was likely overreacting anyway. Besides, part of the plan had been to leave the country once the bonds were safely tucked inside the George Town bank vault. And Miami was much warmer than Switzerland.

"My favourite uncle," she said, and then disappeared to the restroom. She'd call Mercedes while Orlando handled the refueling.

When she emerged five minutes later Orlando was already gone – no doubt already stuffing his face with Ramiro's sandwiches inside the hangar. Come to think of it, she was hungry as well.

Selena stepped into the brightly lit hangar. "Orlando?" No answer. Selena wondered where he'd gotten to. If Orlando was eating, where was the refueling tanker? That would have been his first priority – not food. Selena took a few more tentative steps and stopped. She called Orlando's name again, tried to shed the quiver in her voice. No response. Selena felt a chill. Something was wrong.

In her imagination she saw phantoms crouched behind a half dozen of the stored aircraft, faces peering out from darkened cockpits.

Selena noticed the closed door at the back of the hangar and breathed deeply. *Thank God*. Orlando and Ramiro had to be inside going over the details of the flight. Selena walked towards the office, already rehearsing what she planned to say to Mercedes. That's when she heard the sounds behind her, the sweep of quickly moving feet. She turned. "Orlando…where did–" The words jammed in her throat.

The man had a gun pointed at her face, grinning. "Orlando's not here anymore," he said. "Sorry about wetting your bed."

Selena screamed.

THIRTY-SEVEN

Juan Rodero lowered his shoulders to get a better view of the two bodies and worried about losing his breakfast in the process. He looked at his partner Jimenez, who nodded in the direction of the two backpackers. The woman wouldn't stop crying. Jimenez shrugged.

"Get them out of here," Rodero mouthed, tilting his head back. The vultures of Arrecifes loitered overhead, waiting for a chance to pick the corpses clean. He returned his attention to the grisly murder scene and knew he'd be skipping lunch that day.

The bodies were located in a coppice of shrubs about ten feet from a well-traveled rocky pathway. A male and a female. Older man. Both black. The woman's hands were bound and the man had a bullet hole in the centre of his forehead. The woman was dressed in clothing you normally didn't find on a hiking trail forty-five minutes from Canaveral. She was young and had been pretty. Rodero crouched lower, caught the faint scent of perfume. Lifeless green eyes stared back at him. A gentle face, lips that curled sharply upward at the corners. Otherwise, both bodies were a shambles of flesh and bone, limbs turned and twisted at impossible angles like toys in the hands of an ill-tempered child. As far as Rodero could tell, the bramble and underbrush around them was undisturbed. He looked for tracks and found none. How had they gotten there? In the middle of the park? Even in Tayrona, which had a murder rate to rival a major American city, it was a bewildering tableau.

Rodero looked up to see that Jimenez had herded the two tourists to a shade tree nearby. They were too brave or too stupid to realize the danger they had ignored in coming here. Rodero couldn't decide which. The woman and her husband, a couple of Canadians, had discovered the bodies not long after sunrise. They ran to Arrecifes where a panicked call was made to the warden's office. Rodero and Jimenez arrived about ten minutes later. The two tourists had at first refused to return to the site, though Rodero informed them it was absolutely necessary that the two investigators be led directly to the scene — and quickly.

Rodero returned his attention to the bodies. No one walked victims this far in. No one carried bodies and dumped them on a hiking path for the first passers-by to find. He stared out through tropical forest and past enormous boulders that ran along the coastline, but ruled out ingress by water. It didn't make sense either. Why heft two bodies this far from the beach and dump them here? Rodero wiped a moist hand across his forehead and then focused on the body of the male. Beige pants and a pale blue shirt stained red with blood. Expensive leather sandals. Fine features, like the woman. The man had long slender hands and wore a watch that looked expensive, lots of gleaming dials and buttons. In a robbery it would have been taken. Rodero guessed the man was about six feet in height and average weight. There were other similarities between the two that Rodero saw quickly. Shapes and sizes that defined their faces — bloodline features — the nose, lips, and the delicate curve of a cheek. They could have been father and daughter. Was that possible? Rodero wondered. Sunlight glinted off the dead man's wristwatch. A beacon to Rodero because the timepiece seemed to be leading him somewhere. The forest ranger pivoted forward on the balls of his feet and rested on his knees, then dropped to his elbows and leaned in, careful not to disturb the crime scene. He looked closely and saw the watch was a Breitling, one of those expensive aeronautics models that was popular with pilots. Maybe the guy was a flyboy — lots of work shifting coke until you screwed up and ended up dead. That was a definite possibility. But there was something Rodero still couldn't figure. Why here? And why the woman? She was no pilot. She looked more like one of those high-powered boardroom types. Flyboy ends up dead in the middle of nowhere with his corporate she-wolf. Maybe lovers?

He decided nothing was disturbed in the vicinity of the bodies. It was as if they had just dropped from the sky. That made sense to him so Rodero considered that for a moment. He looked up and went to work formulating a likely scenario. The man was already dead when he took the plunge. A bullet in his forehead before he hit the ground. It had to be a chopper because the surrounding brush was intact. That meant they came straight down. Dropping at a velocity of about a hundred miles per hour, Rodero calculated, while the chopper hovered above. There was something else. The woman was broken but not bloodied – no bullet holes, no stab wounds that Rodero could see. He was certain she had been alive when she was sent out the door. It meant the woman was the key to what happened, the one they'd tormented and tortured until she was pushed to her death. Rodero wondered what she wouldn't tell them. Or maybe she had and they tossed her anyway.

Rodero looked at the twisted forms and said a silent prayer. Father and daughter? Accomplices in something that got them killed? He shook his head. They'd likely never know.

The female hiker had stopped crying and was talking rapidly. Jimenez had his notebook and was doing his best to write as fast as she spoke.

Rodero was leaning back to get up when he saw it. A fragment of something sticking out from the dead woman's clenched hand. He reached forward and gently loosened her stiff fingers until he saw what it was. A photograph. Rodero carefully retrieved it, smoothed it out as best he could. It was a picture of a man and a woman, both smiling as they stood next to an airplane – the same two people who now lay dead before him. The aircraft looked like one of those sleek executive twin engine jobs, fast enough to get you to Miami for dinner and home again in time for a nightcap. Rodero brought the picture closer to his face to read the registration numbers on the tail of the plane. Maybe they'd lead to the pilot. KL-TFC.

Kilo Lima. Tango Foxtrot Charlie.

THIRTY-EIGHT

Mercedes Mendoza wept uncontrollably, drawing pitiful stares from Rodero's staff. The ranger handed her another tissue, leaned back on his desk and waited for her to stop crying.

"Are you sure it's them?" Mercedes sobbed.

Rodero simply nodded, then passed her the torn photograph. "This was in her hand. An Aztec registered to Orlando Santos. He was with her. The victims are the same two people in the photo. Jimenez met your friend when she got here a couple of weeks ago. The day before you arrived. He showed her the way to the bungalow where you were both staying."

Mercedes looked for a long time at the picture before handing it back. She'd recognized it immediately. She'd snapped the shot of Selena and Orlando the day he flew them both to Caracas last year. It was in a frame next to Selena's bed, and Mercedes was sure she had no reason to take it with her when she left for the Cayman Islands yesterday. That meant Montello's men had found out about Selena and had gone to her apartment. The picture led them to Orlando's plane and to them. The photograph was intended as a message. To her.

"It's so horrible," Mercedes said, wiping her red eyes. "They were only gone for the day. She was supposed to arrive back this morning." Selena had called from George Town to confirm the money had been deposited — provided the necessary passwords and other information concerning the account — and then told Mercedes to have breakfast ready — she'd be there early. She didn't arrive. An hour ago Rodero arrived on her doorstep with the news that Selena and Orlando were dead.

"I'm sorry about your friend," Rodero offered, placing the box of tissues on her lap. "But I'm not going to lie to you. The solve rate for this kind of thing is close to zero." Rodero got up to close the door and waved away a group of gawking staff members clustered at the water cooler outside his office. He turned to Mercedes and waited for a break in her sobbing. "But Senorita Mendoza, it is possible you can help us."

"Help, how?" she asked, sniffling.

"We know about Santos's brother — Selena's father." Rodero picked up a manila folder from his desk and held it up to her. "The crash of his plane. She would have been just a kid then." He opened the folder, flipped through some pages. "When the search team reached his plane they found his body and four hundred kilos of coke." Rodero allowed that to sink in.

Mercedes suddenly realized where he was headed. She knew exactly what Selena was doing and it had nothing to do with drugs — at least not directly. "If you're saying Selena was somehow involved in drugs," she said, "you're wrong. Selena wasn't involved in drugs. She hated anything to do with drugs."

"Maybe she wasn't directly involved." Rodero took his time laying it out for her. "Maybe it was Orlando. There's not a pilot in Colombia who hasn't thought about shifting coke. Huge cash — easy work." Rodero had seen it a thousand times, seen the downside too. Flying your plane into the side of a mountain wasn't the only way to die. Sometimes you got thrown out of a helicopter.

Mercedes shook her head. "Orlando felt the same way as Selena. They both despised drugs. Coke destroyed their family...Can I go now?"

Rodero didn't answer. Santos's plane was parked outside a hangar at Santa Marta Airport. They found no drugs aboard. But there was another dead body inside the hangar. That made three. Rodero walked behind his desk and sat. Outside, the sounds of telephones and voices were getting louder. A group of American hikers had gone missing up near Bahia Neguanje, another case that was likely to have a bad outcome. "Will you be staying at the bungalow?"

"Yes. For now," Mercedes replied. She stood to leave, steadying herself against the arm of the chair. "What about their bodies?"

Rodero thought for a moment before standing to walk her out. "They haven't been released yet. When they are, I'll come see you."

Mercedes opened the door and then turned to him. "Bad luck seems to follow me."

Rodero motioned her through the office door and followed her out. He'd already saved her from rape and murder. Now her friends were dead. What more could happen to this beautiful woman? "You're alive. Your friends aren't," he said as they reached the entrance to the administrative building. "I'd say that's good luck in a way."

Alive, Mercedes thought. Sure. But as she stepped outside and into a gathering storm she wondered for how long?

THIRTY-NINE

Everything seemed surreal to Mercedes in the hours after she left Rodero's office. Unbelievable. She cried for hours, but at some point she must have decided to run because she was now holed up in some motel in Taganga, sitting there like a zombie barely aware of the noises coming from the other rooms at two o'clock in the morning.

She wasn't keeping track of time, but the half-eaten meals on trays on the dresser suggested a couple of days had gone by. What did it matter? Selena and Orlando were both dead. Likely, she was too. It was only a matter of time before Montello's men found her.

Mercedes and Selena had stayed for two weeks in the bungalow, hardly moving outside except to replenish their supply of food. Montello would have cast a wide net, catching them the minute they strayed too far from their hideout. It was likely they would be most vulnerable at airports and bus stations.

Selena had convinced her it was safe. The money would be deposited in the Swiss National Bank in Grand Cayman. One day in – one day out. Selena had promised, even though Mercedes had told her it was too soon, that they needed to hunker down for at least another week before making their move. She only agreed when Selena told her Orlando would be flying her to George Town. Montello's men would be concentrating on commercial airliners and couldn't possibly cover the hundreds of private airplanes that routinely took off from dozens of airfields at every hour. Most importantly, Selena was unknown to them. Invisible.

Mercedes had relented, driven in part by cabin fever but mostly her rising anxiety. Having the bonds made them targets for many. With the bonds in their possession their lives were less than worthless.

Selena had successfully made the deposit before she was killed. She'd called. That meant Montello's thugs had taken her on her return to Santa Marta. Mercedes was certain Selena hadn't told them where to find her. Her friend had given her life for her — Mercedes was sure of it. It made her weep to think of Selena's last moments and the horrible way she must have died. Mercedes didn't care about the money anymore — it had already killed two people and Mercedes knew if she didn't get out of Colombia, she'd be next.

She hardly slept that night. The walls at Motel Pelikan were paper thin and seemed to amplify a chorus of flushing toilets and boozy conversations. She decided against a hot bath when she saw the yellowed shower curtain. Mercedes had stared for five minutes, trembling at what appeared to be a large bloodstain on the carpet near the door.

By lunchtime the next day hunger and restlessness drove her out. She'd eaten a little and then taken a walk along the beach, shrinking at the occasional whistles and jeers she attracted from drunken tourists. The most obnoxious was a group of bare-chested Germans who saluted her by hoisting huge steins in the shade of a coconut palm. They yelled at her to join them. Mercedes walked quickly by, seriously regretting her decision to leave the motel. Then the other one caught her attention. He wasn't rowdy; in fact he didn't say anything at all. Though he had stared at her hard. What if he was one of Montello's murderers? Mercedes shuddered, realizing that leaving her room might have been a deadly mistake. She rushed to her car, fumbled with the keys until she was able to start it. She was driving out of the parking lot when she spotted him again. He was thin and blond. A foreigner. Walking quickly towards her, carrying something low on his body, something threatening in his right hand. Mercedes pulled the wheel tightly, accelerating past him. Shaking, she fixed her eyes on the rear-view mirror. He was standing there, holding something in his hands. A weapon of some kind, pointed directly at her as she sped away.

FORTY

Jack knew it couldn't be real. He had realized before: it had all the permanence of a wisp of hot breath on the morning's chill. But he surrendered to it anyway because it brought him a small measure of comfort.

"You're a good man, Jack Doyle." She is smiling at him, and in that fragment of time, Jack can believe she is alive. He is relieved. But he also feels a melancholic déjà vu as their bodies turn, slowly moving, not to music but a vibration that locks them in magnetic embrace. She is whispering something into his ear that he cannot understand, but she desperately needs to tell him. Jack feels her tighten her hold, trying to draw him closer. Then her breath fades, and the whispering stops. Kaitlin is humming now. But to Jack the humming doesn't sound like anything lyrical, or even human – more like the sound produced by a machine, a cyclic pulsing beneath his feet, becoming stronger and louder until it makes Jack regret where the damn dream is headed.

Slowly turning, his arms are wrapped around her tiny waist, and Jack can feel the softness of her breasts press harder against him. He is giving into the illusion, even though there is nothing permanent about this. He's had the dream before, and like all the others, it will vanish.

Her smile disappears, replaced by a look of terror, and Kaitlin shrieks.

It confuses Jack. In his mind he needs desperately to quiet her. But she is slipping away from him, her lips have parted into a scowl and she continues to scream.

Jack woke with a start when the beer bottle cradled in his limp hand dropped to the floor and smashed. That was the first of three things he would regret. The second was his pounding head, and as Jack bolted upwards in the darkness he swore at his own stupidity. It wasn't Kaitlin screaming. It was the radar proximity warning, a screech that caused Jack to leap from his berth like a jackhammer. That was the third thing he did wrong. A shard of glass stabbed his foot, and now there would be blood, lots of blood. He had no time to deal with it. A bloody foot was the least of his worries. His bare feet thumped across the deck, a base drum beating quarter notes. Up the companionway and into the night. Warm air, calm seas, and the spins, a head full of buzzing, and raw pain. Jack tried desperately to focus, to determine what was threatening his boat. He felt it first: the vibrations that came from powerful engines, then the rhythmic sound of water being cleaved under the weight of something big. Very big. Beating relentlessly closer. Jack tried to wipe the hangover from his face, the crud blocking his vision. He swung around and in the darkness he saw it – a sight that settled in his gut like hot rivets.

She was at least sixty feet abeam and four storeys high. Her bridge was a shroud of darkness barely illuminated by the fluorescent lights that ran along her monstrous deck. The freighter was advancing murderously towards him, about three hundred yards off his stern and closing fast.

Jack jumped at the starter, pushed frantically at the red button. Nothing happened. *Turn the key...turn the key first!*

The key wasn't there. *Where is it? On the key ring!*

Jack dove for the opening that led down below, slipping in his own blood. *The key ring, on the galley bulkhead.*

In the dark, his hands slapped at the bulkhead until he found the key, pulled it into his clenched fist. He clambered back up, squinting through the darkness. *Christ!* She had to be seventy-thousand tons, and there was no sign that anyone on the bridge knew he was there. Two hundred yards at best now, at five knots, not much time before he was heading for the sea bottom.

It took Jack three tries before he could seat the ignition key and turn it, and with a trembling hand he punched the starter again.

One hundred twenty-five yards, trudging along, minding her business. Jack was dead because the goddamn watch was asleep. *Pleasant dreams, buddy.*

His engine turned over, but wouldn't catch. Jack punched it again, heard it cough. *Come on. Let's go!*

Jack did the math. Ninety yards now at five knots. Time for only one more try.

As calmly as he possibly could, he pressed the button. The engine caught. *GO!*

Jack pushed the throttle to the stops and leapt at the wheel, disconnected the automatic pilot, and spun *Scoundrel* hard to port. Fifty yards now. Jack could feel her, could smell the churning water cresting at her bow. Even if someone saw, it would be too late for a ship this heavy to stop.

Scoundrel crawled painfully slow out of harm's way, and a few seconds later Jack allowed himself to believe he was going to live. Then the engine quit.

Fuck. Jack couldn't believe his bad luck. He cursed aloud and pounded on something, teeth clenched from the stinging in his foot. Jack rubbed his face and felt muscles of cement. *The life jackets!* Where are the life jackets? Under the aft bench, of course. He knew that. *Life jackets or the engine? No time to think about it!*

Jack pounded the starter one more time. He wasn't religious, but he prayed anyway.

The Volvo Penta turned once, then twice, and then it started. Jack yelled with relief as the boat began slowly to move. Jack measured his salvation an inch at a time. The inches became feet, and when *Scoundrel* was safely away with only five yards between them, Jack could feel a cold wake from the freighter's hull sweeping by him, like a prissy debutante who never even knew he was alive.

Jack had to remind himself to breathe as he collapsed to the deck.

Even with binoculars pressed tight to his face, she was too far away to catch a name. But Jack could make out the large steel containers stacked high on her decks and a white phosphorous wake boiling around her hull. She was two thousand yards away.

Jack returned the Tascos to their case, swallowed another mouthful of coffee, and wiped the back of a trembling hand across his mouth. Two ships in all this ocean and they wind up on a collision course. What were the chances? Jack stroked the bandage on his foot and figured about a gazillion to one. Thank God for the gear, the electronic wizardry that kept him alive when jerks like that fell asleep on their watch. Hold on a moment, Jack. Just who was asleep? He shook his head. Never a dull moment, he thought as he took another swallow and watched her vanish on the horizon. Another little piece of the global economy headed south towards Caracas, or Rio or maybe even Havana.

Have a nice trip, Jack said to no one but himself.

He needed another cup of coffee before starting his daily ritual. Down below he topped up his mug and swallowed two aspirin before moving to the navigation station on the starboard side of the boat, just ahead of the aft sleeping quarters. It was where Jack sat for long stretches, monitoring the GPS and his radios. He listened as shrimp boat captains cajoled one another, usually a sign their holds were full.

The weather forecast said clear skies. Jack wrote that in his diary and made notations about wind speed and wave height – his heading.

The electronic chart which he'd loaded into the GPS showed he was ten miles off the Carolinas, a position he confirmed on a paper chart that included markings for water depth and the warm currents of the Gulf Stream. Then Jack checked the fuel gauge. He needed a fill-up, more water too.

Two hours later he brought *Scoundrel* alongside a rotting wharf in a sandy backwater with one old gas pump. It was the only sign of sea-faring commerce. Beyond the wharf, a couple dozen houses stood like hitchhikers on the road to anywhere but here. Jack saw only two other sailboats. They bobbed lazily at anchorages with grimy dull fiberglass hulls and slack mooring lines that had collected a salad of seaweed. Neither vessel showed signs of life.

Jack went below to retrieve his wallet, stuffed in his shorts, when he was startled by a face in one of the portholes. It stared at him. "Hello there," it said, muffled.

Jack stared back, spent a bewildered moment wondering whether to grab a weapon of some kind, then laughed to himself instead as he made his way up the companionway.

The mayor and his wife were in their sixties, retired from Norfolk. A half dozen others, who might have been cousins, didn't say or do much except walk up and down the wharf studying Jack's fancy boat.

"How far ya going?" The mayor had a pathetic comb-over and a droop on the right side of his face that suggested stroke recuperation – or an old war wound. His hands were huge, fingers like wooden pegs. He said he was thirty years a welder up at the navy repair yard. There was a strange whistling noise when he spoke. Badly fitted false teeth, Jack guessed. Courtesy of veterans' health care.

"Don't know yet. Antigua at least," Jack replied, looking at his watch.

The mayor's wife was a big fan of polyester. She wore a pair of lime-green shorts that surrendered to rolls of fat encircling her thighs. Her name was Beth or Bess or something like that – and she was staring at him. "I know y'all look familiar."

Jack saw a couple of rooftops with satellite dishes. "My mother used to say the same thing, whenever I came in for supper." Jack smiled at her. All three of them laughed, then Earl, the mayor, offered to pump the gas.

"Hard to get good help these days," he said. "Hell, any help." They chuckled at that too.

Beth asked Jack if he'd care to join them for lunch. Jack said thanks anyway, "be heading out again before noon." Then her husband told Jack to stay away from the point because his cousin had run aground there on a drifting sand bar the week before.

"No radio aboard," he said. "Stuck there for ten hours, the goddamn fool."

Scoundrel swallowed twenty gallons of diesel and twice as much water. Jack paid with cash, they said goodbye, wished him luck, and the mayor and his entourage ambled up the wharf.

Jack decided to check his e-mail. He grabbed his Globestar 2800 and hooked it up to his laptop. A minute later he was logged on to his satellite service provider. He typed in the name of his vessel and a password. All of this bounced into space where it eventually found an Inmarsat satellite positioned in a geostationary orbit above the western Atlantic. A few seconds later Jack was downloading his e-mail. There were a bunch of messages from friends wondering how he was doing and a note from his Aunt Muriel in Boston who still couldn't comprehend the wonder of e-mail. She missed him. Was he eating enough? Write me!

Jack looked out the porthole and saw a cluster gathering, more locals who would soon make their way down the wharf to find out more about the new arrival. When he returned his attention to the computer he saw the e-mail from Seth Pollard. Jack looked at it blankly for a moment and saw that it was a couple of days old. Pollard was one of the best freelance cameramen Jack had ever worked with. The last Jack heard Seth was in Afghanistan somewhere tailing remnants of the Taliban – ballsy Brit always looking for the most dangerous assignments. Jack clicked on the e-mail. The page was blank. Strange, Jack thought. Seth was never short on bullshit. When Jack looked closer he saw the e-mail attachment. He double clicked – and waited.

It took a second for the attachment to open and when it did, Jack saw it was a video file. He pressed play and hunkered down to watch. The first thing Jack saw was movement – lots of it. Whoever was shooting the video was running with the record button on, feet stomping along with the camera jostling up and down at shoulder level. The lens of the camera was bouncing too wildly to discern anything but the fact someone was in a hurry. Jack increased the volume on his laptop and heard heavy breathing and an occasional curse. It sounded like Seth's voice. About twelve seconds into the video the shot settled down and what Jack saw next was a dirt parking lot. That was it. A parking lot with about a dozen cars in it. It was surrounded by palm trees, which meant somewhere tropical. Beyond that there was nothing remarkable about Seth's video. Jack continued to watch as a car backed out of a parking space and sped towards the camera. A shit box of a car, green in colour, getting the hell out of a dirt parking lot in some tropical place. OK, Seth, Jack thought. There's got to be a reason for this. Jack bent closer.

At twenty seconds the sound of tires crunching on gravel as the car rolled closer to Seth. Pollard muttered something that sounded like another curse. At twenty-five seconds Pollard zoomed in to check his focus, pulled back out again. At twenty-eight seconds the car came abreast of Pollard and stopped. The driver's window was open because in a car that old there would be no air conditioning.

Jack looked closer and in the shadow of the car he saw a figure. It was a woman driving, a woman alone. The camera zoomed in quickly on the open window. *Still don't get it, Seth*. The car's engine revved to match Jack's impatience. Then at thirty-two seconds someone appeared. When Jack saw who it was he jerked upright, toppled over on his stool and landed square on his ass.

Now he got it.

Jack was stunned. Too frozen in place to get back up. He struggled to regain the air which had been sucked from his lungs while a torrent of blood rushed through his veins and crashed into his skull like waves pounding on a rocky shoreline. Did he ever get it.

A couple of moments passed before he was able to pull himself back up again. He rubbed the back of his neck where his muscles felt like glacial ice.

Not possible.

Jack looked out a porthole, at a pair of kids splashing in the water near a floating dock, gangly limbs beating up a storm to match Jack's mood. He rubbed sweaty palms against his leg and slumped, a man paralyzed in the path of a tidal wave.

Another moment was spent in sheer denial. He clicked on the attachment again – and watched in amazement. A few seconds later he stopped the video. It was the point where Seth zoomed in, the exact second when she leaned out of the car window to look back at the man with a camera. Out of the shadows now and into sunlight – her face fully revealed.

Jack blinked hard at the computer screen, his mind spinning like he was on some carnival ride, the kind that always ends in the joyless calamity of vomit. A moment later he got up and stumbled to the head where he splashed cold water on his face, stood there staring in the mirror at incredulity. A lot of people were going to be feeling the same way, he thought. "Goddamn," Jack cursed, then pulled himself from the head and stomped back to the computer where her image now filled the entire screen. Jack took inventory of what he was staring at: her eyes, her hair, her nose, her lips. Doubt vanished, replaced by bewilderment. That, he could identify, unlike the things which at that moment he could not, the wonders which swirled around him like black magician's smoke.

Seth had dropped a bombshell with no explanation, and at that moment Jack could have strangled him for it. He'd known the Brit for years, since their first assignment in the Balkans when Jack had called New York and told them they were crazy if they thought this freelancer was going to be able to hump a hundred pounds of equipment through a war zone. Jack was eventually amazed at Seth's courage and determination and the speed with which he was able to edit and feed their stories to New York. "Bing, bang, bong, mate. Time for a beer I'd say." The Brit made sure Jack never missed a deadline – or the bar tab.

They traveled light, except for his flak jacket, which had saved his life on three occasions. Seth never wore it because it got in the way of getting the "money shot." An adrenalin fiend, that Brit. Jack was no stranger to the juice either. He and Seth had once talked their way into the compound of an Afghan warlord outside Kabul. Everything was going swimmingly until one of the lookouts spotted the contrail of a B-2 bomber. Jack and Seth were barely able to outrun the concussions when a pair of five hundred pound smart bombs reduced the place to rubble. Even still, Pollard had managed to get "the money shot." To Jack *this* was the mother of all "money shots."

Jack fumbled for the sat phone, which he uncoupled from the computer. He punched in a series of numbers. A second later someone answered at the Reuters office in New York. Jack knew Seth Pollard wouldn't be there, but he asked for the newsroom anyway.

A moment later a gruff voice came on the line.

"Is Seth Pollard on assignment?" Jack asked.

"Who's asking?" the voice said.

"Jack Doyle. Looking for Seth."

There was silence broken by bursts of static. Finally the voice spoke again. "Jack Doyle, Brian Hoskins here. You sound like you're a million miles away."

"Not quite. Brian, I really need to speak with Seth."

"That's the problem," Hoskins said. "Us too. But can't reach him, haven't been able to for about two days now. Fuckin' freelancers operate on their own timeline."

"Where in Afghanistan is he?" Jack didn't like the sound of it. Seth took chances and Afghanistan was unforgiving.

"Afghanistan?" Hoskins said. "That was two weeks ago. Seth's in Colombia, chasing rebel soldiers up near Santa Marta somewhere."

Christ. Seth had seen her all right. "No word since Tuesday?"

"None. And we're getting worried so for Chrissake if you hear from him tell him to pick up a phone."

"I will," Jack promised, then punched off.

Pollard had gone missing the same day he'd sent the e-mail.

Jack rolled the tape again and checked the racing time code. It had been shot shortly after noon two days ago.

The woman on the video was Kaitlin O'Rourke.

FORTY-ONE

It was a good thing Jack was sailing single-handed, because for the next two days he shuffled around *Scoundrel* like an automaton, with no appetite and a foul mood to match the low black clouds trailing his wake and taunting him before moving in to test his sea legs.

The last time he checked, Jack was ten miles southwest of the Florida Keys, in a sector normally thick with gleaming white charter boats hunting grouper and damselfish. Not today. The ominous weather system had driven them ashore. Taking no chances, Jack thought, as he stared glumly at the wall of black on his stern.

He'd printed a frame of the Kaitlin video and tacked it to a bulkhead where he spent long moments trying to figure out how his producer had survived the attack at Café Umbria. But, more importantly, why she had allowed everyone to believe she was dead. Her father, her friends. The whole damn world. Kaitlin O'Rourke, deceased. Killed in a suicide bombing in Cartagena, Colombia. Case closed. Not anymore. The question now was why?

Doyle studied the image, absorbing every feature and angle, every hue of colour, searching for anything that might reveal it wasn't Kaitlin at all, but an illusion constructed from the trickery of light and shadows. Wishful thinking, too, Doyle thought which was to be expected given the circumstances. In the end he decided that it was Kaitlin's face, and he had absolutely no idea how that could be possible.

That morning he'd received the reply to an e-mail he'd sent sixteen hours earlier. It meant a change in his itinerary. He took an hour to plot his new course, and after checking the weather twice he decided he'd make a beeline for his new destination. Lunch was something he ate out of a can while he checked a satellite photo he'd downloaded from the Florida weather service. The lifting wind told Jack he was in for a wet miserable afternoon and quite possibly a sleepless night unless he was able to outrun the weather, which was highly unlikely. At a GPS speed of seven point two knots the separation between *Scoundrel* and the storm was closing fast. Jack ran the mental checklist of things he needed to do to ride out the storm chasing him. The hairs on the back of his neck tingled with electricity as the ocean rapidly turned darker shades of green. He reefed the sails and when he settled into the cockpit the first bulbous drops of water beat like war drums on the deck.

Jack checked the wind-speed indicator and saw it was rising quickly. He darted below to retrieve his foul weather gear, for a moment stopping at the bulkhead where her picture was tacked. She'd survived, he thought. Even if she'd been hurt in the explosion, she was clearly now recovered. What didn't make sense was the charade of her death. He stared into her eyes – windows, they say, to the deepest part of someone. The eyes he recognized, but as Jack pulled himself up through the companionway into the darkening weather, he wasn't at all sure about her soul.

FORTY-TWO

The storm beat on *Scoundrel* for fifteen hours. A merciless harangue of lashing rain and howling wind that drove her stern into the sea with the force of a giant jackhammer. When it was over, Doyle was exhausted. On rubbery legs he came below for food and rest, and after shedding his waterproof gear he plopped down at the navigator's table and bent his sopping head closer to the radio. By the sounds of it, two sailboats had gone down, their crews rescued by the gutsy crew of a Coast Guard helicopter. These guys never got enough credit or pay, Doyle thought. Risking their lives to pluck the doomed from stormy seas. Doyle knew he could have been one of them. Damn impatience had nearly cost him his life.

He spent the morning putting his boat together again, and even though fatigue dulled his vision, six hours after that, Doyle was close enough to Cuba to see white sugary sand and towering palm trees. The GPS showed he was on a straight course for Marina Hemingway, and although the wind was waning, there was still enough to fill her sails as he skirted the coastline.

1500 hours. The sun burned hot on Jack's shoulders as he watched two gulls spread their wings to gain altitude above the deep emerald water of the Straits of Florida before it turned shallow and became brilliant blue. He rubbed at three days' stubble and massaged his bare chest, fingers slippery on a mélange of sweat and sunblock. Doyle thought about the man he was going to meet. A friend he'd contacted. It had been a long time, and for a fleeting moment Doyle wondered whether to trust him. What choice did he have?

Doyle took a long pull on a bottle of cool water, squinted across shimmering waves towards shore, and drew in a lungful of air that slid down with the consistency of honey. He'd shave and shower before making shore, his first shower since leaving Bark Island. Jack checked the compass and corrected his course ten degrees to port to tighten her approach. He then lifted the bottle and poured half its contents over his head, running fingers through thick dark hair until it was slick against his scalp.

He had taken on the colour of rawhide, bronze like the summers when he was a kid aboard his father's boat. He wore tattered denim shorts and leather topsiders that gripped the deck when he made his way forward, hunkering down to lower his centre of gravity as he dashed from port to starboard, sometimes pulling tight a line or checking a cover. Occasionally *Scoundrel* dug deep, soaking Doyle with salty spray, forcing him to grab something before tumbling overboard. What good were man-overboard drills when you were single-handed? No one to throw you a line. Jack didn't know why he'd never learned to swim. He guessed it was because the water in his part of the world froze you to death before you had a chance to drown. On more than one occasion, with ten-foot waves beating on him, he was grateful for his survival suit and the fact *Scoundrel* was as solid as she was. There was a small brass plate in the cockpit that Jack polished until it gleamed. It said she was hull number ninety-five, a cutter-rigged ketch handmade by craftsmen on the shores of the Hudson River thirty years ago. Jack bought her after selling a hundred acres of his family's land to Boston developers, on which they built condos on craggy hillsides with an ocean view and million dollar price tags. Weekend retreats for Boston yuppies. Jack snickered at the fleet of Beemers and Audis parked at Finnegan's Saturday afternoons. He was paid a heap for his land, but he'd also demanded and received final say on the design of the condos. He would never have sold otherwise, and in the end the properties had blended in perfectly. Others didn't agree, including Argus. It seemed O'Rourke didn't agree with anything Doyle did. He figured he'd taken his old man's place on O'Rourke's shit list. In a way who could blame him?

The Russian's e-mail had been short: a time and place in old Havana where Jack would be met by his "associates." Jack was looking forward to seeing his old friend again. He thought back to the time they met.

The Moscow summit was handed to Jack on a silver platter. "Pack your bags and call me the minute you arrive," Carmichael had said to him. "Now move your ass and don't screw up." Twelve hours later Jack arrived.

"Why aren't you asleep?" he asked Carmichael on the phone from the airport.

"Who sleeps?" Carmichael had responded. "Your first feed window is booked for two hours from now. Get going."

Forty-five minutes later Jack joined the media circus — a dozen reporters doing their stand-ups in Red Square with the snow-capped onion domes of the Kremlin behind them. The satellites bounced their stories at newsrooms in New York and Atlanta. The two world leaders were closer than they had ever been to a major agreement on arms control — even Reykjavik. The underlings were sweating the details on warhead reductions and verification protocols. A communiqué would seal the deal for both sides.

Jack first saw the Russian at the hotel on Baltchug Street in Novokuznetskaya near the Moskva River. A meet-and-greet for western reporters and their East Bloc "counterparts" from outfits like Pravda, Izvestia, and state-run television.

Network news anchors swept into the room past tall red velvet curtains. Czarist princes trailing producers and sycophants. Staking territory like rutting stags.

That night, Doyle recalled, an American senator had arm-wrestled a Soviet air force general to the floor. It was front page the next day in a hundred newspapers.

They gulped good vodka and stuffed their faces with caviar canapés. The smoke from Russian tobacco formed a cumulus cloud high in the inverted cup of a golden-domed ceiling three storeys high.

Jack had struck up a conversation with the Russian easily. Raspov, as he remembered, seemed almost too eager. Always ready with the next drink, background stuff on the arms control apparatchiks milling about the room. After an hour his new friend made an offer. "Let me show you Moscow, Jack." Why not? Jack thought. Five minutes later they were racing through Moscow in a wrecked Lada that had no heat and no headlights. They drank till three in the morning at smoky nightclubs along Leninskiy Prospekt.

"Your man's gonna cave," Jack had said to the Russian after his seventh shot of iced vodka. "Thanks for the cigar."

"You're welcome. What choice does Gorbi have?"

"So Reagan wins." Jack smiled.

"Don't fool yourself into believing that. Gorbachev will end communist rule in my country – not Ronald Reagan. He started along that path well before Reykjavik – before Reagan liked to call us the 'Evil Empire.'"

"Gorbi's gonna cave," Jack repeated, looking smug in the flare of a match, blowing cigar smoke towards the ceiling.

"I think so," the Russian had replied.

When Jack and his new Russian friend uselessly exhausted themselves arguing Soviet-US politics, they had talked about sailing and cigars, and Russian women.

On the way back to Jack's hotel the Russian pulled over. In the darkened Lada he handed Jack an envelope. Suddenly he didn't seem quite as drunk. "No questions. Just take it. You'll know what to do."

Jack however *was* drunk. It took him a while, but he finally stuffed the envelope in his pocket as they were pulling up outside Jack's hotel. "Thanks, com…comrade. A re…reporter never reveals his sources. You can count on me."

"I am," the Russian had replied. "Goodnight, Mr. Doyle."

Jack was awakened the next morning by the head-splitting ring of a telephone. It was Carmichael and he didn't bother saying hello or even how's it goin. "CNN says the Russians are going to cave." Then silence.

Jack rubbed his face and reached for a glass of water, instead knocked it over. Cursed. "What are you talking about?"

"Paul Rimbey at CNN is reporting that the Soviets are ready to make substantive concessions on all nuclear weapons. How come we don't have it?"

Shit. Doyle hung up, cutting Carmichael off in mid-sentence. Five minutes after a panicked shower he pulled shut his door and headed for the hotel's media centre. Something fell out of his pocket. Doyle bent over to pick it up, the vice closing on his cranium. He exhaled painfully and with tremulous hands he opened the envelope, extracting a thick wad of official looking papers. Russian was impossible to decipher but "Top Secret" in thick red ink looked the same in any language. Doyle began to read, eyes widening until his forehead hurt. A moment after realizing what he held in his hands, he stumbled, cursing in disbelief, towards the biggest story of his career.

FORTY-THREE

Jack wasn't worried about sailing single-handed in Cuban waters until he saw the speck on the horizon off his bow. He grabbed the binoculars and pressed them to his face. It was the last thing he wanted to see.

He moved quickly to reef his canvas, and in thirty seconds his boat was dead in the water. Jack brought the binoculars up again and spotted the rooster tail, then the sleek cigarette boat, three men in uniforms bouncing in their seats like bronco busters. Cuban uniforms were a problem, especially if you were a drug smuggler which Jack wasn't. Sometimes it didn't matter. They'd rip your boat apart looking.

Creeps in these uniforms once sank a tugboat with seventy-two Cubans on board – forty-one died, most of them women and children trying to escape Fidel's revolution. Jack remembered the pictures of corpses soaked in diesel fuel – faces frozen in horror. Jack was worried. He dropped the binoculars and dove below. The sat phone was worth a fortune, the computer too. He stowed both, and emerged a few seconds later, still as a statue as the boat got closer. Below the surface of the water he spied schools of dazzlingly coloured fish, frantic and directionless as they shot between razor-sharp coral, a tiny biomass sticking to his underbelly. He hoped for the best. It was all he could do.

The thunder of her jet-powered engine rumbled across the straits, and as she drew closer Jack saw the weapons. The gunboat maneuvered through a wide circle. They swept their eyes along the length and beam of *Scoundrel*, leering in a way that made Jack feel the cuckold. When they got close enough one of them swung a grappling hook and pulled *Scoundrel* into them.

"*Buenos dias*," Jack shouted above the rumble of the engine.

One of them jumped on board. The commander, Jack guessed. Mr. Cocky with a practiced swagger that challenged Jack before the man had spoken his first words. He ignored the gringo, ducked his head to take a quick look down below and muttered something to the others.

Jack dropped the smile. Through his peripheral vision he watched the two underlings, who were watching their commander, hands tickling their side arms. The commander turned and straightened, came up an inch short of Jack's chin. Great, Jack thought. The Napoleon complex – with weapons. Jack held out his passport.

The captain took it and opened it to the photo, and after a tense moment said, "Senor Jack Doyle." His accent was thick as espresso, black eyes like lumps of coal embedded beneath a Neanderthal's brow.

Jack glanced at their weapons again. Still holstered. No one seemed to be in a hurry to shoot him – yet. He nodded, waited as the boats rocked into one another, the dull grey fiberglass chaffing at *Scoundrel* like a schoolyard bully.

"Your destination?" The captain flipped lazily through Jack's passport.

"Marina Hemmingway." Jack's throat felt as though it were coated with sawdust.

"No weapons...drugs?" Eye contact then, challenging. Jack thought he heard holsters being unsnapped – decided it was just his imagination. The boats bumped gently into one another. Two gulls squawked overhead, adding to his tension like a colicky child on a white-knuckle landing.

"No. I'm a journalist." It seemed immediately like an incredibly stupid thing to say.

The commander waved the comment away, and then looked again at Jack's passport, like he couldn't decide if the guy standing there was the guy in the picture. Skinnier in the flesh, Jack guessed. The commander positioned his hands on his hips and spread his legs. "I am thinking maybe the gringo's coming to *Kooba* to smoke our cigars and fuck our women."

The two others grunted in agreement.

"What about it Senor Doyle? *Kooban* woman are easy, eh? A few American dollars for unemployed doctors and lawyers."

Jack's heart raced. He didn't like where this was headed. He was sure now the other guys had their hands on their weapons. "Meeting a friend," was all he said.

They locked eyes again. Shiny hair gel, Jack noticed. Gel with flecks of some kind. In a place where soap was hard to come by, this man had hair products. The commander continued to glare at him, mouth clamped shut. Jack searched for the right words because the ones on his tongue weren't going to cut it. *How's the wife and kids? Nice hair*. The damn gulls were back. Heckling him.

Finally the commander said, "Raspov says welcome to *Kooba*." He placed a hand on Jack's shoulder. "The Russian is waiting," he added with a grin. "But first, we're thirsty."

Jack gulped. Smiled his relief. So the old Russian had lots of friends and now they were his friends. Why not? he thought, as he went below to fetch four ice-cold beers.

They followed Jack until he was past Barlovento Harbor where the river Jaimanitas leads to the mouth of Marina Hemingway. The captain of the patrol boat saluted and then slammed the throttle forward. Heat thermals shimmered from her stern as she leapt from the water and headed back out to sea.

Jack radioed in for docking instructions, and thirty minutes later he motored into a narrow slip between a forty-two foot sailboat and a gleaming flybridge with a "for hire" sign. A deckhand stowed shiny brass fishing reels, while a partner swept a bloodied mop across her deck. The skipper barked at the one swinging the mop, spat on the deck and then with a scowl hefted himself onto the wharf and headed in the direction of a noisy bar at the end of the pier. The two deckhands exchanged a look, and then one of them gave their boss the finger. He grinned at Jack and jumped onto the wharf to take his lines. A moment later *Scoundrel* was expertly tied.

Marina Hemingway was a busy place. Forests of towering sailboat masts swayed on the wake of gleaming mega-yachts headed out for evening cruises. Palm-lined canals snaked their way past stucco homes and rentals. There was a large white hotel which was topped by a harbour light and a manned radio post. Farther away Jack saw the low-roofed houses of Sante Fe.

He'd had just about enough of Cuban uniforms when he saw the two immigration officers headed down the dock. There were perfunctory questions and a cursory examination of his vessel. Jack handed one of them his passport, and his tourist card. The guy reminded Jack of Che Guevara, that brooding pose that had long ago become an icon of the revolution. "How long Cuba?" Che asked.

Jack held up five fingers. "*Cinco dias.*" It sounded reasonable, maybe more, maybe less. It would depend.

"No drugs?" Che continued to ask the questions.

"No, senor." Jack didn't think he wanted to know about the Gravol or the painkillers he kept in the first aid kit.

"No weapons aboard. *Si?*"

"No weapons aboard." *Trick question.*

The partner was becoming restless so the two of them went below, messed things up a bit, demanded to look in the bilge, and then stood there looking at all the electronics, trying to figure out what they did. They said something in Spanish that sounded like gringo boat, then handed back his passport and told Jack in bad English to stay out of trouble.

Jack was happy to see them leave.

The ride to Figuardo's was like a trip back in time. The cab driver wore ten dollar Ray Ban knockoffs a full hour after sunset and was leaning against a 1959 Chevy outside the marina's main gate. He picked at something inside the front of his shirt. "Transport?" he asked, showing two gold teeth like shiny vanguards.

Jack nodded, and a door was opened with flourish. The back seat springs had apparently surrendered decades ago. The vinyl was frayed and cracked, but mostly a tapestry of duct tape. Jack wondered how much he'd find under the hood, or plugging holes along the brake lines. There were no seat belts.

They drove for a while before the driver introduced himself as Edmundo. He told Jack he could supply anything he needed, including cheap cigars and young girls.

"No thanks," Jack told him. "Figuardo's."

Fine antiques like the '59 Chevy came with no air conditioning and Jack was soon sticking to the seat. He rolled a window down and sniffed at a warm breeze that carried odours from the old city: sea air and cooking oil, wisps of exhaust and a hint of raw sewage. A potpourri of human consumption and waste as the antique motored beside the old sea wall, the only thing left which offered protection to a crumbling Havana.

"You came by boat?"

Jack realized Edmundo had said something. He looked for the rearview mirror but saw there wasn't one. "Sorry."

"Boat. Boat." Edmundo turned his head and smiled. "Big American boat?"

"Thirty-two foot ketch," Jack said. "Not too big."

"Big enough. Lots of room for cargo. No?"

"No cargo."

"No cargo?" Edmundo was doubtful. Conspiratorial. "My cousin works in a marina in Lauderdale. Likes to send me pictures of the pretty yacht girls sunning their beautiful bodies. He left with the others at Mariel. You know, like Scarface. One less mouth for the Maximum Leader to feed. Many less mouths. Off he goes." Edmundo made a sweeping movement upwards. "Sick boy. Killed his momma, Ezabella. Now the good life. Cleaning shit from toilets on big American boats just like yours."

Jack simply nodded. He stared out the window and thought about the Mariel boatlifts. More than a hundred thousand Cubans flushed out to sea, backing up like sewage along the Florida coast. A smart move on Castro's part, shedding the revolution's convicts and psychos.

The car drove into a maze of narrow one-way streets that crisscrossed Havana Viejo, past decrepit three- and four-storey apartment houses where old men with vacant rheumy eyes sat in doorways smoking cigarettes. In the distance the dome of the old Capitol Building rose into the sky.

Jack was about to relax when the cab suddenly swerved. Tires screeched, followed by a loud pop. In that first adrenalin-soaked second Jack thought, Gunshot. But Edmundo wasn't gunning it to get out of there. Instead he was yelling at someone. Slowly Jack pulled himself straight and nervously looked over his shoulder, realizing what had actually occurred. He felt like an idiot.

A young boy was barefoot and crying and being yanked to the curb by his angry mother. Jack saw something dead in the middle of the street.

"Stop!" He shouted.

"*Loco nino*," Edmundo shouted back.

"Stop!" Jack repeated, slapping the door.

The car slowed and finally stopped. Jack jumped out and began to walk towards the kid and whatever it was they had hit in the middle of the street.

Edmundo got out and shook his head. "Not good idea, Senor Ketch."

"Wait here," Jack said, tapping his wallet.

He walked closer, palms open in apology, eyeing the dead heap in the middle of the narrow street.

Jack finally realized what they had "killed." He bent down to the sniffling boy and in slow deliberate Spanish he apologized.

The youngster looked at him like he was crazy. So did his mother.

Jack stepped forward until they were just a foot apart.

The women's eyes challenged him. In a doorway Jack saw two bare-chested *habaneros* who had come to see what all the commotion was about. Their eyes flicked from the boy, to the women, and finally to Jack.

Everyone was waiting for something to happen.

"*Lo siento*," Jack said to the woman this time. Reaching into his pants, he retrieved a handful of American dollars, held them out to her. A full minute passed. No one said anything.

Sweat rolled down Jack's back. He knew what the soccer ball would have meant to the kid, but this might have been a mistake. The men watched him, fists balled.

Tentatively the woman stepped forward and took the money, stuffed it into her jeans.

"*Gracias*," she said, a smile forming.

While the two *habaneros* walked slowly towards them, Jack turned and walked briskly back to the car.

Edmundo was already behind the wheel when he got back into the car.

"Let's go," Jack said.

"*Mierda*," said Edmundo, like his mouth was full of it, and stomped on the gas.

FORTY-FOUR

Havana was a city locked in time, a washed-up show dancer stubbornly refusing to surrender her gaudy makeup. Once beautiful and charming, now beaten down and clinging to what she had once been.

Four centuries ago tons of gold glittered on Spanish galleons anchored in her harbour, safe in the protective embrace of El Morro Castle and El Castille de la Real Fuerza. Jack was hooked on the stories of buccaneers and plunder, which he read voraciously as a kid. Cuba had always been part of his fantasy.

Jack was learning the difference between a staysail and a jib when most kids his age were starting to read. When he was thirteen he bought a leaking day-sailor twice as old as him for a hundred dollars. It was nineteen feet long with a main sail that looked like a checkerboard. Shanks and Mulligan thought he was nuts. "Better put a bucket aboard her," Mulligan said.

Caleb Doyle didn't know where his son was for two days. The note Jack left was short on details. *Gone to Boston to see Aunt Muriel.* His father was furious – spent sixteen hours in Parker Thom's Cape Islander looking for his boy.

Jack wasn't scared. He spent hours gazing at Orion's belt and Capella, pulsing red, white, and green, learning the things his father couldn't teach him, about being alone on the water, counting on no one but yourself. He followed the stars like waypoints towards his manhood, and ten hours into the journey he thought he was seeing things when the water's black surface parted.

The sperm whale was close. So close a flip of its tail would have capsized his tiny boat. Jack swung away but the whale surfaced directly beneath him, and a second later the boat moved sideways – no longer a boat, just a piece of driftwood. The beast was blacker than the water could ever be, and Jack saw a huge eye staring up at him. The whale snorted moist air and like a black slab slowly fell away. Jack could still remember the smell, that salty mix of seaweed and warm blood. His heart had pumped pure adrenalin, a rush he would never forget. That, and later his father's stinging hands.

It took the cab driver ten minutes to reach the street where Figuardo's was. Edmundo took Jack's money, and a five dollar tip, and sped away, leaving him standing on the sidewalk of a narrow street with barely enough room for two-way traffic. Spray-painted American classics shouldered their way up and down the street, belching clouds of blue smoke. The place was crawling with the night detritus of Old Havana. Bare-chested hucksters swaggered along the sidewalk, looking at Jack like he was lunch meat.

"Cheap cigars. You come look, OK?"

Jack shook his head. Stared at them until they passed and then stood there. He would have had no trouble imagining another decade were it not for the gaggle of transvestites loitering nearby. One of them spied him and sauntered over. Red sequins and black leather atop three-inch heels, hips swaying to some internal rhythm. "Don you worry about those bugarrons," he said, looking Jack up and down. "What dey sell you don want."

"I'm not buying," Jack said, and reached down for his knapsack before turning his head in the direction of a string of bars, any of which could have been Figuardo's.

More examination from the he-she. A whistle. Then three of his friends high-stepped forward. Excited about fresh meat. "You so lone-ly," one of the newcomers said in a voice as baritone as James Earl Jones.

ANGELS OF MARADONA

Ridiculous looking at six feet in white spandex, and an Adam's apple as big as a kiwi. Scuff marks on his white knees.

"Sorry girls." Jack frowned. "But can you point me in the direction of Figuardo's?"

"Such a waste," the one in black leather said, a look of regret on his face as he pointed to a doorway just down the street.

Jack told them thanks, picked up his knapsack and walked away.

The bar's name was carved in wood above a pair of expansive doors which were open to the sidewalk. The place was no more than thirty feet wide, but it ran deep into a cooler blackness where one could sit to seriously contemplate life without the distractions of noise and diesel fumes drifting in on hot muggy air.

There were a dozen places just like it that ran through old Havana. Relics from the old days that were slowly disintegrating like everything else here. In the fifties, places like the Tropicana were ripe with beautiful Cuban girls who satisfied the needs of American mobsters before Castro's tanks rolled into Havana and the Mafia were politely told to leave.

Hemingway had walked these streets. At La Bodequita Del Medio near the grand old cathedral "Ernesto's" famous ode to *mojitos* and *daiquaries* was displayed amid dusty rum bottles near the ceiling.

Jack walked into Figuardo's and took a seat at the bar, ordered two fingers of Havana Club, straight up.

The bartender took his order and walked away.

Jack took a robusto out of his shirt pocket, struck a wooden match, and pulled on the cigar until it caught fire. He drove the first plume of earthy smoke into his sinuses, resonating nostalgically, like an old black and white movie featuring dancing girls with headdresses made of fruit.

The bartender brought his drink and placed it on a napkin in front of him.

"*Gracias*." Jack said. "Dmitri Raspov, *por favor?*"

"Senor Doyle?" the waiter asked.

"*Si*."

The waiter walked to a telephone at the end of the bar.

Everyone's expecting me, Jack thought, unaware that the waiter had a photo of him next to the cash register. Raspov's e-mail had been short and to the point. Where and when to meet, nothing more.

The walls were full of bric-a-brac, black and white photos of Havana's better days. The Gypsy Kings were playing on a pair of Tanoy speakers hanging in the back of the long narrow room. The lyrics sounded raspy, and the baseline hissed like it was coming from inside a wet cardboard box. Needs duct tape, Jack thought. The rum was smooth. He swallowed twice and wondered who Raspov would be sending to fetch him.

Figuardo's had a dozen tables, four more on a tiny sidewalk patio Jack had passed on his way in. About half of them were taken. Nearby a group of young dark-skinned men and women flirted outrageously with one another. Jack watched as a teenager mischievously cupped his hand beneath a girl's rear end, and was slapped for it. An old Harley roared up and down the street. Its throaty roar rumbled through the bar, causing stacked high-ball glasses to jingle. A leggy girl wearing a short brightly coloured skirt clung to the back of the bike, jiggling.

The bartender watched Jack while rubbing sticky rum circles into a faded teak bar that smelled of disinfectant. Jack drove another cloud of cigar smoke towards the mirror over the bar and caught a glimpse of his tanned face, freshly scrubbed and shaven. He unconsciously wiped a strand of dark hair off his forehead. He needed a haircut, but decided overall he looked pretty good considering his shitty diet and the lack of exercise.

Jack finished three more shots of seven-year-old Havana Club and was feeling much better an hour later when a man took the stool next to his.

"Doyle?"

Jack had trouble taking in the size of him. "That's me," he managed to say.

The largest man Jack had ever seen stared back at him. "Time to go."

A Zil limousine was parked outside. Jack guessed it had to be twenty years old with its torn wine-coloured leather seats and gaping holes where the car phone and bar fridge had once been. It was a relic of Soviet influence that had apparently survived the cannibals who hunted for spare parts all over Castro's junkyard empire.

The lights of Havana faded behind them as they headed west along cracked pavement towards Mariel. They passed stands of palm trees and clusters of ramshackle hovels made of tin and wood. Split oil drums burned brightly in hues of orange and purple along the highway. It was usually the children who tended the fires, while their parents watched lazily from underneath patio roofs fashioned from bamboo and scavenged wood.

The shiny black car skirted high ocean cliffs beneath a full moon that hung like a halogen headlight in the sky.

It had been a long day, and Jack was enjoying the ride, actually thinking about pulling his shoes off. Raspov's welcoming committee was an eye-catcher. Two men, *both*, as it turned out, extraordinarily large. Both had shaved heads as round and brown as sun-cooked chestnuts. Uri was driving. The one sitting in front next to him was Pavel, Uri's brother.

Neither of them had spoken since Jack climbed into the back seat. Uri was humming, something patriotic-sounding with lots of base notes rumbling up his throat and around a cavernous mouth. He snapped his jaw to keep time. Pavel had slipped into a kind of standby mode, hunkered low like a predatory lizard of some kind, waiting for a big, fat, juicy bug to wander by. A quick meal at the end of a long sticky tongue. Uri and Pavel wore ridiculous getups. A pair of Brahma bulls in Hawaiian silk shirts, khaki shorts with thick-soled black shoes, which Jack decided were probably good for stomping people who owed them money, or poor unfortunates they just didn't like. Jack didn't know if they liked him, thought it might be important that they do. Maybe a joke to break the ice.

Hey Pavel. Knock, knock.

Who's there?

Who cares? By the way, what's the Russian mob doing in Cuba? What kind of work do you do for Raspov?

The air conditioning whispered like a dying man but neither brother bothered to open a window. Uri had briefly lowered his, but quickly closed it again when Pavel twisted his head towards his brother and hissed something in Russian that sounded to Jack like a warning.

A moment later Jack caught a whiff of something and looked over at Uri who had said something.

"Sorry." Jack said.

"I said, how long you have known our friend Dmitri?"

"Since Gorbi."

"Gorbi's a bad man," Uri said, "Dmitri doesn't like him. Pavel doesn't like him much either. Me, I don't care."

Pavel gave his brother a cursed stare. "You don't care because you're the son of a Chechen whore. Gorbachev's a traitor."

"A traitor to the motherland, eh Pavel?" Uri said in his thick Russian accent. "Doyle, you agree?"

"Didn't come to talk about politics," Jack replied, hoping it wouldn't piss the monster off. Not with two Soviet patriots, he added to himself.

"This is smart American, Pavel," Uri said to his brother. "I like him."

"Raspov likes him."

"Then we like him also." He looked back at Jack, no whites visible in his eyes. "You will like us too, Doyle — when we've gotten drunk together — tasted some of Raspov's women."

"Whatever you say," Jack said. "But politics is definitely out."

"Even a good patriot such as Pavel likes whores, eh brother? You liked our mother, didn't you?"

"Shut up, Uri. Drive. Don't hum anymore. It makes me remember."

Fifteen minutes later they turned right off the highway onto a narrow tree-lined dirt road. Uri wiped a handkerchief inside his shirt, somewhere in the vicinity of his left armpit, sniffed it for odour.

There was no sign of any interest from Pavel, who had returned to standby mode again.

They drove for about half a mile before Jack spotted more lights. They came to a guardhouse on the outside of a tall metal fence topped with razor wire. Jack suspected the fence was electrified and carried enough juice to knock a man down — maybe even the brothers.

Uri stopped the car.

A uniformed man appeared and tapped Jack's window.

Jack lowered the glass and smiled weakly while the man studied him. "Doyle?"

"Who else would it be, Pepe?" Uri said. "Go back to sleep, you fucking monkey."

The guard gave Uri a killing look and disappeared. A moment later the gate opened and Uri drove to a stop fifty yards ahead. They were parked on a circular driveway in front of a sprawling white stucco bungalow. It had a red barrel-tiled roof and front archways divided by wide ornate columns with sky-blue trim. A dark wood, ground-level veranda stretched the entire length of the house while spot-lit palms and shrubs with thick waxy appendages circled a small fountain populated by illuminated urinating cherubs.

Security lighting pierced the darkness at strategic points on the grounds, turning palm trees into towering giants. Jack saw two men in uniforms hugging the shadows of the building, rifles held lazily at their sides.

Jack opened the car door and got out, stretched his legs while Pavel retrieved his knapsack.

Suddenly the front door swung open, spilling light across the veranda. Dmitri Raspov emerged, wearing nothing but a red housecoat and matching beret. "You bastard Yankee," he growled. "Welcome to Cuba. One of the last places on earth you'll find a good communist."

"Still wearing the party colour." Jack smiled, embracing his old friend with a back-slapping hug.

"What would Stalin think if I weren't?" Raspov replied. After a second he pulled away and smiled. "How are you, Jack?"

"Well, Dmitri. Well," Jack answered. "And needing a drink."

"You and I, old friend."

When Dmitri led them into the house Jack saw why Dmitri couldn't meet him at Figuardo's. The two girls were no more than eighteen and excruciatingly beautiful. They lounged together on a red Caucasian ottoman and giggled when they saw Jack.

"*Más esta noche.*" Raspov bent and kissed their brown cheeks, "*A casa ahora ir.*"

They looked hungrily at Jack, pouted, and then swung a pair of astounding rear ends out the door.

Dmitri winked at Jack. "I think they tire of this old broken-down Georgian," he said. "A tall handsome *Yanqui* would be more to their satisfaction."

Jack watched them leave. "Ukrainian, I thought."

"Who can remember when you've had as many covers as I?"

Raspov's housecoat flapped open as he slapped his feet across travertine marble towards the back of the house. "Time for drinks…to catch up on our lost years!" His voice echoed through a palatial foyer crowned with a huge chandelier that cast shafts of blue light through a thousand Murano teardrops.

Jack walked slowly through the house. On his left, above the ottoman, hung paintings of a birch tree forest and to the right of that, the Russian steppes with a Siberian train in the distance. An antique brass samovar sat in one corner. Russian dacha with a Spanish colonial bent, Jack thought. As he walked farther into the house he heard the limo pulling away. Uri and Pavel were probably taking the girls home. A moment later Jack found Dmitri mixing drinks at an island in the centre of a large kitchen which was full of stainless steel, granite, and terra cotta tile. What remained of a suckling pig lay on a sparkling silver tray, exotic fruit half eaten on white porcelain plates.

"My young guests were hungry as Russian bears," Raspov said. "It pleasures me to watch them eat so, to nourish their young welcoming bodies."

Doyle felt a tinge of revulsion. But he chose not to voice what he was thinking.

"Care to eat, Jack?"

"No thanks."

The old spook had gone to fat. Despite the Cuban sun, he managed the pallor of an uncooked bratwurst. His housecoat had fallen open, exposing an ample gut. Raspov removed his beret to reveal grey hair which was still cut to military length, but thinning over visible age spots on his scalp. He wore gold wire-rim glasses that magnified cold grey eyes and had thick generous lips that were his only redeeming facial feature. KGB Bohemian, Jack thought.

"You were met well?" Dmitri brought the drinks, something red and fruity with rum in them. He looked at the expression on Jack's face and retied his housecoat.

Jack tasted his drink, licked the sweetness from his lips, and wished instead for some of Dmitri's iced vodka. "Eventually, thanks to you," he said. Jack then told Dmitri about his gunboat escort.

Raspov smiled. "Good," he said. "A week ago an American yacht pulled a dozen *balseros* from their inner tubes about forty miles out, Cuban exiles coming to take their loved ones to the land of dreams. A gunboat like the one that found you today was dispatched to engage the interloper." Raspov shook his head. Sipped. "Such a stink it would have caused sinking an American yacht. More sword play between Havana and Washington. You remember little Elian? Anyway, Raul retracted his talons and the yacht was permitted to flee. The coastal defense forces want their revenge. I dispatched an escort to make certain it wasn't you."

"Much appreciated," said Jack. He then asked Raspov about the brothers.

Dmitri laughed. "Big-hearted Chechens those two. Gentle as bears until they are fucked with."

"What's with the fresh air phobia?"

Dmitri turned serious. "You haven't seen the flying livestock around here yet." It was a statement. Raspov shook his head and swallowed a good measure of his fruity drink. "They were driving up from Havana a month ago. Pavel was drunk. Had his big fat head stuck out the window singing one of his patriotic songs when something flew into his large mouth."

The image brought a smile to Jack's face.

"So Uri has to pull over. There was Pavel, crawling in the dirt, choking on whatever it was, and Uri is pounding him on the back, trying to save his miserable life. You know, brotherly love. Anyway some great big fucking cockroach with wings pops out of Pavel's throat. He doesn't like it, even a bit. So out comes his big Russian gun and he begins to shoot. Uri has to force him back in the car and get moving quick before he can reload."

They were both laughing now.

After a moment Jack looked at him. "They look like mob, Dmitri?" Jack knew he was pushing into dangerous territory.

Raspov waited a moment. "Uri and Pavel were KGB – not mob."

"Not the charm school types," Jack said.

"No," Dmitri said. "But they had other talents."

Jack cocked an eyebrow.

"They found them as children," Raspov continued. "Not more than two...maybe three. A pair of little savages. Alone with Papa and Mama. Their parents had already killed each other. Who knows why? It doesn't matter. Both were Chechen. Anyway, Papa had a big knife in his chest. Mama with a bullet...right here." Dmitri placed a finger in the centre of his forehead.

Jack imagined the scene. A barren Moscow apartment, naked light bulbs. Two bodies, and two children, though it was easier to image an infant yeti than Uri and Pavel as toddlers.

"Anyway," Raspov said. "When police kick in door, Uri and Pavel have been there four, maybe six days. No way to tell, though the corpses smell very bad, because as you can imagine they are rotting, even though there is little heat. So there they are: little Uri and Pavel, both of them hungry as black bears and trying to force their way into the bedroom where their parents' bodies are ripening. Not because they want love. But because they need to eat." Dmitri stopped for a moment to let it sink in.

Jack grimaced.

Dmitri took another swallow. "The KGB took them both. Their whole lives. School, everything. Like little wolf boys. They taught them human things. And things not so human. Uri and Pavel were good students." Raspov nodded. "With special talents."

Jack preferred not to think about their special talents.

Raspov went on, "No more Soviet Union, no more use for them. So I took them. They are mine now."

"Your retirement gift from the KGB," Jack added. Raspov's KGB service had never been a secret, not after that first night in Moscow.

"Yes, my retirement gift. Like a gold watch." Raspov laughed loudly.

"You were a better spy than reporter, Dmitri," Jack said, remembering that night in Moscow when Raspov had skillfully drawn him away so that at the end of the night a "brown envelope" could change hands.

Dmitri feigned hurt. "Ouch. Eventually, I'll forgive you for that," he said.

"You've done well."

Dmitri waved an expansive hand. "I suppose. But the fucking country is a shambles, and I grow somewhat tired of hunting for toilet

ANGELS OF MARADONA

paper and soap. Even for someone like me there are shortages. Castro, on the other hand. Lavish homes and a personal fortune. Do you know he's paid twenty million per year from the French alone for the Havana Club label? The revolution has served him well, don't you agree?"

Jack did.

Raspov continued, "When the Soviet Union collapsed, I had no job. Hundreds of us, told to go home. Just like that." Raspov snapped his fingers, let the sound hang there a second or two. "It was also bad news for Castro. No more Ladas and caviar or spare parts for anything."

"It shows," Jack said.

"Now he's an old man who still sees the CIA under his bed," Dmitri said. "Word is he still wears a hairnet to protect his precious beard from the Mongoose."

Jack jumped in. "Castro brought you in to head his intelligence apparatus. You were qualified. A KGB colonel, suddenly unemployed, with 'talents' of your own. He pays you to keep an eye on things, especially in the Americas where the socialist spark is waiting to ignite any number of fires. Sounds like your kind of heaven."

"Or hell."

"You left hell, Dmitri," Jack said. "By comparison this is heaven."

"Yes, I suppose," he said. Dmitri refilled their glasses and then led him outside to a small patio where they sat.

Jack smelled the scent of flowers. Soft lights stretched along a wide stone pathway that led in the direction of the ocean.

They both stared into the darkness for a while, and then Dmitri spoke. "You look bad."

"Thanks, pal."

"That's what friends are for."

"Some days are better than others," Jack said.

Raspov lowered his voice. "No doubt."

"This helps," Jack said, raising the glass to the moonlight. "In large amounts."

Neither of them said anything for a couple of minutes. In the distance the surf slapped an easy rhythm against Raspov's private beach.

"I was sorry to hear about what happened," Dmitri said eventually.

Jack brought the glass to his lips, swallowed twice before replying. "Thanks."

"She was a beautiful girl," he said.

"Yeah," Jack said. He thought for a moment. "We grew up in the same place." It seemed like a good place to start. "I left after my dad died. Moved to Boston with my aunt. That's where I went to college. Kaitlin stayed on the island and eventually went to J-school on the west coast. We went our separate ways until she came back east. Not long after that we hired her." Jack looked at Raspov ruefully. "It was my call."

"And a good one by the sounds of it," Raspov said. "You were her mentor?"

Jack looked directly at him. "She didn't need it, Dmitri. She was already good. Very good. Taught *me* a thing or two."

"Including regret."

"Yep."

"Colombia's a dangerous place, Jack, and you're blaming yourself – maybe unwisely."

"My call," Jack repeated. "Besides, who else is there to blame?" Jack gulped his drink and looked at his friend expectantly.

Raspov remained silent.

"Right," Jack said. The same look he'd seen on Walter Carmichael's face the day he came to collect him in Cartagena. "Let's get the hell out of here, Jack, before someone decides to take out the hospital," he had said, dryly.

Jack thought about Seth's video. The picture he'd printed from it. He'd haul it out soon enough, before Raspov got too deeply into the alcohol. In the meantime he'd relax a little, enjoy the company and the sound of the surf. The rum drink, less so. Its syrupy sweetness was beginning to turn his stomach.

Raspov must have sensed it. "Thank God the embassy has a good supply of Stolichnaya," he said.

"Thought communists didn't believe in God," Jack replied, smiling.

"Only when it comes to vodka," Raspov said, before heading back inside.

Jack stared towards the ocean, which was shrouded by darkness behind a line of tall palms. He imagined the waves licking at sand that had the look and feel of refined sugar. For a moment he desired a long walk along the sea, a chance to rethink everything, including the conclusion that led him here – to Raspov. He wasn't sure about it, or the much bigger choice he'd made. He let his mind wander back to the Moscow summit, to the night a brown envelope was dropped into his lap that transformed him into a bonafide network star. Jack's story seriously imperiled the Soviet bargaining position, and thus, the summit. Jack and Raspov had not spoken about it since. To do so would have been dangerous. Though he still wondered, why him? Why had he been the chosen one?

Raspov returned with two frosty tumblers filled to the brim with fine vodka. They toasted and drank and then Jack turned to him – serious. "How did Rimbey get the story before me?"

"We gave it to him. Just the broad strokes. But you were the one, Jack. You got it all. Remember? Our side's position on offensive and strategic nuclear weapons – warheads, throw-weight and the like. The absolute maximum reductions Soviet negotiators could live with. The party apparatchiks were outraged over Gorbachev's readiness to capitulate. They saw it as surrendering their big stick, giving in to the enemies of communism." Raspov adjusted his housecoat, brought his glass up again and paused. "We needed the Cold War to continue. What would we have done without it? Especially those of us who actually wore uniforms and were dedicated to defending the Rodina. Gorbachev was going to bargain away Soviet intermediate-range missiles pointed at Western Europe. What were we to do? Spit at the invading NATO forces? The Warsaw Pact was screaming bloody murder."

"Sounds like Comrade Gorbachev might have been living on borrowed time," Jack interrupted.

Raspov stared at him. "Believe me. All options were considered. Even that one. But in the end we knew that killing the architect of Glasnost would have created even deeper problems. Reagan would have used Gorbachev's demise to ramp up the arms race even further." Raspov rubbed his fingers together. "Hard currency, Jack. We were short on that as you know."

"You were bankrupt," Jack said.

"That's right. So we improvised. Showing Mikhail's hand effectively ruined his ability to reach a weapons reduction agreement that would have satisfied his opponents within the party, the politburo, and of course the Soviet military establishment. As I said, Rimbey was given just a taste so that he would become the spark under your ass, so to speak. It worked."

Jack remembered the pressure from Carmichael to get confirmation and reaction — "but for Chrissake get the goddamn story."

"What happened afterwards?" Jack asked Raspov.

"The great Soviet Union collapsed — and it all became a moot point."

Jack screwed up his face. "I mean before that." *Smart-ass.*

Raspov tipped his head back. "Shit hit the proverbial fan. Gorbachev blamed his enemies for the leak. He exacted his pound of flesh. Many of the patriots ended up dead or imprisoned. Mostly dead." Raspov lifted his hand, squeezed an imaginary trigger and blew phantom smoke from the tip of his finger. "I kept a low profile and somehow survived. Eventually Gorbachev got what he wanted anyway. The Cold War was over. Communism collapsed. The rest, as they say, is history." Dmitri paused, swallowed. After a moment he said, "I know you were interrogated, Jack."

"Our side was pretty pissed too. They demanded to know where I got my information. My source."

"And you didn't give it to them."

"You kidding? For a journalist the protection of sources is sacrosanct." Jack turned to Dmitri. "I told them to eat shit."

Raspov laughed. "Well said, and no doubt you made a lifetime friend of your CIA." The Russian slipped into silence, gazed into the darkness.

Jack looked at him and said, "The kind of friends you don't need."

The moon slipped behind thin strips of low hanging cloud that looked like trails of grey ash from the countless fires that burned in split oil drums he had seen on the way up from the city.

"By the way. Why me?"

"Pardon?'

"Why was I the chosen one?"

"Simple," Raspov replied, grinning. "Your network had the biggest... what is it you say? The biggest 'market share.'"

"Ratings. The highest ratings." Jack felt slightly deflated.

"Yes, more eyeballs watching as you delivered the goods. You were the biggest bang for our buck so to speak. No pun intended."

"Great," Jack said. "Just great." He'd been used by people who didn't like Gorbi's plans for a brave new world. He suspected it then. He was certain of it now. "I don't think I ever thanked you for the story of a lifetime, Dmitri," Jack said. "Even though I felt like a whore."

"Whore? Maybe, Jack," Raspov said. "Whore or a hero."

"The network signed me to a sweet contract when I got home." Jack grinned.

Raspov sneered. "You became a star and I was still lining up for toilet paper and week-old bread."

Jack chuckled, waved his hand across the grounds. "Looks like you haven't done too badly."

"A good whore also," Raspov snorted. "Castro's whore."

"Welcome aboard," Jack said. "There's no whore like an old whore."

"Spoken like a real capitalist pig."

"I prefer pig-dog if you don't mind"

"As you wish. Capitalist pig-dog, with bourgeoisie thrown in."

"That's better. Anyway, we all have our crosses to bear," Jack replied. "Some heavier than others."

They looked at each other, the kind of look between tired soldiers. Faces full of affection.

"So, what can I do for you, my American friend?"

It was time, Jack thought. Raspov wouldn't be kept waiting. But first. "Your charm and your hospitality," he said and then showed him his empty glass. "And another one of these."

"Right this way," Dmitri said, rising from his seat. "I have a feeling we have business to talk about, and as you can see, I'm quivering with anticipation."

"You don't know the half of it," Jack said, as he hoisted himself from his chair.

FORTY-FIVE

They made their way back to the kitchen where Raspov pulled the vodka bottle from a stainless steel freezer. Raspov studied Jack while he poured, then handed him his glass. "How do you like the house?"

"The revolution is treating you well."

Raspov grinned. "The revolution was doomed the day Fidel rolled into Havana. Gorbachev the Traitor stayed here once. You'll be sleeping in his bed tonight."

Jack tested the drink. "Gorbi is long gone, Dmitri. So why the electrified fence and armed guards? Probably find motion and sound detectors around the perimeter fences too."

"The state has many enemies, Jack."

"The state? Or you?"

Raspov didn't answer.

Jack realized his mistake. He'd pushed too far. He placed his drink on the counter and was in the process of reconsidering his reason for coming when Raspov opened his mouth to speak. "It's good to see you, Jack. But I know you're not here for the free vodka and my sparkling conversation."

Jack seemed to be studying his glass. A lazy finger drew something meaningless in the condensation. "What if ..." He stopped. Set it up, Jack. From the beginning.

"They never found her body," Jack said, nearly too quietly to hear. "I mean there were bits and pieces of bodies but some of the victims were never found. A goddamn nightmare for the identification people and next of kin." Next of kin, he thought. Kaitlin's father, Argus. That was another story. Jack pressed on. "We were seated outside in the back behind this wall. Some kind of courtyard. Then she left for a minute. Went inside to use the restroom. They said everyone in that part of the building was vaporized because it was so close to the epicenter of the blast."

Dmitri clucked his tongue.

Jack continued, "Got a bang on my head. A bad concussion, lacerations and bruises, that kind of thing. I got lucky," he added. "No one could be sure of anything except the number of dead. Even that hasn't been locked down yet." Jack sucked in air. "The network flew me to Miami when I could be moved. But I went back about a week later…had to. I cornered the Colombians. The FBI was gone by then, and the Colombians…they claimed there was nothing I could do. They basically told me to get lost, not to come back."

Bitterness morphed onto Jack's face. "The justice minister was the target. Amillo, his wife and daughter too. The next day they found the bomber's wife and kids. All executed in a burned-out farmhouse." Jack pinched the bridge of his nose. Paused a moment. "The network told me to take as long as I needed so I went back a second time and harassed anyone I could. A couple days later they escorted me to the airport and told me to fuck off. I demanded the embassy intervene and *they* basically slammed the door in my face." Jack sipped quietly. "One of the staffers told me I was treading on dangerous ground."

Raspov nodded. "The assassination of their justice minister was a victory for the bad guys, Jack. They didn't need you reminding them of that. The extradition treaty, remember? Amillo was on it – a friend of the Denton administration who was about to open the door to the long arm of American justice. Even with all their Blackhawk helicopters and fancy weapons they couldn't protect Amillo. The cartels are sending a message: no one's safe, especially if you're a friend of Uncle Sam. After a while your friends are no longer your friends. Everyone's nervous, especially the cartels."

Jack knew Dmitri was right.

"The last thing they need is an American news network poking around." Raspov paused. "Talking about the misspent billions and the sham of a war on coca."

It made sense to Jack, but most of what Dmitri was saying had nothing to do with the reason he was here, which was the mind-blowing resurrection of Kaitlin O'Rourke. "There's this thing that's driving me nuts," Jack said. "Something I still can't figure out."

Raspov half listened while Jack spoke. How blind he was to the truth. Kaitlin O'Rourke was dead. *Who knew you'd be there that night?* Raspov thought about the other one. She had what Raspov wanted. Once he found her, Raspov would take it, and anyone who stood in his way. *Well…* Raspov never finished the thought. Jack was still talking. *Forget the O'Rourke woman, Jack. She's not important. Never was. Tell me why you're here, though I suspect I know already.*

Jack got up and wandered to the patio door. He caught the fragrance of something sweet and thought about his mother, her perfume, and strangely, how he felt that day standing in front of her coffin, with Kaitlin at his side trying to be brave. A fragile courage. Jack turned to Raspov. "Kaitlin wanted to tell me something that night, but couldn't. I'm sure of it."

Raspov closed his eyes. *How much was O'Rourke able to find out about her past before…?* Thankfully, whatever it was died with her. "Unfortunately, Jack," he said, "it does no good to wonder about such things. It's too late now."

Somewhere a night creature called out, and Jack caught sight of a small form moving on the grass, a night lizard of some kind, glowing eyes. It scurried into the bushes and disappeared.

Dmitri waved it off. "Keep your windows closed tonight," he said. "They're everywhere."

Jack laughed nervously. "Sure." A moment passed before he spoke again, nearly a whisper. "Maybe not too late, Dmitri."

Dmitri knew immediately what Jack was going to say. *He's seen her. The other one.* Raspov was sure of it. Also sure Doyle could bring her to him. The woman's connection with O'Rourke and Doyle was mind-boggling. An astonishing coincidence. Also incredibly fortuitous.

"Go on," Raspov said, barely able to conceal his excitement. "What's this about?"

"I wish I knew," Jack replied.

FORTY-SIX

Dmitri Raspov was the picture of incredulity. He managed a quick intake of breath followed by a well-timed pause, and then a slurp of vodka to cap his performance. "I will hear that again," he finally said.

Jack knew it sounded crazy but continued anyway. "I have video, Dmitri. And it was shot after the bombing."

Raspov feigned skepticism. "I'd say give me half an hour and I'll show you video of Jack Doyle having lamb with Osama Bin Laden."

"OBL doesn't eat meat."

Raspov didn't bother asking Jack how he knew that.

Jack sat again. "Shot less than a week ago."

"Where?"

"Colombia."

"By who?"

"Someone who knows her." Jack reached into his back pocket and retrieved a folded piece of shiny photographic paper. Slowly he opened it. "I printed this from the video," he said, placing the grainy print on the table in front of Raspov.

Dmitri's breath caught. It *was* Mendoza. Still in Colombia as of a week ago. It's no wonder Jack believed this was the O'Rourke woman. They were identical. Dmitri had met Kaitlin only once, in Montreal after the death of a former Canadian prime minister who was greatly admired by Castro. Castro had summoned Raspov to accompany him to the funeral. Jack and Kaitlin were covering the story. They had met for dinner later in some jazz club.

Raspov stared at the photo for what seemed an eternity, muttered something in Russian, and then lifted his eyes to Jack. "As beautiful as I remember her," he said.

FORTY-SEVEN

The next morning Jack was certain of what he had to do. He'd spent most of the night thinking about it. He just didn't know if Raspov would agree to help. The two of them were taking breakfast in the shade of a palm tree, listening to the waves crash against a strip of sugary white sand that snaked its way east and west along the coast as far as Jack could see. In the daylight Jack saw the ruin that blackened Dmitri's hacienda – grounds that stretched to the ocean were scarred by neglect. Weather-beaten palm trees were stooped and bare. A large swimming pool was cracked and empty, surrounded by filthy ceramic tile. The country was in a shambles. Dmitri saw a look of mild disgust on Jack's face. He shrugged. "Like everything else here, Jack. In need of repair."

Jack smelled the fragrance of roses and orchids clustered in resplendent flower beds that dotted the landscape and might have taken a decade to cultivate. The heat was already stifling. "Some day the embargo will end, Dmitri."

"Thankfully I won't be here to enjoy it," Dmitri replied. "I'm rather homesick lately." Dmitri spooned the flesh from a grapefruit, efficiently gutted it section by section before slurping the pieces into his mouth. He swallowed and then spoke, "It's all very strange that your friend would appear magically in Colombia when she is supposed to be dead. Almost too strange, Jack."

Jack watched as a fisherman pulled his silvery catch from a net a hundred yards offshore. He thought again about Kaitlin's disappearance. *Disappearance?* If news of her death had been so greatly exaggerated, then where the hell was she? Kidnapping didn't fit. There'd been no ransom. Besides, the woman in the video was no hostage. There were other possibilities but they seemed just as unlikely, and Jack cast them aside like mug shots. "Maybe I'm wrong. Maybe it's not Kaitlin. It's crazy in a way to think it is."

"Possible," Raspov replied. "But if you really believed that you wouldn't be here. Anyway, I've seen the picture and I must be crazy too…because I'm convinced of who she is."

"Montreal was years ago, Dmitri."

Raspov looked at him. "That's a hard face to forget."

Jack continued to play devil's advocate. "So she just got up and walked out that night, decided she needed a change of scenery – permanently?"

"Who says she just walked away? It's Colombia, remember? People disappear all the time."

Jack looked doubtful. "Yes, but usually they stay disappeared."

"Good point," Raspov replied. "The video. Where was the video shot?"

In that moment Jack saw something flash across Dmitri's face. Hunger maybe, excitement over a hunt that hadn't yet begun. The old spook trying to catch a scent. *What was it?*

"Jack?"

"I wish I knew," Jack finally replied, feeling strangely uneasy now. "The e-mail had nothing but an attachment," he continued. "Nothing more. And New York hasn't heard from Seth Pollard in a couple of days."

"Mystery upon mystery," Raspov said. "So, as I said before, what can I do for you, Mister Doyle?"

Jack had thought hard about it during the night, the grainy picture of Kaitlin on the dresser next to his bed. It was driving him crazy. A full minute passed before he spoke. "I need to get inside the country," he said, "without the knowledge of the people who basically threw me out. But first I need to find Seth Pollard." Jack unfolded the print again, placing it on the table between them. "And then I need to find this woman."

Raspov smoothed the front of his light cotton shirt and adjusted a napkin which was tucked into its collar. "That's all?"

"Yeah. That's all. And I need to do this…now."

"Deadlines. You reporters and your deadlines."

Jack ignored it. "What about it?"

"You have rather large expectations."

"OK. I know that. So?"

"You could expect no help or protection from the Colombian government. Even your own embassy."

"I know that."

Raspov dabbed at the juice that glistened on his chin. "You'd never survive."

It was a warning Jack wanted to slap away. Instead, he pushed his plate aside, remnants of scrambled eggs in a fiery red sauce. He brought a thick porcelain cup to his lips and gulped the last of his coffee. "I've been in tight spots before," he said.

"Not like this," Dmitri intoned. "The rebels have been on a killing spree for months now." Raspov held up a fist, revealing one finger at a time. "Besides the rebels you've got ELN, the paras and the Colombian army. And don't forget the drug lords. Everyone's a target – judges, police captains, humanitarian workers, and peasants – all fair game. Officials are gunned down in the street every day. The mayor of Bogotá wears a bullet-proof vest with a heart-shaped opening on his chest as an invitation to his enemies. A man who relishes his drama, don't you think?" Raspov stopped to allow it to sink in. "Murder, extortion, kidnapping. It's all about the coca now, no more bullshit Marxist ideology from FARC. Everyone wants a piece of the pie."

Jack listened silently while a warm breeze rustled nearby bushes. After a moment Dmitri rose and gestured for him to follow. He led them inside the villa, down a long hallway to a large cluttered office at the back of the house. Two computers blinked and hummed, a fax machine was rolling out paper, and Jack saw what looked like a secure telephone on an ornate wooden desk. The walls were covered with military maps of Cuba, Colombia, and a number of other South American countries.

"It's OK, Jack, nothing classified for you to spy." Raspov was grinning, motioning him towards a plush sofa in the centre of the room. "No need to dispatch Pavel and Uri to 'eliminate' you."

"You're a real friend, Dmitri." Jack let the sarcasm drip from his words.

"Thanks," Dmitri said as he walked to a large safe in the corner of the office. He punched numbers on a keypad and swung the door open. Then he pulled out a large brown envelope.

For a moment Jack was distracted by a portrait of Stalin on the wall above Raspov's desk. Raspov followed his stare. "He was a sick bastard, yes, but a sick *communist* bastard."

"We all have our idols, Dmitri."

Raspov walked to the sofa and sat. He placed the envelope between them.

Jack looked at it. "Show and Tell?"

Dmitri ignored him, spread his hands out. "We have minor assets in Colombia," he said, businesslike. "Cuba does what it can for ELN and FARC, but mostly ELN. The government is weak. But lots of American money keeps them going. Anti-narcotics money that feeds their military. No secret. Check the internet." Raspov thrust his chin in the general direction of his computer hardware which was buzzing and beeping.

"It's not been the same in Colombia since Pablo. The cartels are fractured. That's good news for the DEA which has been able to pick away at the smaller targets. Divide and conquer, so to speak."

None of this was any secret. Jack watched Raspov's face for clues to where this was headed.

Raspov continued, "There are rumblings the cartels are really pissed, especially with all that talk of an extradition treaty with your country. You remember what happened last time. It was all-out war. Eventually it led to the collapse of the Medellin group."

Escobar, Jack remembered, had surrendered. He escaped custody and was later tracked down and shot.

Raspov laid the photo on the sofa next to Jack. "To borrow a good American expression: it's a shit storm brewing there right now. And this is the man responsible."

Jack picked up the photograph. Studied it. The man was getting out of a limo, immaculately dressed, dark features. Swarthy was the word that came to mind. The man was staring directly into the camera — defiantly. Full lips and sculpted cheekbones that might have been a sign of breeding. He was surrounded by bodyguards with the requisite bulges beneath their armpits. To Jack the man looked like he had something important to prove.

Raspov continued. "His name is Branko Montello. Scares the shit out of your DEA. What's the phrase? Bad ass. He's a hundred bad asses in one."

Jack didn't think the guy looked that tough. "Pablo was a bad ass too."

"You're right. Pablo was a psychopath. Raspov motioned to the photograph, but didn't touch it, as if to have done so would have contaminated him in some way. "A daisy compared to Montello."

Jack looked at the photograph again. "So what's your point?"

"Our friend Montello has declared open season on Americans," Raspov said. "You carry the passport, you die." Raspov stopped. He seemed to be considering something. "It's the whole country, Jack. He's even offering a bounty. I don't have to tell you what that means. For you — and if she's still in country — for Kaitlin."

Jesus, Jack thought. The goddamn country was already one of the most dangerous places in the world. Now this. There wasn't much he could say. "I have network credentials."

Dmitri laughed. "Yes, Jack. Credentials made of plastic, not miracles." He stopped for a moment, then turned serious. "More than a hundred of your kind have been murdered in Colombia. They had credentials too, my friend."

Jack thought quietly about what Raspov was saying. He'd already decided to take the risk. If Kaitlin were alive, he'd find her. He didn't know exactly how yet, but he would.

Dmitri must have been reading his mind again. The Russian looked at Jack, rubbed his hands together and began to speak. "Maybe she found a story," Dmitri said. "A big exclusive that she wants to horde. Become a big network star like Jack Doyle."

Jack shook his head. "It's not the way we work."

"How would I know?" Raspov replied. "An old communist who relishes the good old days when we controlled the great journalistic organs of the state — and crushed dissent like grapes."

Jack laughed, showing the warmth and respect he felt for the older man. "Thank God those days are over."

"You're a cynic, Doyle."

"A democrat," Jack replied.

"Be a realist, instead. This little adventure of yours could come with a high price."

Jack studied his friend's face for a full moment before answering. "What choice do I have?" he finally said.

Raspov nodded. "All right, Jack, maybe it's time we took a trip. Pack your things."

Jack smiled. "I already have."

"Good. We leave tonight."

FORTY-EIGHT

THE WHITE HOUSE.

Frederick Denton was working late when the soft knock came at his door. Only one person would have been permitted to do that at one o'clock in the morning. Paul Braithwaite looked tired and drawn. "Good morning, Mr. President," he said as he shuffled into the Oval Office.

"Is it that late, Paul?" The president looked at his watch. "Well, well. Guess it is. Take a seat." Denton watched as Braithwaite walked to the sofa and sat. "I trust our Colombian friends understood my message," he said, squaring papers on his desk.

"Loud and clear," Braithwaite replied. "And I don't think they liked it."

"No one likes an ultimatum," the president added, rising from his desk. "Especially not one coming from the president of the United States." Denton walked to an armchair opposite Braithwaite and collapsed into it. He ran slender fingers through a head of thick grey hair. "I don't think they'll be getting any sleep tonight either."

Denton took a measure of his old friend. His chief of staff carried at least twenty surplus pounds on a five-foot eight-inch frame and was still wearing the disheveled suit he'd had on when he escorted the Colombian president and his ambassador into the Oval Office earlier that evening. "Even a Yale man sleeps now and then. We were roommates remember. I suspect you're here for a reason at this ungodly hour. So spill it."

Braithwaite studied the president for a moment, measuring something in his tired face. "Reservations," he said.

"Shoot."

Braithwaite unconsciously rubbed his bald head, a nervous gesture the press had learned to watch for when something juicy was happening behind the scenes. Braithwaite rubbed part of his skull blood-red during the Korean mess the year before.

The president crossed his legs and sank farther into the chair. "Don't keep me waiting. This old Yale brain needs a good five hours' sleep, starting in about ten minutes."

Braithwaite knew the president had no intention of turning in for the night. The man hadn't had a proper night's rest in months. "Operation Javelin," Braithwaite said simply.

For a moment President Denton remained silent. It was because of their long friendship that Paul Braithwaite could walk into the Oval Office this late with reservations about a vital military operation that had already been approved by him with support from the Joint Chiefs, not to mention the FBI and the CIA, and likely, when it was executed, every sick and tired American who had voted him into office on the promise of change.

"We've been over this," Denton finally said. "Remember? Thinking outside the box. Playing by our rules, not theirs."

Braithwaite looked at his boss. "Mr. President, not three hours ago you assured the president of Colombia that the United States intends to renew and increase military aid to Colombia."

"That's right," Denton cut in. "If Operation Javelin's not military aid, then what is?"

"With all due respect, Mr. President, I don't think that's what the Colombians have in mind. They've reiterated support for the extradition treaty which could likely be our most effective strategy."

"Look what happened to Amillo. He supported the extradition treaty. He's dead. Don't underestimate the impact of that on the others." Frustration deepened the lines in Denton's face. "For Chrissake, Paul. You know the score. We've spent billions and it hasn't made one iota of a difference. Coca production has doubled in the past three years. The DEA admits cocaine shipments are way up. Those cartel bastards keep getting richer, more arrogant. If anything, our interdiction efforts have only made their 'product' more valuable." Denton got up to pace. "They say the drug problem is America's problem – so goddamn it, the solution's going to be an American solution. It's our sacred right."

"That may be, sir," Braithwaite said. "But what we're talking about here is a direct violation of a nation's sovereignty. That makes us marauders. With all due respect, what kind of solution is that?"

"It's my solution, Paul. It's the solution Americans have been calling for. Everyone who's had someone they know murdered or robbed or had their lives wasted while some third-world country gets fat on our misery." Denton raised a finger to punctuate what he was saying. "They violate our borders everyday with their illegal drugs. What about our sovereignty?"

Braithwaite silently chastised himself for not being better prepared.

"Goddamn it, Paul." Denton balled his fists. "I've had enough of these drug barons flipping us the bird while they peddle their poison and kill our children. Those kids in New Orleans..." Denton sat again, exhausted. "What about them?"

What about Stevie? Braithwaite didn't say.

Denton rubbed his face, loosened his tie and pulled the shirt collar away from his neck. His cheeks puffed with an exasperated breath. "How many more families have to be destroyed?" Denton went silent. After a moment he wearily pulled himself up and walked to the window. "I've met with the ambassadors from every one of those coca producing countries and they all smile and say 'yes, Mr. President, we agree something has to be done.'" Denton stared through the bullet-proof glass at the Rose Garden and the expansive south lawn. "Fine. I say the first step is stopping the criminals in their own countries. Colombia's failed miserably at every turn, like the others. The CIA has had to slave one of its birds full-time just to keep track of the drug labs and the movements of that Montello asshole. And now the narco terrorists and those bloody Marxists have turned the country into a bloody slaughter house again."

Braithwaite understood completely the reason for his boss's frustration. The farmers produced the coca leaves at profits that dwarfed the paltry sums they were paid for legal crops. Programs to encourage the harvesting of harmless crops had been tried and failed. Hundreds of millions of dollars had been wasted. Coca's history in places like Colombia went back a thousand years before Spanish conquerors ever set foot there. Trying to convince Colombians to turn their backs on coca would be like telling American farmers to abandon forever their fields of wheat and barley and corn. Braithwaite realized the president was asking him a question. "Excuse me, sir."

"What are the polls saying?"

Braithwaite opened a folder on his lap. "Fresh numbers confirming a lot of what we already knew. Illegal drugs are rapidly becoming the key area where we're perceived to be losing ground." Braithwaite lifted a page. "Once you cut to the chase. Budget deficit and social security finances are still highest on the list, but there has been a dramatic shift in the numbers on drugs – with a strong sub-group fretting about crime. The hard numbers say seven out of ten are worried or extremely worried about illegal drug use in this country."

"That's quite a shift."

Braithwaite held up a finger. "Those murders in New Orleans could be skewing the numbers somewhat, but I believe this is substantively accurate, at least as a snapshot."

Denton nodded solemnly. "No fiddling with demographics or party leanings?"

"No, Mr. President. As many young as old were surveyed, and across party lines."

"So," Denton said. "What's the upshot?"

"Basically, with the economy humming on all cylinders people are worried less about their wallets and jobs which is good news. The downside, and I mean *if* there's a downside, is the public agenda has swung even more than we thought towards issues that we're having a hell of a time with. Drugs, and to a lesser extent, crime. The states are also ramping up the rhetoric, complaining we're offloading hard costs for the war on drugs onto them. Their jails are overcrowded, even though we've budgeted another four billion dollars on new prisons. Because their prisons are bursting at the seams, the courts are reducing sentences which feeds the cycle of repeat offences and the perception the justice system doesn't care about crime —nor does the White House. Those myths are especially rampant in rural districts which might seem to be a statistical anomaly except there has been a dramatic upsurge in the use of crystal meth — or crank, as the farm boys like to call it."

"It's like a balloon," Denton said. "Squeeze one end, it bulges at the other."

"The pipelines for coke and heroin aren't as well developed in places like Shelby, Montana. Crank is made with the stuff under your sink and a lot cheaper."

Denton shook his head. "What is it, fertilizer and window cleaner?"

"Not quite," Braithwaite replied. "Two days ago a Methodist minister and his wife were killed outside Chicago when a meth lab blew up in the basement of their church. The son was supplying half the town. The church is gone. The kid's facing manslaughter charges."

"Send a note to the congregation."

"Will do, sir."

Denton walked over to his chief of staff and sat, signaling a change of topic. "What are we hearing from Moscow?"

"Only that something's up. We've got assets working overtime on it."

"Good," Denton said. "If there's a Russian angle on this I need to know about it. In the meantime we need to get our hands on those goddamn drug lords." Denton looked with empathy at his chief of staff. "I know you'd prefer to do this by the book. That's what I'd expect from the former dean of Yale Law."

"You're correct on that," Braithwaite replied.

"The law fails us, my friend," said Denton. "Always has." The president turned to stare out the window again and thought about the commitment he'd made to Americans — the promise he'd made to himself, to his dead son — and now the parents of those murdered children in New Orleans.

"Operation Javelin stands as approved. I want an update on planning in the morning. Thank you, Paul, that'll be all."

"Yes, Mr. President," Braithwaite said, pulling his tired frame from the soft clutches of the sofa. "Goodnight, sir."

"Goodnight, Paul."

Without looking back, Braithwaite shuffled from the office and shut the door.

FORTY-NINE

Off the Colombian Coast. 0300 hours.

Jack gazed into a curtain of black and then added a notch of trim to lower her nose and to increase speed. The thrum of powerful engines rolled away on the spume of inky waves as they cut a path through the moonless night.

He shifted his attention to the radar screen radiating a ghostly green light in the dark cabin. Raspov had handed him the wheel with specific instructions about course, and speed, then disappeared to get some rest, leaving Uri and Pavel to babysit. They were sitting on jump seats to the left of the companionway which led below. Pavel was staring into the blackness beyond the bow pulpit, while Uri maintained a stone-like vigil in Jack's direction, occasionally focusing on an array of instruments that Jack suspected the Russian had no clue about. Dmitri's flybridge yacht growled mightily, and although she stretched for thirty-eight feet, she handled like a sports car. Jack suspected down below, where, despite the cacophony of combustion Raspov could still be heard snoring, he would find enough weapons to gratify an army of blood-thirsty mercenaries.

The water in the area they were now operating was mercifully flat. Jack pulled open a window and breathed in the fresh air, then tweaked the trim tabs to lower her bow again, adding another two knots to her speed. He adjusted the throttle to lower the RPMs, and then checked her oil pressure and temperature gauges. So far, so good, he thought. Jack reached over to switch off her running lights, making her nearly invisible to the government patrol boats whose movements were well known to Raspov and the two brothers. Now they both watched Jack as he helmed the motor yacht.

"There'll be a light." It was the first time Uri had spoken since they left Cuba.

"A light," his large brother repeated, pointing through the darkness towards shore. "On, off, on again. Then bring the engine back to full stop."

"Gotcha," Jack said, hand on the throttle as if the signal might come in the next second.

"If you fuck up," Uri said, glaring at him, "they'll get jumpy. If they get jumpy, we're dead."

Raspov had told Jack they'd rendezvous first with a unit of rebel soldiers, on a piece of beach well within the insurgents' territory. "I thought they were your friends?" Jack said, with mild concern on his face.

"We'd be dead already if they weren't," Uri replied.

"Nice to have friends. Maybe we should wake Raspov."

Pavel turned. "Raspov wakes when the engine is silent. Light on, light off. Don't forget."

The radar showed they were about two miles from shore, headed straight for an inlet bracketed on both sides by fingers of land reaching about two hundred feet out to sea. The tiny horseshoe cove made for perfect anchorage. Also, Jack guessed, a perfect infiltration zone for Raspov and his two goons when they had business to conduct with the rebel insurgents.

The water was getting shallower, and in places the depth sounder indicated dangerous invisible shoals. Jack set the alarm for four fathoms, more than enough water to prevent a disabling prop strike, or worse – running aground.

A half hour later Uri and Pavel disappeared, their skulls like huge dark melons sinking into the darkness of the main salon down below. Jack listened to the sound of latches being unsnapped, rounds being chambered. Metal against metal. The acoustics of deadly instruments.

Not willing to admit he might have made a mistake, Jack gripped the wheel, white knuckles like porcelain caps against polished steel. Had even one light been burning at that moment, they would have seen his worry. He closed his eyes and then opened them a moment later and spotted the signal – two o'clock at a hundred yards – a laser poking holes in black velvet. The light flashed on, then off, and then on again. The pattern repeated itself twice more before Jack pulled the throttle to neutral. *Don't fuck up.* He waited.

It was a mere second before Uri and Pavel stomped up the steps to the bridge. Raspov brought up the rear. Wiping the sleep from his eyes, he barked something in Russian to his two thugs, then reached over and pushed a button to drop anchor. It splashed noisily into the water and sank to the bottom. Jack felt it set and then looked at the depth sounder. Only four fathoms of water beneath the slippery fiberglass hull. *Shit.* The depth sounder shrieked.

"Goddamn. Shut it down," Raspov hissed. "Now!"

Jack deactivated the alarm and looked sheepishly at Raspov. "Sorry."

Raspov ignored him. "Go!"

They both turned as Uri and Pavel hunkered down and shuffled to the back of the boat, followed a moment later by a soft hissing and muffled pop. Through the darkness Jack watched the two Russians wrestling with an inflatable black rubber dingy. They dropped it overboard, tossed a huge rucksack over the side, and then climbed onto the transom and disappeared.

A moment later Jack heard the faint dipping of oars – synchronized propulsion – a trickle of water barely audible above the lazy surf.

Raspov whispered, his face close to Jack's, "If they were going to launch their RPGs they would have done so already."

Good news, Jack thought. They were sitting ducks for rocket-propelled grenades. Somewhere on that beach fingers were tugging gently at triggers, waiting for a command to blow them out of the water. Jack had once seen the mess left by an RPG. A grisly scene of blackened flesh in a Serbian APC in Bosnia. Jack shifted uncomfortably, dropped lower in his seat, knowing it wouldn't make any difference if a round punched through the thin fiberglass hull.

"Paramilitary pricks have launched three raids in the past month not far from here. They came in boats." Raspov wasn't being a confidence builder. "Don't worry," he said. "Our friends will relax when they see it's the brothers. Then Uri and Pavel will make sure the area is secure so there're no surprises when we go ashore."

A firefight with Colombian rebels wasn't anything Jack was prepared for. He was about to suggest they take the boat into deeper water when Raspov disappeared below. When he returned, the Russian flashed a revolver, held it up and made a show of driving a clip home. Expert motion, done a million times, Jack thought. Raspov checked the safety and thrust the weapon at him.

Jack stared at it.

"Take it," Raspov demanded.

Jack wasn't comfortable. Taking the weapon meant he was surrendering his moral and professional neutrality. But, then again. He'd done that the minute he'd stepped aboard Raspov's boat. Jack took the gun and stuffed it in the front of his pants. He was a combatant now, and this was a twisted, screwed up, bonafide battleground.

"Welcome to Colombia," Raspov said, with sarcasm in his voice as tacky as flypaper.

To Jack, it had a sickening ring to it.

FIFTY

There were twelve of them.

AK-47s slung around their shoulders, except for the guerrilla stroking an RPG launcher. He was staring forlornly at the lightless shape of their boat limply anchored fifty feet from shore, still as a sculpture on a pedestal of black tranquil water. A tempting target. The man smiled regret at Jack, took a long hard draw on a cigarette and expelled a cloud of thick silver smoke that swirled upwards and disappeared in the darkness.

They were standing on a beach: Jack and Raspov and the dozen Marxists, all staring at one another. Uri and Pavel had disappeared to the tree line where they were looking for a place to hide the rubber dingy. Jack could barely make out their features, but on the faces of the men closest to him he saw a mixture of suspicion and contempt. Cold, hard looks illuminated now and then by the flaring of a match, the glow of a cigarette, a sliver of reluctant moonlight through low hanging clouds. Jack wasn't feeling any better about things, and the gun in his belt wasn't helping any.

One of the FARC soldiers was arguing loudly with Raspov, stabbing a finger at Jack. He didn't know what the two of them were on about, and that worried him. The commander was getting even more animated, refusing to listen to what Raspov had to say. The conversation heated up to the point where it appeared Raspov had lost all control. The rebel commander lashed a hand at Jack and then, in a sign that things were really off the rails, hands flashed to weapons. At that moment the rebel commander said something that brought dread to Jack.

Raspov laughed in the man's face. Not the best strategy. All eyes were on the Russian as he spat at the soldier's feet, thrust out his chest in a pathetic attempt to intimidate, and in rapid-fire Spanish said what loosely translated might have been, "CIA spy, my ass." Everyone watched Raspov, who appeared in both stooped posture and breathlessness to be failing in his bid to save Jack's life. Time to get the hell off this beach, Jack thought. So, with not a moment to spare, he began to inch slowly and silently towards the water. He planned to make a run for it. Go deep fast, swim to the boat and take his chances with Smiley and his RPG. He would fire up her powerful engines, slam the throttle to the firewall and drag anchor until he was a safe distance from shore. Jack believed it was his only option. He felt the Glock in his waistband, calculated the time it would take to draw the weapon if the shooting started. Christ, he'd never fired a gun. What was he thinking?

Raspov must have big balls, or was simply crazy, because in a uicidal move, the Russian's hands went to his pistol. It was a mistake followed by a roar of voices and the clack of AK-47s being raised to firing position. Adrenalin shot through Jack like compressed air, made his ears ring. He was about to shout something at Raspov when he felt the tip of a blade sting his neck, just below his jawbone. Smiley wasn't smiling anymore. His breath stank of tobacco and rancid meat as he stuck the knife into the side of Jack's neck and said something that roughly translated must have meant "Die! CIA pig."

He should have seen this coming. These men were animals. Raspov's warnings flooded back to him. *Credentials made of plastic, not miracles.*

Everyone seemed to be fighting for the same oxygen. No one knew what to do next. The rebel leader resumed a tirade that was now peppered with language that sounded to Jack like an attack on the morals of Raspov's mother. He pressed his weapon against the Russian's chest and spit at

Raspov's boots. The others looked like they couldn't decide whether to shoot the Russian or the American spy. Jack felt hopelessly done for as the knife pushed harder against his throat, making it impossible to deflect the image of arterial blood gushing from his neck, the radiant transfer of his life from flesh to the sand at his feet.

A second or two slithered past with the tension of electric eels. The rebel leader swaggered towards Jack. He brought an oily hand up and grabbed Jack's chin. "A hundred of my men are dead in six months," he growled. "American special forces in Arauca. Do you know they kill us? They kill us for a big fat American company. The 18th Brigade are whores. They protect an American pipeline."

Jack didn't move. Black hatred pooled in the Colombian's eyes, his hatred so volatile it threatened to engulf them both. The soldier slowly pulled his revolver and placed it against Jack's forehead. "Because of a capitalist pipeline we die."

He twisted the weapon harder into Jack's flesh. The smell of gun oil reached him. "Journalist. Not CIA," he said through clenched teeth.

The rebel leader inched closer. "*Journalista?* Why you not tell the American people what your soldiers do here?" His fingers tightened on Jack's face. "How your government kills our people?"

Jack wanted to break the man's nose with his forehead, or at least point out that the noble revolutionary armed forces of Colombia had slaughtered thousands of innocent civilians – *his people*.

"Big American reporter." The rebel leader laughed, teeth stained black. "All fucking liars."

Strangely, at that moment Jack felt more anger than doom. *Asshole.* Smiley pushed the blade deeper into his flesh until Jack felt something warm trickle down his neck. Smiley murmured, "*Journalista* pig dies."

Jack looked at Raspov wide-eyed. Why wasn't he doing something? Then Jack realized the two brothers hadn't returned yet. Apparently, no one else had given them any thought, and the rebels were about to find out just how big a mistake that was.

In Colombia, decades of civil war had killed tens of thousands of people. Many more were displaced, including legions of women who had been widowed by rightist death squads financed by the United States

Congress, a huge sore point for the insurgents. Many of those widows turned to Marxist doctrine, partly to find revenge, partly because they had no other choice because the insurgents controlled most of the villages where they lived. The group of twelve rebel soldiers was actually a baker's dozen, and the unlucky number thirteen was a raven-haired rebel with the curves of a baroque sculpture. She had been watching her *companero* get in the gringo's face when Pavel crept up and snatched her from the underbrush. She was now the property of the two Russians, and Jack was about to discover what Raspov meant when he said Uri and Pavel were taught "human things and things not so human" by their KGB masters.

Uri had his big Russian gun pressed against her skull, and that should have been reason enough for the wide-eyed panic that distorted her face. There was more. Pavel was holding her tight, inching forward from the tree line, one hand covering the lower half of her face. "Pavel is hungry," Uri said. He snapped his jaw open and shut with a crack that echoed through the clearing. His brother grunted something that couldn't be understood because his mouth was full. Pavel shuffled through the sand towards them.

It was the first time Jack noticed the Russians' strange teeth, and now he understood why they had spoken so little. Mouth wide, Pavel's lips were drawn back to reveal enamel daggers that appeared as sharp as surgical instruments. Pavel pressed them gingerly against the place where the woman's wrist and hand were joined. Jack now understood Uri's and Pavel's special talents, and he wondered how much human flesh they had savaged in the dungeons of Lubyanka, their psychoses blossoming like dewy black roses.

Pavel was able to fit her entire hand in his mouth, no problem. Uri laid it out for them. "Drop your weapons or your comrade is separated from her hand." Pavel bit into her. The *guerrillerera* screamed as a thin line of blood appeared on her wrist.

The rebel commander made his move. It wasn't much. Pavel's jaw tightened on her wrist and a trickle of blood became a drip off the Russian's chin, stopping the commander dead in his tracks. Surrender turned to rage as he flashed at Raspov. "If they kill her, you fucking die! On my honour." His words dropped to the sand like pieces of hot lead. Then a signal.

Smiley muttered something with a religious insinuation and withdrew his knife. Jack gripped his throat and dropped to the sand.

Raspov held his hands up in a show of magnanimity as the bewildered clutch of angry soldiers began to lower their weapons. He gazed at them one by one, waited a moment for the display to have its full impact. "We are all friends. Suspicion defeats us," Raspov sighed, a look of mild rebuke directed at the rebel leader who couldn't take his eyes off the two Russians, and his woman.

Resignation crawled like a dark shadow across their olive complexions as the Russians moved slowly forward, blood spilling over Pavel's chin.

Jack was sure he saw the Russian smile as the woman went deathly still in his vice-like embrace.

FIFTY-ONE

Jack cringed at the sight of Raspov slipping onto his ass again. The once decorated KGB colonel had already gone down half a dozen times on the greasy claustrophobic trail. Uri pulled him to his feet while Pavel appeared to be growing increasingly impatient with the old spy master.

A line of soldiers spread out at twenty-foot intervals to protect their flank. Jack would occasionally hear them muttering to one another, the strike of a match or a shifting weapon. They were young, Jack guessed, still in their teens. Too young, he thought. Probably recruited at gunpoint.

They'd been walking for two hours, making slow progress. The heat and humidity made it feel as though they were breathing under water.

Raspov was wheezing now.

The rebel commander and the rest of his unit, including the woman, were breaking trail, several of the soldiers hacking through brush with large machetes, khaki fatigues sopping wet. Chatter was non-existent on point.

Raspov fell again. "Why don't you carry him?" Jack suggested quietly.

Uri nodded at his brother, and then Pavel hoisted the older man on his back. Raspov offered weak resistance but eventually surrendered to the indignity. A moment later the colour returned to his face. With his wind back he said, "He wanted to put a bullet into your brain."

"I think I got that impression," Jack replied.

"I informed him he was suffering paranoia and that's when he spit at my feet, apparently dissatisfied with my diagnosis. Come to think of it you do look CIA." Dmitri adjusted his piggyback position, reminding Jack of an old Mel Gibson movie. Brains atop the brawn. Mad Max. *Two men enter, one man leave.* That was the flick.

"He obviously doesn't like you," Dmitri added. "He'll kill you if given a reason."

Jack contemplated the warning. He stepped over a huge sodden palm frond, unconsciously rubbed the wound on his neck. "I don't plan to give him the motivation."

The rebel commander looked back at Jack. Tough guy, sneering.

Jack casually averted his gaze. "Just another terrorist," he said to no one in particular.

"One man's terrorist is another man's freedom fighter," Raspov offered.

Jack knew Raspov was goading him. "Freedom fighters killing innocent women and children?" Jack thought about Amillo's wife and daughter and the thousands more murdered over the decades.

"You make a good point, my friend, best saved for the debating club. It means nothing here."

Jack slowed his pace, came shoulder to shoulder with Pavel, who was breathing easily, eyes straight ahead while he carried the Russian.

"Amillo was dead the moment he began his march towards the extradition treaty with Washington," Raspov continued. "He signed his own death warrant. The extraditables couldn't allow him to live."

Jack remembered the faces of Amillo's wife and daughter. They had both been beautiful, bravely following a man targeted by some of the most brutal men on earth. "There are cleaner ways to take out a target. Why kill so many innocent people?"

Raspov laughed. "You're talking about collateral damage like it matters here, when in fact it's part of the equation. The more innocents who perish, the greater the terror. The people are shell-shocked. The government is paralyzed and as a result chaos wins the day." There was a pause. "Last December a school teacher was shot dead on a street corner in Medellin after asking his ten-year-olds to pray for an end to the killings. It was a stroke of genius to take him out. Imagine the terror dividend it paid."

Jack was seeing a side of Dmitri he didn't know existed. "You're a bastard, Raspov."

"Just a realist."

Pavel gave Jack a sideways glance. You insult a man with such a word – fists usually follow. He hefted Raspov higher on his back and turned away, apparently satisfied Jack wasn't about to throw any punches, along with his slur on Raspov's character.

Raspov dropped his head until his eyes were level with Jack's. "No offence, Jack, but stop being so soft and gooey. Open your eyes and say hello to Coca Loco Land."

Jack had seen plenty so-called "freedom fighters" and their acts of cruelty. Heinous atrocities by small haughty men who killed and destroyed in the name of something. The Hutu and Tutsi had done that in Rwanda, their gory machetes held high in righteous fervour. Jack also remembered the blood-stained churches in the Balkans, the religious zealots and ethnic cleansing. He'd had to numb himself to the horror and pain of others, suppressing what he feared might one day overpower him. Lesser burdens could turn men into drunks or emotional basket cases. As Jack trudged along the slippery trail he thought again about the suicide bombing at Café Umbria. Amillo wouldn't crumble to the threats, so he had to be taken out, clear and simple. His wife and daughter and dozens of others were sacrificed for the terror dividend. Shit happened. But in this case the shit had happened to him – and his producer. He mentally chastised himself for not acting on his instincts when Amillo walked into the restaurant. Jack rubbed rock-hard muscles at the back of his neck. "Any guesses on Café Umbria?" he said.

"Who knows? Maybe FARC," Raspov replied, thrusting his chin at one of the rebels. "The insurgents don't care much for that extradition treaty either. Big bad America throwing its weight around again. The cartels, ELN? Need I go on?"

"No," Jack said.

Raspov went on anyway. "Sometimes everyone's on the same page, but for different reasons. One group takes a pass, the other takes up the slack. Why duplicate resources?"

None of this came as news to Jack. "Simple stuff. Drug lords, FARC, ELN. Everyone in the same bed humping, but everyone else gets screwed."

"Nicely put. No wonder you're a journalist."

The jungle was long awake with the calls of exotic birds. Occasionally there were the sounds of larger creatures scattering through the rainforest, as well as the persistent thump of heavy boots against hard-pressed mud.

Jack wanted to hear more from Raspov but the Russian dug his heels into Pavel, quickening his pace. Uri slid away into the thick jungle, breaking through the foliage as unstoppable as a trophied linebacker.

Jack thought about Jonathan Short's warning on the phone before he and Kaitlin boarded the Citation in New Orleans. "You're absolutely crazy to be even thinking about it, Jack. The DEA says things are about to explode." Short, ex-CIA now, riding the diplomatic ladder at the State Department and one of their best analysts on South America. "The extradition thing is making the nineties flare-up look like a picnic."

Jack had been warned.

"Sarah sends her love. Watch your back." The click Jack heard when Jonathan hung up that day sounded to Jack like a gunshot.

They continued to march through a wall of humidity, sunlight barely piercing the thick jungle canopy.

Jack was drenched, a combination of sweat and dew from a thousand leaves that reached out to touch him. First they had to locate Seth. Raspov was confident his revolutionary friends would help them accomplish that. After all, Seth was last reported in rebel-held territory near Santa Marta.

"If he's still breathing — we'll find him," Raspov had guaranteed.

As Jack trudged along the darkened trail there were curves around bends, bends around corners, footprints that shifted this way and that on a terrain that constantly changed. Jack preferred patterns of right and wrong, good and evil. Judgments easily made when based on fact. But he wasn't sure about anything or anyone right now, including Raspov. And of course, Kaitlin. She'd been expecting someone that night, Jack was sure of it. Jack was also certain that Kaitlin had already disappeared when the car full of explosives obliterated the restaurant.

What troubled him most and puzzled him more than all else was the possibility that she had abandoned him to die.

FIFTY-TWO

They made the rebel camp three hours after starting their grueling trek through the jungle, and a curious thing happened when they walked through the well-guarded gates into the Marxist stronghold.

It was exactly five minutes past seven. Two hours earlier in Washington and at the National Reconnaissance Office headquarters in Virginia. Time was very important there because spy satellites traveling at mach 25 in a geo-synchronous orbit around the earth opened their all-seeing eyes at pre-determined points and times along their orbital path and, at exactly five minutes after seven every morning, one of those five satellites was perfectly positioned in the black and cold of space about one hundred miles above the hot rainforest and mountains of Colombia. The 3-D imagery from the billion dollar birds told American intelligence analysts a lot, including where the opium and coca were being nurtured, sometimes by peasant farmers who lived in wooden shacks overlooking tiny pathetic crops that made them target-worthy combatants in America's war on drugs.

The Drug Enforcement Agency was mandated, through both

legislation and executive branch political imperative, to stem the production of cocaine and heroin, thereby denying the mighty American appetite. Sometimes that satellite information was used to vector the pilots of Colombian aircraft who, under escort by US Blackhawk helicopters, launched from government-controlled airstrips with their bellies full of a poisonous chemical called glyphosate. In America, Roundup Ultra kills weeds dead. In Colombia it destroys the coca plant and everything else in its path, including maize, yucca and plantain, which American drug addicts can't sniff or inject, and thus crops which the US administration couldn't care less about. No one seemed to care, either, that fumigation chemicals such as Roundup Ultra made people and animals very sick.

The CIA's Keyhole-class satellites, which can see an object as small as five inches, kept a close watch on hideouts of Colombian drug lords and rebel fortresses, and at precisely five minutes after seven, one of these "visible light" birds was snapping digital pictures high above the insurgents' camp where Jack Doyle now stood. Jack had no access to classified information on the orbits of CIA spy satellites, but apparently the leftists did. They knew, because ex-KGB spook Dmitri Raspov knew. And this was why, at the same time every day, a large group of guerrillas, two hundred or more, interrupted their morning calisthenics to send a message to those CIA imagery analysts who toiled along the Beltway. With their middle fingers raised high, they cried out in unison, "Fuck you!" in their best English and then resumed their sweaty regime. Jack couldn't help laughing.

The rebel fortress wasn't really a fortress. Milosevic of the Serbs. Now there was a fortress. Saddam. Another one. Though what good were they in the end? Jack thought. Slobodan wound up a maniacal denier before judges in The Hague, Saddam living like a rodent when American soldiers flushed him out of his spider hole. Jack himself had tried it on for size a week after they spirited Hussein away. He barely fit. Some fortress.

To Jack, this rebel "fortress" looked a bit like summer camp except for the heavy perimeter security and the fact everyone was dressed in army fatigues and saluted. The camp was well into a daily routine. Thigh-slapping jumping jacks were winding down as clusters of soldiers dispersed to Quonset huts and lean-tos which blended into the jungle. A makeshift open-air classroom was filled to capacity with students. Jack caught the odour of food being prepared in a large green tent a hundred feet from where they stood. Even though *muchacho* was against Marxist policy, Jack saw that a clutch of *guerrilleras* were doing the cooking and clearing tables. Pavel and Uri smacked their lips and headed towards the field kitchen. No one challenged them, and Jack found that curious until he realized Pavel and Uri were familiar faces around here. Raspov had mentioned the brothers freelanced their talents here. "Teaching the monkeys how to kill with a hairy little finger and such." The two Russian brothers had taken a table with a half dozen uniforms, and after a moment of back-slapping that looked like a college reunion, steaming plates of food were hurriedly placed in front of them.

Raspov was talking animatedly with a head-shaven uniformed brute who had been studying them closely since they arrived. The soldier caught Jack's eyes, shook his head in a gesture Jack couldn't decipher, and then pointed in the direction of a building at the end of the compound.

The morning sun tore through cloud like fingers ripping at cotton. Groups of teenaged soldiers squatted on well-worn patches of dirt outside barracks where huge Burund trees provided cover and quiet. In one of the groups, an instructor in a tight khaki T-shirt and fatigues carefully demonstrated a small round object.

Anti-personnel Mines 101, Jack thought. "Keep this side towards enemy." Farther on, two well-muscled youngsters circled one another. One slashed a knife inches from his opponent, while a female instructor barked commands. Jack noticed that, the deeper they moved into the camp, the harder the stares. Kids, curious about the gringo. Back home, Jack thought, they would have been playing X-Box, watching MTV, and fretting about pimples and dates. Here they were recruits to a Marxist struggle few fully understood. The next generation. Learning to kill, but becoming fodder in the conflict between stubborn angry men.

Headquarters was a long narrow building with a flat roof that blended in with hills of green and brown that rose gently for miles beyond the razor wire. Of the two dozen buildings in the enclosure, the HQ building was the largest, but still a utilitarian structure with a row of evenly spaced windows along its front, and a plain door at the head of three broad wooden steps. A banner hung above the windows with the FARC logo: a pair of crossed rifles and an open book on a Colombian map imposed on the country's flag. Layer upon layer of righteous symbols.

Jack's muscles ached and when he caught a whiff of himself, he realized how desperately he needed a shower. Raspov had made it clear they would be in and out as soon as they could. "A courtesy call. Let them know we're in the neighbourhood," he said. They'd eat and finagle a vehicle.

Commander Domingo Guzman was a tall thin man with a black beard and glasses with thick dark rims. The standard military fatigues. His office had the charm of a jail cell, the only furniture a metal desk and chair. No place for visitors to sit. The walls were bare, a few maps and propaganda posters. A cigar burned in a huge glass ashtray. Montecristo number two, Jack noted.

Guzman gave him the once over, stuffed the large torpedo in his mouth and nodded at Raspov. "So you bring us a Yankee spy, Colonel." Guzman looked at Jack like he was something stuck on the bottom of his boot.

"Your man overreacted, Commander," Raspov replied, no apologies. "The situation had to be diffused. I expected better from my revolutionary friends."

Guzman ignored Raspov, more interested in Jack. "So this is what a powerful member of the gringo press looks like."

"Media," Jack said, smiling weakly.

Guzman didn't realize he'd been corrected. "I'm not thinking you look so formidable," he continued, moving so close Jack caught the smell of the man. Cheap aftershave and cigar breath. He waited for Guzman to show more of his hand.

"What will you write about me, Mr. Doyle...our struggle?"

"It's not why we're here," Jack replied.

"Humour me," Guzman insisted. "Surely you've made observations... have something to say that's worthy of note." Guzman, like a school yard bully, hands on his hips, a cocksure look on his face. He waited – but not for Jack's lunch money.

Jack thought quickly. He didn't want to tell Guzman there wasn't a hope in hell they were going to win their "struggle" – and that the United

States wouldn't tolerate another communist state in the Americas. That even if they did win, there wouldn't be enough left of Colombia to lead. He wanted to tell him that it didn't matter which side won, they were all blood-thirsty psychopaths who murdered men, women and children. Any righteousness in their so-called "struggle" had long ago been contaminated by innocent blood and cocaine. That's what he wanted to say, and it would have probably gotten him executed.

So he said this instead: "You've never been better positioned to reach a lasting peace. You control more than forty percent of the country and can now bargain from a position of strength. The government is tired, the people are tired. In Washington, Plan Colombia is seen as a dud. The moderates don't want another Viet Nam."

Guzman thought about this for a moment, nodded his head. "The government no longer wishes to talk peace. They are not so motivated with all that American money paying for Blackhawk helicopters and fancy weapons."

"Do they have any choice?"

Guzman struck a match, held the flame against the end of his cigar and sucked until his face disappeared behind flame and a cloud of grey tobacco smoke. "Perhaps not," he replied.

Jack's ad lib may have saved his life. He let Guzman savour it. Guzman backed off to his desk without taking his eyes off Jack, and then reluctantly turned to face Raspov. "Good to see you again, my Russian friend. We have much to discuss." Then Guzman smiled. "Can we offer breakfast, Senor Doyle? It's not what you're used to, but it's a good honest effort."

Jack got the message and left, thankful to be gone. Once outside he spotted Uri and Pavel demonstrating some kind of chokehold to a group of wide-eyed teenagers. Pavel was struggling to free himself, slapping at his brother and turning a shade of blue that brought howls of laughter from the students. Uri released him, and Pavel fell to his knees, but then in a flash of movement drove his head into his brother's gut. They crashed to the ground, cursing at each other. No one was laughing now.

Jack surveyed the camp, out of habit began to count. Soldiers. The ratio between men and women. Number of vehicles. Number of armed vehicles. A unit of soldiers was forming up in the parade square. How many troops per patrol? What kind of weapons? Two of the soldiers carried shoulder-mounted devices. A large white board was nailed to a post off to the side that contained the silhouettes of three black helicopters with red x's stamped on them. Lots of room for more kills. Maybe today if they were lucky.

Jack realized he was being followed. No surprise. They'd want to make sure he didn't see anything he wasn't supposed to. He decided to eat, and then try for a shower and a shave. His knapsack had clean clothing, which he was looking forward to.

The humidity seemed to swallow the sounds of machines and soldiers as they fell into a lazy routine beneath a blistering sun that threatened lethargic stupor before noon.

Jack was fed and watered. And smelling much better after his turn in a makeshift shower hung behind one of the barracks. He'd smiled for the first time in days when a group of *guerrilleras* whooped and hollered at the sight of his nakedness. They scattered under the glare of a superior officer who stared at Jack for an uncomfortably long time before sauntering away.

Raspov, Uri and Pavel had disappeared to secure a vehicle. They planned to head higher into the mountains to the place Seth Pollard was last reported by his people in New York. Given his disappearance it was sadly possible Pollard had met a cruel and untimely fate. Jack said a silent prayer and decided to seek out shade, somewhere away from the activity. Besides, his knee ached and he needed to sit. He was making his way along a narrow earthen passageway between two barracks buildings when he felt a rough hand on his shoulder. Jack spun around to see a kid with an angry look on his face. The teenaged soldier muttered something that sounded like a warning. Jack's Spanish was bad, but he was pretty fluent in body language, and he knew he was about to wander into a restricted area. Jack brought a finger to his lips. *Our little secret, amigo.*

The guard wanted to look like a hard ass, despite the pimples, but at no more than sixteen that would have been impossible. Instead he looked around, lowered his weapon, shrugged and said something that Jack understood as *Fuck it. Why not?*

Jack smiled at him. "*Gracias.*"

When they reached the end of the passageway Jack saw the reason for the boy's reluctance. They had arrived at a small clearing with an enclosure. He was staring at a cage made of high chain-link fence and topped with razor wire. Big enough for about a dozen prisoners and a small latrine. There were half a dozen men inside, half dead by the looks of it. Jack felt sorry for them, baking like that in the midday sun. There were three guards, none of whom looked happy about Jack's presence. They raised their weapons in protest until the kid with the pimples held up a hand. *Take it easy.*

The prisoners were stripped to the waist, sweat rolled down their backs. Several were badly bruised and had swollen faces. The khaki pants they wore identified them as soldiers, but Jack couldn't tell if they were regular army or paras. They stared at Jack with pleading eyes. One of the prisoners muttered something in Jack's direction and then fell to the ground when a guard stabbed his rifle barrel through the chain-link mesh.

Jack pointed down at him. "*Agua...agua.* Do they have water?" No answer. Jack looked beseechingly at the kid with the acne. His shadow shrugged and then shoved Jack towards the way they'd come.

"These men need water," Jack said.

"You must leave!" the guard shouted. His English had obviously improved. "Now!" He grabbed Jack's arm.

Jack slapped his hand away.

The kid leveled his rifle, followed by the click, clack of safeties.

Dread hung on the air. He'd pushed too hard and was about to pay for it. Even the birds went quiet. Then the tense silence was broken. By the clap of hands. One man's applause and a voice not unfamiliar to Jack.

"Bravo, Jack. Bravo."

Jack couldn't believe his ears, and when he turned he could barely believe his eyes. "Seth?"

"I see you got my message." Seth grinned. "Now be a mate and get me the fuck out of here."

FIFTY-THREE

"Fifty thousand quid. Can you believe that? If only they knew, Jack boy." Seth Pollard was trying to keep up as they walked quickly across the compound to where Uri and Pavel loaded a vehicle. Raspov watched them approach.

"You're worth ten times that, Seth. Twenty." Jack wasn't slowing down. "Where's your gear?"

"Thirty times at least," he said, studying Jack's profile. "But you see, none of these committed revolutionaries has ever heard of Pollard Energy."

Jack looked at him. "Or the great Nigel Pollard, no doubt."

"Well, that's another issue, isn't it?" Seth frowned. "Father does hate ransoms, doesn't he?"

"No, Seth. He hates paying them."

"I suppose you're right." Seth scratched his forehead, allowed his fingers to travel backwards through thick greasy blond hair. He wiped his hands on a khaki vest that had nearly a dozen zippered pockets and pouches.

"How is he anyway?" Jack saw the Russians had scored an old Land Rover.

"Nigel? Tanned and probably screwing his new wife in Greece."

"Good for him. Number three?"

"Four, I believe." Seth began to check off fingers, stopped at his thumb. "Five, actually, counting mother."

"Don't forget her." Jack grinned.

The Land Rover was nearly loaded by the time Seth and Jack reached it. Raspov was stone-faced. He'd made the case for the Brit's release, told Guzman he was part of his crew, and in turn the commandant had made it clear the Russian now owed him.

A soldier approached with a large gunny sack and handed it to Seth who immediately checked its contents. Declaring everything accounted for, he carefully placed the bag on top of the other cargo at the back of the Land Rover.

"Breathe easy, lads," Seth said, extending a hand in the direction of Uri and Pavel. "Seth Pollard."

"Fuck off," they said in unison.

"Bravo," Seth said. "We're off then."

Uri was driving and Pavel rode shotgun, a kerchief tied tightly around his mouth like a Mexican bandit. Jack and Raspov were in the back with Seth between them. Jack had purposely waited until they were underway before asking the question that had been on his lips since they'd liberated Seth from the rebel cage.

"Where'd you shoot the video, Seth?"

"Brilliant, wasn't it?"

Jack glared.

"Taganga. It's up near Santa Marta," Seth said. "About a week ago."

Jack had never heard of it.

Seth looked over at Raspov's grim profile. He reached into one of his pockets and withdrew a tube of sun block, pushed it at him. No response.

"Suit yourself, mate. So, anyway. I'm at this beach place eating rice with greasy chicken." Seth stopped a moment, as if regurgitating the memory. "One of those beach restaurants, you know the ones. And I'm just sitting there eating—"

"Eating *arroz con pollo*," Jack said. "I know."

"*Arroz* what?"

"Never mind."

"Right. Anyway, along the beach comes this bird. She's all alone and driving this crowd of German drunks crazy cause she's quite a looker. They're screaming and yelling and so it gets me curious too. I look – and then I realize I've lost my mind or something."

Jack noticed Raspov was listening intently.

"The looker gets even closer. And Jack, no shit. I don't believe what I'm seeing."

Jack was all ears now. "Go on," he demanded impatiently. Seth paused, gathering his breath.

"Seth?"

"It was her, Jack," Seth finally said. "It was definitely her."

Jack looked grimly past Seth to the passing scenery.

"Jack, I know how fucking crazy it all sounds. And I know you'd have every reason in the world to call me bonkers – full stop. But you saw the video, right?"

Jack tried to process what his skinny British friend was saying.

"Make no mistake, mate. It was Kaitlin. Kaitlin, Jack." Seth was sure. Would have bet everything that the woman he saw that day was Kaitlin O'Rourke. "One hundred percent, Jack. You with me, mate?"

"Yes, Seth. Now tell me the rest of it."

It was like he said. Lunch at a beach restaurant in Taganga. Her coming closer and closer to where he was eating his greasy chicken. Wandering along, getting her feet and legs wet in the water, dodging waves. A bit spaced out, in his opinion.

"She kinda just swept on by me as I'm sitting there digesting my pollo or whatever you called it. I could have choked," he said. "She didn't see me. I didn't call out. I really don't know why." Seth paused to taste the regret that left. "Then she disappeared."

Jack was thinking, drumming fingers on his leg.

"You know I wasn't going to just let her stroll away, leave me guessing about my fucking sanity. So I got up to follow her. But she'd gone. I nearly shit. Brilliant, I thought. Just brilliant."

"What happened then?" Jack said.

"I grabbed my camera and ran after her."

The video played again in Jack's head. Seth provided the voice-over. "There was this car, leaving the parking lot. It had to drive right past me. So I waited."

"Why didn't you stop her?"

Pollard stopped to consider that. "I didn't think of it. Shit. Sorry, mate." Seth frowned. "Anyway, the car had to stop for a second for some traffic." Seth paused a moment. "And that's when I saw it was definitely her. Like that time we hunkered down for Milosevic, remember? Caught him and his driver coming through the gates."

"I remember. Your e-mail was short on details."

Seth shook his head. "Now that's another story. Are we stopping for lunch?"

An hour later they slid to a stop in front of a dusty cafetera that advertised *cerveza* and American cigarettes. A Coca-Cola sign leaned against the building, completely bleached of its trademark colours. An old man with a brown leather face sat next to a screen door, watching them suspiciously as they jumped out of the jeep. He wore a wide-brimmed straw hat, and Jack looked twice before he realized it was a rifle propped up against the wall behind the old man's wicker chair.

"*Buenos dias,*" Raspov said.

The old man ignored him, but gave the two Russian brothers the once over as he got up and led the way inside.

The place was empty except for some worn wooden tables, none the same, and a collection of mix and match chairs. A brass fan turned lazily above their heads, pulling hot wet air towards a ceiling stained with some kind of mould. Jack couldn't nail down the smell. The menu board said pork and chicken.

Uri and Pavel muttered in Russian and took a seat next to a window that was cracked and clouded by age and filth.

When the old man came over they ordered, and five minutes later heaping plates of pork and fried potatoes were brought to the table. Jack ate a small bowl of white rice, which he doused with hot sauce. Uri and Pavel looked at him eat, and snickered.

Jack arched an eyebrow. "See who's laughing tonight."

Seth continued his story. "There's a reason the e-mail was short on facts. A pretty good reason." He shovelled a large forkful of dripping meat into his mouth, followed by a fistful of fries, and then took a pull on his bottle to chase the bolus down. "They came for me before I had a chance. Broke down the door to my hotel room before I could complete the message. All you got was the attachment."

Jack noticed Raspov was as interested as he was, which wasn't completely unusual, except it tugged at Jack in a fashion he was unable to analyze.

Seth chewed as he talked. "*Knowing* she's in Taganga is one thing," he said, smacking his lips. "Knowing exactly *where* is another."

Jack looked straight ahead. "Kaitlin isn't the kind of girl you can forget. We'll ask around. Start on that beach strip where you saw her." Seth nodded agreement.

Jack continued, "I've got a disk with her picture on it and I expect they have computers in Taganga."

Seth shrugged.

"Anyway we'll print it off, spread copies around until we get a bite. There're probably not many places someone can hide there." It was all well and good unless Kaitlin had already flown the coop. Jack didn't want to think about that. There was a pause. Then Jack said, "So you gonna tell me? What exactly did you do to end up in that cage?"

Pollard shook his head as if he couldn't believe it himself. "The day I saw Kaitlin, that morning. I'm an hour out of Taganga with Jose. You don't know him. My fixer. Anyway, we run into this roadblock about thirty miles from town and I think: Bravo, I'll get some video. You know, some of the routine stuff – lads on roadblock duty. That kinda thing."

"You should know better," Jack said. "These guys don't like cameras."

"I thought I had carte blanche. Got to know the unit commander pretty good. Guess I was wrong," Seth continued. "Three of them had this girl, you know, in the back of one of their lorries. They didn't want me shooting any video." Seth seemed to be steeling himself. A moment passed. "She was just a kid. They probably killed her afterwards."

"Jesus."

Seth's nostrils flared. "The leftist struggle my arse."

Jack let him speak. He knew what he needed to say.

"I should have done something. Anything. Power of the camera... you know. The minute you flick on the sun gun, the cockroaches scatter."

"There was nothing you could have done."

Seth considered that a moment. "Anyway, they snatched me that day. It was just after I got back to the hotel from my close encounter with Kaitlin."

Seth stopped to stare at Raspov for a long moment. There was something familiar about the three Russians. He'd figure it out later. "The Marxists were going to tag the home office for a ransom. Then you came along. Cheers, mate." Seth lifted his bottled water.

"Some fixer, that Jose," Jack said.

"I found out it was two of his cousins in the back of the truck with that girl," Seth simply said. "Wankers."

Jack was glad he'd eaten light. They were headed west along a deeply rutted road and were still a good ways from Taganga, where Seth had shot the video of Kaitlin. The gear was strapped down in the back, including the black rucksack the Russians had brought with them from the boat. Pavel had earlier removed a pistol-handled shotgun from the sack, which he now held firmly between his legs. Several boxes of shells sat at his feet.

The Land Rover smelled of air freshener of some variety. An evergreen tree dangled from the rear-view mirror. Pavel flicked at it now and then as if to knock more scent out of it. A brown stain on the driver's door looked to Jack like dried blood. Probably some hapless soul had tried to run a rebel roadblock. Lost his life and his ride.

They bounced along a road running parallel to a rain-swollen river. In spots, murky water pooled in huge, muddy potholes. Flights of Blackhawks and *Chachalaca* erupted from low-lying bushes where the landscape widened to reveal undulating hills and much farther away mountain ridges of white, gold and brown. In other circumstances Jack would have enjoyed the vista. The region was controlled by rebels, but hit-and-run paramilitary attacks were not uncommon. Jack nervously scanned the roadsides where rightist soldiers could be nestled just beyond the tree line waiting for soft targets. A familiar edginess began to take hold, a survival instinct fired by adrenalin. It's what kept him alive, especially in places where some fifteen-year-old combatant with a Kalashnikov had his finger on the trigger. South Africa, the Gaza Strip, Sarajevo and Kabul. Jack survived by trusting his inner voice, and sometimes he paid a price when he didn't. He learned that lesson in the Balkans too. A cabbie had driven them into an artillery bull's eye in Kosovo. The driver was probably drunk and definitely lost, and while Jack had a bad feeling about where they were headed, he ignored it. A shell cratered next to the car. Seth wasn't hurt, but Jack was bloodied by a piece of shrapnel just below his third knuckle. He should have listened to that whispered warning.

Jack rubbed the small scar on his hand as the dirt road shot into a tunnel of thick forest. Great spot for an ambush, he thought.

Raspov pointed out the window. "Paramilitaries have been on a killing spree farther west." He drew a hand across his throat and made a scratchy sound. "Killing villagers by the dozens because the rightists see Marxist sympathizers hiding under every rock."

"And if we run into them?" Jack already knew the odds of surviving that kind of a meeting.

"If they don't snipe us first, you tell them you're the famous Jack Doyle doing your work. Here with your skinny cameraman to write about the demon leftists and the heroic forces marshalled to crush them." Raspov studied two shiny domes in the front seats. "If that doesn't satisfy them Uri and Pavel will take care of it. We'll survive as long as they haven't brought their gunships."

"Great," Jack said.

"Faster, Uri," Dmitri shouted, gripping the seat in front of him. They fishtailed through a cloud of dust around a sharp bend in the road, sending Pavel into a spasm of laughter.

"You'd better know where we're going," Jack shouted, with no attempt to disguise his concern.

Raspov laughed. "We'll find the woman if Uri doesn't kill us first."

The jeep swerved to avoid a tree in the middle of the road. The three Russians whooped with childish glee as Uri spun the wheel and gunned the engine. Jack slammed into Seth.

"Hold on to something," Raspov screamed. "This is only the beginning!"

Jack didn't doubt it.

FIFTY-FOUR

Forty-five minutes later they drove into Taganga – and straight into gridlock. The main street was a strip of wrecked pavement that separated a string of cantinas and the town's rocky beach. Cars and people jockeyed for space. Kids and old men on rusted bicycles dodged the potholes between the cars and the people. It was all accomplished to music which blared from tinny speakers mounted on poles that ran the length of the street above the crowd.

Jack looked at Pollard who shrugged. "Must be Saint's Day. Every town has one. The Patron Saint of Fuck It."

"A special day," Raspov said sarcastically. "What a treat for us."

Children wearing brightly coloured costumes ran alongside the Land Rover, screaming at the top of their lungs, and twice Uri had to apply the brakes to avoid running them over. His brother beamed as though he'd never seen happy children before. Pavel then jumped from the vehicle, stomping along in time to the music, but when the children saw his smile, they screamed louder and scattered.

The Land Rover moved slowly through the village and Seth pointed out the few landmarks.

Here and there in the crowd stares made Jack nervous.

"Nothing to do. Nowhere to go. Trust no one," Seth said, thumping the headrest to the beat of the local rhythm.

They found a parking spot on the strip between two monstrous SUVs in front of a nondescript building that had wrought-iron bars on its windows and a heavy wooden door. A doorman watched them exit the vehicle. He had a leathery face and was wearing black pants and a striped gondolier's shirt.

"*Buenos dias*," Raspov said as they approached.

The gondolier nodded beneath a wide-brimmed straw hat and walked them to a table on the sidewalk with a view of spectators' backs. A number turned to stare at the two Russian brothers, who snarled back at them.

Jack watched the top of a float as it passed them, a paper mache spectacle adorned with waves of flowers in pink, green and red. Three smiling teenaged girls wearing white cotton gowns and sparkling crowns waved to the crowd at the height of the contraption. The crowd went wild, a thunder of shouts and applause rolled up and down the strip, drowning out the music. Seth was shouting, trying to get the waiter's attention above the din. The brothers joined the cacophony while Dmitri covered his ears and scowled. Jack stood to get a better view of the float and the crowd. It was difficult because of the crush of spectators directly in front of them. "Back in a minute," he told Seth and then strolled away.

Raspov watched closely as Jack disappeared into the crowd.

The music became louder as Jack walked, and as the crowd thickened, walking became more difficult. He wanted an unobstructed view of the parade so he pushed his way through a barrier of people ten deep and ended up in the street. That's when he felt the hot wet snort of a horse against his cheek and startled backwards. People in the crowd laughed and pushed him forward again. The horse brushed against Jack's chest and stomped off, followed by several more carrying costumed riders.

Jack wiped his face and then quickly lost his smile. He couldn't explain the sudden feeling, no more than he could explain the time he knew Tommy was about to be hit by a truck. Jack's eyes scanned the heavy line of farmers and tourists on the other side of the parade route. The sun flared from behind a church bell tower, causing Jack to squint.

He turned slightly and then bleary-eyed, he saw her.

Mercedes was almost enjoying the parade and had been thinking about *Viernes Santo*, Sister Evangeline's favourite day of the year, when she saw the Russian and his two monsters being shown to a table by the ridiculous gondolier doorman. Two gringos were with them. Now one of them was pushing his way through the crowd and into the street. He spotted her.

They locked eyes and Mercedes froze. After a second she stumbled backwards, bumped into an elderly couple and stammered an apology. Then Mercedes ran.

Faces blurred as she pushed her way through the crowd. Voices cursed her as she shouldered hard and stepped on feet. For a fleeting second she twisted backwards but couldn't see him. She found no comfort in that as she ran.

She cursed her stupidity. The parade had been too great a risk, even though she was driven crazy after a week in that hotel room. The filth, the flea-ridden bed, the bare light bulb in the bathroom, the smell she couldn't seem to wash from her hair. Mercedes had had to get out and it seemed like an opportunity to feel human again.

Now she'd been spotted. Mercedes dashed through an alleyway and emerged on the beach. She had no intention of leading them to her hotel, her only sanctuary. The beach stretched for at least a mile in each direction, but Taganga was surrounded by hills and escape on foot was doubtful. For a second she thought about taking one of the fishing boats that were bobbing near the shoreline. The ropes slackened and grew taut with the rise and fall of the water and Mercedes knew she'd never be able to untie one in time. *Damn!*

Her feet crunched noisily along the pebbled beach as she ran, fifty yards then sixty. Suddenly a rope from a fishing boat snapped tight, creating a trip line running twenty feet to a stake on the beach. Mercedes didn't see it in time and she went down hard, her shoulder plunging painfully into the rocks. The breath was knocked from her and a sharp pain numbed her arm. She tried to get up and run again but she was entangled in the anchor rope. Frantically she tugged at it, cursing her bad luck. He was coming. Footfalls of crunching rock, getting louder. He might have been the one who had killed Selena and Orlando. She was petrified. Closer now. Mercedes simply shut her eyes and waited. It was finally over.

Confusion muddied Jack's mind as he closed the distance. Twenty more yards to go. Anger carried him ten more. Jack swore.

She was face down, not moving. Even from that angle he was sure it was Kaitlin. The same shape and colouring. Her hair was much longer. How was that possible? By the time Jack reached her he could barely stand. He collapsed to his knees and reached out to grab her.

It was the voice inside her head that told her it didn't have to end like this. A voice that might have been Selena's. Except Selena would have been more specific about what to do.

Mercedes needed no instruction. She kicked him in the chest with her free leg and sent him hard onto his back. He grunted loudly in pain and swore aloud.

Mercedes tore at the rope entangling her leg, her hands slipping on seaweed and slime. Her attacker was moving, trying to pull himself to his knees. Mercedes screamed for help, realizing with dread that she would never be heard. Not with the parade. The beach was empty — except for Mercedes and the man who was trying to kill her. Or was he?

He sat there gasping for breath, doubled over in pain. Both of them were breathing hard. He looked at her with eyes that were blood red. Rivers of sweat trickled down his face. Mercedes would never understand why, but she was sure he was no killer. Anger mottled his features but, underneath, she saw traces of compassion and kindness. Maybe this man didn't want to kill her. Still, Mercedes tensed, muscles tightening to the point of pain. Their eyes locked and it was as if the man couldn't believe what he was looking at. His first words puzzled her. "I knew you were going to do that," he wheezed.

FIFTY-FIVE

Seth saw Jack bolt. But he didn't plan on telling the Russians. Problem was they were getting restless, wondering where Jack had gone.

"*Por favor.*" Seth waved an arm at the waiter, and then motioned towards their empty bottles.

Raspov looked at him suspiciously. "It's Jack's round."

"Jack's not here."

"Maybe we'd better go look," Raspov said. "Maybe he's gotten into some trouble."

Pollard saw the skepticism in Dmitri's face but ignored it, instead showed five fingers to the gondolier who disappeared inside the bar. "He'll be right back. He does this a lot. Curious Jack and all that." Seth knew they'd eventually tire of his bullshit.

Raspov barked something in Russian at Uri and Pavel. The two brothers leapt from the table and darted to the sidewalk. Raspov gave Seth a murderous look as he followed them. They pushed their way to the back of the vehicle, opened the gate, and then tore into the rucksack. A second later they vanished into the crowd.

Seth's instincts about Raspov had been right. Now he was sure who the three Russians were. In Bellavista they'd remember too. Jack would never have known about that massacre. Pollard got there two days later and had seen the bodies, had heard the stories. When the waiter returned with their beers, Seth thrust a fistful of money at him and ran. He'd have to find Jack before the Russians did.

Seth ran to the vehicle, hoping to attract as little attention as possible. It was locked. He picked up a rock, stepped back, and in a gesture reminiscent of his famous cricket serve, hurled it. The back window exploded, the concussion drowned out by applause and voices from the passing parade. An eye out for police, Seth ripped open the rear gate. No one watched. No one seemed to care. Seth shoved the bags aside and climbed in. He tumbled forward until he forced his way into the front seat. No ignition key, but Seth expected none. He had other talents. A sinner on a day for saints, he thought, as he reached for the wiring beneath the steering wheel.

FIFTY-SIX

"What's your name?" Jack waited, feeling foolish because he'd asked a foolish question.

She was trying to untangle her leg, doing a poor job of it because her fingers were coated with sea slime. She looked up at him, urgency in her eyes. Or was it terror? She gulped air, coughed. "They will kill. Please help."

That made Jack nervous. He rubbed his ribs where she'd kicked him, and thought they might be broken. He took in a lungful of air and it hurt to breathe so laughing at the ridiculous statement was definitely out of the question. Instead he grabbed the tangled anchor rope, wheezed, "Who's going to kill you?" The strangest words he'd ever had to say. Jack searched her face but saw nothing to explain her crazy act.

"Senor, please!" She struggled to free herself.

What was wrong with her? Maybe she'd hit her head or something and had been wandering around Colombia in some kind of amnesiac stupor. He'd heard about other cases. People who just disappeared only to turn up months later, blank about where they'd been.

"You are also with them." She scowled, tugging at the rope. "These killers — you and they."

He stopped working the rope. The Russians were no angels, but what the hell did she mean? Jack saw the horror in her face as she ripped at the rope. "They are killers," she repeated, shaking. "You too are a killer."

Jesus. Something crawled up Jack's spine. What was it? The woman's insane behaviour didn't seem so insane anymore. Intuition? Maybe. His inner voice again. Jack spun around. Where were they? Still relaxing over cold beers back at the bar? Jack doubted it. He grabbed the rope and a moment later it snapped loose, freeing her leg. What now? Would he tell her, *Sorry, thought you were someone else? No worries*, she might say, then get up and walk back to the parade. *Have a nice day.*

Jack's thoughts were shattered by the crack of a bullet. He flinched. Turned. The Russians were running towards them. Shooting at them. At him. *What the hell?* Jack waved at them. Stupidly, he thought, after Uri raised his arm and fired again. *Killers?*

Uri and Pavel were behemoths, and Dmitri's better years were long gone. They were neither svelte nor fast, heavy-footed and sluggish as they pounded into the sand and rocks two hundred yards down the beach. This was a good thing, Jack thought, as he grabbed her by the wrist and pulled her up.

"You see now?" she shouted, running. Another bullet snapped at the rocks behind them. She was pulling Jack now, surprisingly hard, and after a few seconds they dove behind a flimsy wooden shed. Not much cover. A bullet splintered wood just above their heads.

"Shit!" Jack growled before yanking her into the open again. Fifteen yards at least to another alleyway. They crouched as they ran. Another bullet. It cleaved the air next to Jack's head. *Jesus.* They *were* trying to kill him. He looked back in rage, wishing for a moment alone with his "old friend."

Mercedes picked up the pace, frantically tugging Jack towards safety. "No time," she said as if she'd read his mind.

They lunged into the alleyway opening. Thirty feet more until they reached the safety of the street and the crowd. Behind them Jack heard the Russians shouting, furious that their prey were getting away, were still breathing.

Jack's heart sank. The crowd was gone, thinned to nearly nothing when they burst through the alleyway onto the sidewalk. Jack saw the tail end of a float disappearing around a corner up the street. Bad news. They'd have to move faster. Jack looked back and spotted the two brothers, weapons gripped in their meaty hands. They looked at Jack and sneered. Jack rubbed the sweat from his face and decided the Russians had a clear shot no matter which way they ran. They'd be cut down. With no time to figure it out, a bullet chipped pavement at Jack's feet. He grabbed her arm and flung her towards the disappearing float, their feet pounding towards what remained of the parade, the crowd, and their dwindling chances for survival. Why were they shooting? Who was this woman? Jack knew he had to live to find out, and it was time to get the hell off this street.

They were running full out when an engine revved, careening behind them. Jack glanced back, at Seth's grinning face behind the wheel of the Land Rover.

"Get in," Seth screamed through the windshield.

Mercedes tried to pull away until she looked back and spotted the Russians in a dead run towards them, rapidly closing the distance. One of them raised his weapon to take aim.

Jack shoved her roughly into the back seat and jumped in beside Seth. Pollard gunned the engine and they vanished in a cloud of dirt and dust. Jack swung around to watch his new enemies grow smaller and smaller behind them. He gulped air loudly and whipped his head to the stranger in the back seat, daring her to fool with him any longer. "Now, like I said. Who are you?"

FIFTY-SEVEN

They didn't look dangerous, but they'd been with the Russians and that alone was a good reason for Mercedes to want to jump from the car, though she knew she'd kill herself in the process, or at least hurt herself badly. For the moment she was alive. The Russians were apparently their enemies and that meant it was possible the two gringos were her allies.

They had already been to her hotel, where she grabbed her things. The one called Doyle had watched her like a hawk, and when they saw her car, the one from the video, the decision was made to dump the Land Rover. They took two weapons from a large black bag and then tossed it into the ocean.

The one driving was named Seth. Mercedes remembered where she'd seen him before, that day at the restaurant about a week ago. That day she'd also made the mistake of believing she could safely leave the motel. Seth was the one with the camera as she was leaving the parking lot. They were both watching her. Doyle was twisted in his seat with a red face and hardened eyes that refused to release her. Mercedes averted her eyes to the blur of passing landscape, the dusk clumping in shadows near the road and farther in where the forest thickened. Sunlight settled like brilliant slivers of gold leaf on distant hills. She was hungry and tired. If only she could travel back in time. She'd trade all the money in the world for a chance to correct the mistakes she'd made. Mistakes that had cost two lives already, one of them her dearest friend. Mercedes flashed her eyes. "You stare at me," she said, folding her arms. "This is rude."

"I'm waiting," Jack replied.

The gringo had a deep soft voice that resonated with what Mercedes admitted was warmth. She didn't know how much of it was schooled, how much was natural. He was very handsome except for the anger that lined his face, and his blue eyes were accusing and full of something that might have been hurt. Mercedes thought that under different circumstances she might have found him attractive.

"Mercedes. Mercedes Mendoza. Does this satisfy you?"

Jack shook his head. "Not nearly. Maybe you can start by telling me why my friends got so worked up over you back there."

Mercedes looked past him, nonchalantly. "This is something to ask your amigos."

"We're not on speaking terms anymore," Jack replied. "Apparently thanks to you."

Mercedes continued to glare.

Jack was stunned by the similarity. She was a carbon copy of Kaitlin, a remarkable duplicate. Her face. Her colouring. Her voice. Strange to hear Kaitlin with a thick Spanish accent. Kaitlin was an only child, yet this woman could have been her twin. Jack had no idea what to make of it. He looked at Seth. "Doppelganger?"

Seth's eyes shifted to the rear-view mirror. "They say we all have one."

"Bloody strange to see. Look at the way she bites her lip. Doppelgangers don't share nervous ticks, do they?"

Mercedes hissed something Jack didn't understand.

Seth said something back. "She's angry with us."

Jack squared himself in his seat, quiet as he watched the passing landscape. There wasn't much to look at. Trees and listless signs of civilization. Here and there a tractor or donkeys hauled a wagon piled high with some kind of harvest. Occasionally a farmer waved lazily as they sped by. No surprises yet. Good. Though Jack knew they'd have to quickly find a safe place to hunker down. Raspov was still out there, looking for them. Jack reached for a map.

"You are Jack and Seth." The anger was momentarily absent from her voice.

"Yeah, that's right."

"Jack and Seth. Please to listen. I was watching the parade and you…you came after me. I thought you were killers so I ran. Then I fell and you – yes, you – assault me–"

"Wait a minute–"

"No. Excuse. Your ugly friends shoot at us. Then you pulled me away and into the street, and next you push me into your car." Mercedes rubbed her shoulder.

"A Land Rover," Seth corrected.

"A Land Rover…yes." Mercedes rolled her eyes. "Anyway, here we are. You have kidnapped me, and I demand you release me."

Jack rubbed his face, paused while he processed what she had said. "You forgot something," he said.

"I don't think so." Mercedes folded her arms. "But please feel free to tell me what."

"You said they were killers," Jack said. "The Russians."

"Of course they are killers! They tried to kill us."

"Yeah. But you called them killers before they showed up on that beach. Before they started shooting. I grabbed you after you fell, remember? You said I was with them, and you called them killers."

"I am a good judge of these things," Mercedes said. "And I think you and him," Mercedes pointed at the back of Seth's head, "are kidnappers."

Jack looked at Seth, shook his head, and sighed loudly.

"Sorry, mate," was all Pollard said. "She's a dead ringer."

"Good choice of words," Jack said, the disillusionment showing in his face.

The dirt road was leading them nowhere, a destination Jack was now familiar with. How could he have been so stupid? Chasing shadows from the start. Trusting a gut feeling that, somehow, Kaitlin had survived the bombing. Pollard's video had fit nicely into that fantasy. He should have known better, should have asked himself some basic questions first. Like, how in hell could she have survived? Why wouldn't she want anyone to know? Jack realized now he had been a victim of his own grief, self-inspired folly.

"How far to Cartagena?"

Seth gave him a perplexed look. "What's in Cartagena?"

"An airport," Jack said. "A flight to Havana. Get *Scoundrel* the hell out of Cuban water before Raspov can stop me." Jack knew there was a good chance the Cuban navy would be waiting for him anyway. Raspov could pick up a phone and within the hour, *Scoundrel* would be surrounded by armed guards.

A safer option would be to fly to Miami, wait for things to cool down a little and then fight for the return of his boat. Jack didn't like the thought of abandoning *Scoundrel*, but at least he wouldn't end up in a Cuban jail, or worse.

"We could be there by morning," Seth told him. "But the rebels are pretty thick in this area, and they're always looking for the big fish."

Great, Jack thought. He wouldn't get to decide about his boat because he was going to be shot or kidnapped by FARC rebels.

Mercedes was quiet in the back seat. Jack wondered about her too. He still couldn't believe the similarities between the two women. He wanted to ask about her family, to find a thread that would tie her to Kaitlin. But this woman was clearly not interested in cooperating. Jack had no idea what game the Russians were playing, but thankfully this little adventure was over. At least that's what Jack thought. Then Seth cursed and Jack saw the roadblock.

There were four of them, standing there smoking. Jack recognized the uniforms. *Fuerzas Armadas Revolucionarias de Colombia.* When they saw the approaching car the FARC soldiers stomped out their cigarettes and pointed their AK-47s.

Mercedes gasped in the back seat. "Stop please. Turn. Stop now."

Suicide, Jack knew. "Shut up," he said between clenched teeth. He looked at Seth. "You know the drill."

"Righto."

It suddenly became harder to breathe. Jack felt his own heart, beating like a snare drum when he reached into his pocket.

Seth stopped the car.

The youngest rebel had to be no more than fifteen. Fresh recruit, Jack guessed, leftist drivel still a wonderful mystery to him. The oldest one looked like a veteran not much older. They were suddenly blinded by powerful flashlights, and for a second Jack wanted to shout at Seth to get the hell out of there. Before he had time to open his mouth both doors were ripped open and Jack felt the barrel of an AK at his temple.

They were ordered from the car. Rough hands jerked Seth and Jack into the night while Mercedes tried to sink into the shadows in the back seat. One of them yelled at her, then reached in and pulled her out. Smells of dried sweat on electrified air. Jack immediately recognized the ingredients of a massacre.

The rebels circled them. Whistling and grunting. Sizing them up, Jack thought. He waited for them to make the first move and hoped Mercedes wouldn't do anything stupid.

One of the rebels held a hand out and Jack noticed the Rolex watch. Nice touch. Jack held up his press card. "*Journalista*," he said. "*Journalista*."

The rebel snatched the card. "*Journalista?*" The man looked at Jack and then the photo. "Access Hollywood? Maury? Gerry Springer? Transvestite priests?" He flung the credentials to the ground and stomped on them.

One of the others laughed but stopped abruptly when the soldier doing the talking shot him a look.

The air thickened. How much longer before the shooting started?

Seth kept his mouth shut even though one of them was rooting through his equipment bag at the back of the car. The camera alone was worth forty grand. The leader moved closer to Mercedes, sniffing the air.

Jack tensed.

The rebel brought his flashlight up and shone it directly on her face. He said something in rapid Spanish, words that jabbed at her.

Mercedes slapped him.

That got everyone's attention. Rifles up. Safeties off. They were dead. Jack braced himself for the bullets while Seth whispered what he thought were his last words. "Not a good idea to strike the soldier, my lady."

Mercedes stared at the soldier hard. Spit a mouthful of words that seemed to slice into him.

The rebel forced a laugh and then brought the flashlight closer. Mercedes spoke again, this time with exigency in her voice. The universal language of warning. Jack saw her steely squint and would have given anything to know what she was pulling.

The rebels searched her face, muttering among themselves.

Mercedes wasn't backing down.

Seth looked at Jack questioningly.

Jack tilted his head slightly but said nothing. Whatever was going on, he was glad it was buying them time.

A full minute passed in silence, except for the sound of crickets and the flapping of powdery wings in the shaft of white from the rebel's flashlight. He finally barked something at his men.

Jack was stunned by what happened next. The rebel soldiers backed off. Their leader muttered something that sounded crazily like an apology and lowered his light to the dirt. He bent down to retrieve Jack's press card and handed it to him. "*Grande cajones*," he quietly said to Jack.

Jack exhaled. He didn't know if the soldier was referring to him, or Mercedes.

FIFTY-EIGHT

An hour later they pulled into the dirt parking lot of a rundown motel, an unimpressive flat span of rooms whose main source of ambient light was a neon sign that flickered "Vacancy." There was an empty swimming pool that might never have held water, cracked and littered with green patio furniture.

Seth went into the office to pay for two rooms while Jack and Mercedes hunkered down in the car. They crouched lower in their seats when a couple of trucks turned in and parked next to them. Half a dozen men with hard hats tumbled out, talking and laughing. They dispersed to rooms without even looking in their direction.

The rooms reminded Jack of a place he once stayed in Kinshasa — lino floors worn in places to bare wood with a curtain the colour of a hunter's vest. The furniture was vintage seventies.

Everyone breathed easier when Seth locked the door and Jack pulled the curtains. They both stared at Mercedes. Waited for her to say something.

When she didn't, "Nice trick," Jack said in amazement. "Whaddya call it?"

Mercedes forehead wrinkled. "Trick?"

Roadblocks like the one they ran into were a choke point for executions and kidnappings, especially for foreigners. Not to mention Mercedes had slapped the man. Nice. "What happened back there?"

Mercedes studied the ceiling, focusing on a large yellow stain that seemed to be migrating down a wall.

"The pig called me gringo whore."

Brave woman, but a lousy explanation. The soldier had backed off. No roadside executions. The slap had suddenly turned him into a real gentleman, full of remorse. Jack pointed out the weaknesses in her reasoning.

"A man I know," she explained. "At the roadblock the pig knew of him."

"Powerful friend," Jack said.

"*Si.*"

At that moment something occurred to Jack. The attention Kaitlin got when they'd arrived at the airport in Cartagena, the way the guy at the hotel kept looking at her, and then at the restaurant. It was very possible Kaitlin was mistaken for Mercedes the minute they'd arrived in Colombia. Mercedes, who apparently kept company with a powerful friend. Maybe very public company that made her a familiar face around here.

They could have spent the better part of what remained of the night jousting with one another but Jack wasn't in the mood. He went over to the television, the only thing in the room that wasn't cracked or peeling. He bent down and saw the inputs for audio and video and then said to Seth, "Have you got adapter cables for the television?"

"Absolutely," Seth replied.

It took him a few minutes to string cables from his camera to the television.

Jack removed a videotape from his knapsack and tossed it to him. "It's cued."

Seth shoved the tape in the camera and snapped it shut. He turned on the television and fiddled with some of the buttons on his camera.

Jack swigged from a bottle of water and turned to her. "I want you to meet someone."

A second later the television screen came to life and Mercedes inhaled sharply. Kaitlin filled the screen. She was sitting in front of a floor-to-ceiling window with a million dollar view of the city. Off camera a voice said, "Sit up, Katie."

"Sorry, George," she said, straightening herself. "Forgot how tall Carlyle is." Jack watched the tape glumly. Kaitlin was sitting in for the interview subject, the head of a large New York investment firm. They were covering the latest inflation numbers, the problem child of an overheated economy.

"Mic test," the voice off camera said. George was checking light and sound, the camera angle.

"The increase in inflation signals a worrisome, but predictable trend," Kaitlin recited from Jack's script, never looking down. "The big investment firms are worried how the Federal Reserve will react to today's numbers."

Jack had showed the tape to Walter Carmichael, the VP of news. "She's a natural. Camera loves her." Kaitlin didn't know it, but she'd just made her first audition tape.

On screen, while George continued to roll, Kaitlin stopped to look at her watch. "Come on, Jack. We've got ten minutes with this guy. That's it." At that point on the tape Jack walked into the office. Kaitlin's eyes brightened when she saw him. She smiled. "Thought you got lost," she said.

Jack heard the sound of his own voice.

"Have I ever let you down, Ms O'Rourke?"

In the motel room, Jack winced because he knew what was coming next.

"There's always the first time," Kaitlin said and then disappeared off camera.

Mercedes watched in awe, speechless.

"That's Kaitlin O'Rourke," Jack said, studying Mercedes' face. "And since you're not her, it means she's probably dead."

FIFTY-NINE

It was part trust and part gamble. Mercedes decided it was time to take a chance. She told them almost everything, and when she was finished talking Seth added his two cents. "This Montello bloke is a real piece of work."

Jack shook his head. He breathed deeply. This was bad. "I wouldn't have taken you for a drug lord's type."

Mercedes averted her eyes. "This is not so."

Seth opened his mouth and then shut it again. He shook his head and got up to repack his cables.

"You're absolutely right. It is none of my business," Jack replied. "Good looks. Money. Guy's one of the most powerful men in Colombia. What girl wouldn't fall for him?"

Seth was oblivious to Jack's sarcasm. "Did you mention that he has the biggest collection of Renaissance art in Central and South America?"

Jack rubbed the back of his neck and turned away, fixing his eyes on the wall. She'd been the consort of a Colombian drug lord who was now mightily pissed and wasn't handling it well at all. Killing her friends. Great. But how was Raspov involved? Jack walked to the bed and collapsed onto it. "An acquaintance of mine tried to kill us today. Probably to get to you. Any ideas why?"

"No," Mercedes lied, looking away again.

Jack got up. "Then don't you want to know who that guy was. Shooting at us?"

Mercedes didn't reply, didn't even look at him.

Jack continued anyway, "I'd wanna know everything about a guy shooting at me like that, a guy with two big apes. I'd wonder, what's his bloody problem?"

"They're your friends," Mercedes said. "How should I know?"

Jack sat again at the foot of the bed, buried his head in his hands. "Let's start from the beginning. First there's the suicide bombing and Kaitlin's disappearance." There was a pause. "Then you on that beach back there. Seth thinks he's seeing a ghost and he shoots that video which he e-mails to me. Raspov's ex-KGB and I go to him in Cuba because I'm sure he can get me 'unofficially' into Colombia. I know I have to find Seth in order to find the woman you just saw on that tape. Turns out my Seth here led us all to you, not Kaitlin, and it's no wonder because you could be the same person. Right, Seth?"

"Had me fooled."

Jack continued, "After I spotted you in that crowd today, and tackled you on the beach, that's when my 'friend' started shooting. He apparently wanted to get his hands on you pretty bad. Would have too had Seth not come along when he did."

"You are kidnappers," Mercedes said, accusation flashing in her eyes.

"If you like," Jack said, remembering the look of fury on Raspov's face as they sped away. "Kidnappers or saviours," he added. Jack didn't doubt what Dmitri had intended. Bullets for all of them. The Mendoza woman had a lot more to explain. Everything was somehow connected. Mercedes, Kaitlin and now Raspov and Montello. "So which are we? Kidnappers or saviours?"

Mercedes thought for a long time, the face of a blackjack player trying to decide whether to take another hit – go for broke. Then she began to speak, "The Russian came with his two 'apes' to Montello's villa. A month ago. Maybe." Mercedes looked at Jack, then at Seth who found a place on the floor where he sat against the wall. "I was getting in the car to leave when they came." Mercedes remembered the way the Russian had stared at her. The look on his face. On the way home Mercedes couldn't shake the feeling that she'd been expected to acknowledge him in some way. Her driver and the bodyguard were talking in hushed tones. Had called the Russians *tres verdugo*. The three executioners.

"Then there was after that time. Raspov came with a soldier," she continued. "Branko took them to his study." Mercedes looked from Jack to Seth. End of story.

"That's it?" Jack said. "All of it?"

She paused. "No."

"Go on," Jack said.

"Yes," Seth added. "I can hardly wait."

Mercedes went on. "The Russian – your friend – was mucho…very excited. Castro…Fidel. He talked much about him."

"Hold on a second," Jack interrupted, but Seth asked the obvious question. "How do you know what he talked about?"

Mercedes looked at both of them with the hint of a smile. "I was, as you say, the fly on the wall."

Seth and Jack wiped the surprised looks from their faces and got more comfortable as Mercedes began to tell the rest of the story. Nothing could have distracted the two men, not alien spacecraft crashing through the ceiling or a chorus line of Rockettes splintering through the hotel room door.

It was the second time Mercedes had dared to enter Montello's study. Second thoughts, second guessing. Whatever it was, it pulled her to the safe again. To confirm its contents. To bolster her courage. She couldn't believe her bad luck when she was forced once again to hide beneath his desk.

"You heard them?"

"*Si*," Mercedes said simply. "I hid under his desk. I listened."

Jack pictured her cramped and squat beneath the desk, fearing the one twitch or spasm or panicked gasp that would give her away. The woman had *grande cajones* all right.

Mercedes studied Jack's approval. She continued, "They talked about soldiers. A big attack. The president would be dead because people in the presidential palace were part of it. The soldier who came with Raspov was worried about the United States." Mercedes paused, searching for the right words. "Montello told him the United States would not interfere. It would be taken care of."

Jack looked at her quizzically. "Take care of it? How?"

"He did not say. That's all."

Seth swore under his breath. "Sounds like someone's preparing to overthrow the Colombian government."

"Sounds worse than that," Jack added. He looked at Mercedes. "What else?"

"There was very much I could not hear. Then they went."

"And you're certain it was Raspov?"

"Yes."

"What about the other man?"

"A soldier, I am almost sure. They sound the same. I choked on the smoke from his cigar. Once I nearly coughed."

Jack and Seth were thinking the same man. Domingo Guzman, the commander of the rebel camp.

Mercedes continued, "The next time I saw the Russian was with you and him. I thought you were part of them. You scared me, so I ran from you."

The bed was strewn with junk food Seth had gotten from a vending machine near the entrance to the motel. It was the best they could hope for at one a.m. in the middle of nowhere. Pollard reached for a bag of potato chips and ripped it open, held it out for the others. "*Jalapeño.*"

They ignored him.

Mercedes suspected the Russian had been dispatched by Montello to find her. He'd used Jack to get to her. Seth, now stuffing himself with potato chips, had spotted Mercedes on the beach that day and had taken the video, starting the chain of events. Mercedes didn't know what to make of the girl on the videotape. The girl Jack was looking for. Maybe Mercedes wasn't alone, after all. It was a feeling she couldn't shake. It suddenly overwhelmed her. Mercedes brought a wad of tissues to her face.

Seth munched noisily. "Kaitlin could have been your twin."

Mercedes looked at him through moist, bleary eyes.

Jack shook his head.

Seth shrugged.

Jack walked to the window and peeked through the curtain. The neon sign flickered at the edge of the parking lot above the two pickup trucks. "Colcord Pipeline Services" said the sign on one of the truck's dented doors. There was no one in sight. Jack wondered what Raspov was planning for them. Mercedes had finally revealed how she'd known them. Dmitri Raspov and the two brothers were involved in some scheme, possibly a *coup d'etat*. The plan had probably been sanctioned by Castro to clear the way for a friendly Marxist regime in Colombia. Jack was sure the American government would never allow that to happen – Marxists controlling the illegal cocaine trade would generate unlimited resources to fund FARC's ideological agenda. Lots of hard currency in Castro's pocket too. Everyone got their beak wet. Montello had told Guzman the US would not interfere. How could he be certain of that? What was his "insurance policy"?

"First things first," Jack said, pointing a finger at Mercedes. "We've got to get you out of here."

Seth stopped chewing. "I'll wager the DEA would love to have about two days of her time."

"Good thinking," Jack said. "And no doubt they'd love to hear about Raspov. No doubt he's been opening new markets for Montello with the Russian mob. Think about the market potential."

Seth nodded his agreement and then raised a single finger. "And since Raspov and Montello are mates, Dmitri is recruited to recover Montello's property." Seth looked at Mercedes. "No offence."

"*Si. Bien.*"

Something occurred to Jack. He'd shown up on Dmitri's doorstep with the thread Raspov could follow right to Mercedes. Seth's mystery video. Raspov had known all along who the woman in the photograph was. It had been convenient to nurture Jack's illusion. With Seth's help Jack had unwittingly led him right to Montello's "property." Jack told them what he was thinking.

Seth was still puzzled. "Why do Montello's dirty work? What's in it for Raspov?"

They both looked at her.

Mercedes shrugged.

Jack suspected she was holding something back. He clenched his teeth as he thought about the possibilities. If Raspov wanted her, it was because she held value for *Raspov*. Besides, Montello didn't need the Russian's help in that regard. He had no shortage of resources.

Seth held up a finger.

Jack saw it. "What?"

"There's something else."

"Christ."

Seth's forehead wrinkled in apology. "I wasn't sure until after the Russians showed their hand today. Now I'm sure."

"What?"

"Your friend Raspov is quite the piece of work, Jack." Seth appeared to be steeling himself. "The Rio Atrato massacre. Remember it? A bunch of farmers slaughtered apparently because they'd had enough of the coca. Tired of the fumigation chemicals killing their livestock. I went in to get some footage for Reuters. Not much left but aftermath – and the widows. '*Tres Ruso–*'"

"Three Russians," Mercedes translated, eagerly.

"Yeah," Seth replied. "Three Russians. Two as big as trees. One of the widows said they forced the women and children to drag the corpses of their men into the river and made them watch as they floated downstream."

Mercedes was mortified by the image. Without explanation she grabbed the telephone and retreated as far as the cord would allow. With her back to Seth and Jack and huddled in a corner, she spent the next ten minutes speaking in hushed, but urgent tones. She replaced the phone, a look of relief on her face.

Jack had screwed up, big time. If it were true, it meant the Russian – the mercenary entrepreneur – had been doing the cartel's grisly wet work for some time now. It was even possible that Montello had paid Raspov to assassinate the justice minister – Amillo – patron of the extradition treaty. As outside talent, Raspov would have provided the drug lord with arm's-length deniability, for whatever optical value it provided. Jack turned from the window, unable to disguise his grim comprehension.

Seth detected it immediately. "What?" he said.

Comprehension vanished, replaced by gloom. "The bastards

blew up that restaurant. Killed that farmer and his family. I've put us in grave danger by foolishly trusting a man I hardly know."

For a long time no one spoke.

Mercedes excused herself to go to the bathroom. When she returned her face was freshly scrubbed. Her long hair was tied back tightly to reveal her beautiful face. She moved to the bed, quietly reflective – there, but not really.

She held a stranger's moods, though Jack easily recognized regret and sadness. Her friends had been brutally murdered as a direct result of her actions. Also, she would never know the woman who might easily have been her sister.

Jack wasn't one for self-pity, but he had plenty of it for her.

Seth excused himself. "Met one of those rig workers from 113 at the vending machines. The lads are having a bit of a do and I said I'd drop in for a *cerveza*. Don't wait up."

Mercedes watched Seth leave. After an uncomfortable moment she pulled her knees tight to her chest. "The woman in the office. The videotape."

Jack knew what she was expecting. She'd want to know everything. He spent a moment collecting his thoughts, trying to rationalize the spectacle before him, a stranger who wasn't a stranger, except there was a life's worth of differences separating the two women. Things superficially evident. Mercedes the Colombian. The way she spoke and carried herself. The low-cut jeans and belly ring that glistened below her too-short top. Everything about the way her body responded to its surroundings suggested an almost reckless sexuality. Her hand gently stroked the soft folds of a pillow she was at that moment cuddling at her breasts. The way she used her tongue to moisten full red lips while her eyes searched his face for clues to his meaning. Her head tilted, hair swept back exposing her throat. None of these things seemed any more contrived than the luxurious grooming of a cat sunning itself. But they were qualities not openly displayed by Kaitlin O'Rourke, in the same way a rosebud has yet to reveal the full potential of its sensuality.

The Colombian Mercedes Mendoza was an only child. According to what she told them she'd been raised by nuns at an orphanage after the death of her parents in a car accident. She knew of no other family and was bewildered at her astounding resemblance to the woman in the video.

Jack recalled what the drunken Argus had told him. The peasant girl who had become pregnant. The desperate letter. Giving up her child. Argus had never revealed her name. If Kaitlin knew, it was likely she'd had to beg for it.

Mercedes was waiting. Jack started with Argus and Kaitlin's Colombian mother.

"What was her name? Does she live?"

Simple questions. Astonishingly absent of answers, Jack shook his head.

Mercedes listened closely, interrupting only when she had a question. *Argus?*

"Fire red and stubborn as forged steel."

"A Viking," she said. Why had he left Kaitlin's mother?

Jack shrugged, even though he could have easily guessed. Pairing with Argus – part boiler, part squall – promised a wretched existence. That might have been an exaggeration. In truth he was a caring, good-humoured soul who had raised a fine daughter. Jack offered a tempered assessment on both accounts.

"Kaitlin is beautiful. She received none of him." Mercedes smiled mischievously when she realized how immodest that sounded.

Jack cocked an eyebrow in acknowledgment. "She cherished her father, was pretty protective of him. She was like that with the people she loved, but let me tell you, she had no tolerance for fools and assholes, no tolerance at all."

Mercedes nodded. Even though she didn't fully comprehend, Jack's tone said everything.

Jack thought about the hooded Klansman in Mississippi whom they'd managed to track down for an interview after the fire bombing of a black daycare. She'd gone toe-to-toe and called him *schmuck* before Jack intervened for the sake of the story, and their safety.

He also remembered the time a widow in her apartment building broke her ankle. Kaitlin made her meals and walked her dog.

Mercedes seemed pleased by that.

Jack could have continued except Mercedes curled up on the bed and was dozing off. Jack pulled a blanket up over her shoulders and slipped quietly away from the bed. As he stepped through the open door Jack stopped to think again about the last thing she had sleepily said. "Were you..."

Jack had laughed no, realizing he was embarrassed more by his answer than her question. He turned as she softly snored and studied her a moment. Then quietly he closed the door.

Schmuck, he said to himself.

SIXTY

T‍rinity Orphanage.

The children were half asleep, and some of them were crying, and the oldest among them was frightened. They had been roused from their beds in the darkness and told to pack their belongings quickly.

The nun told Ernesto they were going on a trip. "Help the little ones," Sister Evangeline ordered and dashed from the room.

Without questioning he darted between the small beds with quick hands and now and then words of encouragement for the bewildered children, though Ernesto knew something was definitely wrong. "This way, Dominique," he told the little Choco girl who was trying to stuff everything she owned into a sack no bigger than two loaves of bread. "Put the rest with Luis…he's got room."

Luis didn't protest, looked proudly into Ernesto's face and nodded as he cleared a space for the little girl's clothing.

"Doctor Sam can go too?" the little girl pleaded, adjusting a sticky white bandage she'd stuck to the front of her stuffed animal.

"Of course. Doctor Sam takes care of you," Ernesto told her, understanding that since her heart operation, Dominique couldn't be separated from the small toy bear.

"I take care of Doctor Sam," Dominique replied earnestly, her large brown eyes widening as she carefully placed her one-eared patient into Luis's care.

A moment later when the children were nearly ready, Ernesto stopped what he was doing, sat down, frozen by memories of the last time he was shaken awake in the middle of night. It was his mother, and she was pulling him from his warm bed, screaming at him to hide. Ernesto remembered what he heard next. A loud bang, the sound of splitting wood, and the panicked shouts of his father in the front room. The gunshots sounded to Ernesto like the fireworks the old mayor lit off every year during the flower festival. His mother flinched at each report. "You have to run, Ernesto, now!" He climbed through the window, half pushed by his mother, and began to run. "*Si, amor. Carrera! Carrera! Rapido!*" More gunshots. Ernesto looked back as his mother collapsed. He stifled a scream. Ran faster, his little feet pounding the dirt along a worn pathway that led to the village. After fifteen minutes he reached the mayor's house, where he was found the next morning, asleep next to a litter of kittens beneath the porch, safe beside the small mewing creatures.

Ernesto got up to help Luis clamp shut his suitcase just as Father Govia threw open the door. "Come, children, to the front of the church. Now, Ernesto!" Ernesto thought again about his mother in the seconds after he tumbled from his bedroom window, when her hands pushed him hard away from her, before the bullets exploded into her body.

"Go, my son. Go!" Father Govia shouted, furtively scanning the room for stragglers.

The courtyard in front of the small church was a flurry of activity. Ernesto wanted to look away because the sisters were wearing funny nightgowns. They frantically pushed the children aboard a small yellow school bus and the look on their faces made Ernesto even more frightened.

"Hurry, children." Fat Sister Evangeline's eyes were red, and Ernesto had never seen her move so quickly. "God be with you," she said, silently counting the children.

Ernesto was sure something bad was about to happen, but he was too confused that late at night to figure it out. Father Govia was shaking, in bare feet as he lifted their small suitcases up a ladder at the back of the bus.

Sister Mary-Lynn handed Ernesto blankets. "Get moving, Frog," she said, smoothing his wiry hair. She smelled like flowers. "You'll be the one in charge." She gently touched his cheek and then kissed him.

"Why?" A breath caught in Ernesto's throat. "Why are you sending us away?"

Sister Mary-Lynn silently nodded, her eyes filled with tears. "Ten blankets. One blanket per child, Frog." She pushed him aboard the bus, gently stroking his back as he climbed the steps. Inside the bus the children were crying. Ernesto placed blankets over their tiny bodies. Two of them bolted for the door, but Ernesto blocked their escape, pushed them roughly into their seats, and then shoved blankets at them. "We're going on a trip," he said in a lie. "Stop being babies."

The others knew it was a lie, too. Father Govia always came on their trips, always drove the bus, but at that moment Mister Jeminez, the gardener, was climbing behind the wheel, his shaky hand fumbling around the ignition.

Ernesto sat at the front of the bus, his feet barely touching the floor, the one in charge because Mister Jeminez never spoke, never answered the children when they pestered him about the missing fingers on his right hand and the reason he walked in his funny lopsided way. Mister Jeminez, with a sadness that seemed to be painted forever on his face. He started the bus, and when Ernesto saw the old man's reflection in the large mirror above the windshield, he was more frightened than the crying children. Ernesto peered through the window and saw Sister Mary-Lynn, fat Sister Evangeline and the others with their heads bowed. Their mouths moved like they did on Sunday mornings when they kneeled in their pews, eyes clamped tightly together as they quietly prayed.

Ernesto imagined the feel of his mother's frantic hands, pushing him. "Run, Ernesto!" He had run then, unable to help her.

Father Govia shouted through the open door of the school bus, flapping his arms as if shooing the children away from his hammock after Sunday mass. "*Vamos!*"

Mister Jeminez jerked the clutch to get the bus moving. It growled. Black smoke painted ebony on night as Ernesto twisted in his seat to look back one last time. Sister Evangeline had a white rag to her face and even as the distance lengthened, her wet eyes found his, eyes that pushed him to run. Ernesto wouldn't cry, but he thought about the feral kittens whose purring coaxed him into sleep the night his parents were murdered only a month ago.

SIXTY-ONE

Hernan and his men moved with the stealth of leopards, their shoulders hunched as they crept through the forest surrounding Trinity Orphanage. One of them giggled like an expectant schoolboy. He'd be punished for it once their work was done.

Suarez rubbed his rifle as if to awaken it and then halted to listen. The others watched him, waiting for instructions.

Suarez pointed to the rear of the building and his two men disappeared quietly in that direction. He moved towards the front of the church, a smaller building with stained-glass windows along its side. Suarez decided he would enter that way. They watched them first and had seen the priest lead his flock of nuns inside the church sanctuary. Fools. What did they think? That they were safe there. Suarez smiled as he pictured the children asleep in their beds. He had big plans for them too.

He reached the huge wooden door and slowly opened it with barely a squeak. They knelt at the front of the church, seven of them, heads bowed and muttering. Candles flickered on the altar beneath the Christ, and Suarez caught the smell of burnt wax from where he stood at the back of the church. He enjoyed the feeling of being an intruder. It tingled beneath his skin, made him want to call out and demand they acknowledge his violation. He stepped inside. Only the priest turned to see him. He stared at Suarez without surprise. "Our father," the priest continued to pray.

The bitch had warned them, but Suarez wouldn't let that spoil his enjoyment. His two men emerged from a small door to the left of the pulpit and sneered, one of them gulping noisily from a bottle of wine. *The blood of Christ.*

The nuns continued to pray. "Imps of Satan," one of them whispered loud enough for Suarez to hear.

"May God forgive you," the priest said harshly as Suarez raised his weapon.

SIXTY-TWO

There was no answer when Mercedes called Trinity Orphanage in the morning. She was worried – very worried. Jack reluctantly agreed to a detour. What choice did he have? Mercedes had no intention of leaving the country without assurances that Govia and the others were safe. Then she'd accompany them to Santa Marta where Jack had arranged for a private plane to fly the three of them to Costa Rica. Jonathan Short at the State Department told Jack an embassy representative would be there to meet them. The DEA and "others" would want to debrief Mercedes Mendoza. "We've gotten wind that something's up, Jack," Short had advised him. "But that's all I can say. What's important now is you get your ass to that airplane and you and your friends get the hell out of there." A couple seconds of phone static passed, then Jonathan said, "Sorry your trip didn't end the way you wanted it to, pal." He hung up.

Jack thought about that as they drove from the motel the next morning. How had he expected it to end? Jack wasn't sure he knew – absolutely. He realized he had been foolish, chasing an illusion all along, the promise of something that he understood now simply wasn't possible.

It had seemed so in the beginning, but Jack wouldn't blame himself for the misdirection. The evidence had been too compelling to ignore. Jack couldn't say for certain that Mercedes Mendoza was connected to Kaitlin. He couldn't begin to calculate the odds that she was. Had Argus fathered two Colombian children? Jack suspected Argus would definitely want an answer to that question – Mercedes too.

Jack wanted his boat back, but he didn't know if that would be possible. He'd get to Cuba as fast as he could and take *Scoundrel* to sea, hoping Raspov didn't have other plans for him, or his boat. He immediately shelved those thoughts when he realized something was wrong.

It was quiet. Trinity Orphanage at ten o'clock was disturbingly quiet. No one came running when Jack stopped the car.

They were in a clearing at the end of the road which was surrounded by gigantic trees with broad loping palm fronds. There were several swing sets tucked into shade beneath them. *Empty.* Besides the orphanage and small church there were a number of other buildings, a small dilapidated workshop of some kind and a large wooden storage shed that might have held large machines, or even a tractor, had this been a farm instead of what it was. No one here. A dread slithered down the back of Jack's neck. Where were the children? The nuns?

Mercedes bolted from the vehicle in a dead run for the church. Jack and Seth jumped out and ran after her. They caught up just as she got to the front door. She gasped.

Through the shadows of the church Jack saw the smashed pews and broken glass.

Mercedes walked slowly inside.

Jack saw the blood trail first. He silently cursed, grabbed Seth's arm and frantically motioned in the direction of the orphanage next door. He'd stay with Mercedes.

Seth bolted from the church.

"They're not here, Mercedes," Jack said, trying to sound confident. "It's possible they all left after you—"

"The blood!" Mercedes exclaimed. "*Idios mio.* The children." Mercedes swept past and was out the door. She moved quickly, feet kicking up clouds of dust. Jack ran after her.

"Wait!" He took hold of her arm, blocking her path. "Let Seth check things. When he says it's OK we'll go in." Secretly, Jack was worried they'd grab Seth and use him as bait to get to her.

It must have made sense to Mercedes because she stood still, closed her eyes and exhaled a tortured breath. "Something's wrong."

Jack felt her tremble. "We'll wait for the all-clear. Then we go in," he repeated.

It seemed like an eternity. They were using a tree in the courtyard as cover. "You need to keep your head right now. OK?" Before Jack could stop her, she flung herself towards the orphanage, fingers scraping at dirt in a crouched run. She ducked into shadows just beyond the doorway.

Jack caught up to her again, ducking into the same doorway. "Wait," he cautioned breathlessly. "Believe me. Seth will shoot first. Ask questions later. He gets jumpy sometimes."

Mercedes nodded and then moved behind him. Jack slid the gun from his waistband as they both crouched. They were in a small foyer narrowing to a hallway that ran for a distance until it opened at a room at the back of the house. The kitchen. Light spilled on countertops and brass pots that hung from a ceiling rack. A dark table made of hewn wood was overturned, and pieces of broken dishes were scattered everywhere. Closer to them a large crucifix was ripped from its place on the wall and lay dully on the floor. Jack couldn't take his eyes from it. Mercedes' breathing quickened as he pulled her farther into the house. Jack swept the revolver in a wide arc in front of him. His heart suddenly pounded at the sight of a dark figure standing stiffly against a wall. It was a coat rack. Take it easy. Jack waited for his eyes to adjust to the hallway's gloom. Then it was time to move.

They heard someone moving around upstairs. The floor boards creaked under the weight of slow measured steps. Over the buzzing in his ears Jack heard doors being eased open on rusty hinges. *Seth?* he hoped.

Three doorways were on the left of the hallway. All closed. The next opening was a stairway. Jack grabbed Mercedes and ran to it. He winced at the thump of his heavy boots on polished hardwood. So much for stealth. Jack threw himself against the wall and called out, "Seth, it's us!" No answer. Jack pictured Seth, his finger nervously on the trigger, so jumpy he'd blast a hole in Jack's chest. *Ooops. Sorry, mate.*

Jack mounted five steps that stopped at a landing, Mercedes still clinging to him. A small stained-glass window splashed hues of red and blue across iconic wall hangings, a blur of cherubs, and Jesus, forlorn in the passion of crucifixion. Broken glass crunched beneath their feet. Jack took the remaining steps slowly and emerged into another hallway, narrower than downstairs, but brighter because of a huge window at one end. More closed doors, six by Jack's count, running at long intervals beneath a vaulted ceiling. Seth was nowhere. Jack hunkered down to lower his profile and shifted the revolver to his other hand, nearly dropping it in the process. He realized the safety was still on. *Dolt.*

"Keep her out of here, Jack." Seth's voice came from a room at the end of the hallway, as monotonous as tundra. The tone made Jack freeze. "It's bad, Jack. Fuck. Really bad."

Jack knew Mercedes would not be held back. She moved slowly ahead on legs that shook like spindles of thin bamboo. Jack touched her shoulder. His own feet felt like blocks of Indian rubber on floorboards stained red, boot prints smudged and streaked in a pattern of murderous frenzy. Jack would never forget the heavy burden of dread, the absolute hopelessness he felt as he was drawn forward.

"It's like that time in Kinshasa." Seth was blocking the doorway. His shotgun hung limply at his side. "Remember that one, Jack?" Seth clamped his other hand across his nose and mouth.

Mercedes pushed around him, tears streaming down her face, choking on sobs. "Oh God," she wailed as she collapsed into Jack's arms.

Seth looked back at him with haunted eyes. "Christ, Kinshasa was a picnic compared to this."

SIXTY-THREE

There were ten beds in the room, three more than needed for the seven corpses. Six women and one man, bound and gagged, stretched out on white sheets stained with large red blooms. Crimson pools shimmered on the floor beneath the bodies. There was movement there. Jack thought the flecks looked like white rice.

"Maggots," Seth said matter-of-factly. "It doesn't take long in this heat."

The stench he would always remember. So repellent it took control of the muscles in his face. Jack covered his mouth and steadied himself against the door.

Seth touched his arm and then hefted his camera farther inside the room, kneeling carefully to avoid a circle of congealed blood. There were small, black holes neatly positioned between their eyes, cloudy, hooded orbs that stared vacantly from death masks. Seth coughed, swore silently as he began to roll. He was methodical in his movements, eye plastered to the viewfinder while he framed one shot after another. A stiff hand, bluish fingernails – a gallows pallor that signaled the bodies were now controlled by the efficient soldiers of decomposition. Seth avoided the eyes, colourless and spent and the saddest part of death. On the Sony, the record light strobed, pulsing red in the rhythm of a heart.

Jack had gently drawn Mercedes to the end of the hallway, where she stood sobbing at the window. Shoulders pumping still.

"Looks like small caliber, possibly .22." Seth studied Govia, the priest. He was in a T-shirt, jeans and bare feet, no peace in his last expression. No absolution.

"The weapon of choice of your garden-variety assassin," Jack said, stifling a retch.

"Nothing garden variety about these guys," Seth replied.

The murders were shocking in their cruelty. Their hands and feet were tied with the same blue rope, identical knots — something efficiently fashioned with an expert's flourish. White cotton handkerchiefs were stuffed between grey lips in a homogenous display of evil, bordering on the Satanic.

It had to be Montello's work, retribution on a grand scale, driven by boundless rage. Jack was sickened.

Seth put the camera down and touched the frozen hand of one of the old nuns. A white rag was locked in her fingers. He touched it, allowed his hand to brush against her necrotic flesh. "They could have run," he said.

"Run where? Where could they hide?"

Jack stuffed his hands in his pockets, hunched his shoulders as if bracing for a heavy load. "Remember that Croat village? They had plenty of time to run but they stayed too."

"They were praying for the UN. The UN didn't come."

"They stayed anyway."

"The Serbs came instead."

"Yes. They did." Came and slaughtered an entire village, left nothing but a mass grave to be unearthed later, live to satellite.

Jack looked around the room, a kids' space with its gallery of posters. Britney Spears, the Back Street Boys, and some other teen idol Jack didn't recognize. There was a small stack of children's books on a shelf near the door. "They got the children away," Jack said, barely a whisper. "Thank God, Mercedes warned them."

Seth stood, surveyed the scene one last time before shutting down his camera. "Faith or foolishness?" he said.

"Maybe both," Jack replied. "Maybe sacrifice? Govia knowing they'd have to give up their lives for the sake of the children." Jack looked down the hallway to Mercedes. What had she told Govia that made the notion of escape so hopeless? Another unknown, he thought, as he moved towards her.

SIXTY-FOUR

Jack led her gently down the stairs and sat her on the shaded porch at the front of the building. He sat wearily, poured cool water over his head and offered the bottle to Mercedes.

"I pleaded with him," she sobbed, looking vacantly at the bottle of water. "I begged him to run…one of his silly camping trips with the sisters and the children."

Jack had seen the snapshots pinned to a large cork bulletin board just inside the kitchen. Roadtrips with lots of happy kids. A yellow bus which was nowhere on the property. Jack imagined the scene. Govia and the nuns pushing the children onto the bus and then retreating inside the church to wait. Jack took a swallow from the bottle. "I'm sorry, Mercedes," he said simply, feeling a deep sorrow for her.

"My fault," she whispered.

Jack felt helpless to soothe her. There were simply no words. Instead he watched Seth shooting b-roll at the front of the orphanage. A moment later the Brit disappeared inside the church. Jack knew exactly what Seth was up to and for the moment he let it pass. He'd talk to him about the ground rules later. Mercedes began to weep once more, her shoulders shuddering under deep mournful sobs. Jack gently rubbed her back, swallowed the knot in his throat, and tried unsuccessfully to erase what he'd seen.

The brutality had been ferocious. The priest's wounds as well as the blood on the inside of the church suggested he'd been pistol-whipped before he and the others were herded upstairs. One bullet each to the forehead. The nuns had been raped, two of the bodies had been posed in a macabre display of self-mutilation. They were strangers to Jack, but that didn't diminish his outrage. It was inhuman beyond words.

Her sobbing abated; Mercedes tilted her head back, allowing the sun to dry her face. She'd made astonishingly bad choices. So much had changed for her, her life a sad wreck. Montello had seen to that with obsessive fervour.

"Your ex-boyfriend holds a mighty big grudge," Jack said, regretting it immediately. "Jesus, I'm sorry."

Mercedes glared at him, a copy of Kaitlin in looks only.

Jack averted his gaze to the lush verdant hillsides that surrounded Trinity Church, a place of grotesque massacre. He thought about the children and wondered if they'd be safe. He'd seen the same worry in Mercedes' tired face a moment before. Jack was thinking about the children when he heard Seth's urgent shout.

The rectory at the back of the church was a small room, monastic in its appointments. A desk was cluttered with strewn and torn papers. There was a framed papal photograph on the wall above the desk and below the Pontiff, a crucifix. It seemed right that God's anointed representative on earth held higher position than man's sin against the Son of God. A filing cabinet was tipped over in the corner of the room. The drawers had fallen open and paper was spilled across the floor.

Mercedes took it all in. "Father Govia's office," she said. "We were never permitted here." She walked over to the desk and gently touched it.

Seth sat on the floor, back against a door which Jack guessed led outside. He studied the contents of a folder. "Look what I found." Seth passed some of the papers to Jack. They looked official, something produced by bureaucrats with rubber-stamped dates and faded signatures. The typed documents were frayed and discoloured, no doubt custodial red tape for the children in Govia's care. One of the documents appeared to be a birth certificate, the child's name in fading block letters, the date of her birth. Jack's eyes widened when he read it. He then fumbled at a second piece of yellowed paper which was stapled to it. It was a vaccination record for a number of childhood diseases. Jack brought the paper closer to his face. There were two children listed on the health document. One of them was Mercedes Mendoza, aged eight months, the same name which appeared on the birth certificate. The second child was also eight months of age. Another female.

Jack stared at the date of birth alongside the second name. Then he smiled broadly. Tentatively he offered the papers to Mercedes. "Your sister's name is Angelica," he said simply.

Trembling, she took the documents from Jack and brought a hand to her mouth. She paced as she examined them. There were two names on the vaccination record, Mercedes and Angelica Mendoza, both birthdays identical. Healthy and vaccinated at eight months old. Mercedes stared disbelievingly at Jack and Seth, and then read the vaccination schedule again, mouthing the names. The birth certificate listed Eva Magdalene Mendoza as her mother. Her father was Argus Peter O'Rourke – Kaitlin's father, according to Jack. Tears pooled in her eyes as she pressed the paper against her chest. She had never been alone. There had always been someone.

Kaitlin O'Rourke and Mercedes Mendoza were sisters. Jack had known that as soon as he saw Mercedes, and now the vaccination record confirmed it. Suddenly everything made sense. "Raspov knew the videotape of you on that beach was his ticket to you," Jack said. "He knew there was a connection between Kaitlin and you, because he had actually met you both – separately. Finding adoption records would have been easy stuff for a former KGB spook."

Seth handed Mercedes a tissue. She took it. "The explosion."

Jack knew where she was headed.

"There was no body?"

"None," Jack said. "But that doesn't mean Kaitlin survived. There were others—"

"Yes, I understand," Mercedes said, irritated. "But you cannot say...say a hundred percent...that my sister was killed. No body."

Jack shook his head. "No body. Nothing's a hundred percent. If I didn't believe that I wouldn't be here."

Mercedes sat on the edge of the desk, suddenly deflated. "But you thought I was her. This is why you came to Colombia."

Jack's blue eyes couldn't hide his own misgivings. He lowered his head, brought a hand to his face as if to wipe away her logic. "You're right. It's why I came." She was right, of course. But things were different now, no longer driven by that illusion. Things had changed. The journey — wherever it led — still had legs. Imperative. Jack was suddenly infused by new energy. "Kaitlin took a phone call in her room. I overheard her talking to someone just before we left the hotel. I'm certain she lied about who it was. It's possible — just possible — she went to meet someone outside the restaurant before the explosion. What if she had?" He plopped down next to Mercedes on the desk. "What if it had something to do with you? Or her mother? What if she wasn't in the restaurant at all when it happened?"

Seth looked doubtful. "That doesn't explain the fact no one's heard from her since it happened."

"I know...I know what you're saying, Seth, and I don't have all the answers. Shit, how could I? What if, for instance, she was being held, or unable to make contact? That's possible — right? This is Colombia, after all."

"I suppose," Seth replied, staring at the documents Mercedes held in her hand.

"A most dangerous place," Mercedes added. "For everyone."

Seth pulled himself up from the floor and reached out for the papers. "Please." He took them, then quickly scanned the vaccination record. After a moment he looked up and smiled.

Jack moved closer. "What?"

Seth jabbed a finger at the vaccination record. "Look right here."

It took a moment before Jack understood. *Of course*. How could he have missed it?

Seth pushed the paper at Mercedes. "Where you were born. Look. Maradona. Bolivar Department."

Mercedes grabbed the document and studied it again. "This cannot be true. I was born in Bogotá. My parents died there in a car accident."

Jack allowed her the time she needed to process what she was looking at, to understand the lies she had been told – for reasons unknown to them – by Father Govia. The truth was in her hands – for years squirreled away here in Govia's office. Her father was alive. An Irishman living in America. Maybe Eva Mendoza was alive as well. If that were true, why wasn't she told? Why had she been abandoned? These were things she'd need to know. Did she have a living sister?

Jack suddenly jumped up from the desk. Seth had clicked to it too. Both had a worried expression on their faces. "You're thinking what I'm thinking?" Jack said.

"Exactly," Seth replied immediately.

Mercedes looked at them questioningly.

Jack took a moment before explaining. "Those documents were too easy to find." Jack nodded in the direction of the death scene next door. "It's a message. Like they're a message."

"And the point is well taken," Seth added.

Jack waited impatiently for Mercedes to catch up.

When she had, Jack pulled her off the desk, and in a storm of fluttering paper, they ran from the office.

SIXTY-FIVE

MARADONA, COLOMBIA.

"The name I gave you is Angelica, but your father is an Irishman, so you became Kaitlin. I like that name very much also."

Kaitlin held her mother's arm as they walked slowly from the wide plateau overlooking the village. It had become a daily ritual that Kaitlin enjoyed because of the exercise, which they both needed, and the opportunity to explore this mysterious woman. It was on these sojourns that Eva usually became more talkative, likely the therapeutic benefit which was evident in the way the sick woman straightened against Kaitlin's body and drew her shoulders back to admire the hilltop view. Long and deeply Eva would inhale, savouring fresh air tinged with heady fragrances of the earth, the sky, and perhaps even more restoratively, Kaitlin's companionship.

They'd tied her thick hair back using a gold and red ribbon which Kaitlin had found among an assortment of hair accessories and costume jewelry scattered on the bottom of a small drawer in a scuffed ancient dresser. The drawer was otherwise vacant, except for a dazzling silver box, its lid missing, which contained a set of gold earrings with blood-red rubies cut in the shape of teardrops. There was a beautiful gold locket. Kaitlin looked to Eva who simply nodded. Kaitlin carefully opened the locket and tilted it towards the light of the window. She brought it closer to her face. Into each side of the pendant was tucked a faded miniature portrait. A man, unsmiling with a broad nose, meaty lips and eyes staring out beneath thick brows and a well-oiled mane of black hair. The woman's portrait showed the pretensions of billowing lace and languor on a countenance, once delicate, but since hardened by life and wifely duties.

Kaitlin guessed at their identities, then snapped shut the locket and set it down.

Another drawer was full of neatly folded garments of cotton and raw silk. Kaitlin tugged from the collection a pair of thin berry-coloured buttoned trousers and a white sleeveless shirt with pearl buttons and helped Eva dress. She then scrutinized a face of hollows, shadowed basins that sloped inward from the thin ridge of Eva's delicate cheekbones. The skin underneath her dark eyes presented wanly discoloured crescents. Eva smiled at her own reflection, nearly breaking Kaitlin's heart because she realized at that moment the sheer joy Eva felt as a result of this slight transformation.

On one of their daily walks Eva had led them as far as the graves and stood there quietly, for a long while deep in thought, disposed it seemed to anything but sweet recollection.

"Your parents?" Kaitlin finally said, to break the silence, but also to draw her back from whatever painful place she was revisiting. For some reason, Kaitlin was reluctant to allow the moment to wedge itself between them.

"My father and mother. Yes," Eva replied, vacantly assessing her father's grave. "My father was U'wa. His father was a tribal elder. The ones who remain live mostly in the northern provinces where they fight against big American oil companies. Centuries ago, rather than be dominated by the Spanish, the U'wa leapt to their deaths. They say they will do it again to protect the blood of mother earth."

Somewhere a raven screeched. A winged shadow swept across the ground at their feet and vanished before the echo died. "It was the barbaric traditions I feared most," said Eva. "You were not safe here, so I made a decision to get word to Argus as fast as I could."

Not safe. Kaitlin stared at the grave of Eva's dead father. The portrait inside the gold locket showed a man with thick broad features suggesting an indigenous lineage. Proud. Unconquered. Willing to jump from some sacred cliff rather than accept the ways of the conquerors' descendants' cash culture.

"I had no choice," Eva continued. "After what my father did I had to protect you from the U'wa cruelty."

Her father. Cruelty. Kaitlin felt compelled to ask for an explanation, when, despite her frailty, Eva dashed from the grave as if desperate to flee the reach of the dead man's corpse. Kaitlin caught up with her a moment later near the orchard of Eva's younger years. Slashed and burned to ruin now.

"Mangos," Eva had said simply. "They made us fools for refusing our land to the coca when everyone was fat with it." Eva carried a stick which she dug feebly into the dirt. "In the end it didn't matter because we had no help for the harvest. Only Alejandro and I were left."

Kaitlin could imagine the over-ripened mangos, weeping a syrupy sludge and thudding uselessly to the ground in the irregular rhythm of a dying heart.

"*Pistoleros* from the coca growers' union came in the middle of the night and this is what they did." Eva looked at Kaitlin with deep sadness. "It was a very difficult time for me. You understand."

Her parents were both dead, under circumstances Eva had not yet revealed to her, though clearly it was a loss shrouded by something unspeakable. Ostracized by her people – alone, except for her strange uncle. *Very difficult* was an understatement. Kaitlin doubted anything she said would help at that moment. She nodded sympathetically.

Eva offered a smile in return. It quickly vanished as she gazed back towards the two crosses, beyond the scarred earth where they both now stood.

Kaitlin wanted to hear much more. Her face must have relayed that.

"Your father came for you as soon as he received my letter."

"Argus."

"Yes, Argus."

Argus. Kaitlin struggled to remember. A face. A feeling. The echo of voices. Forms assembled as if beneath water's rippled surface and then vanished to the depths below her consciousness.

They walked together into the cool narrow pathway stretching from the sunny plateau to the clearing in which stood Eva's home. It was a lightless tunnel, veined by thick creeping vines and ribbed in century-old trees which bowed as though they were treading inside the torso of some benevolent breathing beast.

Eva took Kaitlin's hand and squeezed. "I never told Argus he had two daughters. That there were two of you."

Two of you. Kaitlin abruptly stopped. The starburst of that revelation made her tingle. Her stomach felt as if it were tumbling within its own weightless environment. *Two daughters.*

"Let's have a cup of your wonderful tea," Eva said before Kaitlin could say anything. "It'll help your memory. I think you're finally ready to hear everything."

SIXTY-SIX

The two women emerged from the tunnel of trees and walked towards the house on the hilltop high above Maradona, and although they were not alone, they would never have known it.

Suarez thought the older one looked sick. She leaned on the younger woman as they shuffled slowly to the house, where they sat on the porch, smiling and talking. Suarez studied them through the scope of his high-powered rifle, playfully stroking the trigger as the crosshairs danced from one target to the other.

Mercedes Mendoza had come home. Of course she had. Where else would she have gone? Suarez smiled to himself and wondered if Mendoza had seen his handiwork at the orphanage. He hoped that she had. No matter. Even if she hadn't it wouldn't lessen the satisfaction he felt for a job well done. He'd taken his time with the priest and nuns but became impatient when they refused even to acknowledge Mendoza's existence. How fucking stupid did they think he was? He'd watched while the two others had their fun, finally joining in when the screaming became too much for him to resist. Discovering the birth certificate had made it easy to find this place, a bonus after a hard night's work with the old priest and his bitches.

The woman with Mendoza had to be her mother, the woman who had tossed her aside as a worthless child. Maybe this was some kind of reunion. A reconciliation. He congratulated himself for his good timing. The man was there as well. Suarez spotted him earlier in the shed and then he had disappeared inside the house. He would have a weapon, Suarez was certain, and assets he could summon from the village. They could simply storm the house, but it made more sense to destroy them from the safety of their sniping positions. It was his preferred tactic for other reasons as well. The combination of the drug and his ability to bestow life or death made him feel almost God-like.

Suarez pressed his eye against the scope again and realized at that moment that the older one might also have been involved in Mendoza's thievery. The bonds were likely stashed inside the house, though he couldn't say for certain because Mendoza's confederate had refused to speak before he'd thrown her from the helicopter. She had begged him at first and then spat in his face in the second before he loosed her into the darkness. A search of their airplane turned up nothing useful, some jarred food and a briefcase which suggested the woman was some kind of bank honcho.

In any event, Suarez had plans for the money that made his head buzz with anticipation. Or was it the pipe? He'd smoke again in a moment, but for now he was content to study the two soft targets as they loitered on the porch, smiling like old friends who were enjoying the approach of another perfect evening.

Two of Suarez's men were staked out behind trees like this one, a hundred yards from the house, waiting for his signal. They wouldn't have to wait much longer. Good thing too because the mosquitos were beginning to leave purple welts. His nerve endings hummed and lately he'd had a sensation that felt like bugs burrowing under his skin, making Suarez pick and scratch to the point of bleeding. He would break up the family reunion by putting a bullet into Mendoza's mother first. He'd enjoy the look of shock on the younger one's face as her mother crumpled to the ground, blood gushing from the centre of her forehead. Maybe a gut shot would produce a better show. Then he'd take Mendoza, after having his fun with her.

Everything was perfect. Suarez was enjoying the moment as he reached into his pocket for another rock which he placed in a small glass pipe, and in a smooth motion cupped a tiny white flame at its bowl and drew fiercely. The rock turned instantly to grey ash. Suarez coughed but wasn't worried about giving away his position. He knew they were oblivious to him as he pulled the rifle scope to bleary eyes and applied light pressure to the trigger.

He'd be wealthy soon, he thought, exhaling thin smoke between smiling lips.

SIXTY-SEVEN

What this country needs is another Stalin, Dmitri Raspov thought. An iron fist and decent road maps.

Uri traced a blunt finger across a piece crumpled paper containing the smudged directions they had acquired two hours before from a boy riding bareback in the middle of nowhere on a washed-out mare his grandfather might have broken. That was at least a hundred miles back. Now they needed water, gasoline, and whatever food they could come by on this wretched scar of a road which had become as doubtful to the three of them as a Chechen ambush trail.

Pavel stared menacingly at the man who was filling their tank. He had to be a dimwit or a mute, the way he had ignored Uri's demand for directions. The man beamed toothlessly and simply grunted when the crumpled paper was shoved in his face.

"That's enough," Pavel said, spying the pool of spilled gasoline at the dimwit's shoeless feet. Lazily, Pavel swung a steel-toed boot to his rear, raising a plume of dust that settled on the mess.

The man turned abruptly as if to engage, but wisely stood down when he saw Pavel's steely grin. "You come, yes," Pavel taunted, tossing a handful of bills into the wet dirt.

Two minutes later, when Pavel was finished, they drove off, spraying dirt and sand onto the man's unconscious form.

"He does not forget us," Pavel said, removing his hand from the steering wheel to wipe blood-spattered knuckles on the front of his shirt.

Raspov was choking on the dust that wafted in from the smashed rear window. They'd retrieved the Land Rover, but not surprisingly, the sack of weapons and ammunition was nowhere to be found. The only guns they had were the ones they carried, which would have to do, he decided.

They'd been driving the same road since morning, skirting a river for the twenty miles through a series of lush valleys that appeared to them as giant bowls brimming with the morning's mist. The road they could not yet find would carry them higher into the mountains and ten miles more until they reached their destination. At least that's what that cocksure boy had told them, bending forward on his pathetic mount to get a better look at the three strangers in the Land Rover. "*Si*. You pay, yes." Then for five minutes the boy swung his arms like spears on a compass, spouting directions in splintered English. Uri jotted most of it down.

They were close now, Raspov was sure. "Keep your eyes open." He thought smugly about the information he'd obtained from the *Rezident Kulakov* at the Bogotá embassy who knew everything, including the colour of the president's shorts on any given day, and more recently dining habits of his justice minister. Birth records showed both Mendoza women were born to Eva Mendoza, but Kulakov had cursed, "Better records kept in a Chechen whorehouse." There was no trace of Mercedes Mendoza beyond infancy. The mother, he said, was being treated by a doctor in Barranquilla. She still lived in Maradona. Kulakov, former 9th Directorate KGB, now FSO, had offered Raspov a team, but Raspov had declined, thanking his old friend for the intelligence. Raspov was sure the girl would run home. Doyle and that fucking little Brit would help her. Raspov was intent on spoiling that homecoming.

When they found the Mendoza woman, Raspov would have his money, enough to guarantee his place in the new Russia. There'd be a powerful position in the government, maybe even elected office now that democracy was the fashion. Raspov found that distasteful, though things were changing in other ways that Raspov liked, and he wanted to be part of it. As a member of the former communist KGB elite, Raspov would be revered, maybe given special status. After all, Putin the president was one of them. Raspov smiled to himself. No more dancing to Castro's pathetic tune, no more of his silly little Marxist revolution. The psychopath Montello was desperate for the promise of what only Raspov could supply, so Raspov had fed Montello's illusion, Guzman too. As a result the cartels had happily agreed to his price. Let them pay for something they would never have. Dmitri Raspov, colonel of the great KGB, 2nd Directorate, had engineered some of the greatest intelligence operations in the history of the motherland. Deceiving the Colombians had been child's play. It rankled him to think that, were it not for the Mendoza woman, the cartels' millions would already be in his hands. She had spirited away Montello's money in the most brazen of ways. Right out from under his nose. It's what the drug addict Suarez had foolishly confided to him, perhaps stoned, perhaps out of resentment towards his master. Raspov didn't care. He would have the bonds, and be gone.

"Remember, the girl lives for now," Raspov said, leveling a finger towards Uri and Pavel, who both smiled expectantly. "The rest…do what pleases you both."

SIXTY-EIGHT

Eva and Kaitlin sat in wooden chairs on the porch, listening to the soft thrum of powdery wings and enjoying perfumes from a dozen varieties of exotic flowers in Eva's garden. The older woman trembled as if the warm Santa Marta winds swirling around the house were coated in ice. Kaitlin retrieved a shawl for Eva and then watched her closely as she sipped her tea.

"You were born here, in this house." Eva smiled on the memory, cradling her cup tightly to her chest as if she were holding a suckling newborn. "I was in labour for two whole days, but you were the most beautiful things I had ever seen."

"Tell me about my sister."

Eva's smile wilted to a frown. "Mercedes nearly died the night you were both born. Were it not for the doctor's quick hands she would have strangled. It seemed forever before she finally took her first breath."

Mercedes. For a moment Kaitlin pictured the scene of panic as they fought to save her life – the urgent voices, a baby's screech followed by prayers of thanks in the amber glow of oil lamps. A disconnected image intruded on Kaitlin's thoughts. An infant swaddled in a dirty blanket in the death grip of its mother. This infant will not cry again. A bulldozer is pushing dirt into a hole containing row upon row of white sheets. Oppressive heat presses in on her, dust coats her throat. The smell. She is not alone. She and the others share an imperative which is a mystery to her, as they are. In a way Kaitlin is being reborn, swaddled in the fabric of her past.

Her mother continued, weakly now since it was her habit to fade in the same way as a Maradona sunset. "I was a stubborn girl, Kaitlin," she said. "I made the decision that Argus would not know and with good reason. I had no one but my parents. And Alejandro."

Kaitlin was glad Alejandro was back. He'd been gone for a long time, leaving her alone with Eva. He'd stomped into the house two days before, offering no explanation for his absence. Eva hadn't asked for any. Kaitlin cooked her healthy meals and after a week's hard work she'd transformed the kitchen, in fact the entire house, into an acceptable living space. Marginally, Eva's strength returned. Twice the doctor had come but the pills he left made Eva sleepy. He examined the gash on Kaitlin's scalp and carefully studied the reflexes in her eyes for signs of deeper damage, or even clues to her memory loss. Finding none, he said there was nothing he could do, not with the meagre possessions he carried in his worn leather medical bag. A hospital was required for that, but Kaitlin sensed she wouldn't be making the trip to any large medical facility. The doctor told her not to worry. She was doing fine, eventually her memory would return. It was a prognosis she prayed for.

Eva lowered the steaming cup from her lips and traced a finger around its rim. "It was amazing how you mimicked each other. It seemed you were both connected to one brain. When you wailed your two voices seemed like one. Your stomachs and diapers were as if connected to a clock."

Kaitlin was fascinated by what she was hearing. She absorbed everything.

Eva continued, "Once you were stung by a bee and Mercedes cried also – with the same red spot on her tiny foot. Alejandro insisted the insect had attacked both of you, but believe me, this was not the case. You were without shoes at the time. Mercedes had not managed to kick hers off."

The more Eva said, the more Kaitlin felt connected. To what, she wasn't exactly sure, though connected all the same. In the next second the warmth she felt became a chill.

"You were considered bad luck because you were twins."

That was crazy, Kaitlin thought. "Twins are a blessing."

"To the U'wa, a curse, not a blessing." Eva tried to get up but surrendered to her fatigue. She fell back in her chair and stared into the trees somewhere. Kaitlin followed her gaze and thought she saw something move in the darkness gathering at the foot of a tree.

"The U'wa fear twins as an evil omen – demon children," Eva continued. "The father is believed to be an animal. Where you come from these things are hard to accept, but they are the truth for the U'wa – still."

It was an abhorrent "truth," Kaitlin thought, certainly absent of anything human. But in the rough little societies where indigenous people survived, feeding two children had to be much more difficult. Suspicions were sometimes born of common sense. Walk under a ladder and you're likely to get something dropped on your head. Break a mirror and you'll probably cut yourself. Both were hazards steeped in suspicion.

None of this Kaitlin felt compelled to impart at that moment. Instead she remained silent, struggled to keep her face free of further judgment.

"The parents of twins are a curse also," Eva said. "In my case I was unwed which was another shame for my family." Eva paused. "In the village they said I was a gringo's whore."

Argus. Her father. In the part of her mind where the past had retreated a face stared out at her, absent of definable features. Kaitlin clenched her jaw and shook her head as if to dislodge it. She was unable to stop the question that parted her lips, even if she had wanted to. "Why didn't my father take you with him?"

Eva touched her arm and looked at the last of the sunlight as it settled like a golden ribbon on distant hills. "He wanted to and he was very…what is the word?" Eva clenched her fists, pulled her face into a knot.

"Unwilling to take no for an answer?"

"*Si*, a big stubborn fool of a man."

Kaitlin tilted her head. "Then why–"

"I could not leave," Eva interrupted. "Never."

It sounded to Kaitlin like a declaration of innocence. Something she had said a thousand times but had waited decades to be heard. Kaitlin sensed the relief that trailed it.

Eva breathed deeply. There was much more she had to explain. "My father was a very proud man — and very difficult to live with under the best of circumstances. Having an unmarried and pregnant daughter was his shame. But when I gave birth to two of you, well...that was too much for him to bear, so he left us." Eva studied the remains of her tea, tilted the cup to expose the leafy remnants at its bottom. "For weeks he was gone and when he returned it was as if we were dead to him. He wouldn't even look at me. Or the babies."

Kaitlin tried desperately to absorb everything Eva was saying. She thought again about the graves, both marked with the same date of death. A premonition. She braced herself for what was coming.

"The U'wa elders came that night. They stood over there and called out to my father." Eva looked to a spot twenty feet in the distance near the crumbling shed and then snapped her head away as if the ghosts of those men were still waiting to be acknowledged. "At first he refused and yelled at them to leave. They refused. Then my father confronted them."

The only thing missing from the picture were flaming torches, a hangman's rope slung over the nearest oak tree. Hooded figures on a moist Mississippi night. Kaitlin tasted bitterness at the back of her throat. Softly a moth thudded against the window behind them, tugging her back to the moment.

Deep worn lines were suddenly drawn on Eva's face. "We thought..." she said, halting mid-sentence. There was a pause. "We expected him to fight. To chase them off. But Serpez held power over the entire village. There was argument, yes. But in the end Luis simply bowed his head and wept."

It was the only time Kaitlin had ever heard Eva say her father's name, as though the broken, weeping man she had just described was the man she needed to remember as her father. Not the animal who had stolen her children.

Eva wrapped herself in her arms, stooping forward in her chair.

Kaitlin would have told her to stop but knew it was too late for that.

"Your grandfather," Eva continued, "he took you both that night. We could see in his eyes what he was going to do." She tugged a sleeve to her face, dabbed at her eyes. After a few seconds Eva pulled herself as straight as she could. "My mother and I fought him when he returned without the babies but he refused to tell us anything. But we knew what he had done. The U'wa believe twins are animals, not human – the children are returned to the earth." Eva reached over to take Kaitlin's hand. "He abandoned you both. To die."

Kaitlin had heard enough. She clamped shut her eyes and covered her ears, which might have appeared to Eva as though she could listen no more, which she could not. Though, in reality, Kaitlin was also desperate to eliminate distraction because of the whisper coming to her as if through a crowded room. *Kaitlin. Go.* Suddenly there is the warm metallic smell of equipment, tense bodies. They are olfactory touchstones that seem to lock her to the moment elusive. Fade in. A dark, crowded space. Rows of small glowing monitors. Urgent voices. She is terrified for someone.

"Kaitlin?"

The man standing next to her is a cop. *Shut this down. Now!*

"Kaitlin?"

Eva is pulling her back. The tableau, as tenuous as frost sheets on spring grass, crystallizes into a billion luminescent pixels. Kaitlin returns to the there and now. After another moment, "How did we survive?" she asked.

"It was a miracle that Alejandro was in the shed when the elders came, tending to his horse. He heard them telling my father what he had to do and where he should do it. Alejandro knew he wouldn't be able to stop him, not with Serpez and his thugs still there. So he waited until everyone left. Then he raced after you." Eva shivered. "He and that old horse of his found you in the Jaguar Forest and brought you back home to me."

It was the first time Kaitlin had seen her truly happy, though the smile vanished as quickly as it appeared.

"When my father discovered what Alejandro had done he was insane with rage. He and Alejandro fought. Alejandro was badly beaten. Then he grabbed you both again. I tried desperately to stop him but my father pushed me down hard. That's all I remember. I must have blacked out. When I woke up you two girls were wailing in Alejandro's arms. He was crying. My mother was dead. So was my father. She shot him." Eva's face was streaked with tears. She took a moment to collect herself. "Then she took her own life."

Kaitlin couldn't believe what she had just heard. She swallowed hard, stunned by it. The timeless echoes of two gunshots cracked in her imagination. Two graves, the same date. Remains in one, a beloved mother and sister in the other. It broke Kaitlin's heart to see Eva in such pain. There was a moment of silence between them and then Eva, steeling herself, continued, "I knew the U'wa elders wouldn't allow you to live, not after what had happened. I had to separate you to save you. I got word to your father. You became an American. Your sister I sent to Father Govia at Trinity Church." Eva shook her head. "A little while after, the U'wa elders came to Maradona to deliver a warning. You were already safely in America by then but they said I was cursed as long as my children lived. You could never be reunited with your sister. I couldn't leave Colombia to marry your father because I wouldn't leave Mercedes here – not alone." Eva averted her eyes. "After what happened I think I actually believed them. The curse had killed my mother and father. I was afraid it would eventually kill both my beautiful children. I'm sorry," Eva said. "I'm very sorry."

Kaitlin stared at her mother with understanding. She rubbed her shoulder, a simple gesture that seemed, by the look on Eva's face, a sinner's absolution. No, Kaitlin thought. No sin on her soul. How could Eva even think that? This woman had endured a lifetime of pain and even now the barbarians, with their insane tribal dogma, haunted her with the residue of culpability. Kaitlin couldn't remember her life past, but she knew it would have been completely different. A twin sister and a mother she had never known. This place. Her home. Kaitlin exhaled loudly and closed her eyes again. It was unbelievable, yes. But Kaitlin never doubted its truth. Why was that so? She shoved her curiosity aside for the moment. "How did I get here?" she finally said.

A breath whooshed from between Eva's lips. "That's another story," she replied. "But first I think we'll require more of your tea."

SIXTY-NINE

Jack threw the car into second gear and stomped on the gas around a curve in the road. Mercedes squinted at the map. "There's a road. The next right. It looks like it could be a shortcut."

Jack saw the open maw of a turn up ahead, a darkened throat swallowing the day's lingering light. He punched on the overhead light. "Tell me you're sure about it. We don't have time for mistakes."

Mercedes brought the map closer to her face. "Yes, I am sure."

The look on her face wasn't a confidence-builder but he decided to trust her judgment anyway, and a moment later he swung the wheel hard and spun onto a road which was even more potted and narrow than the one they were exiting.

"I didn't even know there were roads up here," Seth said without purpose from the back seat. "The map if you will."

Mercedes passed it over her shoulder without looking back. "I think it could be the smallest place in all Bolivar department – this Maradona."

"Right," Seth replied, studying the map.

"There in the mountains. Do you see it?" Mercedes said. "Follow the shortcut road."

"Yes. There it is. Complete with all the amenities, I'm sure."

"In this part of the country – some of the best," Jack cut in. "Coca plants prefer the high altitudes. The farmers harvest the leaves and then process them into paste. Then they mule it down to drug labs which are basically heavily guarded depots for processing chemicals and cheap labour. That's where they turn the paste into coke. The *campesinos* have satellite TV and haute cuisine, not to mention a paychecque that's better than yours, Seth."

"That's because the coca growers have a better bloody union."

The three of them chuckled and for a brief moment the tension retreated.

Jack stole a glance at Mercedes, dazed and quiet as she stared out the window. Dark lines seemed scorched on her forehead and her eyes appeared ready at any moment to burst. In the hours since he'd known her, Mercedes Mendoza had become a different person. How could she not, Jack thought, after what had happened? Jack was also certain she had wounded Montello in a way she had yet to reveal to them. The bodies at Trinity Orphanage were grim confirmation of that, each corpse a notch on Montello's scorecard.

Jack checked the rear-view mirror and saw Seth's head bobbing against his chest. The man could sleep anywhere under any circumstances. He cleared his throat and quietly began to speak, "Everything changes if you're involved at all with Montello's drug business."

Mercedes snapped around, fire in her eyes. "Excuse?"

Jack returned her glare. "If you're part of what you're running away from, I can't help you. You'll be treated like any of the others – extraditable – indictable and punishable. The DEA might cut you some kind of slack, but I doubt you'll avoid prison. I won't help you if you're one of them."

For a moment Mercedes remained quiet. A storm gathering energy.

"Do you understand what I've just said?"

"I understand that you have misjudged me," Mercedes replied.

"Do you blame me?"

"How can I not? You accuse me of being a monster. Like him."

Jack held up a finger. "Not a monster. I didn't say that. What I'm saying is there's a possibility that you are in some way tied to Montello's drug empire. I don't know. It's possible you stiffed him or something on some huge drug deal. You're on the run. He's killing everyone in your path, past and present. That doesn't sound to me like he's just pissed at you for bruising his ego."

"You cannot understand."

"You're right. I don't understand. But you can help me by telling me the truth. Why is this guy so goddamn determined to destroy you?"

There was a pause. Mercedes opened her mouth as if to say something. Then she abruptly turned to the window.

Damn, Jack thought. Anything would help right now. Even the smallest piece of information could be a life saver if they ran into Montello's men. Knowing the depth of her betrayal could help them anticipate the measure and extent of his response. What if FARC soldiers were now searching for them with their much larger weapons and resources? Jack searched passing shadows at the side of the road, where snipers might be lodged, waiting for their quarry. He wondered what they would find when they arrived at Maradona. Another slaughter? Jack shuddered at the thought, concentrated instead on his driving. The road narrowed, heaping claustrophobia upon his growing apprehension. This mirror image in the seat next to him could have been Kaitlin. His cameraman was now coming awake in the back seat. The crew was together again, Jack thought. Reporter, producer and shooter on another assignment. He shifted gears to gain speed around another uncertain twist in the road, higher into the mountains where night had already taken hold, rooting in Jack the uneasy feeling that this was a story no one would survive to tell.

SEVENTY

Eva wasn't hungry. Neither was Kaitlin. Appetites seemed an intrusion under the circumstances. A layer of cooler air had dropped from the cloudless sky, prompting Eva to ask for a warmer sweater. Kaitlin wore an old pair of her mother's blue jeans and a white long-sleeved shirt that Eva said Alejandro sometimes wore when he took her to the fancy doctor in Barranquilla. As far as Eva was concerned the time for doctors was over. "You would never have found me," she said. "Except for a debt which was owed Alejandro."

Kaitlin listened closely, thinking back to the time when she'd first awakened, Alejandro watching her as she walked into the room. His first words. It seemed so long ago now.

Eva smiled warmly. "The doctor says you'll eventually remember."
"Let's hope he's right," Kaitlin sighed. "In the meantime…"
"You're confused."
"Very confused."
Eva nodded. "On the day you arrived in Colombia—"
"I was trying to find you."

"Yes." Eva smiled. "But it was not the only reason you came."

Kaitlin's brow furrowed. One step at a time, she thought. Slow down. "Sorry. Please go on."

"On the day you arrived you visited the Regional Records Office," Eva continued. "The bureaucrat in charge is a man named Sousa. Alejandro and Sousa go back a long way – to the army. He's a bureaucrat now, but he owes Alejandro his life and doesn't forget. Many years ago Alejandro went to him and asked for a favour which he could not refuse. If anyone came looking for me or the two Mendoza girls, Alejandro would be told. Of course Sousa told you nothing at the time. In fact, the file he keeps locked in his desk."

An image flashed in Kaitlin's mind. A cavernous room. The musty smell of old paper. A long counter and a man with a chubby, round face. The recollection slowly dissolved, making Kaitlin want to snatch it before it vanished into thin air.

"Sousa asked for your name and your hotel, and then he got word to Alejandro that someone was looking for me. Alejandro called you later that day with instructions. You were having dinner that night so he asked you to meet him outside the restaurant at precisely nine o'clock."

"Why the precautions?"

Eva thought about it for a moment. "Serpez and his cadre are long gone, but there are others who nurture the old superstitions. The old resentment. Your grandfather's name has never been forgotten, nor what happened. Alejandro does tend to be overly dramatic at times, but then again, the U'wa still consider twins as evil. Not too long ago the parents of twin boys gave their babies to a clinic not far from here rather than see them abandoned in the rainforest or thrown into the river. The parents were cast from the tribe."

Kaitlin was mortified. "That's unbelievable," she said. "Why isn't the practice stopped?"

"The tribe uses the courts to defend its rights," Eva replied. "They fought for the return of the boys, perhaps to carry out their death sentence. Thankfully it was a case they lost."

Kaitlin folded her arms tightly, as if warding off a sudden chill. She and her sister had been sentenced to die, and would have, were it not for the

ANGELS OF MARADONA

blood which was spilled in this house so long ago. In a flash of anger she cursed inwardly.

Eva told her next about the suicide bombing, easing into the worst part of the story. "Many people were killed, including the justice minister and his family. They believe he was the target. You were there that night."

Kaitlin gasped.

"But you were spared." Eva exhaled. Reaching over to wipe a strand of hair from Kaitlin's shocked face, she added, "When you walked out to meet Alejandro, it saved your life."

She had been thrown into a cement stairwell in the alleyway next to Café Umbria. "A miracle," Eva said as if it were delivered by the hand of God.

These facts simply didn't exist in Kaitlin's mind. Nor did she have any recollection of the old man who hobbled through smoke and fire and debris to reach the stairwell, her tiny fortuitous bomb shelter. His rough little curses, as he hoisted her with sinewy arms on bony shoulders and carried her to a rusted pickup truck parked two blocks east of the demolished restaurant.

"When Alejandro brought you here you were unconscious. The doctor came and cleaned your wounds and changed you into one of my old dresses. He told us you'd be fine, and thankfully you were. Except for your memory." Eva paused a moment. "Wait here," she said.

She went into the house and came back a few minutes later. She placed a folded garment on Kaitlin's lap.

Kaitlin stared at it blankly. "What…"

"Open it," Eva said.

Kaitlin unfolded the garment. It was a cream-coloured dress, stained and torn. Kaitlin savoured the feel of the expensive material. "It's beautiful. Too bad it's destroyed," she said, frowning at the tattered state of what had clearly been an expensive item of clothing. Kaitlin hadn't seen it before, even though she had helped Eva dress on several occasions. It must have been something Eva had squirreled away – ruined, but still holding sentimental value. "You must be sick about it," Kaitlin said.

"Such a dress you have no need for around here," Eva replied. "This was the dress you were wearing when Alejandro brought you."

Kaitlin studied it quizzically, rubbing her fingers across a shapeless brown stain. She traced a long gash that ran from its hem, and then for a reason she could not explain, she brought the garment to her face and breathed deeply. Traces of perfume swept into her nostrils, faint with the hint of seduction. Suddenly, a thousand switches fired in her brain, creating a cacophony of snaps and crackling like dormant embers latching onto oxygen. *Oh, God*. She squeezed shut her eyes. Suddenly, pulsing lights pierced the ebony, tantalizing in their promise, each one a lost moment encapsulated. They began to burst, one by one, and then an entire constellation against a bleeding black universe. *The dress*. It had been so expensive, she remembered. But she had purchased it anyway. *God. Yes.* There was a reason she had wanted the dress. Other memories were painfully just beyond her reach. Kaitlin ached, as though blood were returning to deadened nerves. A moan escaped her lips and she sank into her chair. She breathed deeply again as if to energize the fusion process which was taking place inside her brain. Then, instantly, everything went black. *Damn!* Kaitlin sighed. She was about to open her eyes, until…something else began to appear. Slowly. Flesh and bone morphed on a shapeless frame. Shadows moved like tides around the contours of a forming face, obscure at first as if pressed behind a sheet of melting ice. Kaitlin's heart pounded with excitement and then in the warmth of revelation and relief, she smiled to herself. She whispered a name and before her breath faded she braced herself against the rush of her past. Everything swept in. It was all there now.

Then came the gunshot.

SEVENTY-ONE

Mercedes jabbed excitedly when she spotted the turn off to the left about fifty yards ahead. Jack saw it too, slowed the car, and quickly consulted his mental compass.

A guy in the village, manning a tin shack where you could buy cold *cerveza*, had pointed towards the summit of a distant hill where it was barely possible to see the roof of a house behind some trees at the edge of a broad plateau. Jack decided it made sense that this was the way in. A moment later he braked abreast of a narrow pathway that stretched far away into the darkness, revealing no signs of human activity except for the deep ruts made by off-road vehicles with a lot more road clearance than they had. He felt dread at the sight of it. "We'll walk in," he said.

Mercedes and Seth stared anxiously at the coal black of night which engulfed the car like a malevolent entity.

Seth turned. "You sure, Jack?"

"We've got no choice. Besides we'll be harder to spot on foot," Jack replied, trying to sound as confident as he could.

Seth wasn't convinced. "If you say so, mate. But if they have night-vision equipment we'll look like glow sticks."

Jack pulled into a small clearing at the side of the road and killed the lights. Seth was absolutely correct, but it was a chance they'd have to take. Besides, the car offered little or no protection, and because of the terrain, less in the way of hasty retreat.

No one said anything. Then Seth chambered a round so excruciatingly loud that it made them jump. "Sorry," he whispered.

Jack pulled out his revolver and turned to Mercedes. "You stay here."

She shook her head vigorously and reached for the door handle. "I don't stay here. I'm going with you."

Jack knew argument was a waste of time, so reluctantly, he nodded.

The three of them got out and moved quickly to trees at the side of the road. When they reached the opening, Jack halted them. He peered through the darkness, feeling dread from the sight of it. He wondered nervously who and what would be waiting for them.

The flap of wings startled them; the silhouette of some night hunter appeared above their heads and climbed away until it disappeared to another perch a few tense seconds later.

Jack moved forward, crouching low while he led them into a hardened mud rut. He looked back at Mercedes' expectant face.

"What's the plan?" said Seth behind her.

"Quiet," Jack whispered, not really knowing what the plan actually was. He supposed they would reach the house, hunker down while they scoped the threats, and then assess the situation. Beyond that there was not much else Jack could have told them. Truth was, most of what he was doing at that moment was improvisation, except the praying. Jack searched his intuition but felt nothing. He decided that was a good thing, since his intuitions were normally of the dark variety. Twenty more steps along the path he abruptly stopped. A sound. No, the echo of a sound farther ahead in the darkness. Jack froze. *Shit.* What if they were waiting? Then they'd be walking into an ambush. Something jabbed into his back. He jumped and spun around.

Mercedes mouthed an apology and stabbed the air as a small furry creature scurried across their path.

Jack clenched his teeth on a curse and toed forward, heart still pounding.

Five minutes later the road veered left and opened into a large clearing. The three of them melted into the shadows, which were thickest at its margins. After a few seconds, Jack pulled up short. In the distance there were two buildings, one decrepit and collapsing that might have been a barn or large storage shed. The main house was in better shape, a small one-storey clapboard structure with a long sloping roof that extended to a wide porch facing in the distance a dark wall of scrub, trees and giant broad-leafed bushes.

As he scanned the edge of the clearing, Jack imagined glassy eyes, hard and cold, sighting them from a deadly sniper position. At any second a bullet could rip into his body. Maybe a head shot, he thought gruesomely, or a round that would vaporize his heart. He shook loose the feeling, wiped the sweat from his face and chastised his overactive imagination. Jack inched them forward, carefully searching for signs of danger. There were none, at least none that could be seen. Jack took only a small measure of relief in that. Still, he managed a calm breath which was repeated twice behind him.

Then Mercedes whispered at his back.

Lights were on inside the house. Someone was home.

Seventy-five yards from where Jack, Mercedes and Seth were crouched a radio crackled lightly. None of them would have heard it. Suarez keyed his transmit button and quietly ordered silence, cursing the idiot who was about to tell them what he already knew. Visitors had arrived.

He saw them immediately – two men and a woman. *The woman.* Suarez studied her through the scope and decided he was hallucinating. He shook his head, bringing on a dull throb that threatened a full-blown headache. He wanted to smoke another rock, but there was no time. He'd have his hands full in a moment and he couldn't count on the morons who were similarly entrenched around the house, including the idiot who had just broken radio silence. Suarez touched the spent casing next to his rifle, still warm. One shot, one kill. He could have taken the others just as easily but had decided against it. The shot had produced an enjoyable moment:

the look of terror on the woman's face when she realized death had reached out to them. The terror was followed immediately by her panicked screaming, and then the little man had burst from the house, shocked and confused, before collapsing to his knees when he saw her, her head lolling lifelessly at her chest. Blood on his hands now as he ripped at clothing to find her wound, he had shouted her name, no cried it, a piercing pathetic wail that reached Suarez, making him tingle with exhilaration. The little man spun around, fear and rage as he searched for the source of her death, darting eyes which would never spot the sniper. He'd gotten smart then, hoisting the corpse from the chair, though he should have left her, and then retreating with the help of the other Mendoza woman inside the house.

Now, these new arrivals. He didn't recognize the two men, the woman he did. He could take the men easily and then spend his time with her, produce an even more enjoyable moment, longer than a moment, of course.

Suarez sighted the taller man through his night vision scope, a figure in ghostly green moving towards the house. An easy head shot. Slowly he began to pull the trigger.

Suarez suddenly jerked. A spear of pain penetrated his skull. There was a flash of blinding light and he could pull no more.

SEVENTY-TWO

Jack saw movement through a dimly lit window and his heart raced. He pulled Mercedes to the side of the house, followed by Seth who dropped his shotgun and then bent quickly to retrieve it.

Jack shot him a disapproving look, then said to Mercedes, "I saw a rear door. Go and wait there for our signal."

She appeared to be thinking about her options.

Jack moved his face close to hers. "If there's trouble you can go for help."

She thought for another second and then disappeared at the back of the house.

Jack and Seth moved silently to the front of the porch and mounted the steps. Jack spotted a trail of blood and stopped dead in his tracks. *Shit.* Immediately the sight crushed his prayers for a bloodless night. He motioned for Seth to stay back as he crept to the front door, leveling his revolver, flaunting a bravado he didn't possess. Like drawing down at high noon, he thought. Jack waited a moment and then did something that seemed ridiculous to him. He lowered his gun. He knocked.

Seth looked at him incredulously, whispering harshly, "You're knocking?"

"What do you expect me to do?" Jack whispered back.

Seth thought about it and then shrugged.

"Lower that thing," Jack said, and waited. Knocking may not have been the best idea. No one answered.

There was no lock. Not even a doorknob. Slowly, Jack pushed the door open into a dark room. He tensed. Earlier, there'd been a light on. He was sure of it.

Seth stayed on the porch while Jack stepped inside. Too dark to see anything. Jack took another step. He was sure he heard breathing. Seth? Not Seth. He was still on the porch. Jack rubbed the front of his shirt and listened. There it was again. *Someone behind the door.* He was certain of it. He had two options. He could kick the door and take out whoever was hiding there, or…

Plan B.

Jack stepped back and swung the door closed. It slammed shut, revealing a figure crouched low in the darkness. It sprang forward, swinging something menacing in its speed and trajectory. It came at Jack in a wide arc and with a sickening thud smashed into his head just above the temple. Shards of pain buckled his legs and he collapsed to the floor. Feebly he reached up to protect himself against further blows, but none came. Just a scream which seemed distant as he slipped into unconsciousness.

SEVENTY-THREE

"Jack...Jack?"

Someone was slapping his face.

"I'm so sorry."

The slapping was really irritating him.

"Jack?"

But the throbbing pain in his head was worse. Excruciating.

"Shit." A woman's curse. "He's really out."

Jack sought refuge behind clamped eyelids, though her voice plucked at him. A tone as tight as piano wire. There was Seth's voice then. Further back. "Got a bucket?"

Jack spun away into the blackness, away from the pain, until a few seconds later when a splash of water, cold as ice, jolted him awake. "Jesus," he coughed, driving a dagger into the rapidly expanding lump on the side of his head.

"Jack, I'm so sorry, but you've got to get up now. We've got to get out of here!"

Who the hell was talking? He heard the words but was having

difficulty with their meaning. Everything was spinning and Jack was choking on the bile in his throat. A trickle of warmth ran down his cheek. *God, the pain.*

"We thought you were them," she continued. "When you came to the door and then you kicked it in—"

"Didn't kick," he moaned, still unsure who was talking.

"Not kick, I know, but when you pulled the door shut, Alejandro saw the gun and that's..."

A cane was broken into two pieces on the floor.

"Nice piece of wood," Seth said as Alejandro maintained a vigil at the window, a look of worry on his face which matched Kaitlin's. Something darker than worry. A countenance painted with the doom of Michelangelo's Minos. Alejandro spoke in a rapid and guttural Spanish which Seth found difficult to follow. The old man swept his hand angrily towards a door across the room.

Seth walked over and pushed it open. A child-sized bundle lay on the bed, another white sheet stained with blood. He cursed quietly, cut the muttering old man as much sympathy as he could muster and then walked quickly back to where Jack was lying on the floor. "Jack, get the hell up, mate, we've got to go!"

Jack was seeing double, four faces silhouetted against the dim glow from a ceiling light. It took him another moment before he could raise himself onto his elbows. A large accomplishment given the extent of his misery. In the fog of his pain it didn't make sense that Mercedes would have disregarded his instruction to remain in hiding out back and to race for help in the village at the first sign of trouble. Instead she'd beat him inside the house and then clobbered him. "Mercedes, why..." The words trailed off in surrender.

Kaitlin looked at Seth for explanation.

"I don't think he gets it yet."

"Get more water, quickly," she said. "There's no time."

"Mercedes, no!" Jack shouted, rubbing the side of his head. "What the hell were you thinking?"

"Look at me, Jack," Kaitlin demanded, choking back a sob.

It took him another couple of minutes to pluck the cotton from his brain and for his eyes to begin to focus. Jack cocked his head to one side and fixed on her. "Kaitlin?" he moaned.

"Now he gets it," Seth said.

Jack steadied himself against her as she helped him up. Sparkles floated like confetti in front of his eyes. "What are you..." Jack paused, tried to recalibrate his brain. "Here. I mean how..."

"It's a very long story," she replied shakily, wiping her eyes. Then she carefully embraced him. "And God, it's good to see you."

Her breath was warm against his skin, a soothing distraction from a current of pain in which confusion seemed an undertow. What she said next didn't help.

"Eva," Kaitlin sobbed. "She's dead. They shot her."

Jack stumbled back a step, shoulders against the door. He gingerly touched the large bump on the side of his skull and exhaled loudly. Then he stepped unsteadily towards her again. "I'm just a little fuzzy right now. Could you repeat that?"

Kaitlin didn't have to.

Jack followed her eyes to the open bedroom door. A bloody sheet stretched out on the bed, a pitifully small bundle beneath it. His heart sank. He permitted a minute to pass, silently waiting for his senses to re-energize, for his mind to establish equilibrium. After a moment he took in his gloomy surroundings. Kaitlin's shoulders quivered upon her grief, a red-eyed survivor of some cruel act — not of God or of nature — but of man. There were a million things he didn't know. The body inside the bedroom screamed the one thing he was certain of. Jack took Kaitlin gently in his arms. "I'm so sorry," he said. "But you're right. It's time we got the hell out of here."

"Jack," Seth said, motioning towards the back door. "You're forgetting someone."

Jack's eyes widened. Mercedes. She was still waiting behind the house for the all-clear. He nodded quickly and Seth disappeared down a hallway that led to the back door.

Jack grabbed Kaitlin by the hand and began to follow. Briefly he looked back at Alejandro. "Who's Alejandro?"

"He's a friend," Kaitlin sniffled. "Where's Seth gone?"

"You'll know in a moment," Jack replied. "Is he coming with us? He's got a pretty good arm. We might need it."

Kaitlin stopped dead in her tracks. She held a hand out towards him. "Alejandro?"

Alejandro walked instead to the open bedroom door, where he stood, motionless.

"Alejandro," Kaitlin repeated, eyes swelling again with fresh tears, faintly pleading in her Spanish. "There's nothing we can do for her now. She would want us to be safe."

"From the curse," Alejandro replied without taking his eyes off the bloody sheet.

"Not the curse, Alejandro," Kaitlin replied. "There is no curse."

Alejandro sneered. "Luis, Gabriella, Eva. No curse?"

Kaitlin thought a moment. Her family had suffered immeasurably. Staring at her mother's dead body, she swallowed her grief, incredulous that after all these years the suffering continued. No curse, she repeated silently to herself. "The curse of cruel and foolish old men who had no right to believe in such things," she finally replied.

Alejandro appeared to be thinking.

Jack was growing impatient. He had no time to fill Kaitlin in on everything that had happened so far even though it would have given her a better understanding of their perilous situation. There'd be time for that later. If there was to be a "later." Right now, they needed to get moving. There was clearly a connection between the old man and Kaitlin that Jack didn't understand yet. He hoped he was going to get that opportunity. In the meantime, Mercedes and Seth were waiting. And Jack was sure – when the two women came face to face – more valuable time would be consumed by their mutual surprise.

Jack then turned towards the source of heavy footsteps. Seth and Mercedes entered the room.

Kaitlin went slack-jawed.

Jack stiffened when he saw the three hulking figures behind them.

ANGELS OF MARADONA

"Nice to see you again, Jack," Dmitri Raspov said, sounding as cold as the Siberian landscape. "Sorry about screwing up the reunion."

Uri shoved Mercedes and Seth out of the way; Pavel placed his weapon against the side of Jack's head.

"Time we all got better acquainted, don't you think?" Raspov said with a sneer.

SEVENTY-FOUR

Did she tell you, Jack?"

"Go to hell."

Raspov's eyes swept the room, stopping briefly at the bedroom where Eva's body lay. He jabbed the gun at Mercedes, laughing dryly. "Your little orphan didn't tell you, did she?"

Jack had no idea what Raspov was talking about. He didn't care. He was frantic about Kaitlin. Uri and Pavel had taken her, along with Seth and Alejandro, into the shed. There was no telling what kinds of horrors were underway. Jack's eyes slid to Dmitri's gun. The best he could hope for was an inattentive moment during which he could try and jump him. He'd grab the weapon and take his chances with Uri and Pavel next door. Then they'd make a run for it. It might have been a plan, except Jack was just about incapacitated by the horrible pain in his head. Alejandro had likely given him another concussion when he hit him with that fine wooden walking stick.

Raspov got up to pace. "I saved your life tonight, Jack." Dmitri was full of surprises, Jack thought. Here comes another one. "Those little monkeys had you in their sights when you wandered in here." Raspov moved to the window and stared into the darkness. Jack began to count. Another second and he'd take advantage of Raspov's distraction to make his move. *Shit*. Raspov spun around. "Montello's man Suarez. You wouldn't know him, but he never misses, even though he was a hopeless drug addict. He smoked a rock while he waited for you. The moron. Still would have gotten his head shot." Raspov smiled. "I got mine first. No need to thank me."

"I wasn't planning to," Jack said.

"You're welcome anyway," Dmitri replied jovially. He took a couple of steps, stood directly in front of Mercedes while keeping an eye on Jack. "This one has bigger balls than both of us, Jack. To do what she did. I am impressed with her courage, if not her judgment. She sits there a dead woman, though she may not completely understand that."

Mercedes sat stone-faced.

Jack tried to conceal his confusion. He gave Mercedes a questioning look, unreturned.

Dmitri sat down again, wiping sweat from the back of his neck. "But poor me. I've been robbed. I'm a victim and I deserve to be treated as such. Compensated for my pain and inconvenience. That fits nicely your western sense of justice, doesn't it?"

Jack suffered the dread of a man being ushered into traffic. He'd stall for time. "Robbed?"

Raspov stared at him, contemplating something. "It's a long story, one you'll not get a chance to hear."

"Then what's the harm?"

"You're right. Just two guys talking. Like old times, eh?"

"If you say so," Jack said.

Raspov checked to make sure the safety on his weapon was off, and then began to speak. "Montello and the others are worried. Very worried. They remember Noriega and Hussein, the poor soul, and they know they're next." Raspov leaned in closer. "Like rabid animals backed into a corner they will fight."

"Animals is right," Jack replied. "But not much of a fight for American special forces."

"Perhaps. But what if you could even the odds?" Raspov expected no answer. He got up again, swung his gun before him and took imaginary aim. He looked back at Jack. "Montello and the others have unlimited financial resources," he said. "Which appeals to my sense of greed. After all, Jack, it's the new Russia. Big houses with plasma TVs, and SUVs. Consumerism. What a wonderful concept." Raspov allowed a moment to pass, perhaps to daydream. "I'm going home, my friend," he continued. "Going home with a piece of the American dream in my pocket. A big dacha, lots of cars and women. It's all very expensive."

"Learn to live with less," Jack said. "You'll be happier."

"Perhaps you're right," Raspov replied. "But why should I? I've met an opportunity for unbelievable wealth which is too difficult to resist." The Russian studied Jack's face. "You're hungry for the details, I suspect."

"You're crazy, so spare me the details."

"Crazy with wants and desires," Raspov shot back.

"Just crazy," Jack spat. "We found your handiwork at the orphanage. You're a psychopath."

"You mean Suarez," he replied, feigning hurt. "My dead friend outside with his two dead accomplices. Don't worry. They've paid for their crimes." Raspov paused, jabbing a finger at Mercedes. "See what you've done, my child. You delivered a pox upon that house. All those righteous souls delivered to heaven. Suarez, on the other hand…perhaps not."

Mercedes stared defiantly at thin air.

"No matter," said Raspov. "Here's a headline that may interest you, Jack."

"I'm not interested in anything you have to say."

"You're a news junkie. You'll love it. 'Colombian Cartels Take Desperate Measures to Fight Extradition to the US.'"

"Too many words," Jack said.

"You may be right."

The former KGB spymaster held up a finger. "Then how about this? 'Nuclear Weapons for Sale.' More to the point, don't you agree?"

Jack's ears buzzed. He struggled to conceal his alarm. "You are nuts."

"Don't condemn me so quickly, my friend."

Jack shook his head painfully. "Come off it, Dmitri."

Raspov grabbed Jack by the hair, jerked his head back. "Come on, Jack. You're a reporter. Dig a little deeper for the juicy stuff. It's worth it."

Jack denied Raspov the satisfaction of his misery. He grabbed Raspov's wrist and wrestled it free. "You're a dinosaur, Raspov. Thank God, you're extinct."

"Extinct?" Raspov repeated, tapping the gun against Jack's head. "I wouldn't be so quick to judgment if I were you."

"Get to the point," Jack demanded.

"Deadlines, deadlines," Raspov said. "Very well." He circled them and sat once more.

Jack was glued to the gun, menacing in its deadly purpose. Time was like oxygen in the compressed blue wafer beneath space, thin and sadly gasping. Raspov couldn't be stalled forever. He'd eventually become bored with the game.

"Hawks within the Politburo were extremely nervous," the Russian said. "Because of all the American talk about Star Wars, remember?"

"It was Gorbi's deal-breaker in Iceland," replied Jack. "Old news."

"That's right. Old news. And also no secret that Star Wars would have changed everything. To his credit, Gorbachov resisted at Reykjavik and the summit collapsed. But we knew then something had to be done. There was no way we would have survived a first strike with the ability to retaliate." Raspov fixed his eyes on Jack. "You remember how it was, Jack? The Cold War, tit-for-tat arms buildup. It got rather expensive and we couldn't keep up. Besides that, our ICBMs were becoming unreliable, leaking radioactivity. There were navigational problems because of substandard components in the gyro and computer systems. We couldn't even afford to keep them fueled. Inspectors found empty vodka bottles in one silo." Raspov shook his head as he stood again. "We needed to protect ourselves, even if Gorbi didn't understand that. A group of us did, so we came up with a solution to level the playing field."

"Gorbi and Reagan wanted an end to nuclear weapons," Jack said. "Why not just suck it up, get on with life?"

"It was bullshit," Raspov shot back. "You know as well as I that the American people would not have accepted that. Nor would good patriotic Soviets. The nuclear deterrent had functioned as it should for decades. Why fuck up a good thing with talk of full-scale arms reduction?"

"So?"

"So we decided to take proactive measures." Raspov waited until he was sure he had Jack's full attention. "Loosely translated, something we called Operation Seedling."

"Planting saplings for the environment. Commendable."

Raspov ignored the remark and leaned in until Jack could smell him. "Portable nuclear weapons, Jack. Tactical nukes were to be seeded in twelve cities within the continental United States. Twelve of the most populated."

Mercedes shifted in her chair, drawing a sliver of their attention.

A gasp lodged in Jack's throat. He wondered whether Raspov had heard the groan in his gut.

Raspov offered the hint of a smile, dreamy eyes held Jack in their gaze. "Smuggled aboard German freighters into Los Angeles, Seattle, New York. From there, overland destinations. Chicago, Boston, Detroit. Need I go on?"

The thumping in Jack's head pounded his senses. It was difficult to speak, to find the right words. "Lay off the coke, Raspov," he said. "You're psychotic."

"No. Listen, Jack. This is good," Raspov continued. "The shipping company was a KGB front which was convenient when we needed to ship weapons and military supplies to our friends in Libya, etcetera, etcetera. How do you think we got those ICBMs into Cuba? Old story. Unfortunately a bit before my time."

"Too bad you had to miss it."

"Kruchev had the right idea. Just poorly executed," Raspov observed. "Anyway, those German-flagged ships were loaded with shiny new BMWs, Audis. The American dream, remember? Let's just say that a dozen of these luxury cars wouldn't have met your country's pollution emission standards. Not after what our weapons institute was able to conceal inside them."

Stall, Jack thought. Keep him talking. Raspov cherished his ego. It must be fed. "Soviet tactical nukes smuggled aboard German ships and seeded throughout the country?" Jack said, barely able to believe what he was saying.

"You make it sound so easy." Raspov smiled. "But yes. Essentially that was the nuts and bolts of the plan. Brilliant, don't you think?"

"You are crazy," Jack replied.

"Brilliant then," Raspov sneered. "Brilliant now."

Jack cocked his head slightly, hoping to detect signs of life in the shed outside. There was no telling what the Russian brothers were doing in there. He shuddered to think of Uri's and Pavel's special talents.

Brilliant now? What had Raspov meant by that?

Satisfied that Jack was brimming with curiosity, Raspov eagerly continued, "The nukes were made ready. Twelve of them."

Jack shook his head with disbelief. "It would have been impossible to circumvent the state's nuclear control structure. The nukes would have been missed immediately."

Raspov laughed softly. "Ordinarily yes," he said. "But let's just say accountability would not have been a problem. We had the weapons we needed because back when things were very nasty between you and us – at the peak of the Cold War – the KGB had custody and control of the nuclear warheads. The missiles were separate." Raspov tapped his forehead. "Even then we were thinking. A number of the KGB's warheads were skillfully made to disappear from all official records before we relinquished physical control of the weapons a couple of decades ago. They were our 'insurance policy.' After Cuba we decided we needed one."

"Kruchev backed down. Tarnished what should have been a shining moment."

Raspov's face tightened. "That's right. He did. But never again would that happen. No one in the Kremlin had the guts to do what we were going to do."

Thank God for that, Jack thought. "So…"

"We had sleeper agents in place in safe houses to accept the automobiles with their on-board nuclear devices. All was set to go. Yes, a shining moment in Soviet history as you put it, Jack. Think of the strategic advantage we would've achieved. Soviet nuclear weapons on America's doorstep – literally. Like bringing the mountain to Mohammed, don't you think?"

"Mohammed was a prophet, not a terrorist," Jack said.

"So were we," Raspov spat. "Smart enough to see through American deception concerning disarmament. We would have relinquished the only real weapon we had left, becoming easy pickings for the hawks in Washington."

Raspov was a dinosaur, Jack thought. A dangerous relic of out-of-control times.

Raspov looked at him. "Gorbi and Reagan were talking about complete eradication. No more ICBMs. It scared the shit out of us patriots." Raspov tapped the barrel of his weapon against Jack's knee. "Gorbachev would eventually have given it all up. We were a Super Power for Chrissake, preparing to surrender our might. Mikhail was a traitor."

"Some would say visionary."

"Bullshit. The threat of a nuclear exchange was our strongest ally. It kept both sides on their toes. The Soviet Union would have relinquished its ace card, thereby destroying the balance of power."

"The power to destroy the planet twice over," Jack said. "Some ace card."

"And you — ten times over," Raspov said angrily. "Don't get righteous with me. It doesn't suit you." A scornful look cut lines in Raspov's face. "Gorbachev was to be told only when the devices were in place. Better to ask for forgiveness than permission, right, Jack? You were using the same strategy when you came to Colombia with Kaitlin. And by the way, I still cannot believe the astounding coincidence with these two women. Amazing. And very convenient for me when you came looking for my help."

"Whatever you say."

"What happened was this," Raspov continued. "Gorbachev found out what we were up to — and heads rolled. Most ended up dead or in the Gulag. Not me. I cooperated with them." Raspov's features turned sour. "After that I was basically exiled to Castro's shitty little island. I've made a living, but I'm tired now and strangely I miss the Moscow winters."

Jack thought back to the first time he'd met Raspov. The night in Moscow when they got drunk and Raspov passed him the envelope. "You sabotaged the summit to buy time for your little plan," Jack said, knowing the truth before Raspov answered.

"Of course we did. We would never have been able to proceed with American weapons inspectors climbing all over us with their damn verification protocols. Sniffing around to see if we were living up to our part of the disarmament deal. We were concerned they'd discover the discrepancies in the warhead numbers. By that time twelve were missing. As I said, we knew the best way to scuttle the summit was to expose Gorbachev's hand before he had a chance to play it. That's where you came in. You did your job, that's all."

It didn't feel like that to Jack. He'd been a pawn, played to perfection. "So what next?"

"Not so fast, Jack. I'm not finished yet."

Jack dreaded where Raspov was headed.

"The nuclear weapons were supposed to be returned to the Soviet strategic command," Raspov said. "And although the records indicate that's what happened. It did not."

More slight of hand by the KGB, Jack thought.

Raspov continued, "For more than a decade we've been storing…no, hiding them in a forgotten bunker at an air force base outside of Moscow. We are remnants now but we still control them, Jack. Patriots who believe in nationhood again for the great Soviet people."

Jack shuddered at the thought. Suitcase nukes. What zealot miscreant or terrorist wouldn't want a taste of that kind of power? Jack didn't doubt Raspov's reach. "Which brings us to what?" he asked, fearful that Raspov was about to put an end to this.

"Which brings us to my good friend Branko Montello," Raspov replied. "This man, Jack. He has big balls, this man. Like her."

Mercedes was unsettling in her silence.

"Strangely, I admire him for what he wants to become," Raspov continued. "I'm a greedy capitalist now so I gave him my price."

Price? She'd been holding back, Jack thought. He punished himself for not seeing it. But how exactly was she involved?

"Montello and the others were more than happy to pay." Raspov paused, as if to savour the taste of his words. "Ask her, Jack. Ask her how much she took from her old boyfriend. My money."

At that instant, Jack wanted to shout her deception.

Mercedes continued to stare off into space.

"I prefer bearer bonds over gold or diamonds," said the Russian. "Much easier to handle. Ask her, Jack. Go on. It's why we're all here."

Jack stared at her with reproach. "Well, Mercedes?"

"Fifty million dollars," she replied weakly.

Jack was stung.

Raspov looked at him. "Now that we've gotten that out of the way I know what you're thinking and it is too dark to comprehend. Montello's a psychopath. He'd detonate one of the devices just to prove he has the weapons. Take out a million or so people in say, Houston, or Miami, or something with strategic military significance like Guantanamo Bay or the American military installation in Panama. Montello saying 'Don't fuck with me, Mister Denton. There's more where that came from.' No more talk of extradition to the United States. Thermal nuclear weapons have always been a wonderful deterrent. Maybe Montello wants to be president. Nukes open a lot of doors, maybe even the door to the presidential palace. The insurgents like him, Jack. They're all whores. Everyone's on the coca payroll and politics makes strange bedfellows."

"You sick bastard," Jack hissed.

Raspov chortled. "Give me some credit, Jack." Raspov hefted the gun from one hand to the other, pointed it at Jack again. "The truth is Montello's little problem doesn't concern us. He would have received stage craft, duds or props, for lack of better words. His money, however. That was real. I would have taken his bonds."

"Pretty risky slight of hand. Montello's not that stupid."

"No. Not that stupid. I agree. But the Argentinean physicist on his payroll – the man who was to verify the weapons – was a willing participant in our subterfuge." Raspov reconsidered. "Maybe not so willing until we showed him photos of his grandson leaving preschool."

"The deal is obviously dead now." Jack needed to hear confirmation of that.

Raspov allowed it. "Yes. Dead, I suppose. For now."

"Don't worry, Dmitri," said Jack. "I'm sure there are others who'll pay your price."

"Yes, there are. And we're ready for them. You see, Jack, there are old men in Russia who believe it's the KGB's time again. We're believers now in something you taught us. Democracy. Back home my old KGB friends are winning elections – becoming leaders – stronger leaders willing to return Russia to its rightful place. You've never heard of Viktor Kryshtanovskaya. Mid-level KGB. Great politician. Won a landslide in Voronezh in the south. Now he's in charge of the nuclear arsenal there. What a great thing, this democracy. Even I have a place in the new Russia, thanks to our old friend Putin. The government has a great many places to put us. Raspov, the bureaucrat. Imagine. We're back, my friend, I'm back. But in the meantime we need Montello's money – our war chest. I want the money, Jack. She stole it. It's ours."

"You'll have to talk to her about that," Jack said.

"You're absolutely right," Raspov replied. "I shall." With that, Raspov raised the weapon until it was level with Jack's forehead. "Sorry, old friend."

Suddenly the house went dark.

The first concussion came from the front door, followed by simultaneous eruptions of thunder and smoke from the windows and at the back of the house.

Pain exploded in Jack's head. He covered his ears and lunged towards the spot where Raspov had been seated. He tumbled over an empty chair onto the floor. More explosions were followed by the stomping of heavy boots and American voices shouting hurried commands. Jack heard screams in the shed, followed by loud reports from a killing shotgun. People were dying in there. A pair of sweaty hands encircled his throat and squeezed. Raspov was suddenly on him and he weighed a ton. Jack swung – and swung again – his knuckles cracked as he pounded at the Russian's upper torso. The fingers around his neck tightened, but with a final flurry of punches Jack was able to break Raspov's death grip. He heaved Raspov off and fought to catch his breath. A split second later the Russian was on him again, spittle erupting in curses, sour breath and slimy fingers at his throat again. With his free hand Raspov struck him with something hard, something that made a sickening thud as it struck Jack's skull. Jack was losing consciousness. His arms lay helplessly at his sides. Everything was turning black as he looked up to see Raspov wild-eyed with rage. The Russian placed the barrel of his revolver against Jack's forehead.

"They're all dead out there, Jack. My orders—" Raspov didn't finish. The bullet that killed him entered his head at the left temple and dissected the frontal lobe of his brain before burying itself harmlessly into a wall. Raspov fell limply forward and grunted against Jack's cheek. A soliloquy of the dammed.

Jack must have blacked out. When he regained consciousness it took all of his strength to push Raspov's dead body off him. A moment later the shooting and shouting halted. The smell of sweat and cordite was thick. Jack lay there trying to catch his breath when a pair of boots thumped heavily toward him. A powerful light struck him square in the face, causing him even more pain. He slammed shut his eyes as a voice barked at him, a soldier's voice, gravelly and hoarse with the beginnings of an adrenaline hangover.

"I thought I told you not to come back, Doyle," Colonel Neil Braxton said.

SEVENTY-FIVE

The medic who looked at Jack said he'd definitely live. Jack quietly nodded as he watched the Delta boys stomp around the house, grimly gathering up their hardware, satisfied looks on blackened faces. The guy with the bag of medical supplies leaned in to examine the robin's egg on the side of Jack's head. "You get the guy's number who did this?"

Jack ignored him. "160th Regiment – Night Stalkers. Right?"

"Can't say, sir." The soldier smiled and resumed his examination.

Kaitlin and Mercedes were safe and huddled together under Alejandro's watchful stare. Seth was getting in everyone's way demanding his right to use the video camera he had retrieved, along with the rest of their belongings from the car.

The soldiers ignored him.

Colonel Neil Braxton waited for the medic to finish his work. In the meantime he shook his head in disbelief. "You're a lucky man," he said.

"Thanks. What can you tell me?"

"Most of it's classified," Braxton said. "And we don't have a lot of time to talk about it. Our eye in the sky is telling us FARC boys are headed this way. We definitely want to bug out before they get here."

Braxton's eyes glowed from beneath a shiny layer of dark camouflage paint. He looked larger to Jack in fatigues and a flak jacket. And to Jack he appeared exhausted.

"Intel gave us a heads-up about three days ago when satellites picked up Raspov's boat about fifty miles off the Colombian coast."

I was aboard it, Jack didn't say.

"We know you were a passenger, Jack."

"How did—"

"Not important."

Braxton shouted something about a security perimeter to one of his men, then turned back to Jack. "Raspov was up to his ass in some pretty scary shit."

Jack wondered how far Braxton would go.

"How much of this is off the record," the colonel asked.

"As much as you can tell me," Jack replied.

"Raspov did the justice minister and was planning plenty more — union leaders, mayors, anyone with a title. Anything to destabilize the country, nothing like the candy-ass *violencia* of the past. Harder, faster, much more blood. The president was going down. They had an assassin on his staff inside the presidential palace. The Colombian military was in for new leadership. You met him. Guzman. By the way, how does President Branko Montello sound?"

"Like a nightmare," Jack replied.

"That's why we're here," Braxton said. "Anyway, our Intel was slow on the restaurant job that got you and your friend, otherwise we would have intervened, saved our buddy Amillo. You know what they say, Doyle. Wrong place, wrong time. You were collateral damage. Though it looks like the O'Rourke woman managed the impossible by the looks of it. I won't ask how she got here."

"It's a long story," Jack said, feeling no inclination at that moment to reveal Raspov's nuclear intentions. That was to be his exclusive — and he intended to protect it.

"Anything we should know, Jack?"

"No," Jack replied. "Just a coupla old friends catching up on old times before you interrupted."

Braxton appeared doubtful.

Jack looked past it. He counted six body bags which were being loaded aboard a Blackhawk helicopter. Two others had touched down seconds before, turbines spooling for a rapid exit.

"What about Montello?" Jack asked as Braxton was getting up.

"Let's just say that Montello and two of his business partners are now guests of Uncle Sam. Three Blackhawks like those are on their way to a secure runway in Panama. An army transport is waiting for them. Montello and his friends aren't going to like the in-flight service." Braxton smiled. "How about you? You need a ride home?"

Jack nodded.

Kaitlin and Mercedes got up to join Alejandro who was standing at the bedroom door. They spoke quietly for a moment. Mercedes stepped tentatively into the bedroom and halted. Regret painted her face as she stared down at the death shroud. After a moment she turned and walked back to her twin sister, hugging her affectionately.

Alejandro smiled and reached out to take their hands, mindless of the intrusion of armed men and the racket from a launching helicopter.

Jack walked over. "There's no time left," he said. "We're going with them."

Alejandro nodded.

Kaitlin hugged him. There were more quiet words, and then in a move unnoticed by everyone, an object was tucked tightly into her hand. Finally they said goodbye.

Five minutes later they were airborne. The crew chief brought them coffee, and then Jack and Seth watched the Mendoza sisters shyly studying one another, duplicates inspecting their own special qualities. There were two lifetimes to catch up on, stories of a million words. Kaitlin smiled. "Thank you," she mouthed to him.

Jack nodded, smiled back, and in that moment the guilt and shame that killed his father were forever finished with the Doyle name. Jack stared into the darkness outside the helicopter and breathed deeply. Passing trees and rooftops were barely visible except where home fires flickered brightly.

This time everyone was going home.

SEVENTY-SIX

They spent two full days in Panama City. Jack and Seth were relegated to loungers at the hotel pool while Kaitlin and Mercedes disappeared on long walks or to the quiet shady places on the hotel grounds where people could sit and talk.

"What about it?" Seth said on the afternoon of the second day, an umbrella drink of some kind balanced precariously on his white chest. "Another Emmy's got your name on it."

Jack looked at him reproachfully. "Don't you think you'd better find out if the sisters are OK with this? After all, it's their lives, Seth. Rule one, remember?"

"Understood, my liege."

Seth had documented nearly everything. His videotapes were on their way to New York, including the ones shot with his hidden lipstick camera. He'd managed with that camera to shoot the aftermath of the raid in Maradona and something that happened on a jungle tarmac west of Panama City, where three grumpy and sneering drug lords were bundled in leg irons aboard a C-130 military aircraft.

Jack had asked Braxton for a favour which the Delta leader granted. "Why not?" he had chuckled. "I expect the Mendoza woman's got some parting words for the bastard." Better than words it turned out when Mercedes stepped up to the shackled drug lord and smiled.

"I can't believe she actually kicked him in the walnuts," Seth said. "Great money shot."

"Woman's got spunk. And by the look of agony on Montello's face, good legs too."

Both men laughed loudly.

The day before, they had gathered in Jack's hotel room to watch President Denton and the Colombian president announce the capture of three of Colombia's most feared drug kingpins. Jack smiled as Jeremy Rankin, quoting reliable administration sources, reported details of a cartel plot to overthrow the government and to install a dictatorship under the most ruthless of the country's drug lords – Branko Montello. Rankin, in grave tones but quick to point out the exclusivity of his information, also quoted unnamed intelligence sources as saying the cartels may have been close to acquiring one or several tactical nuclear weapons. "This left the Denton administration with no choice but to act," he reported, as though it was on his recommendation alone that the operation was launched. Rankin went on to say that secret elements of the army's special operations 160th Regiment Night Stalkers, based in Fort Campbell, Kentucky, dropped Delta teams onto heavily guarded jungle fortresses. There they captured drug kingpins Zebe Bonito, Ungaro Alvarez and Branko Montello to whom Colombian authorities credit the assassination of another cartel leader, Carlos Ruiz of Medellin. An unnamed Russian operative, based in Cuba, who is believed to have been a central figure in the cartel bid to acquire nuclear weapons, was tracked down and "neutralized" by American forces. "The operation has effectively decapitated the leadership of Colombia's cocaine industry," Rankin reported. "No Americans were hurt or killed."

At a news conference within minutes of Rankin's live report President Frederick Denton also revealed that Colombia's military forces, aided by American "advisors," swept down on numerous Colombian drug labs responsible for eighty-five percent of the country's cocaine output. Satellite photos, distributed to wide-eyed reporters at the White House briefing, clearly showed pinpoints of light that represented dozens of fires burning at secret jungle locations.

Off camera, and off mic, Paul Braithwaite, the president's chief of staff leaned towards an aide standing next to him on the White House lawn and said, only half joking, "Cocaine just became the most lucrative substance on the planet."

The two presidents fully understood the economic forces of supply and demand. Denton had already been informed of a huge jump in the street price for cocaine. Thus it was expected the drug industry would likely regenerate under new leaders hungry for even bigger profits. Still, Denton and the little Colombian president smiled broadly as they shook hands and committed their respective governments to "the continued eradication of the menace to Colombia's democratically elected government and the peace-loving people of Colombia."

That morning Jack got a call from Lou Perlman. They spoke for twenty minutes, and afterwards Jack spent a long time thinking about what Perlman had told him.

Seth didn't notice that Jack was preoccupied. Instead he tossed aside a cocktail umbrella serving absolutely no purpose in his double gin and tonic and shifted his white form until it was safety hidden from the hard tropical sun. "Angels of Maradona," Seth said, liking the title more each time he said it. "Two women who triumph over dark murderous forces and find each other. Forget the Emmys. This one's an Oscar contender. You'll write and direct. I'll produce. What about it?"

"Not now, Seth," Jack said, rising from his lounger and heading for the shallow end of the pool.

He stopped and turned. "It's their story, not ours."

On the third morning, they left Panama City. Seth said goodbye to all and boarded a plane to New York, while Mercedes was flown to Miami where Braxton's people planned on debriefing her.

It was a short flight to Havana for Jack and Kaitlin, and after they landed, Jack was satisfied that no red flags had been attached to either of them. They were processed through Cuban customs routinely, and an hour later they reached Marina Hemmingway where Jack was now staring disapprovingly at the ring of slime that had attached itself to the smooth hull of his boat. He paid his slip fees and went to work. An hour after that he started her engine and steered *Scoundrel* through the entrance of the marina — towards home. It was good to be back aboard.

Jack thought again about Raspov and wondered whether he'd told him everything. What if? What if those tactical nuclear weapons had already been seeded? What if those safe houses across the United States were already bristling with enough destructive power to annihilate entire cities? It was crazy just to think about, Jack decided. Crazy to believe anything that came from Raspov's mouth. Whatever the truth, it had died with Colonel Dmitri Raspov, 2nd directorate, KGB.

Jack didn't argue when Kaitlin said she wanted to help sail *Scoundrel* from Cuba to Miami. She was lazily steering the boat when Jack emerged from the navigation station down below. He looked at her earnestly. "Some bad weather headed for the Florida coast."

Kaitlin gave him a doubtful look. "Really?"

"Yes, really," he said, feigning hurt. "Probably best if we spend one more night in Cuban waters, head across tomorrow."

"If you say so, skipper."

Jack watched as the anchor slipped silently beneath the surface of still blue water and plunged six fathoms to the sandy seabed. The anchor caught, swinging *Scoundrel* on an invisible current until her bow pulpit was pointed directly at Florida. Kaitlin disappeared below, leaving Jack to contemplate a strip of sugary white which stretched for miles. He listened peacefully to the surf as it slapped lazily on sand that had rarely seen a footprint. Jack breathed deeply the salt air and thought about everything that had happened. He'd been lucky. Everyone had survived. Even his boat was safe. Docking in Cuba usually meant the automatic seizure of American vessels but Braxton had fixed things. "As far as the customs boneheads are concerned you were feet up, drinking pina coladas in the Cayman Islands. Don't sweat it, it's taken care of."

Jack watched the sunset while sipping iced tea and listening to Kaitlin rummage around down below.

Music began to play and a second later Kaitlin climbed through the companionway wearing a white two-piece bathing suit that glowed against her olive skin. She freed her long hair, looked at Jack through half-closed eyes and smiled.

Jack stared at her too long and grinned sheepishly. "Here's to reunions," he said, raising his glass to her. "And second chances."

"Both," Kaitlin responded, tapping her glass against his.

They sat for a second in silence, until Kaitlin turned to him. "My father said he was pretty hard on you."

"You could say that," Jack said. "But who can blame him?"

"No, Jack, that wasn't fair," Kaitlin said. "He was a shit about it and he knows it. He'll apologize with a great big bear hug when we get home – or else."

"Wonderful," Jack said, forcing a smile. "I can hardly wait."

Kaitlin tilted her head to stare up at the darkening sky. "He also said my funeral got rave reviews and that you ruined a good suit of clothes and some city shoes."

Jack laughed. "It wasn't actually a funeral. There was no body. Thankfully you were still in possession of it. You'll get my bill for a new suit."

"Stop it," she said, slapping his arm. "I know it must have been difficult. I'm sorry."

Jack turned serious. "What can I say? Father Doherty was at his best. I was at my worst. And, by the way, it wasn't your fault."

The wind rustled thick woody leaves on shore. Palms bowed gently as if bidding them farewell. About a hundred yards to port a tiny piece of ocean parted to reveal a pair of dorsal fins which flashed dull grey-white against the water's mirror finish. The dolphins whistled, and then vanished as quickly as they'd appeared.

The CD changed to something with a sexy Latin beat.

Kaitlin stood, and without a word, dove into the water. Jack was worried until a minute later she popped up at the boat's transom, spitting water with a wicked smile. "Come on in, Doyle, the water's gorgeous."

Jack leaned over the back of the boat, looking gloomy. "You know I can't swim."

Kaitlin kicked off from the boat and treaded water. "Second chances, remember?" she said with an impish grin.

Jack disappeared down below and returned a moment later wearing swimming trunks. He climbed onto the swim platform and nervously studied the water as though it were some ancient bottomless well.

"Come on, Jack, I'll save you."

"I don't know if I can."

"Jack Doyle, fearless slayer of dictators and despots, afraid of water."

"Hussein can't swim either."

"He swam the Tigris, Jack."

"So he did."

"Just jump, silly."

Jack clamped his eyes tight and jumped. He sank like a stone. The water pressed against him as he descended through its cooling layers. Strangely, he didn't panic. In his mind Jack saw his father on the day they launched his boat, the same schooner Argus's brother Aiden ran aground at Sable Island while Jack's father was too sick with the flu down below to save them. Caleb Doyle is smiling. "One day she'll be yours, Jack. When you're grown you'll be skipper."

"I'll take her to the other side of the ocean, Dad," Jack had said to him that day. "I'm gonna take Kaitlin to find her mother."

Jack was about to inhale his first deadly mouthful of water when a hand locked on his arm and pulled him upwards. When he broke the surface, Kaitlin was laughing.

"You're a good man, Doyle," she said. "But you can't swim worth a damn."

"I told you," Jack coughed. "Thanks for rescuing me."

Kaitlin pulled him closer. "No problem. Now we're even."

In that moment Jack knew it was real. Something permanent. Kaitlin was smiling – he was smiling – happy. Music drifted over the transom and they came together, their bodies turning slowly in magnetic embrace.

Kaitlin whispered in his ear and Jack finally understood what she had always meant to him. Jack felt Kaitlin tighten her hold, drawing him even closer, her hot breath against the side of his neck, their bodies weightless. Kaitlin began to hum, a soothing vibration that tickled his neck. Jack felt the softness of her breasts press harder against him. She felt him as well. He moved her to the swim platform and with one hand lifted them both from the water. Jack stood and pulled every inch of her into him. She warmed him, swept trembling hands onto his shoulders, and looked deeply into his eyes. "The first time I wore a dress it was for you," Kaitlin said. "Argus was flabbergasted."

"It was red, right?"

Kaitlin frowned. "No, dummy, pale yellow with blue lilies, and I had dog poop on my shoe."

"Ah, yes, I remember it well," Jack said, as he dipped his head and kissed her deeply.

EPILOGUE

The moon was his only company as Jack swung *Scoundrel* around the point of land that stretched across the opening of Ragged Hole Bay, and even it was preparing to call it a night. Far in the distance, buoys that reflected bright shades of red and green funneled navigators to the government wharf and the glimmering lights of Bark Island.

Jack heard stirring, muted voices in the darkness down below. A moment later Mercedes' face emerged into the early dawn. There was warmth in her smile, and contentment, which Jack realized he had never seen before.

Mercedes pulled a sweater over her head and shook loose her long hair. "Good morning," she said, rubbing her eyes. "Or nearly morning."

"Sleep well?" Jack handed her a thermos, which she took gladly, and poured a good measure of steaming coffee into its plastic top. "Like the dead," she answered, frowning at her choice of words.

After leaving Cuba, Kaitlin and Jack sailed lazily towards Miami. Kaitlin's memory was fully recovered and X-rays revealed no permanent damage, though a navy neurologist at the base where Mercedes had undergone hours of exhaustive debriefing explained there might be headaches.

It took seven days, with Kaitlin and Mercedes aboard, to reach Bark Island. The two sisters spent long periods of time together while Jack sailed the boat and tried to stay out of their way. Jack was happy the trip was nearing an end.

Mercedes followed his gaze towards the shoreline, where tiny flickers of light signaled early risers and the home she had never known. "It's beautiful," she said. "But…"

"But scary?"

"Yes, a little bit."

"Don't worry," Jack said. "How many men lose a daughter and gain two in return?"

Mercedes puckered her lips as if calculating something. "This arithmetic is good," she replied.

Scoundrel rose and fell on a shallow swell. A light wind filled her canvas, and now and then Jack hardened her mainsail to keep her slicing through the water at a decent clip. They swept past a channel marker, its red light blinking in a nether world that existed between dark and dawn. Jack couldn't wait any longer to ask her about the money. "Fifty million dollars is an obscene sum of cash," he said quietly.

Mercedes looked at him, giving nothing away in her expression except the absence of surprise. "Yes it is."

They looked at each other, both sipped on their steaming brew. Then Mercedes turned away. "I know what you're wondering," she said. "Why did I do it?"

"Maybe you earned it." Jack shrugged. "He was quite the bastard."

"Yes," she answered quietly. "For many of us." Mercedes lowered her eyes to a spot on the deck, apparently not willing to say any more about him.

Jack could only imagine the tragedy which would haunt her, always, the people who had died as a result of Montello's brutality. He exhaled on crisp air, deflecting the ghostly images of Govia and the nuns of Trinity.

"I have plans for the money," Mercedes said after a moment. "But not what you think." It was a secret known only to Mercedes Mendoza that

Swiss National Bank in the Grand Cayman Islands had already begun dispersing the money. None would be kept. Mercedes had provided a list of organizations involved in the care of children, the thousands of orphans created by the insane cycle of violence in her homeland. The bank was to contact each of them with an unbelievable endowment, though none was to be told the name of their benefactor. New orphanages would be built, food and clothing would be paid for, and scholarships would be established for university educations. As Mercedes and Selena had intended all along "dirty money would be made clean." Mercedes wasn't ready yet for the tears she would shed for her dead friends, the mother she never knew. That would come later. So much had been stolen from her, but now Mercedes had the duty to make sure those lives weren't wasted. She promised that the Trinity orphans would be taken care of immediately, the ten children who were forced from their beds by brutality, including a small girl with a one-eared bear. Dominique's heart would grow strong because of the incredibly costly operation which Mercedes and Selena had secretly paid for. That money had come from Selena's bank the first time they were angels. The Trinity orphans would have a new home soon. They would grow up healthy, a new generation, maybe a peaceful one. Silently Mercedes prayed for it. "Fingers crossed," she whispered.

"Excuse me?"

"Never mind." Mercedes smiled. "I was just dreaming."

They glided past buoys, one by one, sentinels leading them closer to land. A foghorn sounded in the distance, too far away to tell where, more a beckoning than a warning.

"What about you, Jack?"

Jack thought about that for a moment. Lou had informed him the senior anchor job was about to become available, if he still wanted it. Jack looked at her and smiled. "There's someone I plan to finish falling in love with," he said. "And she's about to get a promotion, if she wants it."

The sound of wind and waves washed over them. The moon seemed a worn decoration now on the remnants of night, a smoldering reminder to Jack that the radiance of his ambition had never seemed so cold. A fire without warmth, he thought as he captured the last of the heat from his thermos. "The network will have to wait," Jack told her, "likely for both of us." Jack swung the boat's bowsprit ten degrees to port. In another minute or two he'd reef the sails and fire up the engine.

"Good morning, everyone." Kaitlin emerged from the companionway and moved to Jack, snuggling into him to stay warm against a cool grey mist that materialized like gauze in the fading darkness.

Jack felt her tremble, and squeezed gently.

For a moment no one spoke and Kaitlin reached out to take Mercedes' hand. "There's something I want to show you," she said. Kaitlin placed a small object in her sister's hand. It was a tiny gold locket.

Mercedes looked at it with surprise.

"Open it," Kaitlin said.

Mercedes opened it. Inside was a small heart-shaped photograph which brought a smile to her face, immediately. "Eva," she said.

"And her two babies," Kaitlin added. "I am the oldest as you can see."

The two of them laughed heartily. Mercedes brought the locket to her chest and gave Kaitlin a sisterly peck on the cheek.

"You wear it," Kaitlin said. "I have my memories."

"Thank you."

They sailed for another five minutes, expectation gathering in all aboard, until life appeared in the distance.

Kaitlin looked towards the wharf and their home, a home where Argus, their father, was waiting. A moment later, as the last of the wind abandoned the boat's sails, Kaitlin saw him. "Oh, God," she mewed, breath trapped somewhere at the bottom of her throat, hands pressed to her mouth as tears spilled downward.

Mercedes saw him too, and smiled at her sister.

Jack grinned widely and reached down to start the engine. It caught immediately.

Argus O'Rourke stood at the end of the dock, steady as the granite that ran for miles along the rocky coastline. In his outstretched arms were two burning lanterns, not one. They swayed slowly in a signal as old as fathers and the fathers before them.

In that moment Jack understood what his father had suffered that day so long ago. A ship and his crew were lost – his life. "Not this time," Jack whispered to himself. "Not now."

The lanterns swayed. *Welcome back.*

Others stumbled up behind Argus, a dozen or more holding lanterns that flickered like fireflies through the early dawn. Kaitlin and Mercedes seemed mesmerized by the lights, and after a moment the two sisters turned to each other. A fading breeze tickled their faces, like angel wings fluttering, and as icy waves thundered against the boat's smooth hull, a shooting star burned a fiery path towards home.

ACKNOWLEDGEMENTS

I say a heart-felt thank you to the many who provided their advice and support in the crafting of this novel. First, Jayne Leong, who insisted that I stop talking and start writing. Also, Sheilagh Morrison, whose boundless enthusiasm was a constant source of energy throughout the many drafts of my manuscript. There were my perfect readers: Carolyn Stokes, Clarissa Dicks and Julia Wyeth, all of whom gave their time and most importantly, their honesty, in helping to shape my story. As well, psychologist Leigh Minter, whose expertise on Colombia's reclusive U'wa tribe provided the genesis for plot. I owe a debt of gratitude to the dedicated staff at Breakwater Books and especially to my editor Annamarie Beckel. I would also like to thank someone who cannot be named here, a spook who opened a door for me to the murky world of intelligence. You know who you are, my friend. Finally, to Pavel Palazchenko, the omnipresent Cold War interpreter for ex-Soviet president Mikhail Gorbachev, who graciously cleared the way on an airport tarmac for a few inspirational moments with "the boss."

GLEN CARTER is an award-winning journalist who has spent nearly thirty years in the high-pressure world of television news. He has covered everything from national politics and crime to world leaders and deadly disasters. He is now applying his story-telling craft and decades of fact-driven writing to the flight of fiction. *Angels of Maradona* is his first novel.